Advance Praise for *The Shaadi Set-Up*

"Charming as hell and wonderfully witty, *The Shaadi Set-Up* had me grinning, swooning, and sweating. Watching Rita and Milan torture each other is truly delicious, and the tension between them is so thick you'd need several buzz saws to cut it. A pitch-perfect romantic comedy and a new all-time favorite."

—Rachel Lynn Solomon, author of *The Ex Talk*

"*The Shaadi Set-Up* is my favorite ever second-chance romance. Hilarious and emotional, with characters who feel so real I didn't want to let them go, Rita and Milan punched a hole through my heart. I can't wait to dog-ear all my favorite passages. This is an absolute treasure of a love story."

—Sarah Hogle, author of *You Deserve Each Other* and *Twice Shy*

"Funny, sexy, and so full of love! With hilarious and vibrant prose, memorable characters you can't help but fall in love with, and a new twist on modern dating, this second-chance-at-love story is addictively readable. I was rooting for Rita and Milan to overcome their complicated history and find their happily ever after from the moment I met them on the page!"

—Farah Heron, author of *Accidentally Engaged*

"What sets *The Shaadi Set-Up* apart is Vale's luscious prose and deft characterizations. A fun yet thoughtful novel that ties together love for family, friends, and the one that got away, *The Shaadi Set-Up* is a heartwarming debut you won't soon forget."

—Elizabeth Everett, author

"YA author Vale (*Small Town Hearts*) makes a splash with her laugh-out-loud adult debut. . . . Vale evenly balances heart and heat, while imbuing her rom-com with cultural specificity and delicately exploring familial obligation and heartbreak. Hilarious and heartfelt, this second-chance romance proves it's never too late to start again."   —*Publishers Weekly* (starred review)

the
Shaadi
Set-Up

ALSO BY LILLIE VALE

Small Town Hearts

the
Shaadi
Set-Up

A NOVEL

Lillie Vale

G. P. Putnam's Sons

New York

PUTNAM
— EST. 1838 —

G. P. Putnam's Sons
Publishers Since 1838
An imprint of Penguin Random House LLC
penguinrandomhouse.com

Library of Congress Cataloging-in-Publication Data

Names: Vale, Lillie, author.
Title: The Shaadi set-up : a novel / Lillie Vale.
Description: New York : G. P. Putnam's Sons, [2021]
Identifiers: LCCN 2021024140 (print) | LCCN 2021024141 (ebook) |
ISBN 9780593328712 (trade paperback) | ISBN 9780593331149 (ebook)
Subjects: GSAFD: Love stories. | LCGFT: Romance fiction. | Novels.
Classification: LCC PS3622.A42526 S53 2021 (print) |
LCC PS3622.A42526 (ebook) | DDC 813/.6—dc23
LC record available at https://lccn.loc.gov/2021024140
LC ebook record available at https://lccn.loc.gov/2021024141

Printed in the United States of America
1st Printing

Book design by Ashley Tucker

All things work together for good.
Romans 8:28

For my mother, who helps me believe it every day
without an I-told-you-so, and who has read this book
more times than I can possibly count.

the
Shaadi
Set-Up

Chapter 1

I drag myself on a walk around my neighborhood twice, the soup of North Carolina's early June humidity plastering my hair to the back of my neck. Still half asleep, I let my dogs set the pace and try not to nod off behind my enormous incognito actress–style aviators that cover half my face.

Most girls would try to squeeze in a morning cuddle with their hunky boyfriends as soon as the alarm goes off, but I launched out of bed this morning before mine could hit snooze. As a holdover from his college days, Neil's mom still calls ten minutes after his second snooze to wake him up. In the beginning, he'd ignore her second "How are you doing this morning, beta" call, but three months into our relationship, he's comfortable enough to carry on a speakerphone conversation with his mom while he shaves and gets ready.

In almost every other respect, we're fine. But if he just hit reject the way he used to, I wouldn't be out here at the asscrack

of the morning, wincing at the sheer audacity of the sun streaming directly into my eyeballs, despite my sunglasses.

To kill time, I pause at the bus stop and let the kids pet my
French bulldog, Freddie—who pretends not to enjoy it—and my
Yorkie–Jack Russell terrier mix, Harrie—who unabashedly does.
I get to chatting with the Instagram-wellness-peddler-pretty-at-
eight-a.m. moms who've seen my latest upcycled furniture dry-
ing out in my driveway.

"Rita!" a woman calls from across the street, beckoning me
to join her and her friend.

It doesn't take long before the frenemy neighbors vie for the
same vintage Queen Anne dressing table, and their frenzied bids
have already crossed double the asking price on Instagram.

I have to admit it's a beautiful, if somewhat boring, piece.

I thrifted it from a local flea market last month at end of day.
The price dropped because the crusty seller didn't want to load
it back up on their van. Even with its busted cabriole legs, peeling paint, and cracked mirror, it was a steal at under a Benjamin.

I would have loved to paint it a bright pop of color—hot pink,
peacock green, or electric blue—but the clientele around here
prefers their paintwork just like they prefer their neighbors—
conservative. So refinishing to the original walnut color and painting the new legs and drawers in champagne it is.

My phone dings with a new email in between a particularly
fierce volley between the always-glowing skincare ambassador
and the went-vegan-for-the-likes yoga instructor who I know for
a *fact* smuggles home Zaxby's wings and fried chicken from Bo-
jangles.

I don't want to take my eyes away from the bidding war in
front of me; in any case, emails are harbingers of evil, usually
credit card statements or sales bots who have scraped my email
from Dharma Designs Instagram's contact info.

Skincare Lady's final bid takes it up to triple, well above markup, and I arrange to deliver it later this week. Shaking on the price isn't easy, especially when I know my (um, *her*) dressing table is only going to be used as a prop to display her overpriced gunk for sponsored posts (I mean, she has a mini fridge just for her skincare!), but I need the money.

And secretly, I *was* rooting for her to come out the winner.

So I grit my teeth and take her hand, both of us pretending we don't see last month's chipped black polish clinging desperately to my tips.

She has a flawless gel mani. Because, of course.

Yoga Girl smiles through her teeth and says "Oh well, maybe next time!" with neighborly gusto, but her eyes are slits. I'm glad she was outbid. She always responds to my "Hey" with "Namaste" and asks if I know her Indian friends.

My email dings again.

"You sure are popular," says Skincare Lady, who I really should call by her actual name, Paula Dooley.

Every year Paula's brood goes door to door with glossy brochures, drumming up sales for their school fundraisers. She makes it a point to always wave and chat because I buy her kids' seed packets every spring instead of getting them at the store for half the price. They're too cute to turn down when they knock on my door. And though my grandmother would grumble about wasting money, when I was growing up Mom always emphasized the virtue of being neighborly.

I'm so used to ignoring the junk mail I get that I'd already forgotten about the beeps. "It's probably just spam. Are you sure any evening this week is good to drop off the dresser?"

"Any time," she confirms. "Listen, Rita, it's sure hot out here. Do you want to come in for some coffee? I've got to clean up the kitchen because not a one of them kids knows how to put their cereal bowls in the sink. My youngest still hasn't learned how to aim for the toilet, so you can just imagine how well he's doing with pouring his own cereal"—she laughs—"and there's something I'd love to talk to you about, if you've got a minute."

Harrie gives a warning bark.

I back away. If it was just coffee she was offering, I'd say yes just to while away a few more minutes, but there's no way I can afford to get suckered into buying whatever potions she has in her beauty fridge, even if they might make me look eighteen again.

"Oh, um, you know, Paula, I am all set for skincare." With my free hand, I pat my cheek. "Got my SPF moisturizer on right now."

"One of these days you and I are going to have a chat about what you put on your face. But no, I'm not trying to sell you my obviously superior skincare." She huffs, rolling her eyes. "We're looking to remodel and I want new *everything* for the house. I just love your style. You know, I couldn't believe it when I found out that you renovated the Full Belly Deli, our favorite little restaurant! I *told* my husband I recognized their new furniture! You and your Dharma Designs are turning into quite the local celebrity," she adds with a wink.

I hold back a snort. "Please. Half the women on this street are Internet famous. You're, like, all over Instagram. I swear I get recommended your products every day."

I'm not even exaggerating. Paula and her friends are all beauty, fashion, and lifestyle influencers, with follower counts high enough to be Instagram verified, whereas my furniture account, Dharma Designs, is struggling to break ten thousand.

"Anyway," I continue. "I just gave Full Belly Deli some pointers, helped them with the conceptualization, and did a quick sketch. It didn't even take an hour, and they'd just bought all that furniture, so."

Her mouth drops open. "Honey, you did all that? No no no. You do *not* undervalue your time and knowledge by giving it away for free. You should *not* have to pay for your own exposure."

I give her a tight smile. It's easy for her to say. People like me all have to start somewhere, and sometimes that means being generous with clients to get our names out there.

Harrie, getting bored, strains against the leash. Freddie boxes him between my legs, nose to nose, with quite possibly the sternest expression a dog can wear.

"At least think about it? Cost is no object." Her laugh tinkles. "As my husband says, 'Happy wife, happy life!'"

For some reason, I can't shake the image of her at the duck pond in the park, ripping a hunk of bread into pieces and smiling benevolently as the geese scramble over themselves to get what's in her palm.

I stare. "You're serious? But I've never done a home remodel before."

She nods emphatically. "Yeah, but I've seen *yours*. We don't have to talk details right now, but if it's something you're interested in . . . ?" Her voice goes up at the end, making it a question.

It's tempting. Money always is, especially when you don't have a lot of it.

But the idea of being inside her house, making decisions about all of her things, in the same place her family lives . . . It's too much responsibility. A home has a soul of its own and it tends to the people who live there. And I wasn't exactly someone who had a lot of experience with happy homes.

The happiest home I've had is the one I made for myself.

Even if, right at this minute, it was the one I was avoiding going back to.

"I don't— I mean, I do *product* design," I stress. "I'm not an interior decorator. I wouldn't even know how to put up wallpaper the right way."

"Rita, I'm talking about a big project. It's serious money on the table. Carte blanche."

There's literally no good way to phrase this. I'm put on the spot, so I strive extra hard for the right words. "And I appreciate it, don't get me wrong, but . . ."

My friends tell me it's irrational, but I like to be sure all my furniture goes to a good home. My mom, on the other hand, thinks I should sell to whoever can pay the highest. But when I put myself into every piece, it matters where they end up.

"Summer's my busiest time, Paula. I hit up all the flea markets and I still have spring inventory at my parents' place that needs doing." I lay it on thick so she backs off, but not enough to burn a bridge with a neighbor with deep pockets. "You're so generous to give me this opportunity. But you know what? You have excellent taste, so I'm super confident that however you design your house, it'll be beautiful. And if you need some odds and ends to round out what you buy, then I'm more than happy to show you what I have."

Paula's face slumps, disappointed, but quickly morphs into a preening smile.

My mom would scold me for turning down carte blanche, which is exactly why she will never, ever hear about this. We say our goodbyes and my pups and I continue on our walk, Harrie pulling ahead of Freddie, eager to get home.

It's only just half past eight, though, so I stop for a chat with sharp-eyed old Mrs. Jarvis next door. She's always in her front garden ready to rope passersby into conversation about her handsome single grandsons ("Hint, hint, Rita," she says with a conspiratorial wink), *The Old Farmer's Almanac*, and the latest gory true crime docudramas she's fascinated by, in that exact order.

It's because of her that I could even afford to live in this neighborhood for the past three years. After graduating college out west, the last thing I wanted was to reclaim my room in my parents' house, but good luck finding a one-bed or studio apartment in my price range in a good neighborhood.

Just when I'd been about to lose my mind at Aji treating me like a teenager again because I was *temporarily* living at home until I found a place, Doctor Dad had come to the rescue. He'd been the one to set Mrs. Jarvis's arm fracture after a fall, and found out she was looking to turn her Airbnb on the narrow strip of lot adjoining her own into a long-term rental property.

Every Christmas the Jarvis clan doesn't spend here, I get cards from all of her out-of-state kids, grateful that their mom has someone nearby just in case. Last year a holiday-guilted daughter even sent me a three-month wine subscription.

As we finish the update on her latest docuseries, Mrs. Jarvis none too subtly points out for the third time the creeping invasion of weeds in my front lawn. And since I can't be sure Neil's hung up on his mom yet, I squat by the mailbox to pluck a fistful of dandelions and some yellow flowers I think are weeds.

My rule of thumb? If I don't remember planting them, they're weeds. Harrie sticks close while Freddie sprawls on the drive under the shade of a flowering dogwood with his paws over his eyes, too elegant to go tromping around in dirt.

As I pick out chunks of clover in the middle of the lawn, Harrie wanders over to sniff the flower bed. I don't glance up since he usually knows better than to go digging in there. It's really a shame that a plant as pretty as clover is technically a weed, I muse as I rip another cluster out by the roots.

Freddie woofs, short and sharp, getting my attention. When he sees me watching, he turns his head to the right, drawing me to—

The half dug up flower bed.

My heart sinks.

Pink, white, and coral impatiens are strewn all around Harrie, petals sprinkled over his fur, broken stems everywhere. He couldn't look prouder if he tried.

"Harrie!" I scold, pulling him away. He wags his tail, straining at the leash so he can "help" me some more. Apparently he has the same difficulty distinguishing flowers from weeds as his mom. "Thank you, Freddie, you are the very best of boys."

I swear Harrie growls at him.

I chuck the dog poop baggy and the weeds before picking up the morning paper that I never read but subscribe to only to feel like a capital-A adult. Idling by the trash tote, I doom scroll Twitter until my energy bar dwindles from green to red like a real-life Sim.

My best friend, Rajvee, would tell me to quit dawdling. She's always trying to get me to tackle issues head-on, forgetting that I'm the girl who took running leaps to avoid the monster under her bed while she not only made "friends" with Gladys (because what else would you call it?), but also went on midnight snack runs downstairs with her as a convenient "She did it, not me!" patsy. But she's right; I'm not a kid anymore. Maybe it's finally time to be fearless.

I take a step toward the house. *Keep staring, don't blink.*

Harrie cocks his head expectantly.

I hesitate. God, I'm gutless.

Maybe I should check my email. I mean, there could be something really important.

"Just gotta do this one thing and then we'll go in," I tell the boys. Freddie has no opinion and returns to his very busy life of sitting, but Harrie pins me with a knowing stare.

"Don't look at me like that," I mutter, already pulling out my phone. I tap the mail icon, expecting to see a pizza coupon or a panty sale alert. I'm about to mindlessly trash it, except—

Sender: MyShaadi.com

Subject: A sneak peek JUST FOR YOU ☺

Preview: It's been a while! We've missed you, Rita! Now's your chance to meet new singles in your area . . .

I groan. I had totally forgotten that Aji badgered me into signing up for the matrimonial website during my dating dry spell six months ago, pre-Neil. I'd copped an earful from her when I'd used it for dating instead of marriage.

I should have unsubscribed from this a long time ago.

"Goodbye and good riddance." I press the screen with my thumb harder than I need to.

You are now unsubscribed.

I take a deep breath and turn the key in the lock. The next few seconds will tell me how successfully I've timed my arrival back home. But until I push the door open and find out for sure, I hang in a Schrödinger's-cat limbo.

Time to be brave.

Chapter 2

On the days my boyfriend, Neil Dewan, sleeps over, he usually gets the coffee started after talking to his mom while I take the dogs out. As I open the door, my nose tingles with the anticipation of fresh-brewed coffee. I step inside, inhaling, but there's nothing. All I can smell are the skillet fajitas we cooked (well, I *say* "we," if you count him standing around as helping) together last night.

Shit, was all my stalling for nothing? Is he still on the phone?

I strain my ears, but I can't hear him talking, so maybe I'm in the clear. Still, better safe than sorry. "I'm back!" I whisper-shout as I step through the door, paper tucked under my arm.

I almost want to check my soles for broken eggshells.

Crouching, I unclip the leashes and my boys zip off. After tossing the keys in the only *slightly* hideous woven basket I made in tenth-grade art for Mother's Day (which my mother jokes is too ugly to live), I head straight for my bedroom.

The bed's empty, rumpled covers thrown back in that sloppy way I hate when the sheets are fresh. My eyes skip over the sleep shirt dumped on the floor, one of those ugly free ones the credit card companies hand out on college campuses. Neil's pretty fastidious about keeping his own place neat, but when he's at mine, somehow I always end up picking up after him like I'm his damn mother.

I can make out his low rumble from the bathroom, but the water's still running.

Damn it. He's still on speakerphone. Everything I did to stall and somehow I'm *still* not home late enough to miss Neil's daily morning phone call with his mother.

Siiiiigh. Seriously?

Harrie yips and comes skidding into the room. Every morning Neil stays over, two things happen. The first is the clockwork phone call. The second is my normally very good boy Harrie treating my boyfriend like a stranger, forgetting all the chin scratches and belly rubs he's bribed with every time he sees Neil.

"Harrie, no!" I hiss, but it's already too late.

Right on cue, he bounds up to the door and sets off barking.

"Kohn ahey?" Neil's mom asks in Marathi.

Harrie, now convinced there are two strangers in the bathroom, puts his front paws on the door so he's standing as tall and intimidating as he can (which is not intimidating *at all*) and intensifies his barking, eclipsing my scolding.

"No one," Neil says hastily. The flow from the tap doubles. "Just a dog." Then, unconvincingly, "Out in the street."

I scoop Harrie up, a tough task when he's squirming like this, and deposit him outside the bedroom door, closing it quickly before he can scamper back in.

It's hard not to roll my eyes as I catch the tail end of Neil's mom extolling the virtues of some girl. Ah, back to our regularly scheduled programming of the well-intentioned but no less irri-tating *Isn't It Time You Got Married, Beta?*

It depends on the family, of course, but for most Indian kids, at some point in their twenties it's like a timer goes off and it's time to Get Serious About the Future before you start rocking that withered, on-the-shelf-too-long prune life.

Neil's seen me naked, but not daylight naked. So I start to strip out of my sweaty racerback tank and yoga pants in double time, grabbing the closest clothing within reach, which happens to be a pair of grungy denim shorts and a shapeless black tee, knotted at the front, that I'm pretty sure is a forgotten remnant of another boyfriend. It's my favorite at-home shirt—old and softened from wear.

I tug the shirt down over my neck just as Neil's familiar "One sec, Ma" comes muffled through the bathroom door, followed by a clatter as he balances his phone on the ceramic sink's sliver of a ledge.

He pops his head out, all men's-shower-gel-advertisement hot and black hair dripping wet. The mirror's fogged up behind him, like he never learned to turn on the exhaust.

But then he smiles.

Butterfly wings tickle against my soft, squishy heart. Oh boy.

"Hey, beautiful," he says, voice too low for the phone to catch.

Butterflies free fall into my stomach. That smile is doing dev-astating things to me.

He keeps one hand on the knot of his towel slung low on his hips, dark black arm hair whorled the way it does when he uses too much lotion. With his other hand he gestures behind him. *Mom,* he mouths. *Gimme a few.*

I flash him a thumbs-up, smiling over gritted teeth. No problem.

As if his mom's daily morning wake-up calls haven't been a

problem all the other nights we spent together, too. I miss him when we aren't together, but jeez, she doesn't even give herself a *chance* to miss him.

Don't be such a bitch, Rita. He's not even mad about Harrie barking the house down . . .

He disappears back into the bathroom.

"Sorry, Ma, I was getting dressed," I catch before the door shuts.

I gather my sweaty clothing, along with Neil's discarded clothes, and make for the laundry room. The drum's almost full with the week's clothes, so I start the wash.

As I head for the kitchen, passing in front of the doggy bed, Freddie opens his eyes, but otherwise doesn't move. While Harrie, earlier misbehavior forgotten, leaps from doggy bed to reupholstered crushed velvet ottoman (*"Harrie, no!"*) to the seat in front of the bay window, trampling over the library book I left there last night. Tongue out, head cocked, his cute, cheeky little face knows I'm too soft to make him move.

This house is so small that even when I'm in the kitchen waiting for the coffee to brew, the glugging of the washing machine sounds like I'm still in the same room.

Then I hear it—the *click* and turn of my bedroom door.

"Something smells good," says Neil, entering the kitchen looking like he's stepped out of a Ralph Lauren photo shoot. He's wearing a baby-blue button-down and chinos, sunglasses already tucked into the V of his collar, an effortless cool guy. He flashes me a knowing grin.

Neil is Like This when he flirts. Cheesy nineties sitcom-dad humor delivered with a wink.

He drops a kiss at the corner of my eye, bringing with him the spicy and potent scent of his aftershave. Not unpleasant, just a little extra. Much like his flirting. I tamp down a smile.

"How was your walk?" he asks. "Your cheeks are a little flushed."

"Hot," I say, grabbing two of my newest pretty handmade Etsy mugs from the cupboard.

"Rita, you're literally the only Indian I know who can't stand the heat."

"You let your mama hear you stereotyping with that mouth?" I brush my hand through his straight black hair like I'm smoothing it down, when really I'm messing it up just a little.

He laughs like he knows what I'm up to and wraps an arm around my waist, thumb lightly rubbing the tiniest strip of exposed midriff, but doesn't press too close in case I really am as sweaty as I look.

I want him to lean in, to close the gap, to ignore that I'm flushed and unshowered, but I know from past experience he can be a little fussy about that. Would I be a terrible girlfriend for testing him? I shift closer, tilting my chin up for a kiss, but his arm drops away almost immediately. He shoots me an apologetic smile and gestures to his ironed shirt in explanation.

"Yeah, sorry," I say, faking a laugh.

"You know, Rita, you didn't have to leave just because Ma called. One of these days we'll have to tell her we're seeing each other. Or Harrie will." He grins with insinuation. "Seeing a *lot* of each other."

One, yes I did have to leave. Partly because the woman calls him every single morning, like she has no concept how to give her grown-ass children independence and privacy. Partly because I have a suspicion that if I stick around he'll put me on the spot *and* on the phone.

Two, it's easy for him to say all this now, when a few minutes ago it was pretty clear I was still a secret.

The coffee maker stops sputtering.

I pull away to pour the coffee. Just mine.

Neil wraps his hands around his empty mug. "You're upset," he says quietly.

"No." I watch him alternate my hand-painted lavender-sprigs-with-gold-crescent-moons black mug from hand to hand. The fact I don't scream *Careful!!! Not on the tile floor!!!* is a goddamn feat.

"Really?"

I exhale through my nose. "Really."

Anyone else would be thrilled that their partner wanted to get serious. And yet.

If I didn't have hot coffee in my hand, I would flounce myself dramatically into my seat. But I do, and it's filled to the brim, so tentative cat-burglar inching it is.

He gives me an I-know-you-better-than-that look. "So why the monosyllables?"

My right eyelid twitches. "Look. Every time you talk with your mom, you get like this." I see his mouth open, so I race ahead with, "All mature and 'let's tell our parents about us,' like that doesn't break the very first rule we made when we decided to go out together. And quit it with the mug and the hands—you're making me nervous."

Neil sets the mug back on the counter with a mumbled "Sorry." Without something to fidget with, he crosses his arms. He looks like a child who's had his balloon pricked.

I feel bad for half a second. Right until the point Neil opens his mouth again.

Frustration quickens his words. "Rita, come on. We aren't living in a star-crossed-lovers Bollywood soap where our families have a blood feud going back before we were even born."

When he says things like this, it's so obvious he's never met my mother. She lives for *filmi* melodrama like this. Streaming

Sling TV is religion in our house. If there isn't an Indian woman on TV wailing in Hindi about her lost lover and his conniving mother, something's wrong. I'm not supposed to know this, but Dad turns off the Wi-Fi and blames it on the Internet company whenever he needs a break.

It's why Mom hates AT&T.

And Neil's family.

But I'm not playing that card just yet.

It might not be a blood feud, but there is bad blood between our families. And since his side started it, you'd think, you'd *just think*, he'd do well to remember that.

"It's just," says Neil, "Ma might actually get off my back if she thinks I'm in a serious relationship, you know? Every day it's this auntie's daughter this, that auntie's daughter that. If our parents know we're together, then maybe Ma will stop trying to find green card–girls who can roll out round, round rotis."

He mimes a rolling pin motion, except he looks more like a really terrible preppy DJ than a Desi domestic goddess.

I laugh despite myself. "Oh my god, don't remind me."

The last time I'd attempted to make roti, I was eleven and inspired by our family trip to Italy. It turns out that roti and pizza dough don't have much in common except they both glob to the ceiling with the same amount of sticky.

"Or," I add, "you could just tell your mom you're not interested in being set up."

"Me? Tell my Indian ma to quit interfering in my love life?" His eyebrows shoot up in mock horror. "You *must* be joking."

I put on a wide jack-o'-lantern grin. "So sneaking around for the rest of our lives it is!"

His eyes gleam as he walks over to the kitchen table. "Rest of our lives, huh?" He pulls me up midway through a gulp of coffee and a sputter. "So you and me are a forever deal?"

Ajsdfhjfajfdsjf. My top-shelf sarcasm is clearly lost on him, but I'll play along.

I tap my finger to my chin, thinking about it. "I don't remember saying that."

"Hmm, no. I definitely heard it." He tucks my hair behind my ear, rolling his thumb over the curl of cartilage that sends shivers down my spine. It's teasing and not fair at all when he has to leave for work right about—well, ten minutes ago.

I pluck at the stiff lines on his ironed shirtsleeves. First, he brought his toothbrush; later, when he started leaving for work directly from my house, his deodorant, two-in-one shampoo and conditioner, and extra clothes moved in, too.

Neil makes a little noise in the back of his throat. Not a sexy one, more of a panicked please-don't-wrinkle-me whine, so I relent. As much as I love morning banter, I'm more relieved we got off the topic of parental introductions because I know for a fact how that'll play out.

"You must think you're awfully cute or something," I say, proud of myself for not sounding too breathless when his arms wrap around me, tugging me closer.

My heart does a cartwheel. But then I glance between us and there's a solid five inches of space between him and my glistening upper chest. Well, maybe that's okay. We're different people. He can be grossed out about things like my sweat getting on him. I shouldn't be so hurt about it.

His grin spreads. He doesn't even try to hold it back. He's so oblivious, but he thinks he's done his part in making up. "I do," he says, trying to sound solemn but failing miserably.

I lightly jut my pelvis against his. "So cocky."

My erogenous zone still tingles, but it fizzles fast when he doesn't take me up on the invitation, instead scrunching his forehead like he's about to say something I really won't like.

"Rita . . ."

"Neil," I say firmly, warning him off this topic he's returning to dog-with-a-bone style.

He ignores it, because of course he does. "Rita," he starts again, this time in a firmer voice, fully geared up and unwilling to back down. "Hear me out. Our parents are adults—"

Yeah, he *really* hasn't met my mother. Adult. Ha.

"Not up for negotiation!" I snap. The mood is gone and now so is my patience. "Hear *me*, Neil. I told you why this needed to be on the down-low and you agreed. You *agreed*."

Another face, another boyfriend, flashes in front of my eyes. But Neil knows nothing about that, nothing about *him*.

About the high school boyfriend whose name is taboo. Maybe if he did know about him, he'd know why I hate broken promises so damn much.

"That was when we agreed to a third date," he argues. "But we've been dating for three months. What's the lucky number here? Three years? Three kids?" His voice roughens. "When?"

Never.

The answer flies to my lips and I lean forward, chest rising, about to say it, when I realize I can't do that to him. The truth is, if my mother didn't hate his purely on principle, I'd have said sure, Indian parents lose their ever-loving minds about their kids dating, even if they're twenty-six and not looking for input about it. But yeah, let's do it. Let's tell them.

"We don't have to tell them how we met," Neil rushes to say. "They don't need to know it was Tinder. Or that we slept together on the first date."

Honestly, I wasn't even thinking about that, but now it's just one more thing we have to hide. That we were so horny we ordered dessert first (crispy, beautifully flaky caramel apple empanadas) and skipped dinner entirely, driving straight back to his place. The second date was a do-over of the first because I actually did want to eat at that taqueria and was dying for their traditional rope vieja and the decidedly not traditional caramel apple empanadas again, but it still ended up back at his place. What was that phrase? All roads lead to your lover's bed?

It took the third date for us to agree to see each other again, sometimes maybe even with clothes. We might never have gotten to the fourth if we hadn't agreed that keeping our respective parents out of our love lives (and thereby far the fuck away from each other) was the only way this could ever work.

And now Neil wants to go back on that.

He takes my hesitation to push his case. "And you're always telling me that your aji won't stop bugging you about that matchmaking thingy."

That thingy is MyShaadi.com, the number one matrimonial website not only in India, but even for Indians living abroad. And ever since I turned twenty-five last year, it's the number one topic of conversation for my very traditional, marriage-minded grandmother.

Which also means it's the number one pain in my ass every time I go home, which, according to Aji, isn't even close to often enough since they're only an hour away.

"Shit." On reflex, Neil swipes his unused mug, brings it to his lips like he's going to gulp it down, then laughs, embarrassed, when he remembers it's empty. "I'm so late."

I can guess what's coming next. It's like clockwork.

Neil has the habit of pushing a conversation to the half step right before it turns into a fight, then turning tail before it gets serious enough for me to yell at him. He gets to go to work and do whatever data engineers at tech firms do, turning off his home brain and sinking into work-brain seamlessly.

Neil will get over this the second he's out the door. Me? I can't do that. I'll be on a low simmer all day.

I try to never work when I'm angry or upset, not when power tools are involved. That was the first rule of carpentry my dad taught me. So there goes the plan to go to my parents' place to use Dad's band saw. A recent end table I'd thrifted from Lucky Dog Luke's antique mall needed new curved legs I'd hoped to start work on today, but with Neil on my mind—and not in a good way—it looks like the day's agenda has gone up in smoke.

I hate it when that happens; a sense of wrongness is going to follow me all day. No matter what I accomplish today, it's never going to be how it was supposed to.

He comes toward me with an apologetic let's-make-up smile. Another corner-of-the-eye kiss, a shivery "Promise me you'll think about it?" in my ear, and then he's gone.

I scrunch my nose. I wish I'd told him that he applies his aftershave like an overzealous middle schooler.

But most of all, I *really* wish I'd missed his phone call with his mother.

Chapter 3

The next morning, I head for my parents' house, leaving Freddie in charge. I don't think of it as going home, though, not when they only bought it while I was in college.

Their house is one of those sprawling, turreted stone châteaux that wouldn't be out of place in the French countryside but sticks out like a ritzy thumb in the small North Carolina college town of Chapel Hill.

My unwashed, seen-better-days pickup truck doesn't fit with the stretch of manicured lawns, long driveways, and canopies of tall, proud oak trees on either side of me. Usually it all blends into the background as I make the familiar hour-and-a-half trip from Goldsboro, but not today.

Because today is the day there's a gigantic FOR SALE sign staked just outside my window at the four-way stop sign.

It's not the first one I've seen on Franklin Street; because of the volume of the UNC Chapel Hill sororities and frat houses down the way, family homes can have quick turnover. Noise doesn't bother my parents, not after growing up in Bandra, one of Mumba's busiest suburbs, where the braying street traffic of rickshaws and pedestrians starts at dawn.

But because I'm third in line, the radio is playing a song I hate, and I can't look at the NRA bumper sticker of the asshole stopped in front of me for another second, I glance at the sign.

Mistake.

My shoulders tighten, heart squeezing before free falling into my stomach.

I'm arrested by the glossy real estate agent photo of a cute guy with light golden skin and thick brown hair artfully tossed in an Ivy League crew cut. The straight, perfect nose and the thin lips curved into a one-sided, dimpled I-have-a-secret smile. A small cleft in his chin, like a Desi Henry Cavill. Sienna eyes, bright and mischievous like a copper penny.

Milan Rao. Real estate agent for High Castle Realty.

My fingers tighten around the steering wheel. This isn't just any handsome face.

It's my ex-boyfriend's heartbreaking, promise-breaking face.

In my mind, he's always twenty. We both are. And somehow, being twenty again—and nineteen and eighteen and seventeen and sixteen and fifteen, all the ages that I loved him—feels more real to me than the present. Inch by inch, I sink into the arms of the memory. The deep throatiness of his voice, the way he tips his head back when he laughs, the feel of my name whispered against my heart in the darkness of his bedroom. The tickle of his hair against my chin as he kissed across my collarbone, down my breasts, then back up to my ear.

I used up all my firsts on him. My first kiss. My first boy-friend. The first person to steal my breath and the first to give it back.

The memory isn't so soft anymore, not when revisiting it reminds me that maybe it only feels so real because it was the life I was supposed to have.

The car behind me honks.

I'm yanked out of my reverie so fast my vision blurs away the sharp cut of Milan's jaw, the dark straight-across eyebrows, the fringe of kohl-black lashes lining his eyes. All I see now are the lips I'd known so well mouthing a *Sorry* he never actually said.

Another honk, followed by an impatient blaring succession of noise from the line of cars behind me. "Move it, lady!" someone shouts.

The other drivers at the intersection shoot inquisitive looks my way before deciding to skip my turn. I hold my hand up to the rearview mirror as acknowledgment before taking my foot off the brake. Even though I'm halfway across, a yellow sports car doesn't want to wait and takes a turn too fast, tires squealing as they beat me, forcing me to brake hard in the middle of the intersection.

My heart rattles and doesn't stop until I'm in my parents' driveway.

Once, my heart sped up for him. Now it races for a different reason.

Running from the memory of a boy that I used to run *to*.

I close my eyes as I settle against the seat, switching off the ignition.

Milan and I had been together since we were fifteen. Our parents hadn't been thrilled about it, maybe his more than mine, but with stiff unhappiness, they were determined to be just American enough not to be Indian about their teenagers dating.

But then, after finishing our sophomore year of college, he broke up with me.

I told people it was mutual, because he was the kind of boy

who didn't need to win, like some of my friends' exes. And my parents believed me when I said it's okay, we saw this coming, a long-distance relationship was too hard to maintain, a clean break is better for us, yadda yadda.

More lies, like there weren't already enough holding us all together.

Every reassurance meant to solidify that we were both the ones doing the leaving.

What's worse, *I* even started to believe me.

Thinking about Milan Rao makes me feel like a teenager again.

Young-and-dumb fifteen, too-in-love fifteen.

The kind of fifteen I've never been again.

And honestly? I don't think I want to be.

"Arey, Rita!"

I startle, dropping the truck keys from my limp grip.

My grandmother vigorously waves at me from the front door. Something silver glints in her hand. She's dressed in a mustard-yellow nightie that hits at the ankles. When she first came to live with us, Mom told her to stop going out in her nightgown, but with her usual dismissal, Aji pads out to the driveway, leather chappals slapping against the stone path.

She stops at one of the terra-cotta planters by the side of the garage door.

"You're staying for lunch?" she asks as I get out of the truck.

"Good morning to you, too, Aji."

She snorts, then turns her attention to the bright orange and yellow marigolds. "Do you come to visit us or to use Ruthvik's equipment?" With four precise snips, she beheads the pom-pom flowers with a small pair of scissors with pretty floral detailing that went missing from Mom's sewing box three years ago.

With her back to me, she mercifully doesn't catch my smile drop.

We go inside together and the AC blasts me like I've just walked into a deep-freeze fridge. Sparing no expense on the year-round temperature of your home is an immigrant sign of having "made it," even if it means we're too cold in summer and too hot in winter.

The TV is on, thrumming with a duet. I slip off my black high-tops and leave them by the door next to Dad's loafers, Aji's chappals, and Mom's Gucci Double G white espadrilles.

Aji disappears into her bedroom with her flowers. "You're staying!" she calls over her shoulder. A second later, her door closes and pooja music begins, loud enough to drown out the Bollywood. She keeps a temple in her room for her daily prayer and aarti.

I find my mom in the kitchen chopping cilantro on the island. The room is fragrant with garlic, onion, herbs, and spices. She doesn't look up when I enter, but she does smile. "Dad's out back in the workshop," she says, sliding the confetti of green onto the side of the knife. She nods to the large steel pot on the closest burner. "Lift the lid for me?"

I oblige, inhaling deeply. Fragrant steam rises from the simmering pot of golden daal tadka. There's something unmistakably welcoming about Indian home cooking—the warmth of red chilies and cloves, the woodiness of spices sautéed in hot oil. This is my favorite lentil preparation, the savory swirl of ghee tempered with fried garlic and cumin seeds.

Mom sprinkles the cilantro in a delicate garnish before pulling the pot off the stove. "Thanks, sweetheart." She looks at me now, giving a quick once-over. "You look a little flushed. Do you want to run upstairs and freshen up? Change into something else? You've been wearing that old shirt since . . ." She pauses, stretching her mind back, then shakes her head. "Well, for years. Don't you think it's time to retire it? You have some nice dresses upstairs."

It's usually Aji badgering me to wear a dress. I glance down; I'm wearing my favorite old knotted black tee and shorts, unwashed from yesterday, but jeez, it's not like Mom can *tell*.

When Mom and Dad upgraded to this house, they insisted I get my own room, decorated to my taste. To pacify them, I'd even brought over a dresser with a drawer filled with clothes. Not the clothes I actually wore, just the things I was too sentimental to give away. Something to take up space, like the glossy walnut headboard and desk that bookended the room.

Rajvee thinks it's nice my parents went to all the effort to make sure I'd always have a room even though I'd been living on my own for years. And maybe it would have been nice, if I didn't know the real reason.

This was the backup plan. Just in case I had to come back home one day. They wanted me to know I always had a place with them, wherever they were.

I appreciated it and resented it at the same time.

"No, I'm good as I am," I say, hoping I wasn't going to hurt her feelings. Make her think there's something wrong with the room or that I don't want to be home. "I was really just coming over to borrow Dad's band saw. I have work to get back to. I'll get hot and sweaty anyway."

Once, Mom would have made a crack about my definition of work, but now she just nods. Disappointed. "Maybe you could eat here first? I've missed you."

"I've missed you, too," I say automatically.

Her eyes light up.

My stomach twists. It really does take so little to make her happy.

"Why don't you stay for lunch anyway?" Mom lifts the lid of another pot. "I made rice."

That's surprising. I'm the only one in the family who prefers rice to roti, even though I know that under the tortilla warmer will be a stack of fresh chapati.

"I worry all you eat is ramen," she says.

"Don't forget pizza and takeout," I quip.

She gives a short, unhappy laugh. "How are you doing for money?"

My cheeks burns. "I'm . . . fine." I shove my thumbs into my front pockets, balling my fists tight. It's not so easy to squeeze and crumple in on myself, disappearing like my self-worth.

"Do you need anything? We could write you another check."

"No! I'm fine. I promise I'm fine. I sold a piece this morning, see?" I pull my iPhone from my woven circle purse. I tap the Instagram icon, then Dharma Design's most recent post to show her proof. Something she'll claim she doesn't need, but I know it'll make her feel better.

Mom leans in.

The caption under the Queen Anne dresser has already been edited to say SOLD, but she still looks unconvinced. "Rita, you know Dad and I don't mind—"

She means well. God, I know this. I squash the embarrassment.

"Mom, I know." I gentle my voice. "But I'm twenty-six. I love you guys for wanting to, but you don't have to bail me out every time things get a little tight."

"We worked this hard so it wouldn't be hard for you," she says. It's not the first time we've had this conversation. "If you had someone to take care of you, we wouldn't worry as much."

"Someone does take care of me. *I* take care of me."

She sighs. "Oh, Rita."

That isn't what I mean her eyes convey. She stares again at my black tee, a little too long, like she wishes I'd change it. Like it would be that easy to change *me*.

I bite my lip and look away. My money will run out before my pride will.

"I know dating has been hard since Mi—" She fumbles. "Since then. That maybe there isn't someone else you see yourself with in the long term. Someone to settle down with."

Where is she going with this?

"Mom, not MyShaadi again, please," I say with a groan. "I get enough of that from Aji. Chemistry is way more important to me than astrology or algorithms."

"I wasn't going to suggest a marriage website." Mom draws herself up, a little offended. "You know Dad and I have never pressured you into anything, and I've always squashed all the aunties' notions about setting you up with their sons and nephews, haven't I?"

It's true. Even though she worries that I live alone and haven't seriously dated in years, neither of my parents have ever hounded me the way other Desi kids' parents do. They let me date who I wanted, pursue my passion, *and* live on my own terms.

"I just think," Mom says, "you could be a little more open-minded to falling in love again. All I want is happiness for you, sweetheart. Whomever you find it with."

Now would be the perfect time to bring up Neil—well, not the perfect time, but at least it's an opening, and when am I going to get another one that's even half as good? Better to do this now, fast, while Dad's out back and Aji's music is still playing.

Twenty-eight years ago, before my parents met, Mom thought she was going to marry Amar Dewan, her schoolmate and her brother's best friend. Their parents got along, her brother was their biggest fan, and the astrologers concurred their birth charts were incredibly auspicious.

In those days, you didn't step out with a boy unless he was going to put a ring on it. But before Amar could, his parents quietly broke it off. They'd received a proposal from an American Desi family, and Amar's mother saw this as a chance to fast-track his citizenship.

And then Mom married my dad, Ruthvik Chitniss.

When Neil's older brother was ready to get married, an auntie had innocently asked if my parents had started to look for a bridegroom for me. I wasn't even twenty-one and my parents were apoplectic. Dad because I was his only daughter and he wanted me to marry for love, Mom because there was no way I was ever going to marry into the family that thought she wasn't good enough for their precious son.

I still remember Dad's resigned face as Mom's finger jabbed the air, pronouncing "No daughter of mine will ever be a Dewan. *Let them* ask for Rita, she's too good for them. This family is too good for *those people*."

Little did she know that five years later her daughter would be jumping into bed with the Dewans' youngest son.

My heart crushes and drops into my stomach. Who am I kidding?

There's never going to be a good time to tell her about Neil.

Even if he's practically vibrating for me to tell her.

"I'm not going to marry someone just for financial security," I say finally. "And, honestly, it would be nice if I didn't have to go through this every time I come over just because Aji and all the aunties think twenty-six is such a terrible age to be."

Mom widens her eyes in warning, but it's too late.

"Not as bad as twenty-seven," Aji pipes up. "But definitely worse than twenty-five."

She strolls into the kitchen like she owns it. She's changed out of her nightie and into a pale peach salwar kameez that makes the small black beads of her mangalsutra pop around her neck in contrast, phone in one hand, imported *Times of India* in the other.

I'm too weary to point out the ageism. I've had—and lost—this fight too many times before, and Mom is making big eyes at me, trying to head me off before Aji can double down.

My grandmother's WhatsApp goes off in a flurry of notifications, but Aji continues like she doesn't hear it. "When I was twenty-seven I had three brilliant sons and my husband, your aba, was general manager at Bank of India. Your father is a top orthopedic surgeon who can afford this beautiful house."

She fixes me with a stern what-have-you-accomplished stare while fingering her necklace. "I have a beautiful mangalsutra my mother gave me that I can pass down to you." Aji slants her eyes at Mom. "Maybe *someone* in this family will want to wear it."

Mom makes a soft noise in the back of her throat that could be loosely interpreted as annoyance, but Aji ignores it, lifting the lid of the tortilla warmer to inspect the chapatis instead.

Perfectly soft and round, liberally slathered with ghee, and dotted with golden brown scorch marks from the frying pan.

"Little burned, Esha," says Aji.

"The high heat gives the crispy texture and flavor." Mom plucks the lid out of her hand.

"Hmph." Aji turns to me like she expects me to side with her.

I keep my face neutral. "That's true. That's why seared steak tastes so good."

"Shee!" Aji exclaims, vegetarian sensibilities properly ruffled. "Steak!" She frowns at Mom in reproach, like she's to blame for this. Then, just as quick, she gets her own back. She gives me a self-satisfied smile. "At least you're staying for lunch."

Wait, when was that decided? I open my mouth to protest, but Aji's already scooted from the kitchen, face buried in her phone.

Mom waves a hand. "Honey, set the table, would you? And call your dad in? And are you sure you don't want to change? It must be hot out there. You still look so flushed."

Why on god's green earth is she trying to beat this into the ground?

I open the cabinet to pull out three plates and three steel vatis for the daal. "I'm not staying," I remind her as I start to set the kitchen table. "And, FYI, I love this shirt!"

"No, no, not there," says Mom, using one hand to make a shooing gesture. "I thought it would be nice for all of us to eat in the dining room."

Weird. We never eat in there unless there's company coming.

"I mean it," I stress. "Eating in the fancy room isn't going to tempt me into staying."

She calmly reaches for the top cabinet, pulling out my favorite carrot-chili pickle.

"Moooooooom."

"What? Maybe this is for me."

I'm not buying it. "You said your stomach can't handle it after fifty."

She smiles. "Maybe I'm open to reevaluating my opinion."

Right. My mom, giving a second chance to anything? I should be so lucky.

I try to say it casually. "So now that I have a super-evolved mom, I guess she's totally okay with forgiving her old boyfriend and his mother?"

Her face hardens. "Never," she snaps, thunking the bottle of pickle down on the island.

I flash my palms at her. "Okay, okay, I was just testing you."

Her voice rises, trying and failing for casual, too. "Why are you bringing up—"

The doorbell rings.

Mom almost jumps. "I'll get it."

"No, I will." I dart out of the kitchen, heart thumping. I just needed to get out of there before she saw an inkling of truth on my face.

Neil was wrong about this. Nothing good could come of telling our parents.

My mother's grudge notwithstanding, there is every reason in the world his parents wouldn't love the idea of me, either. I'm the daughter of the woman Amar had wanted to marry. In another life, I could have been his daughter.

Would Neil's ma want her husband's ex's daughter in her family as a daughter-in-law? Would a woman who wanted fresh round, round rotis for her son settle for a girl who bought it frozen from the grocery store?

I yank the door open.

And promptly wish I hadn't.

Because standing in front of me, face drained of color, is Milan Rao.

He takes a half step back, glances at the house number, then back at me. He blinks.

My mouth goes dry. How is he *here*. At my front door. Twenty-six instead of twenty.

"Rita?" He says my name like he's not sure it's mine, and for a stunned, awful second, I gape at him. His voice sounds nothing like the way it used to when it was murmured into my ear or ghosted across my skin. "Rita?" he tries again, staring into my eyes.

I think I'm going to throw up. "No," I manage to gasp before slamming the door.

Chapter 4

Hindsight being twenty-twenty, it's pretty stupid to deny it, because of course he recognized me as instantaneously as I recognized him. You couldn't kiss the same mouth for six years without ingraining the face into your memory.

"Oh my god," I gasp, leaning against the door.

Knock, knock.

Right next to my ear.

I leap away, tripping over the shoes and my own jellied legs.

This isn't happening. This is some heat-induced fever dream. I'm still at home in bed. I'm still in bed. I'm still—

"Rita?" he calls out, this time sounding more sure of himself.

My chest heaves. I feel like I'm in one of those Saturday morning cartoons I used to watch, heart bounding comically out of my chest.

The doorbell peals, shooting goosebumps down my arms.

There's no way I'm opening that door. Nope, no way, sorry, no can do.

What is he even doing here? How did he find out my parents' new address?

First the realty sign. Now this. Did the universe *summon* him?

A hand lands on my shoulder. I jerk.

"Rita, kohn ahey?" says Aji, peering intently at the door like she has X-ray vision.

"Aji, don't!" I hiss, but she's already pounced to the slim vertical window to the left of the door. As usual, she does what she wants and pulls aside a lacy curtain to peer out.

Milan's face is pressed to the window. "Hi, Aji," he says sheepishly.

"Arey!" Aji drops the curtain like it's on fire. She spins, hands on her hips, wild eyed.

"Ididn'tinvitehim," I say, words bumbling over my tongue.

"I did," says Mom coolly, gliding across the foyer to join us. I double take. She's—somehow—found the time to change into a hot pink Nanette Lepore shift dress, wavy brown hair slung over one shoulder instead of its usual cooking ponytail, and a Relentlessly Red M.A.C. lip.

"Why?" I whisper-shriek.

She *tsks* as she unlocks the door. "Rita, you left the poor boy out there in this heat?"

"Mom, that is not an answer! And he is not a 'poor boy'!" I say with finger quotes.

I exchange a look with Aji. She looks surprised, too, and not a lot gets by her.

Mom purses her lips and takes me in from head to toe, settling on the grungy black tee with a can't-be-helped sigh.

Oh no. *This* is why she was so adamant that I change?

I gesture to my shirt. "Mom. Please tell me you didn't want me to look cute for *him*."

Mom's face goes innocent. "I have a beautiful daughter," she says. "Shouldn't I want her to look her best?" She reaches for the doorknob.

My heart lurches. "Nonononononono."

There's no way he's seeing me for the first time in six years with hair plastered to my scalp, dog hair on my shirt, and nothing on my face but SPF.

Before Mom can turn the knob, I flip my head upside down to fluff my haven't-washed-it-in-three-days hair. Mom smiles with approval, but Aji stares like she's not sure who I am.

I'm not even remotely ready to see him, but I force a smile to my face while Mom swings the door open like I didn't just slam it in his face two minutes ago. *You've got this, Rita.*

"Mil-uhn," Mom says warmly, hostess face on, pronouncing his name the right way, even though he's only ever gone by Milan, like the city. "It's good to see you again."

He clears his throat. "Thanks, auntie. You, too. But I thought my mom said—"

"Please, Milan, you're not a teenager, anymore. Call me Esha."

"I didn't know this was your hou—I thought I was meeting a client." He hovers in the doorway, looking more awkward than I've ever seen him. With three generations of Chitniss women to greet him, I guess I can't blame him for his squirrelly eye contact and feet shuffling, but I *can* relish in it for a moment. "When did you move?"

He's the one asking questions when he showed up on *my* doorstep? That's exactly the kind of cheek that I didn't miss from him. Not that there's anything I miss about him at all.

I cross my arms and try not to scowl as I tell him, "A few

years ago. Dad lectures at UNC's medical school now, so he wanted to be closer."

Milan follows the movement of my arms, lingering on my chest. His eyebrows scrunch. There's a long pause before his cheeks redden and he says, "He's still got his practice, though?"

I give him a tight nod. Dad loves his work way too much to quit.

"You're letting the AC out," Aji says in a crotchety voice.

Mom takes hold of his arm and hauls him inside. "Rita, Milan's in real estate."

"Really?" My voice comes out too high. "Wow, I had no idea."

Milan glances at me like he's not sure if I'm kidding. A gentle (disbelieving?) smile curves his lips. "I have signs up and down this street. Kind of impossible to miss."

"Wouldn't know. I keep my eyes on the road when I drive," I reply, uncrossing my arms.

"Rita's a good girl," says Aji. She wags her finger, voice swelling as she comes to my defense. "An excellent driver. First try she passed her test."

"Yeah, I know, I was—" Milan breaks off.

There.

The memory hangs between us, wavering like a maybe truce, a maybe something.

Milan is looking everywhere but at me. So it could also be a maybe nothing.

It's been years since I'd thought about it, but now I remember Aji, Milan, and me squished shoulder to shoulder in the back seat of my parents' car as we drove to the DMV for the written test. He didn't have to do that, he *wanted* to be there for me. Quizzing me on homemade flash cards he'd made for his test a few months earlier. Giving me the biggest smile every time I nailed an answer.

I press my palms to the sides of my clammy thighs (or maybe it's my palms that are clammy) to keep myself from folding my arms again. Something tells me he'd read into that.

Mom takes hold of Milan's arm and herds him toward the kitchen. He casts a look back, but I determinedly don't make eye contact. Aji looks disgruntled, muttering something under her breath as she follows them. Ever since we broke up six years ago, she hasn't been his biggest fan.

Please don't let her say anything embarrassing. I trail behind her, dragging my feet.

"Milan, lemonade?" Mom bends into the fridge. "We also have orange Fanta, coconut water, La Croix sparkling water, and prosecco. Oh! And I picked up a whole crate of Limca from the Indian store. You still like lemon-lime soft drinks, don't you? I remember you *ran* on Sprite during AP testing week. Ah! And here's the Coke. Well, not *Coke* Coke. Store-brand cola." She frowns. "I didn't buy this. Who bought this? Ruthvik!"

"Mom," I say. Read: chill.

"Regular water's fine," says Milan, cheeks a little pink.

Mom holds a glass under the refrigerator's cold water dispenser. "Like Milan was saying, he's in real estate." She's straight faced. Doesn't bat an eye.

"Milan was saying, huh," I drawl, noting the none-too-pointed way she's pulled the conversation back to him. What was she *thinking* inviting him here?

He turns to me with a secret smile. Like he knows I'm embarrassed and he is, too, but we're in this together and we'll get through whatever shenanigans my mother has cooked up.

Betrayal sucker punches me.

He has no business making it out like we're a team here. Smiling at me like that. More importantly, I shouldn't be smiling at him, either.

We are *not* in this together.

I tear my gaze away, severing the moment. I feel him looking at me for a beat longer, but I don't look back. *Stay strong, Rita. He was the one to let you down first, remember?*

Mom's kohl-blackened eyes zero in on me with a don't-trifle-with-me steely glint. "I spoke to Milan's mother at the Deshpandes' potluck last Saturday, and she mentioned he'd been having some trouble with a listing, and I thought, Well, that's something my Rita could help with, isn't it?" She plows right on. "Milan, you'll stay for lunch?" She hands him the glass.

He looks at me before opening his mouth. "I—"

"That's settled then." Mom beams.

He snaps his mouth shut. His expression is stunned.

I'm a little taken aback, too. She ripped that move straight from Aji's playbook. It's clear this situation has been a masterminded set-up from the moment I texted Dad and told him I was coming over today to use his band saw.

Now that the shock of seeing him again has worn off, I'm left with a potent cocktail of emotions, shaken not stirred. But the most identifiable feeling is anger.

At Milan, for being here. For *not* being there when I had needed him.

At myself, for still caring—even if it was only the tiniest bit—what he thought about me.

At Mom, for chasing down a happy ending for me because she didn't have her own.

I meet her eyes, willing her to see what she's putting me through. This is the woman who gave birth to me, whose heart once beat with mine. She should be able to read me better than anyone else on the entire planet. One look at my face used to be all it took for her to know when I'd bombed a test, lost out on a solo in choir, or got in a fight with Raj.

Mom mistakes my silence for agreement. "I told his mother you would stage that house for him." In an aside to me, she adds, "You could use the money."

My cheeks flame. Pinpricks dot my scalp.

I don't need the band saw. I can go home, forget all about the curved wood legs I planned to make for an end table. I'll work with the metal hairpin legs I already have.

"I'm doing fine for money," I tightly tell Milan.

"Rita is just about to expand her business to include full-service interior design." Mom grabs additional plates and cutlery from the drawer.

It takes all my willpower not to reel back. I'm about to expand to *what*, now?

The glib lies falling from her tongue amaze me, even though they shouldn't.

Between my scare at the intersection and this, the universe is officially in cahoots with my mother to reunite us.

"I actually wasn't—" I start to say, but Mom jumps in with, "You'll be her first."

Her words hold a double meaning that I'm pretty sure she doesn't get, but by the telltale blush and tiny smile on Milan's lips, he totally does. He runs a hand through his thick brown hair, all hot and casual, and I hate so much that I notice. I make sure to look away quick before he notices me noticing.

"It's a real problem house from what I've been told," continues Mom. "On the market for two hundred and sixty-two days, which your mom tells me is the longest listing you've ever had." She clucks her tongue. "And this is a seller's market, too."

Even though she doesn't see me, I see her. She thinks she's doing this for me, but at least part of it is for her, too. I can see it in the way she holds herself, poised with anticipation, eyes round and hopeful the way they get only when we watch rom-coms

together. This is her falling-in-love face. She's never looked at
Dad with her heart in her eyes like this.

Not that I needed a reminder, but this hammers home how
very much I can never tell her about Neil. Not unless I want to
be the one responsible for breaking her heart a second time.

I settle on a barstool at the island counter, hunching my
shoulders and keeping my voice flat so everyone is aware I'm
here only as an unwilling participant. There's no point in showing my anger, not when it would only wound her. That's the last
thing I want to do.

"Maybe the house is priced too high," I suggest, even though
that's probably Realtor 101.

"No, it's a fair price," Mom jumps in before Milan can answer.

His face is aghast. "Did my mother tell you *everything*?"

Mom waves her hand. "Oh, the basics. Only that you need
help with this house and your job depends on it, you make six
figures and don't live at home, and you're currently single."

She eyes me. *This is an opportunity, Rita.*

I squint. *Nope, can't see it.*

Milan swallows. "Right. Just all the info you need to file my
taxes or make a dating profile. Nothing important or anything."

I choke back a laugh. Because Milan isn't funny. Definitely not.

"I wouldn't recommend putting your salary on a dating
profile," says Mom. "Unless you're trying to attract gold diggers."
Without preamble, she says, "Did you know Rita restores furniture? She doesn't care about money at all. She followed her passion
and does this for love. She even told me she doesn't want to
marry for money. See how well you'd work together?" She blinks,
the picture of innocence. "Professionally, I mean."

Dear god. She's not even trying to be subtle.

One way or another, this is going to happen. The only question is how much I fight it.

Milan glances at me, then down to my black tee like he's trying to read the faded letters.

Jeez, I've filled out since he last saw me, but he could be a bit less obvious about staring.

I return his interest, taking in his appearance for the first time. Broad shoulders, slim hips. Slight build. Ankle-length black pants, gray V neck, and an unbuttoned blue chambray shirt with the sleeves rolled up, one that makes me wonder if it's as soft as it looks.

In high school, Milan mostly stuck to classic black athleisure and Levi's jeans, while my entire wardrobe screamed discount Serena van der Woodsen. Sometime in the last six years, his style leveled up big time.

He's dressed so nice and he didn't even know I was going to be here, which means he just . . . looks like this all the time.

Great, now he's going to think I'm dressed like I don't care because I don't have money. Maybe I should have listened to Mom and changed, after all.

I make a mental note to put some effort into my outfit the next time I see him—

NO. Emphatic, all caps NO. What am I *thinking*? I dress for me, not for men.

I don't have to roll over and go along with this set-up. There isn't going to *be* a next time.

"So . . . thanks, but I'm going to pass," I say between gritted teeth.

One corner of his mouth lifts. "I didn't offer you the job."

I scowl. "Your mother did."

"My mother doesn't speak for me," he counters.

Mom raises her hand. "Rita's mother does speak for her and she would definitely like to accept the job, Milan. With pleasure."

Pleasure and *Milan* should not go in the same sentence.

"Also," Mom adds, "I already told your mother she would."

"What? You can't commit me to projects without even asking." I stand up, scraping the barstool back. "You had no right to speak for me, Mom. This is *not* a playdate! You can't just . . . just arrange things for us like we're children!"

Aji speaks for the first time. "If things were that easy, I'd arrange you a match on MyShaadi.com like *that*." She snaps her fingers.

Milan stares at me. "You're on MyShaadi?"

A beat. "Yes," I bite out. "I'd love to meet some *reliable* men I can actually count on."

He flinches.

Fierce knee-jerk victory shoots through me. He looks *crushed*. Fucking good. Now he knows there is zip, zilch, zero chance of us ever getting together again.

He takes a step closer to me, face impossibly earnest. "Rita—"

"Wonderful." Mom claps her hands. "Rita is dead set on marriage, and Milan desperately needs the help, it's decided. There's no reason you two can't work together, unless . . . ." She lets the pause linger. "You still have feelings for each other?"

I hold my breath, looking at him head on.

If he looks sad right now, it's not because of anything I said. Maybe that's just his default expression. How would I know? It's not like we speak anymore. Rajvee and her mom cater his office's open houses, but ever since junior year of college when she made the mistake of telling me she'd seen him out with some other girl and I spent the rest of the semester stalking their Instagrams and fuming over every gooey caption, we decided that Raj's acquaintance with Milan aside, she wasn't allowed to tell me anything else about him.

"Milan?" Mom prompts.

He doesn't say anything, just worries at his lower lip, which I guess says it all.

Fine. Right. Okay. Whatever. It's fine.

If Mom knew the whole story, he'd be out of here faster than he could say "Auntie."

Aji's WhatsApp dings, breaking the awkward silence.

"That was years ago. I'm pretty sure we're both over it. I'm up for it if you are, Milan." I've avoided saying his name out loud for so long that my tongue stumbles, but I catch myself before he can notice.

He looks at me a little helplessly, like I was his last chance to get out of this, and now he's backed into a corner. "Well, I . . . I guess? I mean, if my mom already talked to you about it."

"Don't you think for yourself," I mutter under my breath.

He doesn't give away any sign that he heard me, but Aji smirks.

Damn it, what's the point of insulting him if I don't say it loud enough for him to hear?

"Vah re vah, kai good boy ahes tu," says Aji, sneering so he knows it's not a compliment. Not when all the praising words are at odds with the stone-cold voice that lands like a barb. Mom shoots her an odd look as if she's trying to puzzle it out, too, but my grandmother ignores us and heads for the dining room.

"Well, you do have the experience," says Milan. "I hope you're okay with this."

My heart starts to wrench like the KitKats we used to split. The last time I'd really heard his voice, it had been on that damn voicemail recording during the worst moment of my life, and he'd been so vehement then, so full of quivering desperation and righteous, finger-pointing anger.

So different from his voice now—conscientious, tentative. The kind of voice that would take back the callous *I think we should take a break* if I wasn't okay with it.

I swallow. That's why my mom thinks the love from before is still strong.

Because I told them I would be okay. Because I didn't know then that I wouldn't be, not for a good long time. Because Mom thinks Milan's always going to be the one who got away.

To her, he's my Amar.

Here's what she doesn't know, can't know, has no *way* of knowing: Milan can't be the boy who got away if he threw me away first.

So am I okay? Seriously, coming from him, the caring boyfriend act is hard to swallow.

"Yeah. It's fine." I can hear how rigid my voice has become. "But let's get one thing straight, okay? I'm not doing it for the money, although, yeah, money's nice. So I hope my mom was right that this will be paid, because if not—"

"No, yeah!" he says in a rush. "It's in my budget."

"Oh. Okay. So then we're . . ." I swallow back my tirade about fair pay. "All set."

Mom busies herself in the fridge again, coming out with a half-full bottle of her favorite prosecco. "Ah, Ruthvik. Finally. Wine with lunch?"

I turn around. "Hi, Dad." My six-foot-two dad comes through the sliding-glass doors, wearing a Seahawk's cap and a big grin that fades when he sees Milan there, too.

Relief whooshes through me. His creased brow and tight jaw tell me one thing—he may have let Mom know I was coming over, but at least he didn't have anything to do with tag teaming me. It's another reason I don't love coming home. I hate being reminded my parents aren't in love with each other. Going through the motions. Making do.

"Hi, chinu-minu." Despite the softness of the endearment, his mouth takes on a hard set as he takes off his cap. He's not exactly Milan's biggest fan, either. "What's going on here?" He shoots Mom a you-had-something-to-do-with-this-didn't-you look.

"So I should probably be going," Milan says, edging toward the hallway.

"Nonsense," Mom says crisply, ignoring Dad's fixed stare at Milan's panicked face. She gives herself a generous pour of prosecco, then fills up Dad's glass, too. "We haven't seen you in years and you're here now, anyway. We can all be adults, can't we?" She makes sure to widen her eyes at me, implying *I'm* the one acting childish. Well then.

"Milan can do what he wants," I say with a shrug. Then, quieter but not quiet enough he can't hear, I add, "He usually does."

Milan stops moving. His eyes narrow. "Yes, Auntie, clearly we're all adults here."

"No need to be so formal, it's Esha," Mom reminds him.

His smile is mostly wince, but with the trademark good manners I remember from high school, he helps Mom carry the heaviest CorningWare dishes of food to the dining room.

Dad slings his arm around me while using the other to down the wine. "Sorry about your mom, kiddo. She means well. She just wants to see you happy."

I know she does. But how could she think for a second that I'd appreciate her interfering in my life any more than she appreciated Amar's mother intruding in hers?

How could she not see that just because her heart was in the right place, it didn't mean that she wasn't breaking mine?

Even though I hadn't actually crashed my car this morning

after seeing Milan's face, it still feels like I'm walking away from an accident.

Dad reads the misgivings on my face and sighs, giving my shoulder a squeeze. "It's just one lunch," he says, using his soothing doctor voice, his let's-see-how-bad-it-is-first-before-you-start-catastrophizing voice.

It doesn't have the intended effect. I'm not nine-year-old Rita who broke her arm climbing the tallest tree in the neighborhood to knock a crowing bully off his pedestal. I think I may have actually cried *less* when that happened.

Because when a bone breaks, it can be set, mended good as new.

Hearts? Not so much.

Chapter 5

When lunch was over, Milan was able to dash off a quickly mumbled thanks before he made his escape, while I was stuck there longer, letting Mom talk at me. While we cleared the table, during the dishwasher's rinse cycle, even following me out to the workshop, all the while keeping up a nonstop stream of one-sided conversation outlining Milan's good qualities.

She can list all the pros she wants; they'll never outweigh the seen-from-space con.

Dad, who had already snuck out to the workshop during the boy talk—something he'd never been that comfortable with—takes one look at my pained face and wordlessly begins cutting the large sweeping curves for my end table legs, the powerful blade of his band saw making quick work of the blocks of wood.

My phone dings, lighting up the screen.

"Who is that?" Mom tries to peek at the screen, making no secret that she's hoping it's Milan texting to set up our collaboration.

"No one," I say. "Raj." I whisk the phone to my chest before she sees Neil's message.

I'll help you move the dresser over to the neighbor's house before dinner.

A sweet offer, even though I can do it myself and never expect my boyfriends to do the "manly" lifting.

Then comes a barrage of notifications. Every sentence is its own message.

And don't think you're off the hook, Reets ;)

We really should pick up the conversation from yesterday . . .

If we're not going to be honest with our parents, where is this even going?

Plus, I'm pretty sure Ma doesn't even know or care about what happened . . .

My dad loves her.

Of course his mom wouldn't care. She *won*.
My mom was the one left behind.
The distinction seems lost on him, why his mom doesn't get to be the one upset.

I promise it won't be weird if our moms meet?

Indians don't do Jersey Shore catfights hahaha.

My right eyelid twitches the way it hasn't done since finals week in college.

I leave him on read, swiping away the notifications.

"What's Raj saying?" Mom asks, leaning forward to peer at the screen I'm angling away.

"Nothing." I stick my phone in my back pocket.

Her smile turns cat-who-ate-the-canary pleased. "Is it Milan?"

"No! I told you, it's Raj. Dad, here, let me do the next leg."

It was the wrong thing to say.

Hurt flashes over Mom's face. She feels excluded from the hobby that had me spending so many hours of high school learning from Dad. Like every other emotion, she wears this one on her sleeve, too. "I'll just pack up the food I made you," she says, blinking fast. "I already set aside extra daal." She turns away hurriedly, heading back to the house.

Dad looks at me. "Go easy on her," he says, and it's not quite a rebuke, but also it is.

Aji cajoles me into staying for tea and digestive biscuits before I head home with leftovers from lunch: a mixed vegetable korma, and piping hot onion and mirchi pakoras.

Even as I accepted Mom's Tupperware I knew I wouldn't be digging into her food tonight, no matter how delicious it smelled the entire car ride home. It was a small, childish rebellion, but it was the only one I could let myself get away with.

And maybe I felt a little guilty, too.

Back home, I got to work mounting the new legs on the end table and painted its first black coat, leaving it to dry in the garage while I started to make my favorite comfort food, masala mac. I vented to Raj on speakerphone about the total absurdity of Mom's scheming with Milan's mom to set us up—they were both watching entirely too many Bollywood soap operas if they thought I'd fall back into his arms after all this time. After years of forbidding Raj to mention his name in my presence, "Milan" fell from her lips with a dizzying, pseudo-unpleasant regularity.

My chest was still heaving from my rant when my phone chimed with Neil's apology text. He wouldn't be home in time for dinner, but would try to get away from work at the earliest opportunity. For once, at least, his ma wasn't the excuse.

Too hungry to wait for him, I went ahead and started scarfing down a bowl of masala mac while making my side salad. But right after mixing in the dressing, Paula's husband, Rick, knocked on the door to ask if I needed any help delivering the dresser. By the time I loaded it up on my truck, dropped it off, and came home, I knew there would be nothing crisp about my Caesar.

Just as I step back through my door, my phone dings.

On the way reads Neil's text message. I leave him on read because he's not on the way, probably not even heading to the parking lot; he only spells it out when he's still spinning in slow circles in his office chair at work because *something* came up and he knows he's going to be late.

His tells are easy. If he was really on the way, his text would have read "On *my* way!," the predictive shortcut of "OMW" that he uses when he's already behind the wheel, because he knows I hate it when he texts at length while waiting at stoplights. Normally I'd tap back a thumbs-up, but I'm fresh out of understanding tonight. Not when he stuck around at work—I check the time on my phone—*two* hours later than he needed to be, missing the dinner he promised to be there for and the delivery he offered to help me with.

Just as expected, by my return the romaine leaves are soggy, the thin radish slices have bled pink into the dressing, and the croutons squish into pulp with the tiniest pressure of my tongue.

If I'm waiting on Neil, anyway, might as well have another bowl of masala mac to change the bad taste in my mouth. But no, better not. If I have even one more scoop, dinner will be too heavy in my gut and I won't feel sexy enough to be on top tonight.

And yet, I'm not sure even solid B+ sex is better than the cheesy, creamy homemade macaroni spiced with diced tomato and onions sautéed in chili powder and garam masala.

I send the picture of my second bowl to Raj and the family WhatsApp group: a judgmental "baap re, so much cheese" and shocked cat face from Aji; a thumbs-up and heart-eyes from Dad; a reproachful "then how come you didn't like the tomato Maggi noodles I made?" to which the *only* possible answer is "that was a crime against instant ramen, Mom."

Which is followed by "Have you and Milan fixed a time and date, yet?" Yellow heart, red rose, emoji with heart eyes, cat with heart eyes, giant red question mark.

All she's missing is the engagement ring.

I send back a string of vomit emojis. The only rational response, obviously.

Later, Raj messages me a flurry of shocked cat-face emojis and tongue-out emojis right as I get in the tub for a soak with a fizzy bath bomb and even fizzier Moscato d'Asti.

IT'S MEAN TO SHOW ME WHAT YOU'RE EATING IF
YOU'RE NOT SHARING IT WITH ME!!!

Talking with her always brings on the rush of serotonin and endorphins of a full-body, gut-busting laugh.

I relax in the tub with my wine until the water cools and my glass runs empty. By the time I'm out, most of the tension has ebbed away like the remnants of the bath bomb on their descent down the drain.

Cheeks flushed from my scrub, eyelashes wetly clumped, shampooed hair clinging to my neck and coiling over large pinky-brown areolas, I look nothing like the self-conscious teenager who pretended not to hate taking her bra off to have sex with Milan. As I gather my hair into a fist to squeeze out the excess water, I brush a nipple, sparking arousal down to my belly.

I let my hand trail lower. My skin is soft and dewy, and I wonder what Milan would say if he could see me like this.

Confident. Proud. Sensual.

Then I think, *Oh god I absolutely do not want Milan seeing me naked.* So I splay my palm over my torso, imagining Neil pressing close, and twist side to side to find my best angle, indulging in a tiny having-sex-while-watching-ourselves-in-a-mirror fantasy.

Now should be the moment he comes home, wraps his arms around me from behind, and takes me. I stare at the steamed mirror like I'm willing him to appear, like a hero emerging from the fog of the moors, dark overcoat flapping open to reveal a shirt with a deep V neck and a slim but toned chest I can run my lips over.

Thick brown hair blowing away from his face. Thin lips crooking into a smile full of wicked promise. Bright honey-brown eyes that could draw a bear. A cute butt-chin where I could nestle my thumb when I cupped the side of his face, drawing him closer . . . closer . . .

Mouth dry, I almost jump at the soft scraping against the bathroom door.

Lightning-rod anticipation shoots through me, heading straight between my legs. My heartbeat slams in my ears. For one unnerving second, I don't know who I expect to be on the other side of the door.

But then I hear a plaintive woof, and I drop my hands from my body, slumping with disappointment. It's only Harrie.

I try to grasp on to the moment of arousal again and discover it's well and truly left the building. Like dandelion fluff floating away before I can remember to make a wish, it slips between my fingers.

I need something to grab on to so I don't float away, too. My fingers clasp the stem of my wineglass nestled in the corner of the tub and backsplash. I toss back the dregs. I'm such an idiot. The only man I'm sleeping with who has the keys to my front door is Neil.

Your boyfriend, Neil, remember?

Deliciously shivery from the chilled wine and still warm from the tub, I slip into a black allover-lace panty, forgo the bra, and wear an oversize flannel so soft and old that the inside collar's more pill than fabric, fastening only the button above my navel.

I consider my reflection, wondering if there's part of me that should feel guilty that Neil wasn't exactly the leading man in my fantasy. I read somewhere once that when we fantasize about people it's not necessarily them we're seeing, but aspects of ourselves. So maybe I'm just horny and need to own that.

I wasn't thinking about Milan, *obviously.* He was just . . . there. Like the new growth of mildew in the grout between my bathtub wall tiles. Appearing anywhere that's susceptible to, uh, excess moisture. My cheeks burn. God, it's hot in this bathroom.

Better open the door and air it out. The steam coating the mirror has already started to dissipate, revealing the "Hey Sexy!" with a generously proportioned penis stand-in, the infamous eggplant, that I drew on the fogged-up mirror days ago, but which Neil hadn't even noticed.

I sigh and scrub it away.

Harrie lightly growls as I pad back into the bedroom, attuned to my mood as ever. He's like the best friend who's always prepared to no-context hate the same guy you do.

"It's okay, bud," I say with a sigh, scratching him behind the ears and ignoring his whine to join me on the bed. If he gets comfortable, by the time Neil gets here, Harrie will have very definite ideas about whose space this is. I can deal with only one boy pouting tonight, not both.

Freddie's read my mind because he ambles into the room with a knowing expression before circling his favorite spot on my rag-rug and elegantly folding his limbs under him.

Unlike Harrie, who flops on his back, arms and legs akimbo, and tongue out. His eyes beseech me: *I'm cute, Mom, take pity on me.* My baby's making a statement, but it's one I don't fall for and Freddie pretends not to see, because Freddie, unlike the rest of us, is a grown-up.

"You two don't know how lucky you are not to have girl problems," I inform them.

The wily look Freddie gives me says clearly: *You're* our girl problem.

"Yeah, yeah," I mutter, falling on my back, only marginally less sprawled than Harrie.

Freddie doesn't give up on me, marching himself right between my dangling feet and fixing me with an imposing that's-bad-posture-young-lady stare that would make Aji proud.

I straighten without thinking about it. God, he has me well trained.

With one last, suspicious look, he pivots back to his spot on the rug.

And because I can't help but annoy my young-but-old-man-at-heart pupper, I slump my back and feign inching back down again. At once, his head pricks forward. He opens his mouth, about to bark, but then catches himself.

Because Freddie does not bark for anything shy of an intruder, and since I've never had one—knock on wood—there's no proof he'd do it then, either, but I'd like to think he loves me enough to deign to do so.

"I'm so sad," I say to the ceiling. "Pestering my dog because I'm bored and pent up and missing him." I want to mean Neil, but as soon as the confession is out there, I know I don't.

I miss you I type to Neil, anyway. And once I've hit send, I know it's the truth.

He isn't perfect, but he wouldn't hurt me. Not on purpose, anyway.

He starts typing back right away. SRY!!! Ma's being a drama queen as usual. Steam-coming-out-the-nostrils emoji. Clenched-teeth emoji.

Then, Can't talk. Tell you later. Blowing-a-kiss emoji.

I resent this woman, his ma, for so much more than just the principle of replacing my mother. This faceless woman I have never seen, never met, and her control over her son, terrify me to a visceral degree. In my mind, she plays the predictable villain-ous mother-in-law in a Bollywood script, the Indian saas ready to browbeat any girl who dares marry her son.

Without meaning to, I remember Milan's mother, to whom I was already as good as a daughter. His parents were so embar-rassed by what he did that they avoided us for years.

Until now.

Tears catch in the corner of my eyes, slide down the side of my nose, tremble over my upper lip, and finally crash-land in the valley between my breasts. I'm ridiculous, driven to literal tears because of some asshole I dated in high school and college. The pressure builds in my chest like a shaken can of soda until finally a laugh bubbles out.

I told Milan I was on MyShaadi.com to meet reliable men. Me, Rita. I *said* that.

I really *was* a mess if I threw that in his face.

My amusement peters away.

Of course, Mom wouldn't have believed me for a second. Despite Aji's harping, I've held my ground on not believing in the divine intervention of the matrimonial website. I'd rather put my stock in the magic of meet-cutes than in algorithmic kismat connections.

Like meeting a guy on Tinder who happened to be the son of the man who scorned your mother, hooking up with him, and hiding your relationship for the next three months because you're pretty sure it makes you a terrible daughter?

Now that I think about it, the only way Neil would be accepted is if MyShaadi.com proved he was my perfect match. Hell, my *only* match. If Neil was literally the last man on earth, my family would give him the red-carpet, cherished-son-in-law treatment, never mind that we're not actually getting married.

"Holy shit." I say it so loud that Harrie and Freddie both raise their heads.

"Holy SHIT." Again, louder.

Ignoring Harrie's confused yips, I grab my laptop from the nightstand and flip it open. Hunched over on the bed, I navigate to the MyShaadi website. The page populates with a huge graphic that reads *Helping You Find Happiness!* and a glossy header with a brown couple sporting beatific smiles, arms loosely around each other, decked out in wedding regalia.

And their promise: *At least one match guaranteed in your first 24 hours!*

Gross, the site remembers me. *Welcome Back, Rita! We're So Glad to See You Again! What's New with You? Please Log In to Update Your Profile.*

Scrolling down, I find dozens of satisfied customer testimonials as well as search options based on mother tongue, caste, and religion. I frown. It feels like I'm basically customizing an online shopping basket, especially when a pop-up tells me I can upgrade to a premium account for more personalized matches based on age, education, and skin color. This is so *cringe*.

Almost ready to talk myself out of this this-is-either-brilliant-or-brilliantly-bad plan, I swipe my thumb across the trackpad, about to close out of everything. But then I think, no, this is fighting fire with fire. If Mom can use trickery to get me and Milan in a room together, then why can't I use my own cunning to devise a ploy to get both my family and Neil's off his back?

I can see the Hallmark—if it wasn't so white—movie trailer right now:

Rita, a single twenty-six-year-old woman, gives MyShaadi. com another chance.

Neil, a single twenty-seven-year-old man, signs up for a new account hoping to find love.

In a surprise plot twist that will surprise exactly no one, they match with no one else except—*gasp*—each other?

My idea has gained steam, enough to play whack-a-mole with my heart. I'm thinking of possible problems that could rear their ugly heads and fucking *annihilating* them. We'll have to fake it, of course, so we can match our answers to each other. Fill our personality profiles with outrageous traits and bomb the compatibility so hard that no algorithm would even *think* we were suitable for other human beings.

We can't assume our parents won't demand access to our accounts so they can check up on eligible spouses—not with a mom as helicopter as his and an aji as nosy as mine.

So all we need to do is be the most troll-worthy versions of ourselves so not even *one* other person matches with us, and even if by some wacky coincidence, one does, they'll be so D-list that Neil will look like Prince Charming in comparison.

I probably look like a total goon, if Harrie's concerned

puppy-dog eyes and Freddie's alert, perked ears are anything to go by, but I can't stop smiling.

My scam will buy us a few months, maybe even a *year*, of dating, if we want it, before either of our families start grumbling about marriage and grandchildren. How didn't I think of this before? The workaround of using a matrimonial site as a defense tactic, a literal shaadi-block, is a sheer genius way of letting Neil and me figure out if we're going anywhere.

I can just imagine the *crushed* expression on Milan's face when he finds out that not only have I met my dream man online, but I'm thinking about marrying him. It would serve him right to see exactly what he'd let slip away.

It can't be too obvious. I can't flaunt how great my life is without him; I have to play this right. Casual and effortless, like his hair always seems to be. That'll show him precisely how *okay* I am. How *not hard at all* I find his unwanted reappearance in my life.

The past is the past, and that's exactly where it's going to remain.

I smile a feral kind of smile.

And of course, he *is* going to find out.

Because when my plan works, and it will, Milan Rao is going to have a front-row seat to my boyfriend bliss.

Chapter 6

I'm still cackling about the whole set-up, and mentally rubbing my palms together like a Disney villain, when Harrie, my personal alarm, starts barking as soon as the living room lights flick on. He gives up trying to annoy Freddie into play, and takes off for the front door, ready to defend me from home invaders and boyfriends in equal measure. There's a small, somewhat undignified human yelp as Harrie undoubtedly nosedives for Neil's leather dress shoes.

I shut my laptop with a guilty *snap*. I hadn't meant to spend so much time flipping between the MyShaadi site and snooping on the High Castle web page to identify Milan's hard-to-sell home. Broken up for six years and I let myself get sucked into—

No, this doesn't count. It's for work. It's not like I'm stalking his social media to see what he's been up to. If I didn't give in back then, there's no reason to break my streak now.

It's not difficult to see why the house wasn't working. In a family-friendly neighborhood full of farmhouse- and craftsman-style houses, next to a great elementary and middle school, the owner-architect who had designed this place really fucked up.

Of *course* people bypassed the ultracontemporary home with huge plate glass windows and forbidding asymmetrical lines. It stuck out like a concrete-and-metal thumb. The furnishings matched the style of the house, which I promptly dubbed the Soulless Wonder.

Very few people would want to buy a cold, sterile house that didn't feel like a home, especially with little kids. Even if they braved the outward appearance, the second they saw the lounge-y inside, they would know it wasn't a home they could see themselves living in, not without feeling like a fraud. The curved-back white designer sofa was a grape juice or red wine spill waiting to happen; the behemoth steel floor lamp arching over half the living room made me nervous just looking at it; and the lack of soft furnishings *anywhere*, including no curtains in the bedroom (!!!), screamed: *This place is waaaaayyyy too slick for you.*

"Harrie, I've only met you a hundred times, minimum," says Neil, his voice drifting in from outside the bedroom door. "One of these days you'll have to acknowledge that you know me as something other than 'Guy You Bark At.'"

He enters my bedroom with his best forgive-me smile and a handful of apology flowers from Trader Joe's.

Good dog, I think to myself.

"Rita, your attack dog has a thing for Cole Haan," Neil says with a weak smile.

At my blank expression, he looks meaningfully at his socked feet.

Oh. The shoes he kicked off next to the front door.

I try for a joke. "You named your shoes?"

He presents the flowers, not looking amused.

I take them, not quite mollified. "Do you want dinner? There's leftovers in the fridge."

"I, uh, ate at home. Ma made idli sambar and mutton curry."

Other women worry about catching lipstick marks on their man's collar; I have to watch out for brown curry stains and onion breath to tell me he sneaked off to his beloved ma's.

Grim, I ask, "What happened to 'on the way'? That was hours ago. You said you'd have dinner here. You could have—"

Been honest. Chose me first, for once. Cut the cord a little.

He unbuttons his shirt, letting it fall to the floor instead of the chair.

Which is *right* there.

"One of the guys caught me right as I was about to leave," Neil explains, "and said the question couldn't wait. And then Ma called me on the drive here and said there was an emergency, so of course I just headed straight there."

Of course he did.

I fold my legs underneath me, curling the toes hard. "So what was it?"

Harrie prances in, yipping once in Neil's direction, and tramples over the shirt with aplomb before settling himself snuggled into Freddie's side with his usual lack of personal space.

"Huh?" Neil pauses midway through taking off his pants. "Oh. It was nothing. You know how she exaggerates sometimes to get what she wants." He drops the pants on top of the shirt.

I clench my teeth. *And yet you drop everything and go running.*

"Oh hey, didn't you need me for something?"

"It was nothing," I snipe, feeling guilty almost immediately when his face falls. "Sorry. It was just a little embarrassing when Paula's husband stopped by to pick up the piece she bought. Don't worry about it. I loaded it up on the dolly and took it over on my truck like usual."

Neil's eyes light up. Nothing ever keeps him down for long. "Yeah, that's right, you made a sale. Congrats, babe. I'm sorry, it slipped my mind. But looks like it wasn't a big deal?" Down to his boxers and undershirt off, he slides onto the bed. "Maybe we should celebrate?"

His cologne has some major staying power. Even with his clothes puddled on the floor. I pull away. "Wait, so, indulge my nosiness, but remind me why she called you over, again?"

"Why else? *You should take the future seriously, beta*," he mimics.

"Marriage?"

"When I burst in the door thinking something terrible happened, I came face-to-face with a girl dressed in the jazziest kurta I've ever seen in my life and both her parents staring at me. See, this is why I keep telling you we should just tell our folks about us and get it over wi—"

Before he can continue his impassioned tirade, I say calmly, "I completely agree."

Neil gapes. He also forgets to blink. "Did you just say you agree with me? But, but, I didn't even get a chance to convince you yet."

"You don't need to." I pivot my laptop to face him, switching tabs to our MyShaadi profiles.

"Oh my god!" Neil's eyes widen. "Shit. Rita. Our parents did this?"

Before he can work himself into righteous indignation, I say, "No, I did."

Again, his jaw drops. "I . . . don't understand." Then his eyes narrow. "Are you trying to tell me something? Look, is this about yesterday? You want us to see other people?"

"Yes, but not the way you think."

"Right, because there's really a lot of different ways to

misunderstand"—Neil gestures to the offending screen with a wry smile—"your girlfriend making a profile on MyShaadi.com."

"Your mom keeps pressuring you to get married. My mom keeps pushing me at—" I stop short. I can't tell him about Milan. "Also pushing me toward marriage," I recover, thinking fast. "And I'm not going to lie, Neil, the weekly digs about how life would be so much easier for you if only you had a girlfriend to bring home to mummy is . . . well, kind of a lot. Especially when I told you that this will break my mother's heart." He opens his mouth, but I race on. "And yes, yes, I know you're going to say your parents are happily married but—" I also can't tell him mine aren't, and I'm pretty sure it's because of his.

"But, Rita," he says when I'm done explaining the whole scam to him. "It'll never work. How is it possible that we don't get any other matches except each other? The whole point of a match-making service is to provide people with the kind of options they don't get in real life."

"I'll show you."

I make him get his work laptop. He brings a gust of cologne-thick air back with him.

After I hand over his log-in info, we each have our own profile on our screen. "Now we just take the personality assessment, fill out all our interests and goals, and identify what kind of partner we're looking for. It says to be as specific as possible so their AI can give us our best matches. Our job is to make sure we don't come across as appealing in any way, while still making sure our interests describe each other perfectly. So, for example, favorite movie, we'd both type in *Coco*."

"Right." He still looks unconvinced.

"What's up, Neil?" I touch his forearm. "Doesn't this solve all our problems?"

Four birds, one stone. His mom will stop hounding him to

meet girls, my mom will stop thinking I still have a future with Milan, Neil and I can date in peace, and if Milan cries himself to sleep every night, it's literally win-win-win-win. The perfect set-up.

"I g-guess." Neil taps at the trackpad. "I mean, it just seems like a lot of work, but if you think it's a good idea . . ."

"So you're in?" I press. "We're doing this?"

He nods.

The pressure in my chest eases. I hadn't realized until now just how nervous I was that he wouldn't be on board, that he'd hate the idea of lying to his ma, or even that he'd identify some oversight that would blow this whole scam apart.

"Should we fill it in together?" I ask eagerly. My cursor is already poised over start.

"How about tomorrow? I'm kind of tired. It's, like, ten-thirty. These online quizzes take forever. Remember that IQ one?" He yawns and stretches his arms behind his head.

Could he *be* any less enthused? "Oh. Oh, yeah, okay. That should be fine." I blink past the disappointment and sink back onto my side of the bed. "You've had a long day."

Neil's work-life and mom-girlfriend balance are two conversations we've had a *lot*.

"Is it really fine or is it the kind of fine that's going to keep you up?"

Delight Bambi-prances down my spine. "See how well you know me?"

He laughs. "Didn't your mom ever tell you not to pester Daddy as soon as he came through the door?"

"She always made me wait an hour for him to decompress," I say. "I wasn't supposed to ask him questions or beg for attention or chatter at him nonstop about my day. Although, if you just called yourself the 'daddy' in this scenario"—I give him a light, quick peck on the lips—"I'll have to kick you out of this bed. Because, one, yuck. And, two, yuck."

Neil grins, grabbing his laptop from the nightstand and settling it on his lap. "Okay. Let's do this." He stifles a yawn. "I swear I'm awake," he says when he catches me watching.

"Thank you. I promise you won't regret this." I'd go in for a cheek kiss, but my nostrils are still tingling from his cologne. I tap start. "Question one—"

"How about we just do it on our own? I mean, you said it yourself. If I majored in Rita, I'd be at the top of the class. A-pluses only."

His confidence is nice, but if we don't match our answers to be equally terrible, there's every chance we'll get matches other than each other. But maybe that's okay. I can reevaluate, I can adapt. The chances of only matching with each other was a long shot, maybe. If we show our parents all the people we want to pass on, it'll just set us up better when we "find" each other.

My mom will only be thrilled about Neil if she thinks he's the only guy I find appealing. So maybe the best way to prove he's my Prince Charming is to show her all the frogs first.

I haven't told Raj about this yet, but I know exactly what she'd say—that I have nothing in common with Neil.

Wouldn't filling out our answers independently and *still* matching, anyway, be the perfect way to rub her nose in her wrongness?

"Okay," I say, drawing the word out like the longer it took the most okay with it I'd be.

"Great!" He turns his attention back to his screen, eyes skimming at a speed that makes me a little worried for him.

It's not like it's a race.

At least, I don't think it is until Neil adds, "Last one done has to wake up early to get Little Shop of Hors D'Oeuvres's donuts for breakfast on Saturday."

Oh. I work my mouth into a stiff game-on smile and start reading the first question, trying to ignore the loud *click-click-clicks* next to me. Neil's already way ahead, typing with the ease of someone who was passed the answers before the test. He's rough with his keyboard in a way that makes me clench my teeth, but I don't want to interrupt him now that we've finally gotten started. And he does know me. So we're fine. This is fine. It's all going to be fine.

Even if I can't shake the thought that he's rushing through it so he can go to sleep.

Question #1: Why do you want to get married?
Because I do not believe in premarital sex and I'm tired of waiting ☺

The sheer cheek of my answer makes me grin.

Question #2: Are you spiritually strong?
Yes, I can hold my liquor with the best of them!

My jaw hurts from this dorky, inordinately-pleased-with-myself smirk.

This time tomorrow, MyShaadi.com will deliver on their promise and tell me what I already know—Neil is the man for me.

Chapter 7

S till can't believe Esha Auntie managed to pull a fast one on you," Rajvee Delahaye cackles. "Indian moms are truly the *most* terrifying. At least tell me there was some"—she waggles her eyebrows suggestively—"under the table?"

"Yes, Raj, in front of Mom, Dad, and Aji, I let him have his way with me," I say dryly.

It's a busy Friday morning at her mom Una's bistro, Little Shop of Hors D'Oeuvres, a mere ten minutes before nine a.m. When I was starting out and struggling to make ends meet on an artist's unpredictable income, Una hired me part time. I still help out a few times a month for old times' sake. The early morning rush is no time to gossip, but Rajvee's not going to let a little something like dozens of expectant, hungry customers get in the way of hearing about my nonexistent rendezvous.

"Attagirl," she crows. As she bends to pry a mini Belgian waffle from the iron, her cut-at-home bangs flop into her eyes. "You wouldn't happen to have a bobby pin, would you?"

It's already fished out of my rattan circle purse. "Who do you think you're talking to?" I scold lightly, sliding the pin into the glossy black hair untouched by her cosmic Violently-Violet-#9-to-hot-pink-ends ombré. "You think my updo stays put with just the power of good thoughts?"

That gets a deep, knowing chuckle.

My fascination with pretty hair accessories goes all the way back to high school, and she knows it. I can always count on tortoiseshell barrettes, velvet scrunchies, and headbands that would have made Blair Waldorf jealous as stocking stuffers.

Rajvee's far from the most colorful thing in the bistro. Someone on Yelp called it kawaii goth for gauche hipsters. Which, fair. The walls of Little Shop of Hors D'Oeuvres are the same pink as her hair, broken up with peacock-green art nouveau picture frames and bottle-blue bookshelves filled with vintage cookbooks. Re-created classic horror movie posters and a cluster of *Little Shop of Horrors* off-Broadway *Playbills* make the bistro an iconic Instagram location for tourists and locals alike. Black wrought-iron tables and chairs are scattered over the checkerboard tile floor that leads back to the kitchen, invitingly angled, begging for someone peering into the storefront windows to sit for a spell.

It's my home away from home: the tables where Rajvee and I did our homework after school; the kitchen where we came up with the entire Halloween menu when Raj's grandmother decided it was too gross at her age to make food look like eyeballs; and the place where I realized how much I loved, no, *needed*, color in my life.

There's a vintage pinball machine next to a Ms. Pac-Man, with the speakers overhead slithering out dreamy lo-fi hip-hop. At the front, an old-fashioned cash register takes center stage on the oak counter, glass domes of rubbery "fake cake" confections on either side. Devil's ivy creeps along wall trellises and spills out of pewter cauldrons suspended from the ceiling, their green heart-shaped leaves prettily twining. And, in a homage to its namesake, a fake Venus flytrap with a placard that reads: PLEASE DON'T FEED ME HAMBURGER.

This place was built as a Victorian hotel, but after a few mysterious accidents too many, it changed owners, tumbling from hand to hand until Rajvee's grandmother inherited it in the seventies. She and husbands one through three fixed the broken banister and the rotted-wood staircase that had claimed the last owner. They threw out the creepy glass-eyed dolls with cobwebs in their hair, pulled the dead birds from the chimney. It took more than two decades of hard work and money they didn't have, but by the time Una, who had just adopted Raj from India, took over, the family passion project had been restored to its original glory.

"So you're really telling me there was no"—Rajvee hums—"magic between you?"

"Raj, it's *Milan*." Is it too childish to make a gagging sound?

"Yeah, and? I have *eyes*, and objectively, Milan is . . ." She shoots me a knowing, played-up wink before sliding the last mini chicken-and-waffle appetizer onto a tray.

My cheeks warm. Needing a topic change, I eye the already packed and ready-to-go trays on the kitchen counter. The labels read: CRISPY MAC AND CHEESE BALLS, BBQ MEATBALLS, FRIED PICKLES, FRIED GOAT CHEESE AND BALSAMIC PEACHES WITH BASIL, BLOOMIN' ONION BITES, BACON JALAPEÑO DEVILED EGGS, and PIMENTO CHEESE-STUFFED FRIED OKRA.

"Jesus." I blink. "Someone order catering or a coronary?"

"Very funny and not at all avoid-y." Rajvee clasps the waffle-iron lid on with a forceful *click*! "You might be interested to know that it's a lunch spread for one of our very best regular clients."

I suppress an eye roll. "Why would I find that interesting?"

Rajvee opens her mouth, but nothing comes out, like she thought better of it.

"And," I add, "you know I adore your apps, but if this is how they eat I'm surprised they're still around for repeat business. Even Super Bowl parties have more veggies."

She smirks. "So I guess I'm best friends with a different girl who once ate a bag of shredded cheese over the sink so she wouldn't have to wash a plate?"

She's talking about the first semester of junior year when I thought that after twenty-one years of being an only child, wouldn't it be great to have roommates? So I called a number on a campus bulletin board ("Sketch," Rajvee had proclaimed), accepted a room in a house just a street away from campus, which was clean at the time ("Bait and switch"), and then had to spend the next few months torn between just doing the dang dishes that kept piling up in the sink or yelling at the roommates who didn't do a thing to keep our place clean.

At least this time Raj didn't tack on the "I told you so."

"One, that was during the depths of my Milan funk." I grimace. Saying his name twice in as many minutes gives me a scratched-chalkboard feeling. "Two, it was, like, the bottom of the bag and there was hardly anything left. Three, it was finals week and I didn't have time to go grocery shopping. Four, you know I was in that sink standoff with my roommates, *none* of whom respected my chore chart. And, *five*, I don't tell you things so you can use them against me."

Rajvee pastes on a sorry-not-sorry smile. "Best friend prerogative."

My phone lights up in my hand.

Reets, guess who's got a MyShaadi match? ;)

Oh sorry, nevermind . . . um it's not with you?

I squint at Neil's message. Then glance at my mail app. Nothing.

My first thought: He got a match before I did?

The second: Ugh, I hate when he calls me Reets. Why would a person ruin Rita, a perfectly good four-letter name, into the objectively awful Reets-rhymes-with-beets? It's one whole letter longer than my actual name!

Raj snaps her fingers under my nose. "Earth to Rita! If you get a text, share with the class!" Her smile turns wily. "Or maybe that's Milan texting you now?"

"Wrong," I say shortly. "Neil."

"Ah, him. The guy you sleep with but have nothing else in common with."

"Wrong again. We like the same things. Remember, *Coco* is our favorite movie?"

She makes a doubtful scoff.

"What happened to not inherently gendering things for girls and boys?"

"Anyone can dig *Coco*." She shrugs. "I'm just saying Neil doesn't. He seems more like an action man."

Our stare off doesn't have a clear winner, but when we both blink down on our strained, watery eyes, I change the subject from my incompatibility with Neil to the real subject at hand.

"Anyway," I say pointedly. "Like I said, Milan had no clue what he was there for. His mom sent him over with some bogus story about a friend of hers with an exclusive pocket listing. He didn't even know it was my parents' place. We agreed for my mom's sake, but I'm pretty sure he's not going to call." My upper lip curls. "Even Aji thinks he's too much of a 'good boy' to say no to my mom, let alone his."

"You said your mom gave him your business card," she points out. "He needs help with that fix-it house, right? If he said he's going to call, he's *definitely* going to call."

Yeah, he said he'd call because my mom was sitting right there expecting him to say that.

What is with these grown-ass men deferring to their mothers over everything?

And it's not like he *always*, finger quotes, does what he says he will.

Exhibit A, our past.

I fold my arms. "Slap a little paint on it. Get the bloodstains out of the carpet. Fumigate. There's a million things he could do instead of asking his ex-girlfriend to help him."

Raj doesn't even put up a good show of trying not to roll her eyes. She plants her hands on her hips, canary-yellow nails popping against her brown skin and cropped, high school hoodie. "Pretty sure if it was any of those things, he'd have fixed it already. He needs you."

Needs is a major overstatement.

"Listen, if there aren't bloodstains there already, there will be by the time this is over," I grind out. "As long as we're walking down memory lane, maybe we could revisit the part where he dumped me after six years of dating?"

Her face blanches, but I can't stop myself.

Plowing on, I say, "On the very same day we had plane tickets booked to London. Just like that." I make a sound of disgust that reminds me of a cat working out a nasty hairball. "We'd been saving ever since high school for this, Raj. *High school*. And he just, what, decided out of nowhere that none of this was what he wanted?"

The noise that comes out of me is half sob, half gasp for air. "That *I* wasn't what he—" I break off, breathing heavily.

Her face softens. "Rita—"

"No, I'm sorry, Raj, but he didn't even have the decency to do it in person. He left me waiting at the departure gate. You have no idea how humiliating that was. Maybe you can still be friends or friendly acquaintances or whatever with him because you cater for his office, but I was doing just fine without him. *I didn't need this right now.*"

She's on my side, always, but Milan is as much a part of her life as mine. From cozy autumn afternoons spent sprawled over a Little Shop table as we did our homework together to his wholehearted will-start-a-fight-with-bigots acceptance of her gender fluidity when she told us *I feel masculine sometimes* and *Would you call me Raj as often as Rajvee from now on, please?* He went shopping for cargo pants and men's short-sleeve patterned shirts with her when she was figuring out how she identified, and felt uncomfortable by herself in the junior men's section.

They spent a lot of time together during the two years she went solely by Raj at their college, and only wore leather and plaid and boots made for stomping before deciding her pronouns were she/he/they and she hadn't figured out any other labels yet and that was okay, but wanted us to take our cue based on her gender expression and social context. While I was in California, he was here for her. And later for Una, when he hired the Delahayes for High Castle's catering after Raj's grandma got dementia and times were hard.

Our lives are a three-strand braided friendship bracelet, even if I pretend it isn't.

Anger and tears go hand in hand for me, and right on cue, my eyes start to sting. "Actually, you know what? I'm not sorry. He doesn't get another chance. I'm fresh out." My throat sticks. "I'm happy with Neil. So please stop shipping us. My mom I get, but I can't deal with it from you, too."

Rajvee looks stricken. "You don't have to put on your armor with me, babe." She pulls her lower lip into her mouth. "I know he hurt you, but you're—"

"I'm *not* in love with him anymore," I fill in before she can. "I'm one hundred percent over him and even if he does call, nothing's going to happen."

The sympathy vanishes. She arches an eyebrow with a knowing look. "Who said you weren't and that anything *was* going to happen? That's so not where I was going. I was just going to say that you never exactly got closure and regardless of what your mom wants to happen here, maybe this is what you need."

My face burns. Even though we never talk about him, at my request, she's hinted a few times over the years that it wouldn't be the worst thing in the world if we got it all out in the open between us. "I—"

I'm saved from pulling something out of my ass by the arrival of Una Delahaye, Rajvee's mom, who glides rather than walks into the prep area. She styles herself like a Mod Cloth–esque Victoriana It Girl, and today's no different. She's wearing a black high-neck dress with amethyst paisley flowers and a ruffled yoke, pointed black boots, and a hassled expression.

"Raj, I just got off the phone with CariDee and her kid's been vomiting since—" Una breaks off as soon as she sees me. "Rita!" She swoops toward me with a wide smile, giving me a tight squeeze before pulling away to scrutinize me. "Have you eaten yet?" To Raj, "Baby, give her a waffle. Did I just hear you two arguing?" Then, rapid fire as always, "Rita, are you on the schedule for today?"

"Hi, Una," I say with a fond laugh. "Yup, I'm all yours today."

"We weren't arguing." Raj smirks. "Rita needs my unparalleled, unsurpassed expert dating advice." She strikes a pose, all angles and sass.

It's hard not to envy them their easy mother-daughter relationship.

"You know, I gave up watching soap operas when my daughter and her best friend became teenagers," says Una, kissing Raj's temple. It's not the first time she's caught us gossiping in the kitchen. "You girls gave me way too many real-life story lines to keep track of."

The difference was that in high school, most of the dating drama had come from Raj, who was once in a short-lived love triangle with the star quarterback and the head cheerleader. Milan and I thought we were so grown up, above the petty jealousies and irritations that broke our peers up after week one. We didn't even celebrate monthly anniversaries because we took it for granted we were together for the long haul. There was no need to celebrate baby steps when we were running in miles.

"You've got to admit, Mom, our shit was way better than TV!" Raj says cheerfully, and she slides me one of the leftover mini chicken-and-waffles cooling on the rack.

My taste buds burst as my teeth sink into the finger food. I can make out the thinnest glaze of manuka honey, just enough to add a touch of sweetness to balance out the smoked paprika and secret spice blend in the beer-battered fried chicken. It's absolutely orgasmic.

Una pulls her blond hair out of its bun, tight curls bouncing over her shoulders. With a worried glance at the grandfather clock, customized to pop out with rodent skeletons emitting ghoulish cackles every hour, she says, "I have to open. Hon, CariDee's out for the day and we have that early lunch delivery. Could you . . . ?"

"Yeah, I'll do the delivery," I say around a mouthful.

"Rita, you're saving my life here. Thank you so much. It's a huge order and today's is . . . Well, it's for someone special."

"No, I'll do it," says Raj, frowning at her mother.

"Raj, I've done deliveries before," I point out.

"And you've got that custom cake order to finish decorating," says Una, matter of fact. "There's no way you'll be able to finish before eleven. Rita's family, she's got this."

"Yeah, which is why the newspaper is going to call this sororicide," Rajvee mutters.

Una holds her hand out for my phone. "You know where High Castle Realty is, right? Oh, look who I'm asking." Her laugh tinkles. She's already Google Mapping it for me, doing it the concerted, forehead-frowny mom way with one finger. "This is what I love about office parties, especially when there's a promotion involved. They always ask for such a huge spread."

A guilty flush spreads over Rajvee's face.

"I think so." I glance between mother and daughter, not sure what I'm missing, but absolutely sure that there's something.

"Mom," Rajvee hisses.

"You girls always make everything such a production," says Una, handing my phone back. "Didn't it happen years ago? Rita isn't made of spun sugar." She throws me a grateful smile. "Thank you so much. Now, I really have to get back out there. Friday mornings are our busiest time, except for Friday nights and Saturday mornings, and, oh, I suppose Mondays . . ." Her voice trails off as she bustles out, calling out more instructions to Rajvee.

A moment later, the bistro fills with chatter like an opened valve, boisterous voices greeting Una, who, in typical Una fashion, carries on seven different conversations at the same time.

I stare at the map and the red pin of the final destination. High Castle Realty.

Oh.

Oh no.

Not *his* office.

Milan freaking Rao. I should have known.

My chest jackrabbits, each beat throbbing twice as hard in my ears.

His face swims in front of me: crooked-lipped smile, sculpted jawline, and knowing eyes.

Of course it's me, Rita. Come on, you had *to know where this was heading.*

I want to argue that I didn't, but the ghost of him I'd been carrying hasn't existed in years, and I hadn't seen the writing on the walls even when it did.

Cut yourself some slack, we were kids. Not like you had precognition or anything.

If there's anything I despise more than grew-up-unfairly-sexier-than-humanly-possible-and-I-hate-that-I-notice Milan, it's earnest, you-can-trust-me Milan.

The universe is doing the most to push me toward him, giant neon-flashing-sign style. I squeeze my eyes as tight as they'll go before my inner Rita banshee shrieks: *frown lines!!!*

"We're still best friends, right?" Rajvee pipes up, shooting me an actually apologetic smile this time. "Listen, I've got this. Mom didn't realize what she was asking; she probably thought you guys were cool again because I mentioned what your parents pulled, and you know my mom isn't, well," she winces, "great at the listening. So if you can just keep an eye on things here until I get back, I can—"

I hold up the hand still holding the phone, brave face on. "I said I'll go."

I committed myself, so I'll see it through. Unlike *some* people.

The steadiness of my voice kind of surprises me, but after all the other surprises I've had, maybe nothing should anymore. I inject pep into my voice, but it comes out a little aggressive instead. "Closure, right? Pack everything up, babe."

Rajvee stares at me, not moving. "You're serious? Because you know you don't have to."

"Raj, it's closure or bloodstains," I say grimly. "I guarantee you, he has as little interest in working with me as I have in working with him." I screw up my face. "Which is the grand sum total of zero. I do this and I never have to see him again."

And that's a promise.

Chapter 8

I feel the guillotine descending inch by excruciating inch the closer I get to the red destination pin on my GPS. Even after I pull into High Castle Realty's parking lot, an imposing mirrored glass-and-concrete four-story building next to a high-end sushi restaurant, I circle like I don't see a prime spot *right in front*. Part of me wants to just zip right on out of there, but I can't.

Time to grit my teeth and get on with it, and not be such a chickenshit.

I exhale and slide neatly into the spot. *You have arrived at your destination* trills from my phone. I pull it from the air vent mount, close the map app, and remember that I'm not just a professional doing my job, I need to do this for me, too. Closure.

"Time to put on your big girl pants, Rita," I say out loud, then cringe. I sound like a mom trying to convince her reluctant child to eat their brussels sprouts instead of a full-grown woman doing what should be an incredibly simple errand.

Step one, turn off the engine.

Or I could just stay put.

Step two, undo your buckle.

Or I could just stay put.

Step three, open the door.

Or I could just stay put.

Squaring my shoulders, I step out of the car, and by some miracle, my legs don't give out from under me. It's not the building itself that's scary.

It's the boy, now man, inside it.

Ignoring my inner Rita horror movie–screaming at me not to go inside, I take off at a brisk march, almost forgetting to look left and right. And then I'm at the door, pushing it open, and somehow, in what feels like all of two steps, I'm . . . there.

In the belly of the beast.

The AC hits me squarely in the face, drying out my contacts. I blink away the sandpaper feeling and head for the young woman at the front desk who's twirling a limp blond curl around a ballpoint pen and yawning without covering her mouth.

"Hi, I'm Rita from Little Shop of Hors D'Oeuvres," I say. "I have a catering delivery?"

Her expression brightens. "*Finally.* Lunch. Do you need help?" Before I can tell her I'm fine, she's pressing one of the many buttons on her multiline phone. "Little Shop delivery out front," she says. "Can I get someone down here to help the caterer?" She hangs up with an awkward smile.

I look around me: at the gold sparkle in the gray marble tile; the white Casablanca lilies peeking out of the floral arrangement on her desk; head shots of realtors lining the far wall. But in true universe-screwing-me fashion, the first Realtor's picture I land on is Milan's, somewhere in the middle.

"That's our High Castle 'Royalty' wall," she says, following my gaze. "Cool pun, right?"

I stare at it a moment longer. How is he ahead of people who look so much older than him? Wouldn't this be based on seniority? It's clearly not alphabetic.

The elevator dings. "Oh hey, here's someone now," the girl chirps.

I make the mistake of turning to look.

My heart bullfrog leaps into my throat.

Milan.

It all happens in slow motion, our eyes meeting even before the elevator doors glide fully open. His mouth drops open and his whole posture changes. His casual slump against the back wall straightens with a quick, hard jerk. I would laugh if I had any air in my lungs at all.

Seeing him in his natural environment is weird in a way I can't put into words.

Has he grown taller since he came over? I wouldn't put it past him.

I can only imagine his eyes are as wide and startled as mine must be, but he recovers faster. He's wearing a three-piece black suit with a slim cut that shows off the impossible length of him. His lean fingers are toying with the half-Windsor knot of his mustard-gold tie.

It's not like one my dad would wear, it's a skinny two-inch that brings out the warmth of his beige skin. I'm quarterback-tackled by the overwhelming, annoying urge to wind that tie around my wrist and pull him closer.

The impulse isn't real. It can't be. It's a fragment of the attraction left over from Rita ages fifteen through twenty. We'd been together as long as we've been apart. There were bound to be feelings I haven't exorcised.

Milan's long legs reach us in a few short strides, crossing the gray marble floor without hesitation. Without a stumble in his step. Professional and collected. How are his legs not jelly?

The fact that he looks amazing—again—isn't lost on me.

I'm relieved to be wearing something significantly cuter than the old tee he saw me in last. Expensive taste and an unstable income stream don't mesh well unless you trawl through clearance racks and end-of-season sales. I look hot and I know it: 7 For All Mankind distressed high-waisted skinny black jeans and a loosely tucked pink satin cami; face-framing layers of hair pulled back with a thin strip of black velvet left over from a handmade curtain; a rose quartz pendant just shy of dipping into my cleavage. I look like my high school senior year photos instead of the college-student-going-to-an-eight-a.m.-class comfy that I've grown to appreciate.

"Hey, Kerstin," says Milan, shooting me a quizzical look. I open my mouth to say hi back, then clamp my mouth shut when I realize it wasn't me he was addressing.

"Aw, the boss sent Mr. Big Shot out for the hard labor?" Kerstin asks teasingly. She perches on the corner of her desk closest to him and crosses her slim legs. "Rough." She turns, including me in her smile, but I'm still looking at him.

"Yeah, turns out that being made junior partner doesn't get me any special treatment," says Milan, dimpled smile as careless and easy as if he's just a boy talking to a girl.

Her laugh spills out of her like a can of soda shaken hard.

When was the last time he looked at me like that?

I shake off the unwanted spikes of jealousy. I am made of way sterner stuff than this, and yet, right now, it's so hard to remember that.

Milan finally flicks his eyes toward me in silent question, smile fading. "Hi."

"So this is Rita," says Kerstin, voice dropped conspiratorially, not realizing we don't need any introduction. "She's here to drop off your promotion yummies."

"They're in the car," I say, hearing the desperation and hating myself for it. "I'll just go grab everything." I jerk my thumb at the door and start to edge toward blessed escape.

"I'll help," he says.

Oh no, you won't. Determined, I push the door open before he can reach me.

His hand lands on top of mine. Shock zings through my fingers, ricocheting up my arms like a pinball arcade game. My grip on the door slackens enough for his fingers to slot between mine, and everything stops.

My back goes ramrod straight. He's touching me. And not just that, we still fit. I suck in a breath and hope he doesn't notice, but I know he will.

I dare to look at him. The light streaming in through the glass door turns his brown eyes, thickly lashed, into liquid honey. He's staring at the tiny outline of a lotus flower on my right pinky finger, an exact match for Rajvee's on her left.

"I thought you hated tattoos," he says, like a question.

And I hate that I still know him well enough to know that's not what he really wants to ask.

According to best-friend logic, I needed to do something totally out of my comfort zone following the breakup, and yeah, that made total sense, putting myself through actual pain to get over the heart-ripped-from-my-chest actual pain. So I got the tattoo (her idea), but only if she did, too (mine).

But I don't feel like explaining any of that to him. He doesn't have the right to know.

Taking advantage of his lull, I push the door the rest of the way and slip outside.

"Rita, wait."

I don't turn around.

"*Rita*." Desperation thickens his voice into a deep rumble behind me.

I unlock my car from a yard away. "What?"

"What are you *doing* here?" Milan pushes his hand into his hair. His ears are a rosy red. His gaze trails down my neck, singeing electricity following the path his eyes take.

It occurs to me that he doesn't know I help out at Little Shop from time to time. My chest squeezes with love for Raj, who must have been so careful over the years to make sure I never had to make any deliveries here. She'd even tried to talk me out of coming today.

"I work there sometimes," I inform him, in as brusque a voice as I can manage while in the supremely awkward position of bending over to haul the insulated food storage containers from the back seat. "Believe me, I'm only here because their regular couldn't make it."

When I make a soft grunt lifting one of the thermal boxes, Milan gets there fast, gently nudging me out of the way with his hip. His lean fingers grip the containers, hoisting them with upper-body ease. His caring boyfriend is coming out, which means my hackles are, too.

"I've got it," I grind out.

"I know you do, but since I'm here anyway," he says with a shrug.

Fine, but we don't have to talk.

Kerstin holds the front door for us as we trek back in, loaded down with heaps and heaps of fried food. Suddenly, this whole menu makes sense. This is absolutely the kind of frat-boy food I imagine a bunch of office bros eat.

The elevator doors close with a *ding* of finality and we start the ascent.

My biceps ache so I put everything on the floor, trying to forget about all the dirty soles stamped over the steel. I glance at Milan to find, to my sour displeasure, he's got everything balanced in his arms and doesn't look tired at all. In fact, the fabric's pulled taut over his triceps, drawing my attention to his slim wrist and soft brown hair and the band of the watch—

He's wearing the Daniel Wellington watch I gave him for his twentieth birthday.

The stinging, spiny pricks of a durian fruit roll under my breast, tearing at my heart.

I'm beyond thankful for the silence; if I have to make small talk, I'll lose it.

Milan's standing close to me, friend close, not strangers-in-an-elevator close.

When our arms brush, I flinch away.

He smells delicious, like citrus and old-school Cary Grant.

No, Rita. Bad Rita. You're not supposed to notice that.

I try to draw Neil's face in my mind, instead, but give up one floor in.

Milan's eyes are on me, I can tell, because goosebumps skitter up my arms and chest, tickling the base of my throat the way his kisses used to.

I scoot three inches away.

His smile is amused, like he knows exactly what I'm doing, and why.

I forgot that he knows me, too.

It occurs to me that I'm behaving like a brat. The child that wouldn't eat their brussels sprouts and threw a tantrum instead, who's now counting down the agonizing minutes of their time-out like it's an hour instead of just ten minutes.

"Sorry," I say on an exhale. "This is . . . This is weird, right?"

"Not really," he says, signature lazy yearbook smile back in place. "Our moms are still friends, kinda. I'm surprised we haven't run into each other sooner."

He doesn't sound upset about it. Which annoys me all over again.

Does he think this makes us *friends*?

"Speaking of our moms," I start to say, about to make sure he knows he's off the hook, but the elevator lurches to a stop and the doors slide open. Men's raucous voices overwhelm our small space, and Milan motions for me to precede him.

My first thought is: This is a nice office.

The carpet looks plush and the lighting is flattering, with plenty of sunlight coming in from the abundance of naked windows. Tall plants in heavy planters in each corner of the room, and gleaming walnut desks paired back to back. Family pictures line most of them, along with half-empty bottles of Mountain Dew and mugs with the company logo.

If he's made junior partner, would his desk be out here, or does he get his own office? If we never broke up, we'd probably be married now. He'd have *our* family's pictures on his desk.

I try to banish those thoughts before I start imagining little girls with his honey eyes.

A loud, obnoxious laugh peals out.

The room is empty, but the chatter is coming from somewhere.

"This whole building is High Castle?" I ask. "This is the *third* floor."

"Commercial and residential real estate are on the first and second. This is luxury," Milan explains, and if it were anyone else, I'd think it was a brag. He leads the way across the room to a glass partition with the words BOARD ROOM emblazoned in gold on the door.

I hang back while the room erupts in whoops and cheers. While Milan is swarmed by his colleagues, I take all the food out and set it up on the long conference table, and I do it all without looking at him. I refuse to dawdle in what-ifs and what-could-have-beens.

I'm about to duck out without saying goodbye, the straps of empty insulated containers dangling off both arms, when I hear my name.

Ugh, what now. They've already paid. I just wanna get out of here.

Milan's waving me over, his circle of silver foxes, handsome young men, and chic women with ridiculously good blowouts all looking at me with interest and polite smiles. None of these people seem to have heard of casual Friday dress code.

"This is Rita," says Milan.

"*The* Rita?" says a young smirking white guy, standing there like a man who thinks he's inherited the world, so I automatically decide not to like him. The way he up-downs me validates that impulse.

Milan's cheeks flush and he darts his eyes away.

"You're the young woman who's going to help my firm out," says an older man with ice-chip blue eyes and graying brown hair. He sticks his hand out. "Josh Bell."

Help out High Castle Realty? It takes me a second to realize he's talking about the house that Milan hadn't been able to sell for two hundred and sixty-two days. Now sixty-three.

Bell's the boss, I realize, taking his hand. His grip is firm and doesn't linger, and he doesn't bat an eye when one of the containers on my arm bumps his knee.

"Milan tells us that you design furniture and are a rising star of the interior design world," he continues, his tone warm. "We're very glad to have you on board."

I wonder what he thinks about a "rising star" making deliveries.

"Ha! That place?" Smirky Dude snorts, and it sends a ripple of anger over my chest. "Good luck. I don't usually believe in cursed properties, but if I did . . ." He looks at Milan meaningfully. "Hey, boss, shoulda maybe held off on the promotion until that place sold, huh?"

Almost everyone scowls, including the boss.

"I have every confidence in Milan," says Mr. Bell, who's so dignified looking I can't even think of him as Josh. He glances at me as if he's taking my measure, but without an ounce of creep.

Milan's cheeks bloom a patchy red. "Would you like to stay for the party?"

I really would not, but the question requires a circumspect answer. "I have a lot on today, so I better jet," I say. "Congrats on the promotion."

"Yeah, no. I get it. Thanks." He scratches the back of his neck. "I'll walk you out?"

I mean, I'm pretty sure I could find the exit on my own, but he's already at the door.

As we head for the elevator, he makes a swipe for the catering containers, which I swing out of his reach just in time (Rita: 1, Milan: so in the red he'll never dig himself out).

Victorious, I pick up my pace, power walking like Aji at the mall when she wants to calorie-blast after too much Diwali mithai.

"Rita, are you trying to *outrun* me?"

"No." I walk faster.

"You remember I run two miles every morning, right?" he drawls.

My blood pressure spikes. Oooh, his nerve. His smug nerve assuming my brain hasn't already recycled all the stored info about how he only likes the obnoxious novelty creamer flavors in his coffee, the two ABC sing-throughs he does when brushing his teeth, and the abject refusal to order a salad at a restaurant even if he really wants one because of the hideous markup, let alone remembering his cardio routine. I mean, *really*.

"Why would I"—I huff—"remember that kind of inconsequential detail?"

He makes a rough sound in the back of his throat that could pass for a growl, but I just can't imagine Mr. Brooks Brothers behind me doing something that flagrantly uncouth.

I whip around to search his face, but he's smoothed away his frustration into a picture of Bambi-eyed innocence as he once again lets me get into the elevator before him.

After a soft warning chime, the doors slide closed. But for me, the sound is the kickboxing bell popping off.

I cross and uncross my arms. "Why did you tell your boss I'm working with you?"

"Because you are?" Milan stretches out the sentence, head cocked to the side.

My mouth, primed and ready for a sharp repartee, snaps shut.

He lifts a brow. "Oh, are we not?"

I try not to squirm. I can't tell if he's genuinely asking or throwing a challenge. When my mom accepted a job on my behalf that he didn't even intend to offer, I'd assumed, by some unspoken agreement, Milan and I were just being good sports about her interference.

I grind my molars. No one *wants* to work with their ex.

Especially when it's not even their decision.

His eyes appear darker in here with the harsh fluorescent light that casts us both in a sallow yellow tint. They drink me in, no longer syrupy, leonine brown, but infinitely more intense. And yet his voice, when he asks, "I thought it was settled?" is unsure.

I can't help it; I relish that hesitation in his voice, so unlike his hotshot real estate agent confidence.

It only takes one moment to unsettle something. He, of all people, should know.

Milan pushes the emergency stop button even though we've already hit the first floor.

I startle. It's a very Milan-from-high-school move, and I have a feeling that Rita-from-high-school wouldn't have taken long to push him against the wall and muss his coiffed hair into disheveled make-out oblivion.

When will I stop thinking about all the Ritas I used to be?

"You said something before about this being weird," Milan says. A flush climbs up his neck. "And don't get me wrong, it totally is. But I wasn't kidding when I said it was only a matter of time before we were in the same room together. I didn't expect it to happen, uh, quite like that, though." He lets out a short laugh. "But I can't deny that I am happy about how it worked out."

It's not because he still has feelings. It's because he needs help.

I swallow past the sour film on my tongue and try not to hate him.

"I was hoping we could stop by the house before the next open house." He touches my shoulder, electricity zapping us both. "Sorry." He guiltily draws his hand back to his side, then against his chest, then up to scratch his shaved-smooth chin, as if in afterthought.

I draw back, horrified to find that I'd instinctively leaned into his touch. He doesn't seem to notice, which makes it worse, in a way.

Rajvee's voice rings in my ears: *Stop being such a messy bitch, Rita.*

Okay, so she's never actually said that to me, but whenever I need to give myself a WWJD moment, it sounds like her.

Milan chews his bottom lip. "But if our history makes this too hard for you . . ."

It goes silent so fast that I swear I can hear the soft, even clicks of his watch hands.

Anger flares under my skin, turning my arms hot. He's got some nerve thinking this is one sided, that I can't handle working with him without my heart re-ripping along its fault lines.

And what about him? Thinking back to his awkward chin scratching, there was something about the piecemeal movement that tells me it wasn't what he intended. Like he didn't know what to do with his hands, like he didn't want me to see how discomfited he was in my presence. Sure, he's giving me an out, but it's not one I want to admit. Especially now that I suspect he's trying to give *himself* an out, too.

"Please, we were six years ago. Pretty sure I'm over it." My laugh is brittle as I punch the door open button. I shrug. "It's just business. A one-off."

His face turns a little pained.

Aha! So I was right. He *was* hoping I would be the one to blink first.

"And then we go back to our own realities," I finish. First. I give him the condescending-dude-pat on the shoulder, delegating the task with victory smooth as Macallan single malt whisky. "Just shoot me an email and we'll set it up."

And then I step out of the elevator before he can say a word, heart sledgehammering, making sure he can see just how good the view is watching me walk away.

Chapter 9

To make up for missing dinner last night, Neil brings over all my favorite Chinese takeout for our usual Friday night date, plus apology strawberry Pocky and shrimp crackers. It takes him forever to pick out a movie—even though I'm pretty sure it's my turn to choose. So while he browses the trailers of the newly added blockbusters, I check my email.

There's a small red bubble on my mail app.

Could be nothing. Could be 5/$35 panties. Could be my match with Neil.

I tap the screen.

Palpable relief whooshes through me. As promised, MyShaadi had delivered on their guaranteed match within twenty-four hours. Even if they only sent it with one hour to spare.

Sender: *MyShaadi.com*

Subject: *You have a match!* 🎉

Preview: *Love is in the air tonight, Rita! Log in to your account to chat with . . .*

"Neil!"

"Huh?" He glances over, swears under his breath, and rewinds the explosion he missed.

I fist pump. "We've matched! Check your phone!"

He shoots me a distracted smile before pulling his gaze back to his movie.

I work my mouth side to side. A little excitement would be nice, but I guess it's easy to be blasé when he's had not just one match, but three. Still, I'm stoked. My plan fucking *worked*.

"You should check your phone," I say, telling, not asking.

This time he listens, pressing pause. I follow the email link to the web page, glad I asked the site to "remember me" so I can skip the annoying password step.

You have a match! runs across the banner on my home page in a Devanagari-style script.

"Let's read it at the same time," I say, biting my lip to hold back the victory cheer. I'm in the mood to be corny, to pretend confetti and trumpets are bursting all around us.

"Want some fanfare?" Neil offers.

"Always."

He grins and begins to drum his palms against his thighs. "And now . . . the moment . . . we've all been waiting for . . . the moment . . . of truth!" he bellows, like a ringmaster.

I click the link, holding my breath.

Any second now, the name and face are going to pop up.

And it does. It's just not Neil's.

"Uh, Reets?" He squints at the screen. "That's definitely not me."

Congrats, Rita! You have a 100% match with Milan Rao!

Normally I'd listen to the universe when it sends a sign as big and glaring as this one, and normally I'd *never* accuse fate of rigging itself against me, but there's nothing normal about being informed that the man who broke my heart is my perfect match.

This is the guy who started a lawn-mowing business with his buddies when we were in high school in order to afford our college sophomore summer backpacking vacation. Who left me waiting for him at the departure gate until he finally returned one of my many texts to say he'd meet me at our connecting flight in Jersey.

I had turned on my phone as soon as we'd landed at Newark. As soon as the wheels bumped the tarmac. Was Milan already here? Would he meet me at the arrival gate?

It would be our first time meeting since Christmas. My family had gone to India during spring break to see the cousins and Aba, my grandfather. He never stayed in the U.S. as long as Aji, who was determined to get every possible day out of her tourist visa.

Milan and I had been disappointed we wouldn't be together IRL, and with the time difference we'd only be able to talk during his mornings and my nights, and vice versa, but it actually hadn't been that bad.

I was over the moon to finally see him. Even though I was seated in the middle of the plane, I'd jumped into the aisle to grab my backpack out of the overhead bin as soon as the fasten-seatbelt light turned off. I didn't want to spend a second longer in my seat, forced to wait as the aisle crowded. Not when Milan was out there.

Only he wasn't.

I speed walked out of the skybridge, heart in my throat, phone in my hand. I'M HERE!!!! CAN'T WAIT TO SEE YOU!!!! typed out and ready to go, except he wasn't standing at the door with a goofy sign the way boys always did in movies. He wasn't slumped in one of those crumb-lined airport seats, earphones in, fishing the last crumbs out of a Pringle can like the other young men in the arrival's lounge.

He wasn't there at all.

And that's when I saw the voicemail.

Hey, you're probably already in the air so you'll only get this when you land at, um, Newark, but I wanted to— Shit. My parents. [heavy sigh] *It all just hit the fan over here.*

I had to ask them for the money to pay for summer classes when we get back from Europe, because I'd spent my money on the plane ticket already and I needed the rest for food and hostels and stuff. [long pause] *They didn't buy my wanting to do school over the summer and Dad was on my back until I finally had to tell them that I'd failed three of my classes and I wasn't doing too great in the other—* [staggered breathing]

Rita, I . . . I lost my scholarship. I don't know what I'm going to do. My parents, they've never been so disappointed in me. I've never been so disappointed in myself. This isn't me, or at least it didn't use to be? I don't know how it got to this. I mean, I do. But. [loud exhale]

But, um, anyway, that's not the point, I just wanted to say— [voice rises] *I have to stay here. Stay home. This summer. Mom wouldn't stop crying, I've never seen her— And Dad. He . . . I think it would have been better if he'd shouted at me. The silence was worse. Then Mom started giving me a rundown of everything they'd paid for college and how much I'd wasted, and how was I going to pay them back, and I just—* [choked sound, long pause]

Dad calmed her down. They're going to pay for me to retake the classes I failed, but I can't go with you, Rita. None of this would have even happened if I hadn't been thinking of you all the time. I need to focus on school and get my grades up. It's not fair on you when you've spent all this money, but you don't know how pissed my parents are and it's because of you, and I think maybe we should take a break—

It was lucky I had a four-hour layover for my connecting flight to Paris, because the second I heard his voicemail—his rambling, messy voicemail—all the way through, my legs were incapable of moving beyond my gate.

I collapsed into the nearest seat, almost dislodging the tuna sandwich balanced on the knee of the woman next to me. I was too out of it to apologize when she huffed at me, could only squeeze my phone to my ear and listen to Milan's voice over and over until it made some sort of sense. My phone was hot enough to turn my palm pink and leave a fiery rectangle on my cheek by the time I realized that it didn't make sense.

He was *failing* three classes?

He *lost* his scholarship?

He wasn't *here* in Jersey?

He only worked up the courage to tell me while I was *mid-flight*?

And somehow—somehow (!!!)—he had the gall to say it was *my* fault?

My heart slammed in my chest. Over and over.

It's because of you, and I think maybe we should take a break—

Every time I heard that sentence, I waited for him to complete it.

I waited for there to be more. Something to come after it that would make it all click into place, the *Aha, so* that's *what happened* moment. There had been so many stops and starts in his voicemail, a jumble of blame and accusation that arrowed straight through my heart.

Maybe this was just another stop. A pause for breath.

But no. It just ended there.

We ended there.

When my phone slipped from my hand, cracking against tile, I was too numb to even notice.

Unable to sleep after the horror of matching with Milan, I'd stayed up past midnight tweaking my MyShaadi questionnaire to ensure I got Neil the next time. After tossing and turning the rest of the night, skin clammy and head throbbing, I was late getting to Little Shop for our usual Saturday morning pickup and it was slim pickings.

A sugar rush was a surefire fix for my migraine, and by some stroke of luck—the sole, single, *solitary* stroke I'd had this week—Una had already set aside my favorite dark chocolate iced donuts with icing googly eyes and candy-corn teeth.

After fending off Harrie, who started barking his head off as soon as a sleepy Neil wandered into the kitchen, we had breakfast together, but instead of him spending the day at my house, he had to go back to his mother's for the rest of the weekend, something she insisted on.

"You can get some work done without me here to distract you," Neil had said, pecking my nose. "I've gotta do this, but I'm all yours next weekend. Promise."

I didn't wave him goodbye from the front door like usual. Talk was cheap. I should know.

Neil was right about one thing, though—I did have work to do.

Milan had already sent an email with more details about the Soulless Wonder listing. He'd staged the empty rooms himself according to the style of the house and a Pinterest deep dive into interior design after the owner moved out, taking everything with him.

So I spent the rest of Saturday sketching mock-ups and finishing up my mood board; going to Lucky Dog Luke's, the flea market my friend worked at, to pick up some accessories; and trying not to refresh my Shaadi account every five seconds.

Can I get the key? I'd like to get in there to get a feel for the space, I'd emailed Milan. *When's a good time?* I had zero intention of seeing him in person again so soon.

I hit send before I mean to, just so eager to get this over with. Fingers racing faster than my heart, I shoot off a follow-up: *I can send you my designs once I have the floor plans and dimensions.*

Better to keep it strictly professional. The more technical-sounding words I throw at him, the more barriers I have between me and whatever smug, arrogant thing comes out of his mouth.

No worries, he sent back a minute later. *I canceled the Sunday open house and removed the furniture so we can check it out together. I'll meet you there tomorrow morning.*

Chapter 10

I'm at the Soulless Wonder five minutes early and he's still here before me.

Even from this distance, through the dusty, bug-spattered windshield of my truck, he cuts a striking figure. He's wearing a navy suit, smart black aviators, and a dubious expression as he examines a bunch of wilted, straggly flowers in front of the house that someone, at some time, thought added some much-needed charm.

I start to slow, but then panic seizes me. I'm nervous enough to see Milan, but what's worse is if he sees what an absolute fraud I am.

I've never interior designed anything, let alone a place this expensive. What do I even know about selling a house? If I go in there and tell him he got all the design wrong, I'm going to show my ass. Milan's been selling houses for years and he's just been made junior partner at one of the best agencies in town. My palms begin to sweat. What if my sketches are amateur and not to scale? What if my dimensions are totally off?

Maybe I should have digitally rendered everything instead, brought it in a nice portfolio instead of the only folder I could find, an old and obnoxiously hot pink Lisa Frank with soft, peeling corners that no self-respecting adult should bring to a business meeting.

I move my right foot to the gas pedal. Fuck this. I'm going to drive right past.

But then Milan looks up. Recognition crosses his face. He takes off his sunglasses and waves them high above his head like he's one of the guys on the runway bringing in a plane.

My insides shrivel. Too late.

I turn into the driveway without signaling to the car behind me. As I turn off the engine, the driver blasts me with one, two, no, *three* honks that take about ten years off my life.

"I see your driving has gone downhill since I helped you study for the test," Milan says playfully, tucking his glasses into his breast pocket. He takes in my truck as if he's surprised to see it. "I *wondered* whose that was in your mom's driveway on Thursday. Thought your folks were getting work done or something."

I scowl. Perspiration is already gathering in my cleavage and dotting my forehead. It doesn't help that just being around Milan makes my temperature go up at least ten degrees.

Just because *someone* has a sleek cherry-red Alfa Romeo parked next to my dusty pickup does not mean he gets to diss my vehicle *or* my driving.

Heatedly, I say, "That honk was entirely unnecessary, and you know it. I'm sure he didn't even have to tap his brakes."

"Honks, plural," says Milan. "The second and third were overkill, I'll give you that. But if I didn't know any better, I could have sworn it crossed your mind to pretend you didn't see me."

There's a chuckle in his voice that's hard to ignore. I whirl away to grab my stuff from the back seat, trying to cross my arms so he doesn't see the rainbow that vommed all over this folder.

I will be a professional about this. I will not rise to his bait. I will not *banter* with him.

"Let's get inside and get to work," I say, keeping my voice cool and even-tempered.

I start power walking to the front door.

"You do realize I have the keys?" he calls after me.

My shoulder blades tighten. I'm glad I wore my hair down so he can't see me go rigid.

Milan strolls up the walkway, tossing the keys high in the air. Probably higher than he meant to, because mild shock crosses his face for a split second before he fumbles for the keys with both hands instead of a suave one-handed catch. His cheeks bloom like spring roses.

I fight a smile; the smile wins. "Yeah, you sure have the keys all right."

He keeps walking as if nothing happened. He slides the key in with the ease of someone who's entered a lot of houses in his time, and opens the door. "After you."

It's blessedly cool inside and smells like tart apple room fragrance and rubbery vacuum burn. We both wrinkle our noses at the same time before catching ourselves.

"I'll have a word with the cleaning crew," says Milan. "We had a lot of people here at last Sunday's open house. These carpets get a lot of action. I had all the old furniture moved out of here. Do you wanna walk me through your plan?"

"Let's go to the kitchen so I can spread it all out," I suggest.

He nods. "This way."

The house is open plan, which means the lack of any human touch is jarringly noticeable. The kitchen is straight ahead, all the way in the back of the house, cabinets arctic white and appliances shiny and high end. The limited counter space is made up for with a giant marble-countertop island with one of those fancy motion-activated sinks.

"What you're selling isn't a house. You're selling a way of life," I say, opening my folder and taking out my sketches along with the photos I'd printed from the High Castle website.

After spreading everything along the length of the island, I stab my pointer finger at the kitchen photos from the listing. "This glass table? Pretty, sure. But sharp edges. If I'm a mom, I'm not thinking how great this space is for entertaining. I'm thinking my kids are going to get hurt running around. The table corners are, like, eye level for children. These weird, ceramic petal-shaped bowl things on the island? Other than the very disturbing fact they look like a vagina lineup, again, I'm not congratulating myself on my artsy-fartsy taste, I'm wondering if it's going to survive the damage if Billy throws a baseball in here."

"This all makes a lot of sense, Rita, but you're forgetting the niche market of parents who *want* their kids running around in a demolition zone."

He's grinning. It takes me a second to realize he's making a joke. I'd been rambling. Getting excited about this project. Slipping into the familiarity of talking to a friend.

"You're making fun of me." My face feels like a hot pan.

Without thinking about it, I snatch at the papers, crumpling them between hard, rushed fingers. What a colossal mistake. He didn't care about the hours of my weekend I'd spent sourcing the perfect paint colors and soft furnishings and tasteful art pieces. He wasted my time the exact same way he wasted all those years of my life back when I still loved him.

"Rita, stop." His hand lands on top of mine. His fingers settle between my knuckles, eliciting a strangled gasp from me. His thumb, just a little rough, grazes the soft part of my thumb. Slow, relaxing circles. The friction, the *sensation*, of his skin rubbing against mine is heady and familiar, bringing me back years and years to his warmth and comfort.

It's exactly how I remembered it.

It's the kind of small intimacy he probably didn't even think twice about, but which I can't *stop* thinking about now.

I jerk away. We are *not* having a repeat of what happened in the elevator.

"I'm sorry." Milan swallows. His hands look strangely empty. "I was just . . . It was just a joke. The way we used to joke. I didn't think that you'd take it as a dig."

It's been six years since we used to riff like that. We aren't those people anymore. The idea of sharing anything with him, even humor, makes this wide-open space seem cramped as a shoebox. My stomach tosses the way it hasn't since my first time on a ferry, and my fingers close around the hard edge of the counter. I exhale until the room stops rocking and my heart stops pounding in my ears.

My fingers relax and fall away from the island. "It's fine," I hear myself say, even though it's decidedly not. I want to work up a smile, albeit a forced one, but I can't seem to look at him.

"I'm sorry, Rita. I wasn't thinking. I just wanted to make you laugh." His voice comes out small, which surprises me enough to look at him, because never in my life have I heard Milan speak in a library voice before, not even in an actual library.

"Do you think I can finish my presentation without having to talk about us? Because, frankly, I'm not here to pick at old scabs."

Milan's mouth twists to one side. "Right. That's the last thing we want to do."

I dart a quick look at him. There's nothing about what he said that indicates he's offended, but now it's his turn to avoid me. He busies himself with the forgotten sketches, keeping his head low. He's fixed on the feature walls separating the living spaces. "I like this wallpaper," he says finally. "What is it, a map of vintage London?"

"Yeah." My voice comes out a little croaky. I clear my throat, finding my voice. "So a roll of this actually runs pretty expensive, but if we just do the narrow wall with it, the warren of streets won't look so busy, and we can prop a bike against it. It's such a young, progressive neighborhood and so close to schools and colleges that I think buyers would appreciate the nod to sustainability. Living green, you know?"

At his nod, I keep going, "And do you see how I picked out the gray and green and navy from the wallpaper to echo throughout the rest of the house? This bottle-green paint color would make a great feature wall for the living room and here's a stone gray that would be perfect for the kitchen and dining area.

"I want the living room to look really cozy and inviting, so the other main living spaces on this floor are a little pared back, color-wise. I've sourced these amazing, funky dinner plates to put up in the dining room to add a pop of color back in, though.

"And, oh! See how the plates carry the story through the house?" I point to the living room sketch. "This cluster of round rattan wall mirrors on the opposite side of the house to the plates add the symmetry that über-modern houses usually lack."

Milan is staring at me.

I smooth my hair, self-conscious with the way his eyes are moving between my sketches, the house, and me, because he hasn't signed off on anything I said.

He hasn't said a word.

In fact, all he's done is stare at me like I grew a third head somewhere between my panic attack and my word vomit about paint chips. Oh my god, I butchered my whole presentation, didn't I? I rushed through it because I was nervous and trying to get it over with, and he couldn't keep up with anything I was saying, let alone get in a word edgewise.

"What's this?" He plucks a sheet sticking out from the Lisa Frank folder. I immediately recognize it as my mood board, but he doesn't look at it right away. He flips my folder open instead.

He didn't *need* to open it if he's already got what he needs to make a decision. I make a small squeak that I quickly mask with an indifferent expression when he shoots me a look.

Because I've just remembered the pink gel pen heart with our initials I'd drawn on the inside flap when I was fifteen and heartsick with wanting to be boyfriend-girlfriend.

Who knows what he'll think if he sees it now? That I can't splurge for a new folder in more than a decade or that I deliberately chose this one to use today?

Oh god, there's no upside to either scenario.

I stiffen, trying to keep from anxiously rocking back and forth on my heels.

Please please please don't let him have seen it.

He closes the folder with an expression that gives nothing away.

"Well?" I burst out.

His eyes widen. "I haven't even looked at it yet! Give me a chance."

He turns his attention back to my mood board. It's not one of those nice cardboard ones, either. It's four sheets of computer paper laid lengthwise and taped at the back to make one giant rectangle. The front has glossy magazine cutouts, paint chips, fabric samples, inspirational words, and "notes to self" scrawled in my small, bubbly handwriting, a blend of cursive and print.

Milan looks at it for so long that I can't take it anymore.

If he's going to tell me none of this is workable, I hope he rips it off Band-Aid quick. Lingering disappointment is worse than a swift dropkick.

He meets my eyes. "I love it."

"You do?"

He shoots me a small smile. "Don't sound so skeptical, Rita."

The way he says my name makes me think of his fingers smoothly slotting between my knuckles. The pad of his thumb moving in slow, languorous circles on my hand.

I swallow. "Great. I'm glad you li—love it."

He flips through my sketches as if it's just a matter of course, nods to himself, and tucks it all back into my folder. "Your mom was right to make me hire you."

My smile falters. *Make* him. His choice of words dims his earlier praise.

Somehow he manages to hurt me without even trying.

"Mmm," I say in agreement, the only sound I can muster that he won't read into.

He looks at me sharply.

"Um, so everything on the mood board that I haven't already sourced has a dollar amount next to it," I say. "And on the back is my total expected invoice for everything, including my time and labor. If you need me to keep costs down, there are some things I can get rid of, like—"

"I'm happy with how it is."

"—the leather barstools, the jute area rugs, the wood entryway console table—"

"Rita!"

I break off midsentence.

"It's fine," he says. "It's great. Don't get rid of a thing."

I slow blink. Granted, it's my first time interior designing for anyone other than myself, but I'm pretty sure there's supposed to be some pushback on how necessary some of my choices are. I didn't go for the most expensive items, mindful of the budget Milan had emailed me, but I didn't scrimp, either. I didn't actually expect him to sign off on everything.

"Even the banana plant in the corner of the living room?" I ask suspiciously. Large houseplants can run expensive even when you're friends with the local nursery owners like I am.

"Everything," Milan says, enunciating every syllable.

Confused and a little annoyed with his obstinacy, I point out, "You didn't even flip it over to see all the prices. Or the *total*."

"I don't need to." His eyes crinkle when he smiles. "I love what you've come up with. You came highly recommended, remember?" Then softly, "I trust you, Rita. I want you."

All the air is sucked out of the room.

"I want you to *do* this for me," he says, words stumbling out in a rush. "I mean, for High Castle. Do the job. Exactly like this." He lays his hand across the mood board, fingers splayed wide.

My eyes follow the movement. I crack a smile, daring to look at him again. For once, it's nice to see him a little off balance.

"My dream house isn't this contemporary," he says, "but if it was, I would want you to design it just like this."

"So in this dream reality, your dream house would still be designed by your ex?"

His mouth drops the slightest bit. Then he offers me a smile that isn't as open as the ones before. "When can you start?"

"Now is good." I came prepared to work in overall shorts and a tank top. I don't want him to think I dressed to impress him. "All the furniture I got on consignment is in the back of my pickup already. Could I borrow you to help me move those things inside?"

"I'm all yours," he says without hesitation.

God, is he saying this stuff on purpose?

Ignoring those three little words, I go through my mental

checklist. "I can pick up the paint from the hardware store and do two-day rush shipping on anything I need to order online, but as far as possible I'm sourcing look-alikes from local thrift stores and flea markets."

He didn't ask me for a rundown, but I figure it's important to assure him that I've got a handle on everything. I pause, letting the silence ring with *So if that's everything . . .*

"Wait."

Milan flips open my folder again to run a long finger down the sketch of the wallpaper in the master bedroom. My body imperceptibly shivers. The wall is a cream mural of a tree-lined vista, feathery, cloud-shaped trees in neutral shades of brown.

When I'm done with it, that Ikea-white room is going to be chic and simple, with a calming nature vibe that brings the outside, inside. The kind of room that should not inspire the feelings rising in my belly and slinking over me, mirroring Milan's traveling finger.

The backs of my knees tickle. The way he's trailing his finger over the gently winding trunks and branches reminds me of the way he learned the curves and dips of my body.

I exhale to get his attention. It's meant to be a huff, but it comes out as a pant.

He draws his head up as though startled to see me. But what's more surprising than that is the transparent look of yearning and regret in his eyes. It's the last thing I expect to see there, and it swarms to fill the entire room until there's no getting away from it.

Even when I blink, I see that look imprinted on the back of my lids.

"Do you . . . Do you want to do a walk-through of the rest of the house?" he asks.

He's stalling, I realize.

He wants to linger here, in this safe space that has nothing to do with our past, nothing to do with each other. All those things we've never said, the closure we've never had . . . We can fill this space with everything left unspoken. Unload everything in my truck and make this concrete block of a house into a home.

Like the one we should have had.

"If you want," I say, offhand, when what I mean is *I do want, I reallyreallyreally do want*.

But I will deny it if anyone ever calls me on it.

Chapter 11

As promised, everything I ordered arrives on time. After that first day we met at the house, Milan stays out of my way. No surprise drop-ins, no follow-ups second-guessing my plan.

Even though he gives me my own key, I spend all of Tuesday and most of Wednesday wondering when he's going to drop in—but he doesn't.

He trusts me. Not regular trust, but blank-check trust.

The realization sticks to me like a wet sweater.

I'm not sure if he wants me to check in, because he never said—and I don't want to be the one to reach out first. So I say nothing and get on with doing my job.

It's better that he's not here. It would feel too much that this was our place, our first home together. In my fantasy, I can pretend I have enough money to buy more than twelve square feet of it.

I fight a smile as I dress the king-size bed in the master with luxurious brown and warm hazelnut throw pillows. The cream linens are good quality, and the fitted sheet snaps tight over the corners without a single wrinkle.

Milan would have pouted about this bed being too big.

The few times we'd managed to spend the night together, he always hated it when I scooted away from his warmth in the night to find an untouched cool patch. He liked to cuddle, to sleep with me tight against him. I loved it in winter, called him my personal furnace and slid my cold toes over his bare calves until he yelped at me to wear socks. It turned into a joke between us; socks in my stocking every Christmas. Novelty ones, the kind with cheeseburgers, pugs in tutus, and sushi rolls with faces.

Ugh, I shouldn't be thinking about him. I should be thinking about getting back *at* him.

And definitely not back *with* him.

I suppress every single warm fuzzy. Squash it down flat.

Nope. No. Not me thinking about Milan all wistful like that. Certainly not.

This is MyShaadi getting in my head, nothing more.

I had a solid hour with Milan on Sunday showing him my designs and doing the walk-through, and I couldn't find a single window of opportunity to bring up my successful MyShaadi.com match with a "reliable" man to throw in his face.

Which would have been easier if I actually *did* have a successful match with Neil. But like he pointed out, maybe my dumbass answers threw the AI for a loop. He, on the other hand, already had three matches, and the number was growing. How? And, I ask again, *how*?

I take a step back to survey the room. It's perfect, just the way I drew it. The room is draped in soft earth tones, from the vista of trees to the soft furnishings to the reclaimed barn wood I sanded and stained myself.

It's weird, but I'll be a little sorry to leave when all this is done. It was nice to pretend I was an interior designer. Someone who Milan needed.

I want you, Rita, echoes in my mind.

Yeah, for a job.

Not in his life.

Maybe it would be easier if I could point to one thing that happened and say, yes, *that* was the moment it all changed, that's why we fell apart. That's the catalyst that lead to his voicemail. That's the moment when I fucked up. When he did.

But I have no clue who's to blame.

We'd dated since we were fifteen, which was early in Desi families like ours. Most of the time you were questioned to the third degree if you wanted to go anywhere a boy might live, work, or even breathe in the vicinity of, frankly. But our parents put on their understanding, our-kids-are-growing-up-in-a-different-time game faces and decided to be okay with it, probably because it was better than the alternative of us sneaking around.

Even if they had forbidden us from being together, Milan would never have listened.

He even had this funny shirt he slept in for years, a joke present from his mom, that read: I'M NOT BOSSY, I'M THE BOSS. He wore it until the armpits yellowed and the letters faded off.

He was possessive about his tees that way. He refused to let his mom use anything for window rags until it was practically falling apart; even then, it was a fight.

"Hey," says a voice from behind me.

I spin, heart jackhammering.

Milan steps across the threshold, taking in the whole room for the first time. "Wow."

Wow, yourself.

He's low-key today in dark indigo jeans and a short-sleeve white-collared shirt sprinkled with tiny blue sailboats, all pulled together with a camel-color belt that matches his shoes.

I can't take his silent absorbing anymore. "Do you like it?" comes out before I can stop myself. I cringe, hearing the eagerness in my voice.

He doesn't tease out his praise. "Fuck yes."

I stifle my knee-jerk laugh. "Well, that's . . . that's good to know."

"I promise I'm not here to check up on you," he says. "I was just passing by."

"Oh, you've got another house in this neighborhood?"

A beat passes before he answers. He scratches his neck. "Yeah."

When he's not any more forthcoming, I say, "It wouldn't bother me if you were. Um. Checking up on me." Quickly, I tack on, "I mean, it's your money. You have every right to see how I'm spending it. Sorry about the drop cloths and the paint smell. I'd throw open the windows, but I don't want to waste the AC, so . . . um. Should be gone by Sunday's open house. And then you'll finally see the last of me." I pretend to mop my brow, miming relief.

Something shifts in his face. He doesn't respond, but moves deeper into the room.

An arm's length away from me. I tuck my elbows into my side, digging in deep.

His brown eyes travel the room, landing on each of my new additions. I can almost see him cataloging everything in his mind, matching it to the sketches I showed him.

And then, last of all, he ends up looking at me.

The seconds drag on, a string pulled taut enough to snap. What is he thinking?

He smiles like he's read my mind. "You asked me if, in my dream reality, my dream house would still be decorated by you," he states.

The words are familiar in a way that I can't place.

I draw my eyebrows together. "When did I—"

"There's no reality in which I wouldn't want you, Rita," he interrupts.

I'm rooted to the spot, throat too fuzzy to speak.

"—to design my house," he concludes.

My lips part in surprise. That's . . . not where I thought he was going.

That feeling in my gut isn't disappointment. It's *not*.

Milan scratches the back of his neck. A flush rises to his ears, but he doesn't take the coward's way out by looking away. "I wanted to clarify that. In case there was . . . confusion."

All I can think is: Today is Thursday and he couldn't stop thinking about something I said on Sunday, and it bugged him enough to come here and tell me I had it wrong.

"You wanted to clarify," I repeat, heart hammering in my ears.

He clears his throat. "For the sake of accuracy."

Faintly, I manage, "I see."

"So I'm just gonna . . . ." He jerks his thumb over his shoulder toward the door, taking a step backward with a rueful grin. "Let you get back to work."

I could just nod and let him go, but I've done that once before. So I follow him out, down the hallway I lined with small black-and-white abstract prints, past the kitchen and living room that now look so welcoming any family could see themselves growing here.

I don't know if I'm waiting for him to say something or for myself to.

Why did you break us? Why did you let me go?

In the end, he breaks the silence first. He stops at the door, but makes no move to open it.

"Did you mean it about being on MyShaadi to meet reliable men?" His lips twist, about to make a face, before he catches himself.

He reminds me of Una, able to pick up conversations days later, juggling threads in his mind palace until it's time to trot them out again.

This is different, another way he's changed since I knew and loved him.

I haven't answered his question. There's something in his steady gaze that begs me to tell him it was a joke. But I made a plan, and *I* haven't changed—I see things through.

I gather every ounce of fortitude I have. "Yes," I say, proud my voice doesn't quaver the way I'm afraid it will. I tip my chin up. "In fact, I'm surprised you're not already one of their 'Success Story' testimonials."

I wait for him to bring up the elephant in the room that we've been tiptoeing around—the fact that we'd matched.

He just looks back at me.

"I mean, you're the kind of guy who'd do really well. Especially dressed like . . ." I wave my hand over his general area, trying not to zero in on his slim-fit jeans. "You."

Milan glances down at his torso, amused. "Spend a lot of time thinking about my qualities, do you, Rita?"

It crashes into me that I may have inadvertently complimented him.

"I don't think about you at all," I say through my teeth, plastering on a smile.

His eyes light up. "I might have actually believed you if your mouth had moved even once during that sentence."

I relax my grimace-smile.

"Thanks," he adds.

I squint at him. "For saying you dress well?"

Is it that much of a surprise to him when he looks as though he just waltzed out of a Ralph Lauren Nantucket photo shoot?

His voice lowers, turns serious. "For making a house into a home. I always knew you'd be good at that." He smiles, but it's strained and doesn't reach his eyes. "Whoever you find on MyShaadi, the person you make your home with is going to be ridiculously lucky."

I blow past the tenderness in his voice. He's on MyShaadi, I'm on MyShaadi, but we're both going to pretend that we didn't match?

I used to feel so bad, and maybe even a little superior, when couples from high school would be draped all over each other in first period and icing each other out by fifth. I was sure that would never be us. Walking down the hallway without even a chin lift to acknowledge the person whose tongue had been in their mouth a few hours ago.

Is what's happening with me and Milan now just the adult version of that?

I want to be brave. I want to ask him if he saw that we matched, but if I ask first, he'll have the upper hand. For the same reason, I want to—and I *don't* want to—ask about what happened six years ago. Why he'd been struggling so much with school and why he'd never said a word to me about it before the voicemail.

But he can't ever know that I'm still hunting for that closure.

I'm scared to be the one who cares more, who cares too much. I might have been a girl who waited, but he can't know that a part of me is waiting still.

Milan pauses, about to say something else, then shakes his head. "I'll see you soon, Rita."

Neil comes over a couple of hours after I leave Milan's listing, which I can no longer in fairness call the Soulless Wonder after all the work I put in to make it family friendly.

I'm just about to pull the sheet pan of loaded nachos out of the oven when the key turns in the lock. Harrie's attention darts from the cheesy yumminess I'm sliding off the rack—which he's hoping will fall—to the door. He bullets toward Neil the second he's in the house, the cacophony of his shrill barks going straight to my temple.

"Harrie!" I shout, pulling the chilled pico de gallo out of the fridge. "Stop it."

"See, this is why I hate kids," says Neil, raising his voice to make himself heard.

I accidentally dump the cilantro-lime mixture in one place. "You what?"

Mercifully, Harrie stops barking, but not before shooting me a wounded look. He trots back to the nachos, staring with expectation.

"Smells delicious in here," says Neil, sliding his keys back into his pocket. He sniffs the air appreciatively the same exact way as Harrie did five minutes ago.

"Rewind to what you said about hating kids?" I drag a fork through the diced jalapeño, tomato, and onion, spreading it out evenly across the layered nachos.

"Figure of speech." Neil smiles as he enters the kitchen, side-stepping Harrie, who's now ignoring him totally to make a point.

My laugh comes out awkward, strangled. "Yeah, but a pretty revealing one." I take off the oven mitt, but don't put it back in the drawer. "You don't . . . mean it, do you?"

It bugs me, even though we've only been together three months and I'm not even looking at Neil in that way. My womb is hardly rushing to put together a sperm welcome party, but that doesn't mean I *never* want kids.

"Ma says I'll feel differently when it's my kid," says Neil. "That's how it was for her, apparently. But she's always doted on me and my brother. Still does. She's always saying we're her biggest achievement. That's why she likes us over there all the time. We're her world."

He comes close, about to go in for a hug, then spies the reddish-brown stains on my apron and stops an arm's length away. "Why'd you chop the avocado instead of making guac?"

Because I'm tired of him stealing the nucleus chip with all the guac on it.

"Slicing is easier than mashing. Maybe next time you could help cook and do it the way you like it," I say tartly.

He looks thoughtful, but puzzled, like he's not sure I'm deliberately trying to be passive-aggressive or aggressive-aggressive.

It's the latter, for sure.

If we've started to have these little domestic squabbles, the honeymoon period is over.

That *should* be a good thing. It means we're comfortable enough to zing at each other. Which makes this officially my longest relationship since Milan.

By the time Neil washes up and we sit down on the couch to eat ("No, Harrie, not you."), I'm still thinking about what he said, and the fact that his mom maybe didn't want kids but now revolves around them so much that she can't let them live their own lives.

"What do you want to watch?" I ask, pulling up my Netflix list.

Freddie and Harrie curl up against each other on their doggy bed, the prime location for both TV watching and human watching.

"Anything other than romance," says Neil. He pokes a broken chip corner into a glob of melty, bubbly cheese. "If I have to watch another movie about a woman who moves to some rural small town and falls in love with the local lumberjack, these nachos are going to come up."

Harrie looks disconcertingly pleased at the prospect of secondhand ground beef.

"Those guys are rugged and outdoorsy," I protest.

"If they wear flannel, they're a lumberjack," he insists stubbornly.

"*I* wear flannel." I stab my own tiny chip triangle through a runaway pinto and a black bean in one move.

Stumped, Neil shovels in a chip. "Fine, then I'll watch anything other than a Christmas movie. I mean, it's June. Who's craving snow when we have all this awesome sun? And how many movies can you make with 'Christmas' as an adjective, anyway?"

"As many as they want because they are absolutely delightful."

"Hey, what about *Die Hard*?"

How can I deny him Bruce Willis when his eyes light up like that?

I'm pretty sure I hit a maturity milestone for not telling him plenty of people—not me—also consider *Die Hard* a Christmas movie, don't ask me how. Ex-boyfriend number five would attest.

With an internal groan, I hand over the remote and let him add about a dozen movies I'm never going to want to watch to my queue, start two different WWII movies before giving up ten minutes in, and half listen to his rant about all the great TV series that left Netflix this month before he got a chance to watch them. He switches to Hulu, asks me for the millionth time why I didn't pay for the more expensive ad-free subscription, and points out the fact that I'm clogging my queue with things I've never watched for as long as he's dated me.

Dinner's over by the time he finds a movie with high-speed chases and big explosions. I swear he's the only guy I know who thinks jumping back and forth between ten different things counts as "watching TV." After I do the dishes, I return to the couch just to be polite. I've missed the beginning of the movie and I don't care enough to ask Neil to catch me up, and he doesn't offer. He's slid beyond the middle cushion, verging onto my seat. I curl into the armrest and pull out my phone, tucking my feet partially under him.

Neil sucks down air like there's been a horrifying on-screen death. He inches away from me. "Maybe you should wear some socks if you're cold. Or turn down the AC."

I draw my knees up to my chest, cold toes curling.

His eyes flick to my screen. I wait for him to ask me if we've matched yet, but he doesn't.

Part of me thinks it's because he's never really believed in the Shaadi scam in the first place. He'd chuck it aside and introduce me to his mom even without it. I bet he hasn't even checked his account more than the once.

It wouldn't surprise me a bit if he's relying solely on me to give him the—fingers crossed—good news. Neil's so fixed on the TV that he doesn't notice my soft gasp of recognition when a name from my childhood shows up in my matches.

Sanju Khanna, the boy my entire fourth-grade math class had caught slurping down a rope of his own snot the day before winter break. Two weeks off from school hadn't made anyone kinder, and our first day back in the New Year was full of creative nicknames for him.

Not me, though. And not Milan, who was sitting next to him when it happened, either.

"Neil," I start to say, reaching out to poke him with my foot without thinking.

The giggle evaporates in my throat. Slowly, I draw my leg back.

He has no idea who Sanju is or why the snot anecdote will forever make this man singularly repugnant. Sure, he'll make the right faces and laugh about how it's just my luck, but he won't really get why it's so funnily horrifying, because he wasn't there.

If I'm being honest, Neil isn't the one I want to tell.

He's not listening anyway.

Chapter 12

"The place looks great."

I don't need to turn to know who it is. I'd recognize that voice anywhere.

It's been playing on repeat in my mind ever since Thursday night, so my entire Friday and Saturday were spent in cramping dread that I'd run into him here.

Milan didn't show either day, which meant that the figurative nail-biting time I spent worrying about whether he'd make an appearance was nothing compared to how much time I'd have lost if he actually *did*.

I hate this about myself, but being in the same room with him still does something to me.

It's the always-there-just-buried grief until I feel the biting urge to hurt him like he hurt me pressing against my chest like the strike of a snake, but mostly it envelops me with the memory of coming home to soft thumb rubs and stomach-plummeting pronouncements: *Making a house into a home. I always knew you'd be good at that.*

Well, I am. It's what he hired me to do.

And I did a damn good job.

But now that job is over.

I take a deep breath before turning around. "Thanks," I say coolly.

He closes the distance between us, alternating his Starbucks coffee cup from hand to hand, mapping the entryway and the living room and what he can make out of the dining and kitchen area.

There are a few new additions: baby Zebra haworthia succulents floating on an invisible shelf in colorful ceramic reject planters that didn't meet the quality standards of the local pottery studio; a mid-century modern armless leather accent chair thrifted from Lucky Dog Luke's; a tattered ottoman I reupholstered in mint-green velvet; and underneath the flared leaves of a majesty palm, a bench woven with Goodwill belts in varying shades of caramel and espresso.

"It looks so much better," says Milan after he takes it all in. "You were right. I shouldn't have followed the modern, minimal style through the whole house. I should have showed people how they could live in it. Those extravagant other things I brought in . . . the art, the glass table, they were just things."

He doesn't say it, but I understand: *This is a home.*

I wait a beat too long without saying thank you. Waiting for the rest of it.

I'm still waiting for him to make a crack about matching with me on MyShaadi, which he had to have seen by now. He would have received the same email notification at the same time as I did. It would be a great opportunity—my last opportunity—to throw Neil in his face.

Even if I had to lie to do it.

So what if I matched with you? I imagine myself saying. *I also matched with this totally hot other dude who—*

Okay, so it's really hard to think about Neil right now, annoyingly, for some reason.

But there's no sign of recognition on Milan's face, no knowing quirk of his lips.

"You did a fantastic job," he says, his voice too loud in the silence. "One hundred percent." I dart a suspicious glance at him. "It's everything you said it would be, and more. I couldn't have even imagined how terrific everything would come together." He stares at me, trying to drive home his compliments, to make sure I hear him.

"I . . . ah." I swallow past the sandpaper in my mouth. "Thank you."

Relief passes over his face. "For a second there I thought you'd gone into shock because I said you were spot on with your design instincts, Rita." Goosebumps pimple over my skin when he says my name. "I think I'm a big enough man to admit when I was wrong," he continues, flashing me a crooked smile.

"It takes a lot more than that to shock me," I counter.

His smile spreads. "Should I take that as a challenge?"

We stare at each other for a long, heated second.

"So the finishing touches are all . . ." Milan waves his hand. I catch the glint of the watch I gave him. "Finished?" His cheeks twitch, like he can't believe he said something so inane.

I half smile. It's nice to see him discomfited for a change. "Yeah, I'm done here."

His eyes widen. "Yeah, but not *done* done, right?"

Annoyance prickles in my fingers. "Not unless you can think of something else," I say slowly, making a show of looking one-eighty degrees around me. "The open house is in less than an hour. You're going to have to let go of me at some point."

He blanches.

I can't bring myself to apologize. I didn't mean it like that. It was supposed to be a light joke, but it didn't land. I was right, before; joking doesn't work out well for either of us.

Milan watches as I pull my scrunchie out of its messy bun and let it drop on the entryway console so I can shake my hair loose. I don't want him seeing me with the bumpies. It's another memory between us, the way I used to lay my head on his chest and he'd run his hand over my crown, playing with each bump, wiggling his finger into the loop of hair that stuck out.

"You're still obsessed with those things," he says, nodding to the scrunchie.

"I could say the same about you and all your T-shirts."

"Now that's one thing I *did* outgrow."

So there were other things that he hadn't?

"And don't even pretend you don't love my shirts," he replies, so fast that I don't think he realizes he wasn't speaking in the past tense. His eyes get a wily glint. "You slept in them all the time. In fact, there's a couple that went missing that I always suspected you took with y—"

"Patent lies," I bite out. Why does he have to remind me of old times?

He grins at me, slow and easy. Arousal unfurls in my stomach, tickling my rib cage with want. Need. It's shameless and pathetic how much I want him to keep smiling at me like that.

NEIL, I remind myself in all caps. *NEIL IS YOUR BOY-FRIEND. MILAN IS SO FAR BACK IN YOUR REARVIEW THAT HE'S JUST A PINPRICK ON THE HORIZON.*

Falling into this easy banter is dangerous. MyShaadi was laughably wrong about us being a perfect match. If that was true, we would never have broken up in the first place.

You can't fix something this broken.

Not Mom and Amar, not me and Milan.

Right as I'm about to accuse him of trying to waste my time, he asks, "Oh, do you want this? I only had a sip. They messed up my order." He extends his Starbucks cup, its sweetness wafting up to me.

If he'd meant to offer it to me, why hadn't he given it to me as soon as he entered?

Reading the question in my face, he says, "Sorry, brain fart. Lot of things on my mind this morning. This week has been a lot."

Paranoia has me clenching my teeth. A lot, why?

Because we've seen more of each other in the last ten days than we have in six years? Because he's weirded out we matched on MyShaadi and he doesn't want to have a horribly awkward conversation about it?

Doesn't want me to say: *Hey, maybe that AI is onto something! What do you think, wanna make our moms' day by giving ourselves another chance?*

"'Brain fart'? I don't think I've heard anyone say that since high school." I take the piping-hot cup with a mumbled thanks.

"Yeah, you know me." He laughs, but it's strained. "I'm sentimental about the past."

We both freeze. Because I do know him. And it goes both ways.

I clutch harder at the cup. "Right. So. Thank you for the coffee. I didn't have time this morning to grab anything since I wanted to get in and out by nine, and it's already past that, so I better go before people start arriving . . ." I edge toward the door, which unfortunately means moving closer in his direction.

"Rita, it's 8:50 a.m. What time did you get here?" He sounds fondly exasperated, which sets off giddy somersaults in my belly, especially when he reaches out to touch my shoulder.

I stop in my tracks. "It may have been seven," I say grudgingly. "But only because—"

"You wanted to avoid me?" There's a laugh in his voice.

"What? No! That's not even—you're so off base—it's laughable—!" I sputter.

I can't stand his lofted eyebrow.

"Uh-huh," he says. "Don't think I don't remember that you almost caused a car accident in front of this house last week because you were going to pretend like you didn't see me."

I glare at him, unblinking. "I *told* you that wasn't how it happened." My chest rises and falls like I've just gone on a three-mile run.

"One hundred percent that's what happened." The statement is accompanied by a smirk that brings out a faint dimple in his cheek and accentuates his barely there butt-chin.

Wait, this is the second time he's said "one hundred percent."

The blood drains from my face. He's playing with me. He *did* see the notification that our profiles matched and he's acting like he didn't to fuck with me. Or is he waiting for me to bring it up first?

"I guess it's good you weren't trying to avoid me," says Milan, "because I was thinking about you last night and I wondered if—"

Last night? Thinking? About me? My head spins.

"—you'd be interested in getting together to—"

"We're not getting back together. I matched with someone on MyShaadi," I blurt out my lie at the same time, swallowing half his sentence.

Any second now, victory is going to sweep over me. I watch his face carefully, expecting him to roll his eyes and say: *Yeah, Rita, I know, because it was me.*

"Um . . ." His forehead scrunches. "Okay? That's not at all where I was going, Rita."

"Oh." My mouth tastes chalky. "Sorry. I missed whatever it was."

"I just thought that, well, since we worked together so well, maybe you'd be interested in— Wait, I'm not telling this right." He lets out a short laugh. "Let me start over. The other day we talked about dream houses, remember?"

"How could I forget?" I say wryly, hoping I don't give myself away by going red.

Now it's his turn to look embarrassed.

I get the feeling he'd revealed more to me that day than he'd intended to.

"I bought a house. I mean, it's not mine outright. But it's mine enough. Mortgage and all," he says. "Out on Rosalie Island. You remember that B&B we stayed in?"

"Of course." Our families had vacationed there together the summer after senior year. Sentimentality is all well and good, but why is he bringing up—

"Milan," I say, aghast, for the first time saying his name without creepy-crawly weirdness going down my spine. "That beach house was gorgeous, but it had seen better days even *then*." I tilt my head to the side. "Don't tell me that you . . . No. You didn't."

He shoots me the most sheepish of sheepish smiles. "I did."

Why is he telling me this? Is he trying to re-create the past by bringing up Rosalie Island?

"Congratulations." I start for the door again. "I'll send you my final invoice, okay?"

He throws an arm in front of me, inches away from touching. "Rita, please."

Abruptly, I halt, anxiety and annoyance spiking. "What? Aren't we done?"

He opens and closes his mouth.

"Yeah, that's what I thought." He makes no move to stop me,

but I wrench myself away. Hard. "We're done. We've *been* done. Maybe you thought all this was going to soften me up, the compliments, the coffee, the island, the . . . the talking about the past, but we're done. One hundred percent done," I say, throwing the phrase back in his face, just in case it is a game we're playing, pretending neither of us saw our match on MyShaadi. "*One hundred percent*," I repeat for emphasis. "I hope this place sells, but now there's nothing left between us."

"Rita, is that what you think?" He seems truly taken aback. "I think you're talented. I think you're smart. I wasn't asking you for anything right now other than to go into partnership with me to flip the house I bought."

I still. "So you mean . . . you weren't trying to . . ." I gesture helplessly.

"When I'm wooing you, you'll know it," he says, cracking a smile. "It was really just business. Listen, don't answer me now. Think on it."

It was one thing to work with him when I was put on the spot, but another to voluntarily jump in the ring again. "I don't think it would be a good idea," I say. "We're like cats in a bag."

That gets another grin out of him, the butterfly-inducing dimpled one that makes me press my knees together.

"Hear me out. Sure, the house could use a little love, but you could say that about most any place, couldn't you?" He spreads his arms, comes so close to grazing my chest that I flinch out of the way. "Look at this one. You transformed it."

"I rent, Milan. I have no clue how much a mortgage on a place like that costs, and I don't have the money to pitch in for my share." It's less embarrassing to admit than I expect.

"We can work all that out, Rita," he says, leaning toward me in his eagerness. "It used to be a beautiful home and it could be again. It's a little broken down, sure, but isn't it worth putting it back together? Giving it another chance? Restoring it to how it used to be?"

I move to the door, putting my hand on the knob. Twist, release. "Maybe," I admit. "Or maybe it's better not to pin your hopes on lost causes."

Chapter 13

"And the weird thing was, Raj, that the coffee drink he was served 'by mistake' happened to be my favorite salted caramel mocha frappe," I complain, placing my phone on the floor so I can tighten the laces on my Nike running shoes.

It's not the first time I'm having this conversation with my best friend in the week since the open house, but it's the first time we're FaceTiming. So while all she sees of me hunched over on the couch is a ceiling view and hopefully none of the un-flattering double-chin angle, I can make out the weariness on her face.

Usually when we video chat she's distracted with posing for the camera, showing off her great bone structure and Instagram hair, and I'm okay with her half listening and she's okay with me droning on in her ear, but today we both seem out of sorts.

For a split second I feel bad about rehashing last Sunday to death, but I can't help it. Even though he paid my invoice ridiculously promptly, thus severing our working relationship, I still feel the need to exorcise *him* out of my system.

I'm already dreading having to go back to get all my stuff out of the house when it sells. With my luck, he'll be there even though there's zero reason for him to be.

"And you've gone back to not using his name," says Raj. "How's that closure coming?"

I make a face. "You make it sound like it's that easy. Like I ask and I get it. It's been six years. If I ask him now, when I didn't back then, he'll think I'm not over him yet."

"But you're not, are you?"

I sigh at the glib remark. "I'm not you. I don't just *talk* about these things. Look at my family. Not exactly big on the heart-to-hearts."

Raj looks crestfallen for a second before she switches subjects. "And how are things going with Neil?" She treats me to an irascible grin. "Did you tell him that Milan asked you to jump into bed with him?"

"Raj!"

"Figuratively!"

Harrie barks, refusing to be left out. He immediately trots over to shove his face into the screen. He recognizes Raj at once and starts wagging his tail, bumping his nose against hers.

Her delighted smile widens. "Nose boop!"

I pull Harrie onto my lap to kiss the top of his head, forgetting all about the laces. "Your questionable use of idioms aside, no, I haven't. I mean, he knows about the Soulless Wonder, I just didn't go into all the details of my mom and Milan's setting us up after not seeing each other for six years." Defensiveness punches through my chest as I hear how it sounds. "It's not like it's a secret. There's no reason to tell him about Milan's offer because I'm not going to say yes."

I make sure to use his name so she doesn't call me out again.

"Why not? You could use the money."

"Sure, but I'd have to invest in the project in order to be a partner. Helping him last week was different, it was a relatively quick in-and-out job. Who knows what kind of time and money commitment this would be? I looked the house up and it didn't look *too* bad, but you know pictures never tell the whole story."

"What I *know* is that you could have said no and dismissed this immediately, but you took the time to look it up and now you're actually thinking about what would be involved in saying yes."

"That is *not* the takeaway from what I said!"

Harrie gives me a comforting chin lick. It's cold, but it's the thought that counts.

"Oh, Rita, don't squawk. I know you. You're tempted. That's why I'm currently looking at your ceiling instead of you, because you wear your heart on your sleeve. And *that* idiom is one hundred percent accurate."

I groan. "Every time I hear that percentage, my blood pressure goes up."

"Why?"

"No reason," I say quickly. Too quickly.

Her eyes narrow.

I need to get off this topic fast. If I tell her about MyShaadi's one hundred percent match, it'll confirm all her suspicions about our compatibility, and that's the last thing I need.

"It's just a matter of time before I match with Neil anyway. *He's* my boyfriend."

It rings hollow even to me.

"You bitch *all* the time about him being under his ma's thumb," she says, huffing. "I mean, after his mom set him up with that girl the other week, did he even tell her she was out of line?"

I release a short laugh. "Yeah, that's not a conversation he's going to sit down and have."

"And that's not a red flag?"

"I'm not marrying him. We're just having fun. Seeing where things go. If we level up our relationship, *then*, maybe, and *only* then, it might be a yellow flag."

I have no clue why I'm on the defensive when this is the same question I've asked myself from the beginning. How okay am I, really, with a guy—a kind, honest, sexy guy—who still puts his mother first? Someone who's shown time and time again that he *is* his father's son?

While I'm waging war in my mind, Harrie wiggles to be let down. The moment I do, he bounds back to the phone, circling it like a new playmate.

Raj coos at him, slipping into baby talk, but then snaps back to her usual no-holds-barred self. "You're fighting for the wrong guy."

"That implies Milan is the right guy." I snort.

"Maybe he isn't," Raj allows, "but that doesn't mean Neil is just by default."

The lump in my throat is boulder-sized by now.

Thank god she can't see my face, which, evidently, I wear every single emotion on.

"Rita, you turned down Paula's blank-check house reno. Now Milan's offering you one. What if it's a sign that you *should* do it? You said before that the universe was conspiring to bring him back in your life. What if you're ignoring what fate is trying to tell you?"

"It's not the universe," I grumble. "His mother probably forced him into it. That's literally the reason we were even in this situation to begin with, remember? He said it himself. 'Your mom was right to make me hire you.' That's what he said, verbatim."

My heart squeezes. "I was useful to him, that was all. And he thinks I can be useful to him again. I don't think he actually gets that this might be hard for me."

He should have known, even if I told him that I was over it. Over him.

Milan Rao knows me.

Even though I hate it, he should know me enough to get that nothing about this is easy.

"I think you're the one taking away the wrong message," says Raj, quietly now. "To me, it sounds like he's admitting how good you are. Take the win. I know you're a little jaded about Indian moms, but Milan isn't a puppet on strings dancing to his mother's tune."

I fidget with my forgotten laces. "I can't believe you of all people are encouraging me to consider this. Little Shop of Hors D'Oeuvres took your mom and grandma two decades to complete."

"Oh, come on." Raj scoffs. "Do you genuinely think the house on Rosalie Island is going to take that long or is this just an excuse not to do it?"

No. In fact, it's pretty doable. We could finish up by autumn.

Wait, what am I saying? There's no *we*.

"I'm just glad it's over and I don't have to see him again," I say, pulling the laces tight.

She sighs. "Okay, that's the millionth time I've heard you say that in the last week, Rita. We keep talking about him, and not enough about me, which is fine if there's anything new and exciting happening, but there isn't, so can we please return to my favorite topic of me?"

"I thought I was your favorite topic," I say, amused at her whine.

"Yeah, but you're my best friend, so you're me-adjacent," she says with a straight face.

"You're hilarious. Okay, spill. What's new in Raj-land?"

A gusty sigh. She brings the screen close to her face. "I swiped right on Luke."

"Luke? As in Lucky Dog Luke?" It doesn't surprise me he's on Tinder.

"Can we not call him that?" I can see Raj's wince. "It's just a reminder of his—in less crude terms—*prowess*. I didn't even mean to swipe on him, it just happened! He just looked like a hot guy and I didn't think. My thumb has a mind of its own."

"Babe, it's a nickname. And it's not even one he earned. It's because he works at his grandpa's antique mall. And it really doesn't help that he wears a huge name tag that says 'Ask me my name,'" I say with an eye roll, getting up from the couch.

The first time I met him, I made the mistake of asking him. By the end of it, I knew everything about him, his dad, and his gramps, all named Luke, and the entire history of the Lucky Dog Luke's antique mall where he worked when he wasn't an adjunct English lecturer.

She groans. "How am I going to look him in the face when he knows I swiped right on him, though?"

I hide my smile. "Raj, the only way he'd even know is if he swiped right on you, too."

Her jaw drops. "Shit."

"Guess you don't know everything, do you?" I tease.

Harrie's waiting at the door, ready for his walk, but his brother is another matter.

"Freddie, come," I say, patting my thigh. "Raj, can I call you back? I promised these guys a walk and if I don't return my mom's call she might actually badger my dad into coming over to check on me, make sure I haven't keeled over from too much instant noodles or something."

Mom still thinks I can't take care of myself unless I have a partner.

What would have happened if I'd managed to tell her about Neil that day Milan came over? How would my life look now? Would our Friday night date be replaced with a family dinner, Neil nervous to meet my folks, me nervous about the round, round rotis Aji would undoubtedly force me to practice?

I shake the thoughts from my mind, refusing to dwell on them a second longer.

Like I told Mom, I take care of me. I make my own decisions. And even if they're the wrong ones, at least they're mine. I can't second-guess myself now.

Chapter 14

I don't call Mom right away, just WhatsApp her that we'll talk tomorrow.

She sends me back the middle-finger emoji.

Since I'm cajoling Freddie to pick up the pace, I don't see it until after her follow-up message, the see-no-evil monkey emoji and an Oops, didn't have my glasses on. Clicked the wrong one. Meant to do a thumbs-up. And then, to prove her innocence, three halo emojis.

Wrong one, my ass. My right eyelid twitches.

When did my mother learn to troll me?

It's not that I don't want to talk to her, but since she invited Milan over two weeks ago, it's literally all we've talked about. She sees us as her chance to right the wrong that happened to her, to give me a happy ending—and I love her for it, but I'm also exhausted.

Harrie's pulling ahead, straining against the leash. He turns around every few minutes to make sure we're still there and yips to make us walk faster.

Freddie tips his head back to look at me. Unlike Harrie, he never begs for anything. Not food, not cuddles, not attention. But his expression right now plainly pleads with me to pick him up, French bulldog eyes growing big.

"Freddie, you've barely been walking for ten minutes," I scold.

Harrie comes running back, but even his encouraging nuzzles won't coax Freddie.

I give in with a sigh, bending to scoop him up. His perked ears tickle my chin, and his head butts against my chin as we keep walking. I get a few amused looks and snickers from the neighbors, who know Freddie's reluctance to be taken on walks all too well.

It's a little tough to carry a dog, albeit a small one, and hold my phone, but somehow I manage. Hey, want to pick up some takeout on your way over to my place? I type out. Your choice. I'm good with anything.

Send. It whizzes off to Neil.

Takeout means I don't have to do any cooking or washing up. We can watch the next *Die Hard* in the franchise, we can try to tweak our MyShaadi answers so we get a match, we can hit "decline match" on the other girls that he apparently *did* match with, and enjoy ourselves.

My phone starts to ring.

I answer without glancing at the name on the screen, assuming it's Mom. "Hello?"

"Rita, hey."

"Neil?" I furrow my brow. "You didn't have to call me. I told you, I'm really okay eating anything you choose."

"No, it's not . . ." His voice is rough, frustrated.

"What's going on?"

"I need you to not freak out, okay?"

Worry whittles at me, my mind racing with all the things that send me into panic mode. "Neil, whatever it is, spit it out," I say sharply.

"Okay, so you know how"—he blows a long breath straight into my ear—"I got all those matches and none of them was with you?"

My voice comes out tighter than my throat. "Yeah."

"I have a date tonight."

Singular pronoun.

It takes a moment for my mind to grasp the subtext: not with you.

"With a MyShaadi girl?" I ask, drawing out each word until it's a question.

"It's not, like, a big deal or anything," he rushes to assure me.

"No, of course not, it's perfectly normal, my boyfriend going out with someone he met on a *matrimonial* website."

"You're mad."

"Obviously. What the fuck are you thinking? Why would you— I don't even get why that would even cross your— WE WEREN'T SUPPOSED TO GO OUT WITH OUR MATCHES, NEIL. HOW DID THIS EVEN HAPPEN?"

"It's not my fault."

It's the wrong thing to say, and from the short inhale on his end, he knows it, too.

"Neil." My voice is flat. "What the fuck."

"It's Ma! She's been hounding me all week to tell her what I thought about that girl I met at dinner. What was I supposed to do? She wouldn't take no for an answer. I had to finally say I wasn't interested in meeting that girl again, and then Ma said because I'm not being proactive in finding somebody, she *has* to set me up with eligible girls. So I *had* to tell her I joined MyShaadi."

In other words, he'd rather face my anger than hers.

Bitterness twists my voice. "Bet that just made her day."

"I mean—" Neil sighs. "Yeah."

"So you just . . . what? You agreed to go out with all those girls?" And there were a baker's dozen of eligible young women to choose from. Thirteen dates? At least?

"Not . . . exactly."

"Don't hedge," I snap, tightening my arms around Freddie, tucking my phone between my ear and shoulder. I squeeze him close and take deep breaths. Harrie stands close to my leg, brushing against my ankles to remind me he's there.

"Ma wrestled my log-in away from me."

"As in, she pinned you down and grabbed your phone?"

"No, of course not." He has the nerve to sound affronted. "She asked me for it."

We obviously have different definitions of the word *wrestled*.

"And," I say slowly, "you *gave* it to her?"

"Well, yeah."

The silence stretches between us.

"Why the hell did you even make us do this?" he asks, frustration in every word.

I walk faster. I need to be home, not out here, exposed and alone and with nowhere to curl up and cry. "How is this *my* fault?"

"You made us those profiles on MyShaadi!"

"Yeah, for us," I grind out. "So we could date in peace instead of bringing on the band baaja baaraat. Not so you could go tomcatting around because you're too gutless to tell your mother to back the fuck off and let you be a grown-ass man."

He scoffs. "You want to talk gutless, Rita? Seriously? The

whole reason we did this was, yes, to convince your mom. Because you didn't want to tell her whose son I was. Because you thought she'd care about some grudge from a lifetime ago more than she cares about her daughter's happiness. How's that for gutless?"

This is our first actual fight. And it's objectively terrible.

I don't know what to say. I can hear him breathing. It's out of sync with mine.

"It's not my fault," he says finally.

"You could have said no." My voice is small.

More silence.

"I'm sorry," says Neil.

But I don't think he knows what he's sorry for.

I hang up without saying anything.

My chest burns and my eyes sting, but my house is within sight. I can cry as soon as the door shuts behind me. *Hold it together, Rita.* Just another few yards.

That's when I hear the sad "Oh, honey" behind me.

I freeze. Turn slowly.

Paula Dooley is behind me in hot pink, zebra-striped leggings and a matching sports bra. Water bottle in one hand, phone in the other. One earbud is in, but the other dangles over her glistening chest. She must have heard everything.

Harrie yips at high volume, even though our walks have taken us past a speed-walking Paula hundreds of times.

Rallying, I say, "Hi, Paula."

She comes closer, clucking her tongue. "You poor thing." Before I know what's happening, she's hugging me. Freddie makes an unhappy cry squished between us.

"Really, I'm okay. Thank you, though." I pull back, eyes dry.

She couldn't have just let me escape inside?

That would have been the more sympathetic thing to do.

Paula's mouth forms a you're-so-brave smile, but then her attention is caught by something beyond my shoulder. "I think your boyfriend's here," she stage whispers.

"No, it can't—" I start to say, turning. The words shrivel on my tongue.

A red Alfa Romeo has slid up to the curb. Classic black-and-white Adidas emerge first, then charcoal-gray joggers and a fitted white tee.

I close my eyes. Milan.

Paula looks with curiosity as he approaches, the car beeping as it locks behind him.

Freddie feigns disinterest, turning his head away, but I can still see his eyes peeking.

Harrie's head perks toward the newcomer and he takes a few steps forward, glances back at me. I brace myself for an onslaught of barking, remembering his contentious on-again, off-again relationship with Neil.

But then he begins wagging his tail, being a Very Good Boy.

"Hey, Rita," says Milan. He crouches and holds his hand out for Harrie to sniff before scratching Harrie's chin. "What a handsome pup, yes you are."

Warmth swells in my belly. A man and a dog shouldn't be so cute, and yet, here we are.

I guess introductions are in order.

"That's Harrie with an '-ie,'" I tell him. "And this is Freddie with an '-ie.'"

Harrie's named after three of my biggest teenage crushes, all named Harry: Prince Harry, Harry Potter, and Harry Styles. Likewise, Freddie: Freddie Mercury, Fred Weasley, and Freddie Prinz Jr.

"You're not her boyfriend," states Paula, who's seen Neil often enough to greet him on her morning jogs.

He looks up at us with an unsure smile. "I'm not."

"He's a colleague," I say, because I can't tell her who he really is to me. Reluctantly, I add, "And this is Paula, my neighbor."

"'A colleague'?" Paula's thin eyebrows skyrocket to her hairline. "I see." She glances between Milan and his expensive car, then comes back to me. "I see why you turned down my renovation offer," she says with a wink. With a wave, she continues on her way, earbuds back in place.

I squint at Milan. The setting sun casts him in bronze and he looks a lot more like the boyfriend from my memories than he did in those expensive threads. "What are you doing here?"

That's when I notice the scrunchie on his wrist. It looks like the one I wore Sunday to—

My lips part. *Oh.*

"I wanted to tell you in person that the house got an offer. Actually, it got a lot of offers."

There's no way I can play cool about this. "It did? How many?"

He grins, straightening up. "Four offers, and a fifth that blew the others out of the park." He pauses for effect. "Above asking price. They made an offer, scheduled the inspection, and we're all set to close the deal."

"That's amazing! I'm so happy for you. I guess you'll want the house cleared out?"

He shakes his head. "They want everything as is."

"Fully furnished?"

Harrie makes a soft whine to get Milan's attention, tail wagging ferociously.

Milan gives an obliging *scratch-scratch-scratch.* "The new owners love your design. I knew they would." His smile takes over his entire face. He seems even more thrilled than I am. "They even asked for your card in case they want you to do anything else. And, of course, we'll pay you for everything they're keeping. I know you made a lot of it yourself, so just let me know tomorrow what you're charging and I'll send a check your way."

Before I can respond, he darts his eyes down to his wrist. "I almost forgot about this." He snaps the parakeet-green velvet scrunchie against his wrist, and I don't even panic about him loosening the elastic. "You left this the other day."

"I didn't even notice it was missing." I take the scrunchie, still warm from his skin.

Milan returns to a crouch so he can ruffle Harrie's head. "Yeah? Doesn't surprise me. You had about a hundred even in high school. How has the hoard grown since then?"

"Wouldn't you like to know," I say with a laugh.

The smile fades from his eyes. "I would, actually," he murmurs.

Involuntarily, my gaze drops to his lips.

"All right," I find myself saying.

He tips his head back, forehead scrunched. "To what?"

For one wild moment, I want to tell him: *everything.* Just to see what he'll do.

"I'll go into partnership with you. I kind of want to get away from here for a while."

"Anything wrong?" He says it like he's the one to make it right.

I shake my head. "Nothing that some time on Rosalie Island won't fix."

He raises an eyebrow. "What about 'lost causes'?"

"I'm up for the challenge. Besides, with the money coming in from the new homeowners, I'll be able to invest into flipping the place."

"You're actually agreeing to do this with me," he says, his voice low, stunned. As though in all the possible ways he imagined this would go, my agreeing wasn't even top ten.

"One hundred percent in," I dare to say.

Our eyes meet. Looking at him too long is like staring into the sun.

I tear my gaze away. But that's when I notice he's staring at my chest. Goosebumps skitter down my arms. There's nothing that cute about what I'm wearing, since I knew I'd be out in the sun. An old loose black tee, knotted at the waist, and denim mom shorts.

"I was meaning to ask you," he says. "Why are you holding him?"

Of course. Embarrassment washes over me. He wasn't staring at my boobs. He was wondering why I was carrying Freddie.

"I take it you've never met a diva dog before," I say with a laugh.

Milan sticks out his hand. "Hello, Freddie," he says with a disarming amount of gravitas.

Freddie extends his paw to touch Milan's fingers, every bit as solemn.

Mom would be appalled that I haven't invited him in, especially on a day this hot. *It's bad manners, Rita,* she chides. *Let the poor boy in and offer him a drink. Let bygones be bygones.*

But if I invite him in, it's crossing the threshold into my *life,* too.

I take the plunge. "Would you like to come in?"

Milan seems surprised. "Yeah. Yeah, I'd like that. Let's talk about the future."

Chapter 15

The noon sun beats down mercilessly as the ferry approaches Rosalie Island. Stomach still churning from the choppy waves, I can't help but wonder if I've been hasty in agreeing to work with Milan—again.

After I gave him my word last week, I tried not to overthink what it would mean, what it would change between us. It would be so easy to talk myself out of it if I went down that road. It's the same reason I still haven't updated my mom regarding Milan, because I know she'll be so ecstatic about our extended reunion and I don't want to validate what she pulled.

Neil and I made up the morning after our fight. He'd swung by my house with flowers, one of those big bouquets of roses that Dad gives Mom every Valentine's Day and wedding anniversary, without even needing to be reminded by me, Mom, or Aji. I don't know how I feel about getting roses as an apology bouquet, but if his stumbling to my door sleepy-eyed and rumple-haired was any indication, Neil woke up at the crack of dawn to go to the florist. It was touching that, for once, he didn't care about his appearance.

I'd also figured out a way to get us to match on MyShaadi. It took some convincing, but he came back on board, full of contrition that he hadn't been able to keep his ma an arm's length away from his MyShaadi account. I'd made a mistake, too, banking only on the best-case scenario rather than the most *likely* scenario. But I wasn't ready to give up yet. All I had to do was change my wiseass answers. Last night I'd sent him the screenshots so he could update his, too. Now that our answers are the exact same, we *have* to match.

Una's pulled me off the Little Shop schedule, I've made the last of my furniture deliveries and deposited the checks in my bank account, and I sweet-talked Mrs. Jarvis to drop in on my pups a few times a day when she gets bored with her true crime docudramas, the brain teaser workbooks Aji recently got her hooked on, and gardening.

"Yes," she said with a peremptory sniff as she looked at Harrie. "I've *seen* how he appreciates flowers."

I don't take it to heart. She may act grumpy, but she always has head rubs and treats to dole out, spoiling the boys rotten.

I had plenty of time the last few days to back out of working with Milan, and now, swaying on the gangway as the ferry gently bobs beneath me, I sort of wish I had.

"You're still looking a little green there, Rita," says Milan, looking over his shoulder with a teasing grin. "I told you not to be on your phone if the ferry was making you sick."

"If I'm green, it's because of overexposure to you," I grouse, forcing my feet to keep moving as we get off the steel gangway, which squeaks in protest beneath us.

He laughs like he doesn't buy it for a second.

The gangway wobbles as people crowd on behind me. A metallic screech splits the air.

My stomach turns.

I press forward, hurrying to get on solid ground.

Milan gets there first. "Need a hand?" He offers me his, palm up.

Voluntarily touching him was categorically *not* going to happen.

"No, thank you." I hop off, stomach settling almost at once.

Bluebill Cottage is close enough to walk, but Milan takes one look at the perspiration beaded on my forehead and the red flush on my cheeks and decides to call a taxi.

Which would be a good plan, except we get stuck at a stop sign for at least five minutes. I lean slightly to the left to peer through the front windshield. My shoulder brushes against Milan's.

I feel his eyes on me, but I pretend it didn't happen. "What's going on?" I ask.

The driver, a middle-aged man with graying red whiskers, half turns to say, "Horse crossing. Hope you're not in a rush. I don't honk at 'em." He glares at me in the rearview mirror as if to make sure we're not going to complain about the fact the meter's still running.

"It's fine. I'm enjoying the scenery," says Milan, a smile tugging at his lips.

I catch his eye.

I would, actually, like to get out of this hot taxi where the cheap leather is sticking wetly to the backs of my thighs and the broken air conditioner is blasting warm air right at my face. But sure, let's be polite.

He shifts closer to me as he leans forward to look out the windshield. I can feel his heat through his short-sleeved white linen shirt. "You've got to see this," he breathes as his bare knee bumps against mine.

There's something oddly captivating about his tan knee, knobby and sprinkled with light brown hair beneath his aquamarine Bermuda shorts. Are men's knees usually this attractive?

I rip my gaze away, hoping any blush is mistaken for heatstroke. I can't hold back my gasp. Stocky, short-legged Banker horses, including soft, fuzzy foals sticking close to their mothers' sides, are crossing the road in front of us. Their beautiful coats are a rich sable and almost all of them have white star markings on their foreheads.

They're indifferent to our presence, except for one inquisitive yearling who starts to take a step in our direction before another horse gives a sharp, warning whinny. The yearling pauses, as if trying to determine if exploring is worth another scold, before hightailing it back to the herd.

"I forgot about them," I whisper. "I remember when we were here before, I wanted to see one so badly but we never did."

"You thought you saw one that last night on the porch before we went home," says Milan. "And what did it turn out to be?" He's trying not to laugh—and failing.

He's really going to make me say it?

"A large dog," I grumble.

Even our driver laughs. "Tourists love them, but these horses destroy a lot of other local wildlife. Most of 'em are adopted out from the Outer Banks because of overpopulation and inbreeding, which makes them our pests now."

With that, the last horse makes its way to the other side, and the car lurches forward.

I fall against the headrest, tucking my arms close against my sides and craning my neck back until the herd disappears around the bend.

My mail app pings.

Milan glances over, but when I don't acknowledge him—despite watching him out of the corner of my eye—he folds his arms and stares out his window.

I waver. He's been trying to draw me into conversation ever since he picked me up this morning, but other than a few short sentences on the forty-minute ferry ride over from New Bern, I haven't really been a stellar conversationalist. I tighten my fingers around my iPhone. I shouldn't feel guilty about this, like I'm letting him down, when all I did was agree to a business relationship.

I open my mail, expecting it to be my online bank telling me the funds from a deposited check are now available.

Sender: *MyShaadi.com*

Subject: *Rita, you have a new match waiting for you!* ♻

Preview: *Don't let your pyaar get away, your jaan is closer than you think! Log in to your account to chat with . . .*

I roll my eyes at the cheese of their message. Don't let love get away? Who writes this stuff?

This came way faster than I expected, but I'm not about to look a gift horse in the mouth.

I can't stop the goofy smile from taking over my entire face.

"What are you reading?" Milan asks.

I startle. He's studying me thoughtfully, drumming his phone against his thigh.

"Nothing, just some good news." I carefully angle myself away from him. There's no way he can make out anything on my screen, especially with the sun streaming in, but better safe than sorry.

He waits for me to expound. When I don't, he goes back to whatever he's doing with his phone. Probably answering emails and delegating paperwork on our recent sale.

I mean, *his* sale. I've seriously got to stop thinking of us as a team.

Milan out of my mind, I log in, holding my breath.

Seeing Neil's name and picture on my dashboard is going to be *so* vindicating.

The Internet is slow, so it takes ages for the page to populate, thanks to the enormous graphics the site splashes all over the place.

Come on, hurry up.

I stare at the screen until my eyes water.

"We're almost there," says Milan.

My shoulders are tight, rigid. I force myself to relax, but I can't. The driver takes a turn too fast and my body moves with it, bumping against the door. We must have moved just out of reach of a dead zone, because suddenly, the screen floods with color as LTE data returns.

The hope I clutched in my hand plummets toward my stomach like a rock in freefall.

No.

No no no no no.

Milan's face is on my screen.

His frozen smile, which was just so soft when we looked at the horses, taunts me. *You thought you'd seen the last of me, huh?* it seems to say, smug and victorious. *You thought.*

There's no way this is right.

I squint at him while trying to make it seem like I'm not squinting at him. He's still busy with his phone, not typing anything, and not doing anything else, either.

What if he got the same email I did?

What if he's logged in to MyShaadi right now, staring at *my* photo?

I'm back on the ferry again, tossed side to side, queasy as fuck.

No, my rational mind pipes up. You know Milan. If he'd matched with you for the second time, there's no way he would keep quiet about it. He'd crow. You know he would. He'd stick his phone under your nose like an *aha!* moment and give you that smoldering eye thing he does.

"I see it," says Milan.

I jerk. His voice sounds perilously close.

A second later, the taxi comes to an abrupt halt.

My phone slips, falls out of my hands, and skids under the seat in front of me.

"Fuck." I thrust my leg forward to try and hook it back, but I can't reach. "Um, excuse me, sir, could you pull up a little? My phone's gone under your seat."

The driver grunts and hits a button to stop the meter. "All right."

While Milan hands over some bills, I frantically toe at the carpet, coming up with nothing. Frustrated tears spring to my eyes. This can't be happening.

"Rita." Milan tucks his wallet away. Hands now free, he reaches for my right hand. My fingers, dug into the hot seat, release in shock when he takes my hand in his. I swear I can feel the phantom memory of his distracting thumb circles.

"Rita, stop," he says gently. "You probably kicked it farther away from you. Sir, would you mind looking under your seat?"

Another grunt from the front. Then, "Got it."

Please please please let the screen have gone black.

The man looks at me in the rearview mirror. I can see my red face staring back.

"Huh," says the driver. "Give this to your pretty girlfriend."

I'm too panicked to bristle. Neither of us dispute that I'm his girlfriend.

The phone is passed between the gap in the front seats.

The screen is lit up bright with MyShaadi's colors.

Milan hands it back to me, eyes never leaving my face, not once. He doesn't see the screen, or notice the keenly embarrassing fact that his face is on it.

I take the phone with my free hand. In a horrible twist of fate, the screen darkens the second it's in my palm. I pull my other hand free, but my fingertips skim along the length of Milan's, leaving trails of shooting stars rocketing up my arm.

If he's startled, too, I don't stick around to see it, launching myself out of the taxi before I can see the look on his face—and, more importantly, before he can catch mine.

Once outside, without the proximity to Milan, I can breathe without a rubber band around my chest. My eyes squeeze shut against the bright rays of the sun.

Something hard taps my shoulder. I almost fly out of my skin.

"You forgot your sunglasses on the seat," says Milan.

"Thanks," I mumble, slipping them on.

The taxi takes off as we start making our way toward the house.

There's a wooden driftwood sign, rough at the edges like it was ripped straight from the side of a boat, sticking out of the sand. BLUEBILL COTTAGE is written in faded baby blue cursive, the first and last letters of each word made fancy with a swash.

We tramp our way up the slight incline to the front door. I can see why Milan fell so hard for its coastal charm. Cozy bi-level porches on all sides show off the scenery to the fullest, lined with potted fruit trees and tinkling wind chimes. I can't see it from here, but I remember the veranda in back has a narrow boardwalk leading to the sea.

"Obviously needs some new paint," I say, flicking a peeling strip of white railing.

"Saving it until the end since it's just a superficial fix," says Milan, unlocking the door. "The inside was where most of the money went. Do you remember that awful seventies wallpaper and the dirty wall sconces with the dead flies?" He grins when I make a face. "I gutted most everything, put in new appliances, wiring, and floorboards, and then I— Well, you'll see."

He holds the door open.

Once inside, it's clear how much work has already gone into restoring Bluebill to its former glory. The hardwood floors are stained and sealed the same glossy walnut as the steps of the cantilevered staircase leading to the second floor. The foyer is open above us, two stories tall, with a Jacobean pendant light dangling from the ceiling.

Milan closes the door behind us. The air-conditioning isn't on, so it's a little stuffy. But we're close enough to the water for a breeze to pass through from somewhere.

The open floor plan continues through the first floor. The living room has dramatically vaulted ceilings and sunny windows, plus a gorgeous gas fireplace surrounded by a white chimney breast that could use some color.

The oversize kitchen is ridiculously spacious, with a blue soapstone cooking island, high-end stainless steel appliances, and a ten-foot-long breakfast bar. There's a formal all-glass dining room tucked toward the back, overlooking the beach and leading out to a covered porch for informal dining.

Everything is high quality, but plain. Unfurnished. But the bones are there.

He bites his lip. "First impression?"

He's let me explore in silence, but there's a shiny, expectant look in his eyes, like he's awaiting something important. This time, the shoe's on the other foot.

"It's gorgeous," I tell him honestly.

Relief breaks across his face. "No regrets then?"

"No regrets. You've done a fantastic job."

He has. Gone are the musty settees and threadbare rugs that I remember always smelled wet. Gone are the mismatched yard-sale furniture and chipped ceramic shepherdesses in the dining room hutch.

The upstairs is just as improved, I discover, as I wander from room to room. The bedroom windows are bare of the heavy drapes that used to hang there, and the floral wallpaper, a sickly pink, has been replaced with a coat of white paint so fresh that it still hangs in the air.

"Check out the view," Milan urges, nodding to the balcony.

I precede him outside. Salt air fills my lungs and I breathe it in, deep as it can go. The water below is calm, a confetti of sunlight playing across the glassy surface. While they're slightly too far away to borrow a cup of sugar from, there are houses overlooking the sea on either side of us. With cars restricted to residents, there are no sounds of traffic to compete with the tranquility here. Rosalie is still as untouched as I remember her.

Our arms brush as he comes to stand closer. "Before we got on the ferry, you got kind of quiet. Were you thinking about your parents' old house in New Bern?"

"You noticed that?"

"I notice everything about you, Rita," he says, low and gravelly.

I swallow. "I can't believe you remember. I don't think I mentioned it more than a couple of times." When he opens his mouth, I sigh and say, "Please don't say something corny like 'I remember everything about you.' You can't reuse the same line back to back."

His lips quirk. "Okay, I won't."

Despite myself, I smile. "I wondered if we'd pass it on the way to the ferry parking lot. I hadn't even thought about it consciously until we passed the WELCOME TO NEW BERN sign. Then I remembered the house Mom and Dad bought to flip. They used to watch all those DIY shows on television. That's how Dad got into woodworking."

Milan's smile feels like a call for more information, so I find myself saying, "I used to beg them to let me paint, but they wouldn't budge because Mom thought eight was too young to do it right. I would read Mom's *House Beautiful* magazines in the car every time we went there, until I'd get carsick and she'd take it away."

Little did she know that Dad had tossed me a wink and a package of grid paper in the back seat so I could play architect and interior designer, long before my days playing *The Sims*.

"How long has it been since they sold it?" asks Milan.

Sixteen years.

They bought it when I was eight, sold it a little after my tenth birthday.

I'd thought the second house was supposed to be a family project, but it just seemed to drive Mom and Dad apart. Most of my childhood, I'd wanted to see them laugh and giggle and kiss when I wasn't looking, and sometimes even if I was. To hold hands when they watched romantic movies. To swat each other's bums when they cooked in the kitchen the way I'd seen my friends' parents do.

To say "I love you" to each other and not just to me.

I didn't understand why my parents didn't act in love. Why fixing the New Bern house made them fight and shout at me to leave the room, when my gentle father never raised his voice, not even in the heat of a football game.

It was only sometime in middle school when I started to join Mom and Aji in watching Bollywood movies that I understood what an arranged marriage was.

"What kind of marriage did you have?" I remember asking, pressing the mute button on the remote during a song-and-dance number. "What happened if you fell in love with someone you wanted to marry?"

Mom reached for another kachori from the coffee table and popped it in her mouth whole. She wouldn't talk with her mouth full, so I stared imploringly at Aji.

"My parents told me *no love match*," my grandmother said, wagging her finger. "Not in my day. They wanted a same-caste marriage with in-laws that they knew and trusted would treat me well. Shared values are important."

I'd frowned, not liking the lecturing tone this conversation had taken.

Aji paused, looking at Mom, who wasn't looking at her. "But even with an arranged marriage, love can follow. From both sides."

That seemed encouraging. Had love followed my parents?

I waited for Mom's reassurance, but she quietly sipped her tea.

"Rita, rewind. I want to listen to the song," said Aji, voice a little cranky, except for the fact she took my hand in hers. She hadn't done that for years, not since I was young enough to sit on her lap. "Eat a kachori," she urged. "Enough questions."

By this time, Aji was already living half the year with us. We never talked about it—and I wasn't supposed to know, or remember—but there was one month Mom moved out and lived in New Bern, in the house she and Dad had given up on.

We've never talked about her leaving. Or about why she came back.

The house was just sold one day and that was that.

"Rita?" Milan's voice breaks into my thoughts.

"What? Oh, sorry." I shake the cobwebs out of my mind. "It's been sixteen years. I think they bought the house because they were trying to repair their marriage." My voice drops. "It took them a while to realize that broken things always leave a crack."

We fall silent. Not an awkward silence, but the companionable kind where you don't have to say anything and that's just fine. I don't want to talk about this anymore. I've already said too much that I can't take back. The seconds pass with only the calls of the birds overhead and the gentle ebbs of the sea below.

"Hey, Rita." Milan points left of us, grinning. "This is the exact spot we stood in when you said you saw a wild Banker horse."

I follow his finger. "I really did think I saw one! It was dark!"

He presses his lips together, but his mouth gives a telltale wobble.

"You're laughing at me," I accuse, but I can't stop smiling.

"Far from it," he says, still unable to keep a straight face.

I roll my eyes. "You're incorrigible. Come on, let's make a list of everything that needs to be done to get this place ready to sell."

Chapter 16

It's unbelievable that, despite coordinating our answers almost three weeks ago, I *still* haven't matched with Neil. Rubbing salt in the wound, MyShaadi keeps sending me daily notifications about Milan's one-hundred-percent compatibility.

Unlike me, Neil's ma leaves nothing up to chance. Armed with her son's log-in information, she goes full-steam ahead in arranging his dating schedule and, after the requisite vetoes she deigned to allow him, she books his weekends with prospective future Mrs. Dewans. With the single-minded determination of an Asian kid trying to get an A, she gets to work screening them with the kind of scrutiny usually reserved for political candidates.

As long as Neil's weekends are double-booked, there's no reason I can't stay on Rosalie Island for a few weeks with Harrie and Freddie. If I drag out some of the salvageable furniture that came with Bluebill Cottage, now residing in the dusty shed out back, I can live on-site for a while. It'll be easier to attract buyers while we're still in the high season. Even with Milan's head start, there's still so much to do, and not a whole lot of time to do it.

"You're not seriously going to live with another dude in that wreck, are you?" Neil had asked with a pretty significant amount of alarm when the shock had worn off. "It's not like we won't see each other. I can get awa—I mean, come over more during the week."

"One, it's not a wreck. It just needs some love. And two, Milan has a job and won't be there for much except overseeing my progress. My contribution to this partnership is the elbow grease and know-how. Trust me, I'm barely going to see him."

Neil had snorted, but he'd let it rest. I knew he would. He'd put up with anything so as not to blow his cover with his ma.

The last I'd seen Milan was approximately—I ticked off on my fingers—six paint cans and two weeks ago. After our first visit, we'd ferried everything over from the mainland. When we loaded up the rental van, we'd been mistaken for a newlywed couple and got an earful about how great it was that Bluebill Cottage was finally going to be filled with love again. Both of us had gone red and stiff, not correcting the gossipy older woman who'd spent forever inputting Milan's ID into the computer and filling out the paperwork.

So we'd spent a very awkward fifteen minutes driving in silence until I couldn't take it anymore and started saying, "Oh, look, a mom-and-pop clam shack! A real malt shop, did you even think they had those anymore? Holy shit, a *seagull*."

That last one was pathetic, even for me. But he'd smiled, hummed in agreement, made little shocked noises ("Oh my god, really? Where?"), and peered out the window obligingly.

For a seagull. As if we'd never seen one before in both our lives combined.

Since helping me settle in, Milan has made himself scarce. Which is fine. This isn't his full-time job. That's what I'm there for. Well, me and my dogs. Even though we've missed two of their weekly Saturday playdates at the dog park with my friend Luke and his own fur babies, they've adored being on the island.

I knew Harrie wouldn't be a problem, not with his nose for adventure and chasing birds who don't want to be chased. Even Freddie is enjoying it; I caught him tentatively dipping a paw into the sea before yanking it back and looking around surreptitiously to make sure no living soul saw him.

Harrie barks, his small feet making pitter-pats across the floorboards as he scampers to the front door. He stands, front paws pushing against the screen.

"Not again," I say under my breath. He just went out ten minutes ago when I took my paint fumes break. A plaintive bark answers me. *Yes, again, more outside time, please!*

I rise from my crouch, my spine actually creaking as I straighten. If Milan had gotten this done at the same time as the painting, I wouldn't be in agony now. I flex my fingers experimentally, wincing at the fresh ache of having to sand down the several years' and layers' worth of paint from the baseboards. While my electric sander can handle the bigger jobs, for more finicky work, fine-grit sandpaper smoothed by hand is the way to go.

"You poop more than anyone I know!" I shout, stomping from the living room to the front door. "You are so lucky you're cute."

Cough.

A very human cough.

I come to a screeching, anime-comical stop in the foyer.

"I can't refute that I'm cute, but I'm not sure about the first part." Milan smiles sheepishly from the other side of the screen. He looks casual in khaki shorts and a white linen button-down.

"I . . . ah . . ." I wave the sandpaper.

He nods as if it's in any way an explanation, then scoots inside, nudging Harrie aside so he can't run out to the beach. "Sorry to swing by unannounced. But I brought lunch?" He holds up a large brown paper bag like a truce.

Right on cue, my stomach audibly grumbles.

Even Harrie stops pawing at the door long enough to stare at me.

It's ridiculous this should embarrass me when Milan's heard me make far more embarrassing noises.

Stop thinking about that time you banshee shrieked in pleasure in his ear when he bit your neck at the same time you came.

God, why does *that* have to be the first thing that comes to mind.

"You feeling okay? You're looking a little . . ." Milan takes a step closer, forehead ridged with worry lines. "Why isn't the AC on? You're looking hot."

"What?" I give myself a mental shake. "No, I'm not hot, you're hot."

The corner of his mouth twitches.

Good job, Rita, that sure convinced him. If he hadn't already replaced the floorboards, I would have welcomed them swallowing me whole.

"Who's a cutie patootie?" Milan opens his arms toward me.

I stare in horror at his outstretched hands as he takes a step closer. Instinctively, I shuffle back just as Milan drops to his knees to scratch behind the terrier's ears.

Of course Milan wasn't calling *me* a cutie. Ridiculous that for a second, no, half a second, I thought he was. I snatch the bag and escape to the kitchen before he notices my face has turned tomato.

He follows me, sidestepping the dogs that circle his legs. "I got us each a spinach-beet salad and a crab cake with a basket of waffle fries to split," he says. "And a couple cans of Arizona green tea. You still like that kind, don't you?"

I must be imagining that nervousness in his voice. "Yeah, I'll drink any kind of iced tea."

His shoulders relax. "Cool. I would have just gotten a bunch of things to share, but I didn't know if you . . ." He trails off, running his thumb up and down the side of the can, wiping at the condensation.

We used to split all our plates so we could have a little bit of everything. It's strange to be reminded of how much time has passed.

I pop the tab on the can to take a long draw. My mouth is worryingly dry. I must be more dehydrated than I thought.

The spinach-beet salad is delicious, topped with chunks of tart and juicy blood oranges and thin cucumber slivers. The garnish of chewy dried cranberries and salty roasted pepitas is my favorite. It's the exact kind of brown-bag salad I used to bring to high school, despite Aji's deep suspicion of eating raw vegetables that weren't camouflaged in bhajis.

My stomach backflips with the wonder that he remembered.

I fluff the salad to spread the balsamic vinaigrette, content not to talk, but Milan has other ideas. Over our working lunch, I go over everything I've crossed off the to-do list, ignore Harrie's wide, pleading eyes when I break into the jumbo lump crab cake, and carefully dissect everything Milan says for the slightest indication he's noticed that we've matched on MyShaadi.

Again.

But he doesn't give anything away. It's almost as if it never happened.

I tamp down my disappointment. I should be *glad* that he's so oblivious.

Milan finishes eating first. He rolls up his sleeves, exposing creamy, tan forearms and a few scattered freckles. "Can I take your plate?"

I'd just shoveled in the last mouthful. My tongue pushes everything to my cheek, trying not get flustered. "Oh, I can—"

"Nonsense. You've been working hard all day. Doing the dishes won't kill me."

Before I can argue, he whisks everything away. In record speed, he does the washing up and even has time to get on the floor for Harrie's belly scratches while I sit there and try to remember how to swallow.

I down the last sip of green tea, tipping my head all the way back to get the last drop. When I set the can down on the table, Milan's looking at me. I bring my hand to my throat as a reflex. He darts his eyes away, ears turning red. Harrie whines, rolling around on his back to bring attention back to himself.

"Lunch was delicious," I say, chucking my can into the recycling under the sink. "I was getting a little sick of the meal prep I brought over, so I was planning a trip into town later to get groceries. I would never have ordered that jumbo crab cake on my own, so thank you. I really enjoyed everything."

Everything on an island is expensive compared to the mainland. The two morning walks into the town center I'd taken with the pups had taken me down labyrinthine, Europeanesque cobbled streets filled with fruit and vegetable sellers who left everything outside in baskets, old-fashioned general stores that sold nostalgia candy in vintage glass jars, and bakeries that smelled like the center of a cinnamon roll, but the prices made me reel.

Milan gets up. "No worries. You've been out here two weeks doing everything. This was the least I could do. And I, uh, know you love crab cakes." A beat passes. "Actually, I don't need to head back to the office, so why don't I stick around to help? Give me a hammer and tell me where to point it."

I try not to think about those taut forearms wielding a hammer. His lean fingers clenched around a smooth, thick wooden handle. I try not to think about any of Milan's body parts in general.

"No banging required," I say. "But I wouldn't mind getting you on your knees."

"*That was a* dirty trick, Rita!" I catch in a far-off, fuzzy way as my cordless electric sander powers down.

I glance up, squinting at the back door, where Milan is . . . shirtless. Bafflingly, wonderfully, dizzyingly shirtless. Even through the screen door, I can see that his once-lean abs have transformed into a defined four pack. His pink flamingo-print swim trunks hang low on his hips. Swim trunks that he just happened to have. Somewhere. Mary Poppins–carpetbag style.

Between tricking him into the backbreaking work of sanding the baseboards and now, we'd worked in silence. He'd done the hand sanding without complaint, deftly masking the baseboards off so he could prime them for tomorrow's coat of fresh white paint. Almost like he'd done it before, though it's a little tough to imagine Mr. Business Casual rolling up his sleeves.

Milan's mopping the sweat from his brow with the back of his arm. "Stay," he tells Harrie, who's bounding around his legs in anticipation of a walk. "I'm going to take a break!" he shouts to me, trying to keep Harrie from squeezing himself out the door.

"Okay!" I'm set to turn the power back on the sander when I see Milan look down at Harrie, then back at me. They're both wearing identical looks of longing.

It was always a sore point for him growing up that he couldn't have a dog like the other boys. The arguments against ranged from "Your mother's allergic and we *just* installed brand-new cream carpet" to "With all your activities and friends, you're hardly at home, anyway, why can't you play with your friends' pets?"

It tugs at my heart before I can squash it. "You can take the boys with you if you want," I call. "They're fine off leash as long as someone's with them."

Milan's answering grin lights up my neurons like a Christmas tree. Like he was just waiting for the offer, he disappears from view only to reappear a moment later with Freddie scooped up in his arms. With both dogs in tow, he jogs toward the water.

The tide is low, gently lapping at the sand, and Harrie splashes into it with the total lack of dignity I've come to expect from him. Freddie is rigidly unhappy in Milan's arms.

He was never squirmy, not even as a puppy. It was cute the way he held himself aloof, with fixed ideas about how he liked to do things. I was charmed by his strange, sweet self-assurance. Harrie came along two years later, a rambunctious rescue puppy I'd fallen in love with even though I'd told myself I was just looking.

It would be so easy for Milan to favor Harrie with his emotive, vivacious personality.

But no. There he is, sitting on the sand, legs stretched in front of him with Freddie in between. With his back to me, I have no idea what he's saying, but I imagine he's trying to coax Freddie into getting his paws wet. Freddie just barely tolerates sand, and that took me days to accomplish. There's no way Milan is going to be successful with Project Draw Freddie Out.

Even if my heart grows three times its size knowing that he wants to try.

The next hour passes in sanding back the ugly, uneven varnish on the bookcases I'm working on. Dad found them left out in front of a house in their neighborhood and made me crown molding for the top that I've already attached with wood glue, a nail gun, and some putty to fill in gaps in the seams.

By the time I finish cleaning away the wood dust, Freddie is ankle deep in water while Milan floats on his back, Harrie doggy-paddling around him. I get the feeling he's trying to show off. It's a sweet, arresting sight. The way the setting sun makes Milan's droplet-dappled body shimmer. Like a *Twilight* vampire, I think, and immediately want to tell him this. It would make him laugh to tease me about my old obsession, I know it would.

Instead, I keep my head down and get back to work.

I start to prime both bookcases so all the natural wood is covered. I'll leave them to dry overnight before following up with a few coats of soft white semigloss paint tomorrow. They'll slot perfectly on either side of the chimney breast, giving the effect of faux built-in shelving. It's one of those luxurious extras that adds so much character to an old house, and something that can be updated on the cheap.

My stomach rumbles, reminding me that it's almost time to start prepping dinner. I can cook for two, if Milan's planning to stay, but it occurs to me that I don't know an awful lot about what he does when he's not here or at work. Does he grab beer with the guys? Go out on dates? Do the Raos still have their weekly family dinner?

Most Fridays mean date night at my place with Neil. But he's spent the last three with other girls, and I've spent mine alone.

You wanted it that way, says Devil's Advocate Rita, who is nowhere as nice as literally any other version of Rita. *You wanted extra time to match on MyShaadi.* And then, in a sneering little voice, *And how did that work out, Rita, hmm? Did your brilliant*

plan work out the way you thought it would? Has anything in your
life happened the way you thought it would have?

God, I want to vote this bitch off the island so fast.

When my phone rings, I grab on to it like a lifeline. "Hello?"

"Rita, hi." Neil's voice is relieved. "I've been calling you for
the last ten minutes."

There's no hint of suspicion or accusation. I can think of at
least three exes who would have jumped down my throat about
whether I'd been with Milan.

"Yeah, sorry, reception out here is spotty," I say. "Not the
most reliable. So what's up?"

"Can't a guy call his girlfriend because he misses her?" His
voice lilts, teasing now.

I smile. "Of course he can. How's work and everything? Oh,
and did you get a chance to look at the Before and After house
pictures I sent you?"

"Loved them," he says, enunciating every syllable a ridiculous, silly amount. "So listen, about tonight . . ." My heart
launches into my throat. He's going to ask me if we're on for date
night. "I have a dinner lined up with this girl from MyShaadi,
but do you want to do something after? I could come over to your
place."

It's a forty-minute ferry back to New Bern, plus more than an
hour's drive on US-70 to Goldsboro. I'm looking at two hours in
travel, assuming I don't get stuck in traffic.

"I'm not going to be in the mood if you've just come from a
date with another girl," I say flatly. Without thinking about it, I
dig the paintbrush into the details of the crown molding. "I'm in
the middle of a project. I can't just drop everything and rush
home right now."

"No, of course, I didn't mean I just wanted to fuck." Neil
exhales noisily. "I just thought it would be nice to see you, is all.

You know, Rita Chitniss, my actual girlfriend? The girl I'm actually hoping to match with so I can tell Ma we can stop looking for a suitable girl? She's going to love having another daughter-in-law." He laughs, like he hears himself say it a beat too late.

The bristles squash, splaying out every direction. Shit. At least the brush isn't ruined.

"Neil, you get that we're not getting married for real, right?"

The hesitation comes all the way down the line. "What do you mean?"

I swallow. "We did this so we could date hassle free for a few more months. Buy ourselves some peace without your mom hounding you about settling down."

As though that's the milestone for being a real-life grown-up.

"Yeah," says Neil, drawing the word out, "until I pop the question."

I stare out at the beach. At Milan laughing as Harrie vigorously shakes himself dry, spraying Freddie with water. He readjusts his trunks, slung low across his hips, before flopping on the sand with his hands tucked behind his neck.

"Rita?" Neil's voice parts my thoughts. "You do want to marry me, don't you?"

I'm remembering that time we went out to this seafood restaurant in our first month of dating and a woman sitting at the table next to us shrieked so loud that my bottom tooth cracked on a mussel shell. While I was cupping my jaw and trying not to cry, the woman triumphantly slid a goopy, chocolate-covered ring onto her ring finger and screamed "Yes, I'll marry you!" to the man sitting opposite her. It was loud enough that even the chef poked his head out of the kitchen.

All Neil had to say on the ride home, after I'd left a voicemail at my dentist's for an emergency morning procedure, was, "That chocolate cake was kind of a cool way to propose, wasn't it?"

And then he'd looked at me with this secret smile, like that would be me someday.

How many other times had he been looking at me with that wistful smile when I wasn't looking? My blood shouldn't be running cold at the thought of him proposing.

"We haven't even been dating for six months," I say, hoping he'll see reason.

"So what? My parents hadn't even been around each other for six minutes before they agreed to get married."

He makes it sound so reasonable, but I really don't need another reminder of how easy Amar found it to break my mother's heart.

"And you don't think that's a problem?" I grind out.

"I agree it's a hassle to go through this whole song and dance, but I mean . . . our parents want what's best for us. Sure, it's a little antiquated, but what's wrong in making our parents happy? We like each other. We get along. The sex is— I mean. You know."

How is he so okay with this? Getting married because it'll make Ma happy? Marrying a girl based on a few months' worth of good sex?

"Neil, that's not enough. I thought you understood this was just so we could date. I'm not ready to marry you—to marry anybody. In a vague future-y way, yeah, one day, but not with a ticking clock hanging over my head."

I don't say it, but I hope he gets that the ticking clock is his ma.

He's silent for so long that I think our connection cut out, but then he sighs.

"So what are we doing here?" His voice comes from far away. "Why are you with me? Why did we even join MyShaadi if it wasn't— I mean, fuck, Rita, it's in the goddamn name."

He's right. Maybe MyShaadi had it right all along not to match us, despite our trickery.

"Neil, can we talk when I'm home?"

Delaying this conversation won't change either of our minds, but at least we don't have to do this *now*, when I'm feeling a little too peeled back, a little too brittle.

"Fine," he says, more sad than mad. "When will that be?"

"I . . . I don't know. There's a lot left to do here."

He interrupts, voice edged with aggravation. "You're not using working on the beach house as an excuse to hide out there, are you?"

Raj's voice hisses at me to go home tonight, to have this conversation out with him in person. To not hide here, out of reach of Neil and my family.

Without my realizing it, my gaze lands on Milan. The sand sticking to his hair, Harrie nudging his ribs with his nose to get attention, the sun dappling man and dogs in a beatific glow.

Is Neil right? *Am* I hiding?

"Should I come over there?" he asks, hesitant. "We can grab dinner on the island. I— I think I can catch the next ferry. I'll cancel the MyShaadi date. You and me could talk things out."

My skin itches. Is that what I want? Part of me thinks it would just be easier to call it quits, instead. What's left to work out if he's ready to get married but I'm not?

We should call the whole thing off.

Even I don't know whether I mean us or the scam.

Neither. Both.

"No, I'll let you know. It might be a few days," I tell him. "We'll talk then."

He makes a sound of agreement, or maybe it's disbelief, but I can't tell the difference anymore.

When we say goodbye, I'm the first to hang up.

Chapter 17

L isten," says Raj as we mill through Lucky Dog Luke's flea market the next weekend. She stops in front of a painted dresser and vanity set. "This fight had to happen for you both to realize what you want. Out of your relationship, out of the scam."

I fidget with the vintage white-and-gold mirror tray I'm holding, hooking my thumbs into the tiny handles. "I still don't know what I'm going to say to him. I feel so guilty. I've never broken anyone's heart before."

"I've had plenty of practice." Her dramatic purple metallic eyeliner catching on the dim fluorescent lighting, looking not just Extra, but extra sparkly. "And it's never easy." She stops me to tighten the bow scrunchie in my high ponytail. "Just be honest."

I groan and dive into one of the many little shops branching off the main walk. Booth #293 has stacks of lace and thick, folded quilts on rickety tables and tall bookshelves. The space is fragranced by cut glass bowls of potpourri and giant vanilla candles. QUILTS $20/EA reads an index card taped to the shelf below some homespun cross-stitched proverbs. While Raj frolics in the aisle or does whatever she does, I sift through the stacks.

There's a beautiful patchwork quilt with black, rust, and khaki stripes, something that would be far more at home in a rustic log cabin than in a beach house. But below it is a quilt in soft shades of blue, with solid cornflower squares and floral calico.

It's practically *made* for Bluebill Cottage.

Raj pops her head in to finger an ugly moose cross-stitched on a pillow. "Classy."

I set my mirrored tray down on a doily-layered end table. "Hey, help me hold this one up, would you? I need to examine it for stains."

She releases a long-suffering sigh, but takes the quilt by the opposite corner, pinching it between two fingers. "It smells a little funky. Plus, it's kinda . . ." She side-eyes me as she searches for a polite word. "Grungy. And I thought you said bedrooms look fresher in white."

"Sheets, definitely. But fold this up on the bottom third of the bed and it makes a room look super cozy, super fast," I explain.

"I regret letting you drag me out here to pick up stuff for a house you're not even going to live in," she grouses. "You used to be so sentimental about giving away your pieces to people like Paula because '*I want them to go to a good home,*'" she says with finger quotes and a falsetto voice that sounds nothing like me. "And now you're all, like, 'Let's buy this sexy mirror box thing that can look up someone's nose and these cottage-core not-your-grandma's-quilts I *love* that people I don't know are going to have lots of sex on!'"

I cringe, but luckily we're the only people nearby. "The point of the tray is not to look up anyone's nose."

"Then why do you need a mirror on it?" She flashes me an I've-got-you-now grin.

Fond exasperation and Raj go hand in hand. "It's for the *aesthetic*," I remind.

"Oh, the aesthetic," she says gravely.

That does it. It takes every single muscle to keep the delicious smirk off my face as I widen my eyes and do an exaggerated peer around her shoulder, hugging the quilts against my chest. "Hi, Luke."

She pales. Wide-eyed, she slowly turns around.

I hold my snicker at bay until she rounds on me.

"I deserved that," Raj admits, a rueful grin pulling at her mouth. "I can't even be mad. Actually, wait, yes, I can. Because you totally bamboozled me into making a pre-lunch stop here when you *know* I only look deli-cute right now and not seeing-hot-guy-in-bad-lighting cute."

"There's no such thing as deli-cute," I inform her. "Also, you have a full face of makeup on so quit your mental gymnastics."

She hmphs. "Fine, but I'm telling you now, if I see him, I'm gonna duck and cover."

I bump my hip against hers. "When did I get braver than you?"

After picking out a few more blue-toned quilts, we head to the front to pay. It's a win that we get sidetracked only once when Raj stops to model in front of a wall of rusted license plates and stolen road signs, insisting that I get her "good angle" (which, let's face it, is *all* of them).

Luke's working the counter wearing his "Ask me my name" name tag and a yellow Henley that brings out the color of his hair and the warmth of his summer tan. He's wrapping a customer's glass swan paperweight in brown paper when he catches sight of us.

Raj stiffens and turns aside to another booth, like that's where she was heading all along.

"Rajvee!" I hiss.

She all but presses her face to a glass showcase filled with costume jewelry and brooches. And one hideous life-size rooster with a chipped beak, glass eyes that follow you around the room, and a successful Mardi Gras' worth of shiny beads looped around his neck.

"I'm just looking," she mumbles. "I'm an interested customer. I would love to grace my home with this"—visible twitch—"fetching fellow."

I give up, figuring she's *gotta* be nervous if she's lying about the most hideous creation known to man. I awkwardly return Luke's grin as I wait in line, shifting the quilt-laden tray in my arms.

After snapping pictures for Milan and getting two thumbs-up, I couldn't resist the charm of these handmade quilts. They're just coastal chic enough to be draped over a rocker in the master bedroom or thrown cozily on the armrest of the sofa. Soon, we'd be moving into the kind of weather that made people snuggle up with blankets, and these are so, so perfect.

"Find everything okay?" Luke asks when it's my turn to be served.

I suspect he enjoys playing up the helpful employee bit when it's me. It's sort of become our inside joke after all these years.

I give him a gratified thank-you-so-much-for-asking smile. "Oh, yes. No problems at all."

Except, of course, maybe for my little problem still feigning interest in the jewelry case to avoid coming face-to-face with Luke.

He nods toward her. "Is this because we matched on Tinder?"

I pull out my wallet. "Partly."

"'Partly'?" With a bemused smile, he pulls my purchases across the counter to peer at the seller's tiny white price tags.

"She's also a Sagittarius."

He laughs as he punches numbers into his printing calculator. "That explains everything."

I glance at Raj, who's shuffling toward the door and freezes guiltily when I catch her. "Trust me, I know how weird it gets when you run into someone you know online."

He rings me up with a small, secret smile. "Hey, I don't know about that. Could also look at it like the universe is giving you a little nudge in the right direction. And it's eighty, even."

"You believe in signs?" I ask, surprised. I'd calculated the total already, and have my bills ready to hand over. I try not to dwell on the fact that unless I hit up an ATM soon, I'm down to a couple of ones and a ten.

"I mean, I don't read my horoscope every day or anything." Luke shrugs and hands me my receipt. "But I don't ignore the obvious, either." He cushions the tray with a wad of brown wrapping paper and piles the quilts on top. "All this for that new place of yours?"

My eyes fly to his. "I mean, it's not mine. But the place I'm helping the owner flip, yes."

"That's what I meant. Kinda surprised me, if I'm being honest. Never known you to take on such a big job like that. You've turned down so many others for— Was it artistic reasons?"

I can sense the question inside the question. "Something like that," I hedge. "You know how I feel about giving too much of myself to a place. It's weird when everything I do is handmade, to leave so much of my work behind in someone else's house."

"No, right, I get that. But how is this any different?" He runs his hand over the quilts before sliding them into an oversize plastic bag. Gently, he says, "I've been to your place before, Rita. I've seen all your thrift hauls on your Instagram Stories. This stuff is exactly the style you'd buy for yourself."

He's reading too much into a few pieces of decor. So what if I'm revamping Bluebill as if I'm the one about to move in? It doesn't *mean* anything other than the fact that I have really excellent taste, which any prospective buyer will love.

I can let go of the house. I can. I will.

"Thanks, Luke," I say, snatching the bag from the counter. "I'll tell Raj you said hi."

"By the way!" he calls after me. I turn. "The gang's missed seeing you at the dog park on Saturday mornings. Alanna and George miss their buddies."

"Harrie sends kisses," I say with a grin, slipping through the door Raj holds open for me.

Luke clutches at his heart. "And Freddie doesn't?"

"Maybe I should get a dog," muses Raj as she turns onto my street. "Then I'd have a reason to go to the dog park."

"Maybe you should get a rooster, instead, since you like them so much." It's hard to keep a straight face when she gives me a dagger-filled stare. "It was *painful* to watch, babe," I say. "That thing was absolutely cursed and you eye-sexed it for five minutes."

"Hey, I gave you fair warning I was gonna be chicken if I saw him."

"This is an ideal time to make another rooster joke, but I'll refrain. Please clap."

Raj lightly thumps the dash. "There you go. So, do you know what you're going to say to Neil yet?"

I squirm in the front passenger seat, throwing up a prayer. "I wish I did. Then at least I could rehearse it. You know I've never had to do this before. Most of my relationships just kind of fizzled out before the three-month mark. It was never a big deal since neither of us thought it was serious. Like *serious* serious."

"But Neil's out here wanting to introduce you to his ma almost from the start." Raj clucks her tongue. "Jesus, Rita. How did you miss the warning signs that he was ready to settle down?"

We're slowing down. I can see my house up ahead, small and rented, but mine.

"I like him, Raj," I confess, "but when we met on Tinder, I wasn't expecting forever. I liked the right now. I didn't see—didn't *want* to see—that he was already looking to the future."

"I wish I had some advice," she says. "But between you and me, I would never have bet on the Shaadi scam when there's a Desi mom in the ring. What can go wrong, will go wrong."

Speaking of, Neil's car is in my driveway. Right on cue, he gets out of the car, hand up.

"Someone's early," she comments, gliding to a stop. "It's too late to keep going like we didn't see him, right?" She reluctantly waves at him without letting go of the steering wheel.

I step out to gather my stuff from the back seat, sliding my bag of thrifted treasure from Lucky Dog Luke's up my arm so I can grip my takeout box of falafel pita leftovers in one hand and my keys in the other.

"Tell me how it goes," Raj says from the corner of her mouth.

"You don't have to talk like that. He can't hear you."

"He's looking right at me," she says anyway, barely moving her lips.

"Good job not looking suspicious," I say, shutting the back door. "Thanks for the ride."

When Raj leaves, there's nothing left to do but face Neil. He's hovering by his car like he wanted to come over and say hi, but talked himself out of it.

"Hi," I say, not sure how to greet him, so I lean in for a kiss on the cheek. Somehow the wires get crossed and his lips smoosh against mine for a millisecond before he pulls back.

"Oh, wow," he says.

He's not talking about the unintended kiss.

"Sorry. I, um, had a lot of pickled onions on my falafel." (And garlicky zhoug, a spicy green-chili-and-cilantro herb sauce. And harissa. And tangy mint yogurt.)

I unlock the door for us. Before, Neil would have gone in and held the door open for me, but now he waits for me to go in first. Waiting to be allowed in, as if he's a guest and not someone with a key who's slept over here at least twice a week for months.

Harrie's underfoot, barking at Neil with a vigor he's lately reserved for Mrs. Jarvis's fence-scaling cat and door-to-door salesmen. Another reminder of the Before that seems so foreign and far away.

"Harrie, no," I say firmly. *"No."* When Harrie downgrades to suspicious looks and mild yips, I say to Neil, "Sorry, he never did this to—"

He never did this to Milan.

"To?" Neil closes the door and waits by the couch.

I recover fast. "To . . . anyone on Rosalie Island."

"Oh. Did you have a lot of neighbors? The pictures you sent didn't look like it."

I busy myself with putting the leftovers in the fridge. "Thanks for coming over. You didn't have to leave work early, though."

"No, I didn't. I . . . I took today off. There were things I needed to think about."

Things? Me and him things? "Oh," I say, turning around. "Sit, please. You don't have to be so formal." It puts me on edge, the way he's poised like he's ready to drop onto the couch, but isn't yet because he's waiting for my invitation.

He exhales, then sits, slow enough to give the impression he thinks there's a minefield under the sofa cushion. My heart clenches to see him act like a stranger. *Feel* like a stranger.

I fill two glasses with tap water and bring them over, sitting cross-legged on the other end of the sofa. He's not quite looking at me, even though I'm facing him, so I talk to his profile instead. "I owe you an apology, Neil. I should have come home earlier to talk about this. You were right. I-I-I *was* using work as an excuse. I was hiding out on Rosalie because I didn't know how to have this conversation with you. How to tell you . . . god, so many things?"

I blow out a breath, bracing myself for the next sentence I have to say. "Part of me fell for you before we even met. I fell for the version of you I saw on a screen. Handsome, funny. You were the only Indian guy—guy in *general*—on Tinder who wasn't a creep. Do you have any idea how many dudes saw 'furniture restorer' in my bio and messaged me with some ridiculously unoriginal jokes about wood?"

I pull a face, thinking back to all the "Wanna get your hands on my grade-A wood, baby?" and "I bet I can get you hot and hammered" jokes.

Neil gives me a sidelong glance before angling his body toward me, more open now. "And the bar was so low that I seemed like a good choice."

"No!" I shake my head, fingers squeezing around my glass. I take a hurried sip. "You *are* a good choice. You're a great guy, Neil."

He leans in a little closer at the same time I hesitate. We both know the "but" is coming.

"But you're ready for marriage, or your mom's ready, and I literally want to puke at the thought of telling my mom that I'm dating the son of her first love. I can't break her heart, Neil. It would be different if . . ."

If I was in love with you.

I don't say it. I hate that I even think it.

". . . If I was ready to take the next step, but I'm not. You're my longest relationship in years. I told you that after my high school boyfriend, I never . . . I mean, they were nice guys and everything, but they weren't my epic love." What I mean is, they weren't Milan.

Neil brings his fist to his chin. "Then what was I?"

"Fun," I respond. "Sex-on-the-first-date fun. Keeping-it-a-secret fun. It was easy to be with you. It was dating without the incessant questions and badgering and everything that comes with dating in our culture."

I take a sip of water. "But your ma is the number one woman in your life. You can't say no to her. You agreed to date *other girls* while you had a girlfriend, and you didn't see a problem with it. You go along with everything she wants. After what happened with your dad and my mom, you *know* why that's a problem for me."

I can see from his face that, just like the first time I told him, he still doesn't quite get it.

He can't see it as a bad thing when his parents got their happy ending.

"You had it right, Neil. MyShaadi. *It's in the name.* I thought it was so clever, so foolproof. Stalling our parents from the marriage melodrama long enough to keep dating to see where things went, but . . . your ma really grabbed the bull by the horns." I give him a wry smile. "I didn't count on her being a wild card."

His forehead scrunches into a half dozen creases. "What if we dropped MyShaadi and kept seeing each other? I could tell Ma I'll find someone without her help?"

The trouble is that what he calls help, I see as intrusion. He's telling me what he thinks I want to hear. He's okay with his ma pushing him—us—toward the predetermined next stage in life.

I'm not.

Neil reads it on my face. His shoulders slump and his sigh fills the room.

My nose itches and I rub it fiercely. "The girls you went out with," I say, swallowing. "I should have been jealous. It should have been driving me bananas that you were making jokes, rolling out all the charm to impress a cute girl. And it's not that I don't trust you, because I do. It's that I should have wanted to be in their place . . . and the thing is? I was okay that I wasn't."

His fingers flex around the glass and he leans forward to carefully set it on the wooden coffee table without using one of the crotcheted cat coasters. "You know, when you called me . . . I had the feeling you were going to break up with me. I couldn't think straight at home, so I came here early. I thought, even if I was just in your driveway, I'd find the words, the magic words."

I open my mouth, about to tell him I'd searched for the right words, too, but there aren't any. There's only the truth. He holds up a hand, *Let me finish, please.*

"The only thing on my mind was how to talk you out of it, but I didn't know what to say until now." He takes the half-drunk glass from me and sets it next to his. He clasps my hands in his and utters, in the gentlest, softest voice I've ever heard him use: "I understand."

I go absolutely still. "You understand?"

He lets out a short laugh. "Yeah, I mean, weirdly, I think I do. I won't lie, Rita, I'm not against marrying you. You know, growing up, it's like Desis just have two options: have a love marriage with someone family approved that you probably met in college, or some kind of arranged marriage. Even if it's not done via MyShaadi or the old-fashioned way with our parents arranging everything, it always involves *somebody* conspiring. It's like this uncle has a niece who's here on a work visa and hint-hint, nudge-nudge, or that auntie I randomly met in line at Patel Brothers used to live on the same street in Mumbai and"—his voice lifts dramatically—"guess what, she has five single daughters!"

I try not to laugh. I get the feeling both of his examples are from lived experience.

"When I met you," he says, lower now, "on Tinder of all places, I thought I could still have a love marriage. Someone I met by chance who I could see a future with. It didn't have to be one or the other. And for so long, I thought it did. The one girl I brought home for winter break sophomore year of college, it's not like Ma ever came out and said it, but she wanted me to be with an Indian girl. I could tell from everyone's frozen smiles when we walked through the door. She could tell, too; there's a reason we didn't make it to next Christmas."

"Neil," I say, a little taken aback. He's never revealed any of this to me before. "You're twenty-seven. You can absolutely still meet somebody a thousand different ways. There are always hot girls at the gym, getting ice cream at the marina, getting groceries at the store."

"Who would dump me in ten seconds flat once they figure out I can never stick to a cardio routine, don't own a yacht, and basically live off ready-made deli sandwiches, frozen pizza, and

Cheerios because Ma cooks double and brings half over to my apartment."

"Okay, I did *not* know that," I say. "Jesus, Neil, is that why you never help me cook?"

He has the grace to look sheepish. "I never had to learn."

It makes sense now why our couple cooking always turned into me cooking.

"Anyway," he adds, "people only meet like that on TV. In real life everyone keeps to themselves and stares at their phone to avoid making eye contact." He eyes me, weighing something. "To tell the truth, I thought *you* were my meet-cute."

I can give him this. "If it wasn't for our parents, maybe you'd have been mine, too."

His smile is rueful. "Maybe. But maybe not. Either way, thanks for saying it."

"Some of those things you think people would break up with you for? You can change them. You can do your own grocery shopping, learn how to cook. I can help."

Even as I offer, I know he's not going to take me up on it. He'd rather go from his mom to his wife, not lifting a finger. Not because he's lazy or sexist, because he's neither of those things. He's just used to seeing himself as a little helpless when it comes to doing things for himself. When it comes to thinking for himself.

And even if we continued dating, what if tomorrow his mother tells him I'm not the right girl for him? Will he listen? Will he fight for me? Or will he be his father's son?

Either way, I want more.

"You're sweet, Rita," says Neil. He presses his lips together and tries to smile. "I wish I was as brave as you. But I like things simple and easy. If it's not for you, I'm not looking to go up against Ma. She and Dad were arranged, and they made it. And they made it look really, really good. I don't think I ever thought they weren't in love with each other a silly amount."

He bites his lip. "Maybe MyShaadi had us pegged from the start."

There's no use trying to talk him out of re-creating what his parents have. And who knows, maybe one of his MyShaadi dates might actually be the One. I hope so.

Neil comes to the same realization as I do.

He pulls his key from his pocket, rests it in his palm for a moment like it weighs the world, and then places it gently on the coffee table.

I lean forward and graze his cheek with my lips. "I wish you all the best."

Chapter 18

I take the first ferry out of New Bern in the morning, the thermos of coffee still hot after the hour-and-a-half trip to the port. This early, it's barely half capacity and peaceful.

I dump my duffel bag on the seat next to me, Eiffel Tower keychain dangling from a zipper next to the god Ganesh, remover of obstacles, a carved wooden figurine that Aji had bought from her temple shop in India to bring me good fortune.

My aviators have been on since the second I stepped out of my car. As I walk past some familiar faces, I return their smiles, but push my sunglasses higher up my nose and take an empty bench farthest away.

After Neil left, I spent the rest of the night curled up on the couch with Harrie and Freddie, shoveling in forgotten freezer-burned mango sorbet. It might not have been a heartbreak, but my heart still hurt. We watched one of the shows that had been on my Hulu list for months, and it was unmitigated trash, but I didn't change it.

While Harrie was glued to the TV, Freddie laid his head and front paws on my lap, eyes on me. His French bulldog face was gentle and concerned, as if he wanted to make sure his human was going to be okay. I pulled him onto my lap and didn't let go for the rest of the night.

The ride doesn't make me seasick anymore, but I still don't feel quite myself. Eyes puffy and longing for sleep, it doesn't take much for me to succumb to the gentle rocking of the ferry. With my dogs leashed and dozing on the floor, I shut my heavy eyelids, hoping to sleep through the next forty minutes.

Harrie's tail brushes against my bare calves. It happens a second time, then a third.

I ignore it, keeping my eyes closed, but then there's a tug on the leash. So much for sleep.

"Why is your timing always the worst?" I murmur, yawning without covering my mouth.

"I wasn't aware it was," comes the amused response.

Since Harrie obviously can't speak English, I startle into consciousness. Through my tinted sunglasses I see Milan sitting next to me, with only the smallest of space between us. He's bent forward to pet the dogs, looking altogether too awake and cheerful this early in the morning.

"Hi?" I cast a glance around the ferry. There are plenty of empty seats.

But the one he's currently occupying is the one right next to mine.

"Morning." He grins and raises his transparent coffee cup to me. It's more ice cube than anything else, a ring of whipped cream remnants clinging near the top.

I straighten, self-consciously pushing my aviators higher up my nose. "You're here on a Sunday? Don't you have open houses?"

It's a reflexive question, but I immediately want to kick myself for starting a conversation when all I want to do is keep to myself and not talk.

He shakes his head. "We generally only host an open house when it's an exclusive property, otherwise the cost of organizing can get pretty up there. No luxury listings today."

"Mmm." I close my eyes and prepare to go back to sleep.

Just when I think we're about to settle into silence, Milan says, "Most people don't know this, but open houses are more for the agent than the homeowner."

Making conversation is the last thing on my mind, especially about something as dry as realty. "Ah," I say, hoping if I don't show any interest, he'll stop talking.

He gives Freddie a final pet before leaning back in his seat. "For me, the biggest payoff is the free networking. Sure, some people who show up are just nosy and know they wouldn't qualify for the bank loan, and I get the occasional neighbor poking their head in, but these meet and greets are prime time to prospect for more clients for my other properties. Serious home buyers usually already have an agent to arrange a private showing. Otherwise it doesn't really move the needle."

"But what about the Soulless Wonder? It sold for big bucks. That wouldn't have happened without—"

"You," he says, soft enough that it's not an interruption, not really. "It would never have happened without you. I had that house on the market for almost a year, my longest listing ever, and it didn't move until you came along."

"You mean when my mother *conscripted* me."

At my gripe, his smile reaches his eyes. "Regardless of how we were *both* recruited, you can't deny we got a great result. One could even say we made quite the dream team."

"One could." But one wouldn't.

"If one didn't wake up on the grumpy side of the bed this morning, maybe one would," he says lightly. "Late night?"

I freeze. There's no way he can tell how tired and red-rimmed my eyes are.

"It's just . . ." He taps where sunglasses would sit on his face if he were wearing any.

The move brings the sweet toffee scent of his coffee cup even closer to me. One of the ridiculous, overpowering flavors he loves.

I can't stop myself from adjusting the frames, making sure they're covering me from eye bags to eyebrows. "Oh. Um. Yeah. I didn't sleep well last night."

Concern knits his eyebrows together. "You didn't have to come to work today."

"I want to." I don't point out that I could have got my forty winks if he hadn't shown up.

His brows still haven't unfurrowed and I get the feeling that he wants to say something.

"So," I say before he can, "you're going to be here all day?"

"I'm all yours for as long as you want me."

My teeth accidentally bite into the meat of my inner cheek.

He doesn't see my grimace, because in the lull, Milan's eyes have found my Eiffel keychain, Pepto Bismol pink and glittery. Cheap tat from a sidewalk stall I bought on a whim just because it made me smile. That trip, I was always looking for small joys.

I wait for him to ask the way he asked about the lotus tattoo on my pinky finger.

Instead, he says, "There was a time not so long ago that I was hungry for sales. Sell, sell, sell. It's what made my open houses so successful. My name recognition. Josh promoted me because he knows how much money I bring in, but ever since I bought the house in the spring . . . working on my own place is way more exciting than selling other people's. That's why Bluebill means so much to me." A self-conscious smile tugs at his lips. "Six years at the same place, doing the same things day after day . . . I think it's safe to say that all work and no play makes Milan a dull boy."

"Work-life balance is important," I say as Rosalie Island starts to fill the view out of the smudged front windows.

"Does that mean you've got it all figured out?" He stretches his legs. "What I wouldn't give for a social life like we had in high school. I looked at my recent calls and other than work calls, the person I talk to the most is the guy who takes my Chinese take-out orders."

We again, his words lumping us as the team we haven't been in so long.

Maybe it's just my breakup with Neil that makes my mind go there, but it's interesting that Milan's mom isn't a regular name on his recent calls. And as far as my social life goes, it's entirely comprised of Raj, Paula, Luke, and the regulars at the dog park that Luke introduced me to. I'm not exactly thriving in that department.

"Hardly," I say, snorting. "Coming here is the highlight of my week."

His smile is sweet. "Mine, too."

As we reach the end of the gangway, we're greeted by the all-caps letters on the yellow event banner strung high between two wrought-iron streetlamps: FARMER'S MARKET 9 A.M. – 1 P.M.

"This is every Sunday?" asks Milan, sidestepping two little girls in blond pigtails as they run squealing past him. He's sport-ing a silly, bewildered grin.

Harrie whines as he tries to scamper after the children, eager to follow the smells.

"Yup. Sometimes I buy lunch here," I say, pointing to a stall where I bought an egg-and-smashed-avocado waffle last Sunday and a blueberry-acai smoothie bowl with an almond croissant the week before that. The most gorgeous aroma of sizzling bacon wafts over, and my stomach rumbles for the breakfast sandwiches I see handed to a smiling couple.

Dozens of vendors work busily behind their stalls while the square buzzes with people, most of whom are carrying heavy grocery totes drooping almost to the stone cobbles. An all-weather pavilion has been erected from one end of the square to the other, so customers can browse to their hearts' content in the shade.

Local farmers with their just-pulled-from-the-earth produce and small businesses set apart with sustainability and verve always appeal to the tourists. Root vegetables, hairy and dirt-smudged enough to retain their charm, are piled high on tables, while unblemished fruit and cardboard tubs of plump berries line wooden crates.

As we get closer, Milan can't tear his gaze away, but I stride determinedly past.

He loves the tableau in front of him because it's charmingly novel, a curiosity he wants to explore. I get it. I was the same when I stepped off the ferry that first Sunday so many weeks ago and felt that diluted, though familiar, rush of being in a Parisian market.

I know what we'll see if we step into the pavilion tent: fresh flowers and sachets of dried lavender competing with the perfect char of a crisp-skin rotisserie chicken on a spit, dripping fat onto the tiny golden roasted potatoes below. Salmon burgers and tuna melts ready to go in gingham containers next to cold pasta and quinoa salads. Skewers of seasoned jumbo shrimp, heads and all, sizzle away on the grill, the lemony, garlicky smell drawing a sizable crowd.

A bit farther away, the leather satchels and wallets, still pungent from tanning, where the men tend to linger. And on the tables nearby the delicate gossamer metalwork that their wives slip onto their wrists and fingers, turning it this way and that to catch the light.

"Let's stop," says Milan. "I'm ravenous and my coffee feels like forever ago."

I don't say yes right away. I'm in no mood to wander around and make small talk. I'll tell him he can stay if he wants, but I'll go on ahead to Bluebill.

"Come on," he says, wheedling me the way he used to when he wanted to sneak out on a school night. He stops me with a touch to my wrist that makes me jump, then freeze in place.

"You go and enjoy," I say. "Honestly, I don't need you, so have fun."

I think I'm being gracious, giving him an out, but his face falls.

Too late, I hear how he must have heard it: *I don't need you.*

It was the kind of thing I'd have wanted to fling in his face six years ago. Five years ago. Even five *months* ago, before we'd reunited. Hell, I'd itched to hurt him the first moment we met at my mother's. I relive my taunt about MyShaadi, and suddenly, the jab doesn't feel anywhere close to satisfying.

Annoyingly, seeing him hurt makes me want to take that hurt away.

And seeing that same expression on two men's faces in as many days is a gut punch.

Swallowing, I say, "I didn't mean it like that. I just meant I think I should get to work. You already put in practically all the money, it's not really fair for me to accept your time and labor when that's supposed to be my contribution to this partnership."

"All work and no play make Rita a dull girl, too."

I search his face for any sign of a dig. When I can't find one, I shake my head. I'm not being a goody-goody, like he teased me in high school, and it's not because I've never shirked or postponed work, because I have. But: "I still have work to do."

And throwing myself into work is exactly what I need after the breakup yesterday and my sleepless night.

"The work will be there when we get home," he says gently. "We can still put in our hours, Rita, but if there's one thing I've learned, it's that the work won't love you back."

I relent. "Fine. But no more than an hour."

It's definitely been more than an hour.

Milan has already bought hand-poured soy candles and wax melts ("They smell like Christmas trees and mango lassis on a warm, sandy beach, Rita, how can I not?"), juicy Carolina peaches (so juicy that he got it all over his chin and I had to hand him a napkin with a long-suffering sigh), and a double dresser painted the most odious Shrek shade of lime green.

We're still in Second Chance Shores, a charming little thrift shop on a quiet street behind the square. The frosted glass windows with loopy gold lettering and blurred twinkling lights made Milan almost press his nose against it to see inside. On entry, we were greeted by a smiling woman who introduced herself as the owner and decidedly unsmiling, fierce-faced mannequins draped in vintage sundresses and jean jackets, costume jewelry adorning their wrists. I left my sunglasses on indoors, peeking from the top when he's not looking.

The back wall is stamped with picture frames and mirrors, a handful of square and rectangular spaces hinting at recent sales. I catch my reflection in an ornate gilt mirror and cautiously lower my sunglasses. My eyes are still strained, so back up the aviators go. Straw and felt hats hang on a rack next to a towering, paint-peeled bookshelf and end tables decorated with ceramic lamps perched on a footed base. But none of that is what got my attention first.

It was a pair of trestle dining tables that caught my eye as soon as we stepped inside. Painted white and distressed to look coastal-shabby, a very "in" look at the moment, they were large enough for ten, with six chairs and a long bench seat. It wouldn't fit with the warm color scheme and dark wood furniture I'd already sourced, but I could see the possibilities. Once the table was stripped and sanded down, I could bring back its luster with a few coats of Danish oil.

The plan was to sell the house as is, completely furnished. There was, of course, always the chance that the new homeowners wouldn't want every single piece inside, but Milan said most rich people wanted a turnkey house. "If it's move-in ready, it saves them the additional time and cost of getting a decorator in," he'd explained during my tour of Bluebill a month ago. "I know what I'm talking about. I've sold hundreds of furnished houses."

For this, anyway, I can hand over my trust.

I grab the measuring tape out of my purse and pull it taut, squatting.

When Milan ambles up to stand next to me, I make the mistake of glancing up at him.

"Seriously?" His face is the picture of amusement. "You carry that with you?"

"Oh, just a girl being prepared." I give him a daggered smile. "Size matters."

"Do you think it'll fit? Or is it too big?"

Catching on to his game, I say smoothly, "I've seen bigger."

He bites his lip to keep from laughing.

We buy the trestle table.

"You two make such a cute couple," says the owner, beaming at us. "Warms my heart to see a couple share a laugh. Makes me miss—" She looks heavenward, then back to us, eyes misty. "People forget how important it is to be with someone who makes them laugh."

My cheeks burn, but it feels cruel now to tell her she's off base.

She writes down the delivery address before we can give it to her. "We've all been wondering when somebody would buy Bluebill, make it a home. Bet it needs a lot of work."

"Thank you," says Milan. "A lot can be fixed with a little love, I've found. And the best things are worth the time."

I throw him a sharp look, but he's tucking his credit card back in his wallet with a blasé smile, as though there weren't a myriad of other ways that statement could be interpreted.

"And now," I say, as we leave Second Chance Shores, "we work."

His eyes are innocent. "Isn't that what we've *been* doing?"

So, naturally, after all the "work" of shopping, he's worked up an appetite.

"Crêpes," he decides, and drags me off in that direction. "We can eat and walk."

We both choose the same one, folded into a triangle with a smear of Nutella. He insists on paying, thrusting the bills at the vendor before I can open my purse.

"It's as good as the ones I had in Paris," I say absently. Crisp outer edges and a soft, fluffy middle made even sweeter with the chocolate-hazelnut spread.

The roads aren't too busy so the two of us start to walk side by side back to the house. With the occasional car passing by, we make sure to keep Harrie and Freddie close.

"Really?" He shoots me an unbelieving look. "Rosalie Island crêpes go toe-to-toe against the crêpe capital of the world?"

I nod and take another bite. "Perfect crêpe to filling ratio, too. Some places don't make them right, so when you actually start to eat, it oozes out onto your fingers and makes a mess. And yes, before you ask, I *am* a crêpe connoisseur, because it happens to be one of the cheapest foods you can eat on a budget."

"You don't talk about that trip much," says Milan, very much in the tone of someone broaching a topic that's likely to bite him.

On top of not being one of those obnoxious people who can bring every conversation back around to *When I was in* . . . I also have no idea how to share memories of a trip with the man who I'd wanted to share it with in real life.

He thinks I haven't noticed, but it's glaringly obvious after adding up all the little distractions today—he knew something was wrong and he wanted to cheer me up.

So I'll tell him, but I'll curate the nostalgia, leaving out the experiences I know he'd had his heart set on.

I start with Mick and Kayla, the American newlyweds who asked me to take their picture under the Eiffel and gave me tips on the best open-air marchés and high-key *insisted* I had to try the roasted chicken and potatoes before leaving for the next city.

We move on to boyfriends Nick and Gustav from the Paris hostel, who insisted on cheering me up with a night out, their treat, when they found out I was all alone in the city of love. I know Milan well enough to know his smile is forced. "They got married last year and we still send each other Christmas cards," I finish. "We're planning to meet in New York next year."

After Paris comes Italy and Faridah, who shared my hostel

room and gave me all her guidebooks to make room for the souvenirs she was taking home for her family. My crêpe is finished by the time I get to Priya, the competitive surfer, who traveled with me through Spain because her Australian boyfriend had dumped her and she didn't want to go home to an "I told you so" from her Indian family.

We'd thrown back *way* too many solidarity cavas and sangrias and danced with strangers, and my surfing was no better now than it was when she'd first started to teach me, but I gloss over all this. I have a standing invitation to drop in on her next time I'm in India.

There's only one person I'm not in touch with: my cabinmate, Kristoffer, who'd leaned out the window to ask me for my phone number right as the train pulled away from the station, who never called because the train whistle swallowed the last four digits before it picked up speed.

"Do you wish he did call?" asks Milan, a note of *something* in his voice.

"At the time I thought it was a shame," I answer honestly. "But I wasn't ready. And I still thought that . . ." I bite my lip. No, I won't tell him that part of me had thought he'd be waiting for me at the airport when I came home, that it would all have turned out to be a mistake and we weren't broken up after all.

When I don't finish, he changes tack. "Top three favorite French meals?" he asks. "And no desserts. You'll make me too jealous." He says the last sentence in a strange, hoarse tone.

I don't think he's necessarily talking about the food.

The idea that he's jealous over this faceless guy he doesn't know is strangely thrilling, and part of me wants to put him out of his misery.

The bigger part wants to keep him there a bit longer.

I take off my aviators, feeling the deep, rounded indents left behind on my nose.

Why are French words easier to say than the English language? My tongue doesn't trip once as I rattle off, "Moules marinières, salade Niçoise, and cheese soufflé. All delicious, cheap, and filling. Perfect to pick up and eat in a park somewhere."

There's a yearning on his face that arrows straight into my heart, lodging deep. It's not for the food, but for the museum of memories he's being led through, gazing upon each one with wonder, but never able to stay in one long enough to experience it before it's time to move on.

We can't re-create the past. We can only visit it.

Desperate to retreat to a safer footing, I tell him about the whole entire day I spent at the Louvre. It's just the kind of story that he would have been glad to escape in real life.

"That completely sounds like something you'd do," he says through his laughter. He bends to scoop up Freddie, who has pointedly stopped walking. "And I'd spend more time trying to steer you to the exit than actually looking at the exhibits."

"Hey, who knows when we're going to go back?" I ask, too relieved to be defensive at his teasing. "I'm getting my money's worth."

The mirth freezes on his face. His face slackens, all trace of amusement gone.

Too late, I realize that I said *we*.

By the time we get back home, the dining table, dresser, and table lamps are waiting on the porch with a yellow Post-it saying: *Thank you for your business!* Smiley faces in all the *u*'s.

With the *we* still hanging between us, Milan disappears out back with a shovel, presumably to finish planting the ornamental grasses and purple beach asters he started last week. Without hesitation, Harrie bounds after him, Freddie following more sedately.

I throw myself into hand sanding the distressed white paint on the trestle table, using fine-grit sandpaper to keep the character of the grain. I don't want to sand in too deep, butchering the darker, circular knots.

My arms weep by the time I'm done. The sun's fallen since the time I started, turning the pale yellow planks to a burnished gold, the color it'll turn after a few coats of Danish oil. I run my hand over the smooth surface.

Me. I did this.

After a lot of elbow grease—okay, a *lot* of back, shoulder, and elbow grease—this project is halfway to being the table I imagined.

A meeting place for a family to share lazy Sunday breakfasts, for parents to help their kids do their homework. For paying bills and writing letters, the kind no one writes anymore because we all have eight different social media platforms to chat on. But damn it, this is the kind of table I want to write a letter on, using the painstaking Austenesque cursive I've never actually had to use since passing second-grade English.

And then, just like that, this work-in-progress table no longer belongs to a nameless, faceless family. It's mine. I want it. Not just the table, but everything that comes with it.

I want the life.

I want tiny little faces with dimpled smiles and Disney-round eyes crowding around this dinner table. I want kisses exchanged over morning cups of coffee, too long and languid, making our kids screech. I want to argue and know we'll make up, mop up spills, and synchronously clear the table after a long day, not needing to speak in order to be understood. I want to bicker at Trader Joe's over the date night wine (I love white, he loves red, rosé disgruntles us both).

I want this—all of this—for me.

I just never wanted it with Neil.

My eyes sting. No matter how much I'd wanted to buy extra time with him to see where things went, I realize now that I never envisioned it ending in marriage.

A shadow falls over the table. My palm lays flat against a man's shadow chest, right over his heart. I yank my hand away.

"Hey. Sorry. I lost track of time playing with the dogs on the beach," says Milan with a rueful smile. "Even Freddie enjoyed himself." He pushes his wet hair away from his face. Sand sticks on his feet and dusts his shoulders. "Can I help?"

"No, I'm almost done here," I say, swiveling my gaze back to the table. I keep it short as if that'll put some distance between us, but he doesn't get the message.

"That looks amazing," he breathes. His damp, bare shoulder brushes against mine. He catches my eye and nudges me again, this time on purpose.

He reaches out to smooth his fingers over a knot the size of a fist. He traces the swirl with hypnotic reverence, exploring for the first time. "You know, I was always a little jealous that you had this passion for what you studied. I was never that excited about investment management."

"Is that why you went into real estate?" I ask, because this piece of the puzzle still hasn't slotted into place. "When I went to High Castle, and saw your photo on the wall, I almost couldn't believe it at first. You were an adult. Wearing a tie and everything."

His mouth quirks.

"I mean, obviously there's more to being an adult than that, but you know what I mean," I rush on, a little annoyed with myself. "It's impressive the way you climbed the ranks so fast. Did Mr. Bell mentor you? I mean, you were promoted to partner. That's huge."

"No, I'm just that good," he says, then winks when I roll my eyes. "No, Josh looked out for me when I started. Said I had pluck, but what I really needed was hunger. You know how I am, I throw myself into things two hundred percent. Work is the same. Not like I have a lot of other things vying for my attention these days."

No wonder he's on MyShaadi. With how hard he works to get where he is, he has zero time to meet anybody. Sympathy tugs at me.

"But what about MyShaadi?" I ask.

Milan meets my gaze steadily. "I'd prefer to meet someone without it."

"It's hard to believe you're single."

He grins. "Careful, Rita, that almost sounded like a compliment."

"Oh, like you don't already know you're staggeringly good-looking." I roll my eyes. "You dress to impress."

"I dress for myself," he corrects. "Although I do like your description of women staggering back when they see me for the first time."

"That's not what I—"

"And, I mean, that does explain a lot. The way you staggered back and slammed the door in my face at your parents' house, for example. Surprisingly accurate."

It takes every muscle I have not to react. Instead, I take a half step back and study the table, squinting like I'm taking its measure. "Do you think we'll have the room?"

"For what?"

"To get this through the door, along with your massive ego," I deadpan.

That elicits a whoop of laughter that turns into a cough that turns into me thumping him on the back until his coughing subsides. There's a slight chance I hit him a little harder than strictly necessary.

"I don't know," he says, wiping tears from his eyes. "Why don't we try?"

"Don't think I'm forgetting the timing of your coughing fit," I say, moving to grab the other end of the table. "Totally saved you from having to come up with a witty repartee."

"Rita, Rita, let's just agree I'm staggeringly handsome and leave it at that."

"Dream on, Milan," I grumble, lifting the table at the same time he does. "Hurry up and help me bring this in. The sooner you're out of my house, the sooner I can get back to work without being distracted by the totality of your youness."

"That's not the insult you think it is," he says cheerfully, then stops, his grip on his end of the table slacking. "Hold up. *Your* house?" His dimple winks.

"*Our* house," I backtrack.

His grin widens.

"*The* house," I say. "The one that I have absolutely no attachment to whatsoever."

We both know I'm lying.

It's only after he leaves to catch the last ferry back to the mainland that I realize he never filled me in on his meteoric rise at High Castle Realty.

Chapter 19

I t's not just the house I'm getting attached to, and I'm not sure I like it.

By mid-August, we fall into a strange domesticity on Rosalie Island, a limbo where we don't talk about the past. Which, of course, makes me want to bring it up with renewed intensity every time I see his face. Since that day at the farmer's market, Milan's over every weekend, and an afternoon or two during the week, too, when he can get away from work.

With every week that passes, I grow more and more used to having Milan around. Helping me wallpaper; bringing me a second phone charger when Harrie decides to hide the first; joining me on jogs even though he gets winded before I do and has to fall back to carry Freddie. If he happens to stay late enough for dinner, he cooks and I do the dishes. Simple meals, because that's all either of us has the energy for, and then he catches the last ferry back at nine.

It's so easy to see how this could have been my life if he hadn't broken up with me over voicemail.

It's so hard to see how this could have been my life if he hadn't broken up with me over voicemail.

He claims he's helping me, and he does. But when he brings fancy food and bottles of chilled sauvignon blanc in insulated wine jackets, it starts to get a little suspect.

After another of our Saturday "working lunches," Milan heads to the small hardware store in town for new drawer pulls, and I use the reprieve to call Mom.

She picks up before the second ring. "Rita, I've been calling you all morning!"

"Mom, I *told* you the reception here isn't great."

She makes a soft scoff. "Why didn't you tell me you were on MyShaadi?"

My stomach bottoms out. There's no possible way she could have known. "W-what?"

"Rita, ahey?" Aji's voice asks, faint, but no less imperious. "Speaker lau."

Mom sighs in acquiescence, putting me on speakerphone. "Why did I hear from Mrs. Khanna that her son matched with you on MyShaadi?"

I drop the silverware into the sink with a loud clatter.

"She also said you haven't accepted him," adds Aji. "Why not? Sanju Khanna is a *doctor*," she adds, with a hint of reproach.

Now Dad's voice chimes in, "Technically he's a nutritionist."

"*Technically* means doctor," says Aji.

Dad sighs. "I promise I'm not being elitist here, but *technically* he didn't go to medical school. He has a master's degree in food and nutrition science."

"He works in your old hospital," counters Aji. "So, doctor."

I can imagine Dad now, pinching his nose and regretting

even getting into it with his mother. While Aji goes on to chatter about what qualifies someone to be a doctor to Dad, an actual doctor, I zip over to Safari on my phone.

You have several unmet matches! Unlock more by upgrading to a premium plan.

An icon of Sanju Khanna's broad, beaming face, showing way too many teeth, is still in my match list. I hit reject and scan the other faces, relieved when none of the other men are Neil. It would be the worst timing.

The first match, right on the bottom, is Milan. I haven't rejected him. Yet. And he hasn't rejected me. If we haven't talked about the elephant in the room yet, we never will. What am I waiting for? Maybe I should just do it.

Just put my finger there and—

Reject. Done. It's over before I can regret it.

"So you weren't lying when you told Milan you were looking for men," Mom says, as soon as there's a lull in Aji's lecturing. "But I thought—"

"Of course Rita wants to meet reliable men," snaps Aji. "And why shouldn't she?"

"'Don't go out on the street in your nightie' goes in one ear and out the other, but *this* she remembers," Mom mutters.

Aji makes a loud harrumph. "Should she live alone the rest of her life because of him?" Without waiting for an answer, she says, "Sanju Khanna, the *doctor*"—Dad groans—"was very interested in you. And he could get *anyone*. Ekdum handsome zala ahey."

"But what about Milan?" Mom continues. "When you told me you agreed to flip a house with him, I thought you and he would get back together. It's been *weeks*. Has anything happ—"

"Arey, forget Milan. I was telling her about Sanju," says Aji, snappish and irritable. "You can ask him what diet to put your fatty on so he can go on a proper chakkar without being carried."

My stomach clamps when I think about my match with Milan, gone forever. I pass my hand over my face. I'm getting a headache. I love my family, and I love them even more when they're miles away, but not when they're all squabbling in my ears like gerbils.

"It's Freddie," I say, apparently to no one, because they're all talking over me. "And in his defense, he's not out of shape. He's *lazy*."

Only Dad laughs. "Tell Freddie it's not personal. She's been trying to get me on the treadmill more, too."

"So go accept Sanju and I will WhatsApp his mother to tell her the good news," Aji says, voice encouraging. She's not great at drenching her iron will in syrupy gulab jamun sweetness.

I stifle a laugh. The way the older generation uses technology is eerily reminiscent of the way me and Raj would race to the family computer room—back when those were a thing—after school to log on to AOL Instant Messenger—AIM, if you were cool—to whip out our phones and text each other "Get online!!! I'm already here!!!" on our ten-cents-a-minute phone plans because we were only cool enough for AIM, but not enough for a Verizon phone plan.

"Snotty Sanju, the nutritionist," I say slowly and very deliberately, "once slurped a thick string of his own snot in fourth grade, and not even because anyone dared him."

"Shee!" Aji exclaims.

"Does my love life really need to be a four-person decision?" I ask, pressing my palm over my mouth to catch a stray giggle at Aji's horror.

"Rita's right," says Dad. "We don't all need to talk about this. It's her business."

"Thank you, Dad," I say with emphasis.

"Elders should be consulted in these matters, han?" says Aji.

"Rita, you have a second chance," says Mom. "How many people can say that?"

Even though she delivered it softly, it quietens the line like the sullen silence that follows a slamming door. Splitting the moment into a before and an after.

I know she's thinking about Amar. She has to be. He's the second chance she never got to have, and the whole reason why she thinks I need one with Milan. So I don't grow up to be her age, married to a man who would only be second best, hoping my child would be happier.

Aji seems to have had the same thought. "Not everyone deserves a second chance," she says in the steely it's-my-TV-time-now voice I remember from when I was younger and we frequently skirmished over control of the remote. She switches to Marathi to say, "Sometimes we have to live with what we've done. We can only learn from the past, not rewrite it."

Dad's voice holds a smile. "My mother the philosopher."

"There's no need to make your bed and lie in it if there's still a chance to get what you want," says Mom. She ignores Aji's snort. "Right, Ruthvik?"

Thank god we aren't on video and they can't see my expression. It's unfair she wants him to agree. I hope he doesn't know why my second chance with Milan means so much, what it represents to her.

"Esha, you are wise and correct as always," said Dad, generous to a fault.

Right when I think the crisis has been successfully averted, Milan's boisterous "Rita, I'm hooooooome!" breaks the silence. "Let's get those drawers down and start stripping!"

Over Aji's startled gasp, Mom starts to ask "Who is—" but I

cut her off with a hurried "Nothinggottagotalktoyoulaterbye!" before hanging up.

And to think I was grateful for audio a minute ago.

"Did you have to do that?" I ask, stalking to the foyer where Milan's dropped his bags.

"Sorry?" He gives me a quizzical frown.

"Pulling down drawers? Stripping?" I raise both eyebrows. "Are you trying to tell me that none of that was meant to be suggestive? My folks are going to think I have Magic Mike in here."

Understanding passes over his face. "Shit."

"Yeah. 'Shit' sounds about right."

"Would you believe me if I said I was genuinely excited to strip the ugly paint from the bedroom dresser?" he asks, holding up a jug of Citristrip. "Even found the brand you wanted."

I sigh, relenting. "I'll believe you only because I know how much you've been looking forward to the sheer magic that is paint-stripping wood furniture."

His eyes light up. "I'm going to go put this stuff away. Grab the stripper, will you?" As he turns away, he pauses. "You're going to show me how to use the sander, right?"

Before I think better about letting a total shop-class virgin like him handle my power tools, I find myself promising, "Later, only to get those last stubborn streaks of paint that refuse to come off."

"Dresser, we're about to get to know you very intimately," he says with an irascible grin.

"Please don't talk dirty to the furniture!" I yell after him.

As Milan dashes off to put his purchases away, I stand there staring after him, taking in the surreality of the moment. His eagerness is—dare I say it—adorable. The giggle bubbles out of me as I remember the horrifying, uncomfortable silence that followed Milan's announcement that he was home.

God alone knows what my family thought.

My phone vibrates again in my palm. I recognize Mom's WhatsApp icon, her and Dad standing in front of Niagara Falls sixteen years ago.

"Hi, Mom," I say, inwardly groaning.

"Don't 'Hi, Mom' me," she says, voice hushed and gossipy like we're girlfriends who share everything. "I locked myself in the bathroom, the only place I get to myself in this house, so we could talk in private. That was Milan, wasn't it?"

My heart races. "No."

Mom cuts through my bullshit with a knowing, *"Rita."*

The Citristrip is still sitting in the plastic bag it came in. I crouch down to crinkle the bag an inch from my iPhone. "What's that? I'm losing you? I did tell you the reception here is—"

"Don't pull that *Parent Trap* phone trick on me, missy. I *bought* you that VHS. And don't distract me. Your aji has made up her mind about him, but you can be honest with me. Things are improving between the two of you, aren't they?"

I flounder for an honest answer that isn't *too* honest.

When I don't answer right away, Mom says, not without some relish, "I *knew* it."

"Don't you and Mrs. Rao clap yourselves on the back," I warn. "This is just business."

"What if you and Milan mixed a little business with plea—"

My brain short-circuits. "BYE, MOM!" I yelp, hanging up before she can finish.

There is no way that *pleasure* and *Milan* go in the same sentence.

"Hey, Rita," he shouts from the garage. "I'm ready for you! Are you coming?"

Chapter 20

Back the next Monday, I figure out five things:

1. Milan looks sexy as hell with his sleeves rolled up his forearms, wielding power tools with a buff-dude-from-the-Brawny-paper-towels ease.

2. He's called Bluebill Cottage "home" . . . more than once.

3. Harrie, my traitorous second son, quite possibly loves Milan more than me. That or Milan hides bribery biscuits in his pockets.

4. The auntie grapevine moves faster than the speed of light. In the time between the Chitniss-Rao breakup six years ago and rejecting Sanju Khanna, I've gotta admit I've had a good run. So I take my lumps when well-intentioned

aunties start peppering me with information about their sons, nephews, and neighbors' sons.

But the biggest realization of all is:

5. Milan has called me on *all* my shit. When I unintention-ally tried to pass off a large dog as a wild pony. When I tried to drive past the formerly Soulless Wonder and al-most wrecked on the curb. When my tongue slipped and called him staggeringly handsome. So why hasn't he yet called me on matching on MyShaadi?

Does he think I want it that way? Or has he noticed that I rejected him and now he wants to avoid the face-to-face awk-wardness?

Milan didn't show up Friday, Saturday, or Sunday. Nothing weird about Friday; he doesn't always get a chance to come out during the week. And Sundays are reserved for his open houses. But he's been here every Saturday like clockwork, usually with lunch for two.

I don't tell Raj about his absence. I don't ask her if she knows if something came up at work, either. She'll read into that, think I miss seeing him or something.

It's not like we argued more than usual. Sure, we mildly got into it last weekend when he'd tried to convert me to open shelv-ing, but he saw my point of view eventually. I mean, it wasn't even a real argument. ("When was the last time you saw some-one with all white, matching dishes who wasn't an influencer? The average homeowner does *not* want all their mismatched clutter on show!")

We'd compromised on a slim, exposed wall-length shelf above a counter to put little pots of herbs against a feature wall

of blue-and-yellow William Morris wallpaper. I added a strip of
LED lighting beneath the high-gloss cream cabinets, spotlight-
ing the open cookbook propped against a wire stand. He thinks
I don't notice, but every time he comes over, he flips the pages to
a new recipe. I used to think nothing of it, but today the thought
creeps in: This is what we'd make for dinner if we lived here.

I know better than to think he'll be here on a Monday, but I
wait until one p.m. to eat my lunch anyway, a softened peach
from last week's farmer's market, Greek yogurt with honey and
granola, and a fried egg with scallions. This is what I normally
make on the days he's not here, quick and yummy meals that
won't stink up our new kitchen, but it's never been quite so lonely
to eat by myself.

So when Milan does arrive, just past three, empty handed,
looking no worse for the wear, without a word of where he's been
or why he's late, I bite my tongue. I don't want to admit that I
kinda sorta missed him if he was out there not missing me.

I can't wait for him to see everything I've accomplished. But
other than a somewhat terse "Hi" before he got to screwing the
new lightbulbs into the lamps we bought from Second Chance
Shores, he's been uncharacteristically quiet. No teasing statements meant to provoke, no fussing over Harrie and Freddie, not
even his usual swim to unwind after he gets here.

He's even gone into the downstairs bedroom to put one of
the lamps on the dresser we'd just upcycled, but he didn't say a
word about the copper-framed pressed flowers hanging on the
wall opposite the bed. It's just a small touch, those little clusters
of tiny white Queen Anne's lace flowers, taffy-pink and baby-
blanket-blue forget-me-nots, palm-sized ferns, and sprigs of lavender tied with twine. But I want him to notice.

"Hey, do you want to go to the master bedroom?" I ask when
he emerges.

His eyebrows draw together. "Sure?"

I lead the way upstairs, biting the insides of my cheek to keep from smiling. He may have missed the flowers downstairs, but there's no way he'll miss this.

When we enter the bedroom, I can practically feel my soul expand, filling every corner. The quilts all look fantastic folded at the foot of the beds, just like I knew they would, and I put my favorite one in the master. Formerly the "honeymoon suite" when Bluebill was run as a B&B, the mammoth master comes with its own balcony and a more spacious bathroom than the others. If I hadn't worked on it myself, I'd never believe the Before and After that took this room from dingy and worn to fresh and inviting.

Milan takes it all in, eyes exploring the jute rug in front of each nightstand, the egg-shaped wicker chair with the plump cushion seat, and finally, *finally*, landing on the dried flowers next to the sunrise macramé wall tapestry.

He's going to notice that the forget-me-nots are the same exact ones he gave me before I left for college. I'd laughed, thrown my arms around his neck, almost knocking our chins together in the process, and promised him *Never, not in a million years, you goof. How can you even think that? We'll be talking to each other every single day.*

I still have the entire bouquet dried and pressed into the pages of a phone book, along with all the other flowers he's given me: Valentine's Day roses, my prom corsage, even the bunch of daisies snipped from his mom's garden that he gave my mom the first time he came to dinner as boyfriend-girlfriend. It's silly and totally sentimental of me, but I liked the idea of sharing a few of those blooms with this house. Something of ourselves to leave behind.

Milan's gaze finally returns to me. My heart leaps into my throat.

"Very nice," he says.

My forehead furrows. That's it? That's all he has to say?

"You did a good job in here," he adds, taking a few steps back.

Not an over-the-top you've-blown-me-away stagger, but a leaving-the-room-thank-you-and-goodbye reverse.

"Did you recognize anything?" I ask, following him out, but not without one last, desperate glance to the flower frames.

He answers without looking at me. "The flowers."

Yes! My chest surges with elation. I *knew* he wouldn't have forgotten.

"Weren't those the frames we saw last week in Second Chance Shores?"

I wither. I swallow past the dryness in my mouth, fingernails pinching into my palms hard enough to leave half-moon indents. "I—um, yeah. You've, um, got a good eye."

But his memory is shit. I'd second-guessed and almost talked myself out of it twice, but *nooooo*, I'd decided to be brave and take a chance on him. Show him that despite rejecting him on MyShaadi, I still wanted to give him—give us—another chance. The flowers were a baby step in that direction, showing him how something old could be renewed, even though I'd spent so long thinking we'd been broken too long to ever be fixed.

But maybe it's not about you at all, inner Rita reasons. *Maybe he's got something else on his mind, something that's making him distant and terse.*

Inner Rita is right. Something is definitely up, even if he's being tight-lipped about it. He's so noncommittal and blank-faced that I can't even make a guess at what he's thinking. Where I skirt around issues until they come to a tipping point, Milan's the type to push things to a head.

People admire him for being a straight shooter.

People. People in general. Not me.

So I don't get why he's staring at the pinch pots of herbs like we didn't spend last Sunday morning at the Rosalie Island farmer's market picking our parsley, mint, and basil.

I glance at the cookbook. It's still on Sunday's shakshuka recipe.

Are you okay? I want to ask, but I won't, since it'll reveal I've been paying more attention to him than I want to admit.

"It looks great, right?" I say instead. "You were totally right about not buying that baby cilantro plant."

While facing the herb shelf, I sneak a peek at him. There's no expression on his face, just bland interest that makes me think of how Neil's eyes used to glaze over when I'd talk about a day at the flea market.

"Mmm," says Milan.

"I mean, the amount of cilantro Indians use," I say with a laugh. "We'd finish off the whole plant for one meal."

That doesn't even get a smile.

I tell him he was right, make a joke at my own expense, and get zero reaction from him?

"I didn't think you were going to come over today," I say, more in an effort to draw him out than anything else. "I missed you on Saturday."

At this, he twitches. "Why?"

I open my mouth, then snap it shut. Something about the way he asks puts me on the defensive.

"I guess," I say with a deep breath, "I got used to you being here."

His mouth takes on a disappointed set. "I see."

"What do you want me to say? That I enjoyed spending time with you? Okay, you got me. I like wondering what lunch you'd surprise me with. I like debating whether the fireplace tiles should be Oxford blue or Prussian blue, even though they're basically both the same. I like getting to work knowing that you're in the house. Is that what you wanted to hear?"

10 . . . 9 . . . 8 . . . I count down, giving him the chance to reply. My fingernails dig into my palms as I stare at him, unblinking, until my eyes burn.

Waiting for him to feel the same way.

Instead, with each second that ticks by, I'm back in that arrivals lounge.

Waiting for him to show up.

3 . . . 2 . . . 1 . . .

Milan looks everywhere but at me until finally his gaze drops to the dining room floor, where I've propped frames against the wall, waiting to be hung. He glances up at the wall, where I've plotted out where each frame goes in pencil.

He studies it for a moment, then starts to hang the vintage seaside prints and Rosalie Island postcards we picked up at the farmer's market. I found plenty of cheap wooden frames for literal *pennies* on my solo return trip to Second Chance Shores that I painted with our leftover admiral blue and buttercup yellow.

I pause, waiting for him to compliment the color scheme. To say, Hey, Rita, these look amazing. Chalk paint was a good choice. They don't look like you made them yesterday. If a buyer walks in here for a viewing, they'd totally buy that these frames have been in the house forever. How did you get that distressed look? Steel wool? Wire brush?

Okay, so he won't have a clue what half those things are, but still. He was never this stingy with his praise before.

Before Raj's voice pipes up that I'm fishing for compliments—which I'm *not*—I get to work, starting to paint over the pencil sketch on the newly ombréd blue dining table legs.

If I didn't know any better, I'd say he was pissed I shot him down on MyShaadi.

That can't be it. Not when he's never *ever* acknowledged our match in the first place.

The only thing I don't get is *why*. He's never beaten around the bush before.

Focus on the work, Rita. That's what you're here for. That's all this is.

This house is my only link to Milan. Once it sells, it'll probably be another six years before we run into each other again. My chest stress-ball squeezes. I shouldn't give a fuck, but now that he's back in my life, a part of me wants to keep him there.

I can't not know him for another six years.

Painting the house, the sand, and the beach grasses are done in no time, but when I move to the last, final details on the two figures walking along the beach, frustration sets in. I clench the green-tipped paintbrush hard enough that my fingers turn white. Then I unfold myself from the dining room floor, ignoring the rippling soreness that washes over me. I stare at the finished paintwork until my vision blurs, and the faint lines and curves bleed together: the calico scallop shells; the round whorls of the moon snails; the tiny orange clam shells the size of a baby's ear.

"If I wanted to spend my time *not* talking to you, I would never have accepted your job offer or this partnership," I say before I can stop myself, heat rising in my cheeks.

He stops mid-strike, slowly bringing the hammer down to his side. "What?"

"You heard me." I tip my chin defiantly.

I'd said it now. There was no going back.

"I'm sorry, did you want me to sing and dance for you?" He doesn't say it with mockery. He just *says* it, and I feel a fool all the same. "We're here to work, Rita, not play house."

"Don't be an ass. I know perfectly well why we're here. You asked me to flip this house with you. We could have gone our separate ways after the first house sold, but no"—I jab the pencil in his direction—"*you* wanted to keep me around."

"Yeah?" He fixes his gaze on the wall. "Why do you think that is?"

That's the last thing I expected him to say. I suck in a sharp breath. "W-what?"

He turns to face me with aggravating slowness. "You heard me," he says levelly.

Seeing the look I must be wearing, his face softens. "I didn't mean what I said about not being here to play house."

Childish spite rises in my throat. "So we *are* here to play house?"

He puts my hammer back in the toolbox with a *clank*. "Ugh, Rita, instead of having a knee-jerk reaction to everything I say, could you let me finish? Please?"

"Fine," I say, clipped.

He gives me a long look, making sure I'm going to keep my word. Then he says, pointed enough for me to know he thinks it's *my* fault somehow, "It's weird sharing this house with you. It was one thing to imagine where you were, what you were doing, who you were with, when I never saw you."

Before it sinks in that he *thought about me* these past six years, he keeps going, talking faster and faster, like he'll chicken out if he doesn't do this now.

"When I didn't know what street you lived on and what flowers you grew in your yard. The names of your dogs." Milan's voice roughens. "The way you say my name. How it sounds different from the way anyone else says it, even though it shouldn't, and it makes no sense. But I swear, Rita, when you say it, it's like I have a soft place to land."

I gasp in too much air and the soft burn collects in my throat. That's the last thing I expected him to say. It's too hard to look at him, but it's even harder not to, so I settle for zeroing in on a freckle on the underside of his jaw.

"Last weekend, everything crept up on me. How much I looked forward to our weekends together." He runs a hand over his face. "Wrapping up my work early so I could be here. Do you know, after the first few times, you weren't even surprised to see me? You got *used* to me being here, even though we agreed at the start that the day-to-day would be yours. How easy it was to be Milan and Rita again. How fucking stupid it was that we ever stopped."

My mouth hangs open. "So you're *blaming* me now for getting used to you?"

His laugh is short and bitter. "You took it for granted I'd be here for lunch on the weekends and some Fridays, and I . . . I liked that you did. I wanted you to. Because then maybe it would be like no time had passed, nothing had driven us apart." His breath catches. "A world in which I hadn't fucked everything up."

I keep my focus on his freckle, trying not to hold my breath, which I tend to do when I'm emotional. So even when he wanted to show it the least, on the inside he was as much of a mess as I was. As affected by being back in each other's orbit again.

He reaches out like he's aching for me, but doesn't come close enough to touch. His fingers curl in empty air. Rough with anguish, he says, "It was so much easier when you weren't close enough for me to—" His arm drops back down to his side. He blinks fast, tilting his head back as though the ceiling is infinitely fascinating. "So if I'm quiet around you, it's not because I don't care. It's because I *do*."

Why is it that I'm feeling *everything* right when my mind blazes white as sun glare on snow and goes blinking-cursor blank? Words have ceased to exist. Or, at least, my ability to form them.

"Milan," I say, his name a plea. I have no idea what's going to follow it, especially not when he swings his startled gaze to mine.

"Say it again," he demands.

"Milan," I whisper. I know even less, now, about what I'm asking him for.

His lips part, and what he says steals the air from my lungs. "I have no idea how to be around you," he says, low as a secret, "when all I want to do is lose myself in being *with* you. But then, inevitably, I have to go home, and then the real world comes rushing back."

Milan flexes his finger like he has to keep from reaching for me again. The words keep tumbling out of him with abandon. "The one where we can play at being a happy couple again in this beautiful place . . . but it's not real. It's a dream of the life we could have had. And here you are looking on MyShaadi for something solid. Not a redo of the past. Not someone 'unreliable,'" he says with a self-deprecating laugh.

"That's not fair. You're throwing all these grenades at me now when you're the one who acted all this time like it wasn't hard for you." My breath catches. "Like I meant nothing except a slice of stale teenage history."

His forehead pulls into a wrinkled frown. "I knew if I didn't challenge you, you'd back out. When you came to High Castle with Raj's catering, do you think I couldn't tell you were getting up the courage to blow me off? To back out? I know you." Then, as if he's reminding himself as much as me, he repeats, "I *know* you."

"You baited me on the first house," I realize aloud. "You got my hackles up. You called me on trying to run when I went for the elevator." And I'd been such an easy mark. "I would have done anything to wipe that smug, stupid grin off your face."

"But I didn't bait you for this house," he counters swiftly. "I just had to ask."

The way he says it, though, like he crooked his finger and I came running. I had my own reasons for accepting this job, and they had nothing to do with him.

"If you remember," I snap, hands curling into fists, "I turned you down the first time. Sure, I did change my mind but *not* because of you."

His jaw tightens like he doesn't believe me. "Yeah? So what was the reason then?"

I glare. Neil's name is on the tip of my tongue, but the way Milan's standing there, so sure that he's backed me into a corner, makes me clamp my mouth shut. My petty victory would be fleeting and pyrrhic. Mean in a way I don't want to be. Not to him.

More satisfying to let him stew, make him wonder if he doesn't know me as well as he thinks he does.

"Why are you saying all this now?" I fling at him. "Why not the morning of the open house? When you pretended the coffeehouse got your order wrong, but it was the exact flavor I've loved my whole life? Or how about the time you swung by my house to return a scrunchie you *wore* around your wrist the way you used to when you'd pull them out of my hair? Honestly, you say you're not here to play house, but it sure seems like you came here to pick a fight."

"I told you. Spending so much time with you, laughing with you, getting to know you again. I wanted to catch up on everything we missed out on, but it's like trying to hold on to a cloud. It slips through your fingers and it's gone." He snaps his fingers. "Just like that."

Harrie comes skidding into the room to make figure eights around our legs.

Milan and I stare at each other in a stalemate. I don't understand him. He's being honest and vulnerable about everything else, except one thing.

MyShaadi. He's conspicuously avoiding going there. It makes no sense.

I stare Milan down. "That's the only reason?"

"The routine we settled into. It . . . it scared me, Rita."

I grind my back molars. "Yeah, you said."

Harrie gives up trying to get our attention and retreats under the table to watch us.

I'm not being short to hurt him, but I don't buy that his speech wasn't prompted by the fact that I rejected him and now he's worried that I've found someone else.

"Right. So it has nothing to do with MyShaadi?" I scoff. "The fact that we matched on there and you didn't mention it for weeks? And you coincidentally just *happen* to want a heart-to-heart with me right after I reject you?"

"What? I—" Milan's eyebrows shoot toward his hairline.

"You heard me."

"What are you talking about?" He blows out a long, irritated breath. "I used to have an account, but I haven't been active in a long time. There's no way they're still matching me."

He can't be serious. It was one hundred percent *his* name and photo on the profile.

I could prove it if only I hadn't already deleted all of my MyShaadi emails.

"Hold up. Rewind." Hurt blazes in his eyes. "You rejected me?"

There's a horrible, lurching sensation in my stomach. Like the ferry ride over but ten times worse. It's the sixth sense right before you hurl after drinking too much cheap beer and all-you-can-eat wings at sports bars with short-lived boyfriends two and three.

The room stills, almost as disorienting as the rocking.

"I didn't know what else to do. It's not like I set out *looking* for you, Milan," I say.

When I say his name this time, it gets a completely different reaction than before.

He flinches into himself, face closing off. "Yeah, but rejecting me. That's cold."

"Probably still not as cold as you breaking up with me with a Dear John voicemail."

His lips flatten. "*That's* what you think happened?"

"This whole pretending-you-don't-know-what-I'm-talking-about thing is getting real old," I hiss. "You know perfectly well what happened. You blamed *me* for you failing your classes." Tears spring to my eyes. "Told me you wouldn't be coming on our trip, and if that wasn't shitty enough, you dumped me while I was in the air!"

When it looks like he wants to say something, I plow on, "You didn't even have the guts to see me after I came home."

"Because you had the time of your life! You made friends at your hostel, you had drinks with guys in clubs. You were so used to us being apart that you didn't even miss me when I wasn't there."

I didn't miss him? Blood rushes to my ears. I didn't *miss* him?

I have spent the last *six years of my life* missing him.

His mask slips for just a second. "You Instagrammed the Ladurée macarons, Rita." He has to swallow before he can speak again, and when he does, there's a wrangled vulnerability in his voice. "Did you forget what we promised?"

I hate that he's reminding me as though I've forgotten. But he's got it wrong.

We said we'd feed each other those macarons under the Eiffel Tower on our first night in Paris, at the exact moment it lit up with those magical twinkling lights.

Of course I wouldn't forget a thing like that.

His flush dims, returning his cheeks to their normal color. Voice cracking in a way it hasn't since he was fourteen, he says, "You went off on an adventure like it didn't matter if I was there or not. Just like college. So fucking fearless on your own," he says with a laugh, sounding strangely proud. "You didn't need me at all. How was I supposed to know you'd need me when you were back?"

How can he think I was fearless? I was anything but.

I make a strangled sound in the back of my throat. "My god, you're one to talk about promises. What was I supposed to do? Waste my money moping in the hostel over you?"

"Yes! No. I mean, just a little. Of course I didn't want you to miss out." He rubs at his forehead. "I never wanted any of—"

"See, now I'm thinking that's exactly what you wanted."

"All I want is y—"

It's not the repartee either of us expected, judging by the way he goes ashen and throws his hands up, caught out.

Want. Present tense.

This? This *mess* is what MyShaadi thinks makes us such a good couple?

His eyes sear into mine. "I never broke up with you, Rita. I wouldn't do that."

"But you did!" I half shout, splaying my hands in front of me.

He vehemently shakes his head. "Believe whatever you want." He moves forward, as if he's about to walk out, then pauses to glance back at the still-unhung wall art. "I'll get out of your hair. I should have never spent so much time here."

He leaves without a backward glance, the screen door banging shut on Harrie as he tries to follow. I hover where I stand, rolling on the balls of my feet. If I run, I can catch him.

But what do I say? I can't tell him to come back so we can yell at each other some more.

Why am I even bothering?

He said his piece and now he's gone. I hear the six-year-old voicemail in my head over and over. It's engraved on my mind, word for word. Every run-through, it ends the same: *It's because of you and I think maybe we should take a break.*

Harrie barrels back into the dining room to fix me with an accusing stare. He doesn't understand what just happened, but he's never heard me get into it like this with anyone before.

That it's happened now, with Milan, baffles me as much as him.

He wants to be a couple again, but not just any couple. The one we used to be, Rita-and-Milan. He can't see that we aren't the same people anymore, and I can't be sure it's not the Rita I used to be that he misses. He might be able to draw those old feelings out, but I'll never be that girl again. She's not the only Rita I've ever been, and who I am now isn't the only Rita I'll ever be. I'm still becoming, and so is he, and those two people need to see each other.

If we're going to have a chance, we need to look forward instead of recapturing the past. I don't want to pick up where we left off—I want to know Milan for who he is *now*. But he's happy for us to fall back in each other's arms like it's just been a semester apart instead of six years.

How the hell did MyShaadi think Milan was my perfect match?

Chapter 21

After Milan leaves, I make sure to double-check the ferry schedule, timing my departure so there's no chance we're on the same ferry home. Rosalie Island suddenly doesn't feel like my safe haven anymore. After the said-too-much-we-can't-take-back fight with Milan, we definitely need a break from each other.

You'd think we wouldn't need *another* one after six years, but here we are.

So I go home, and even with Harrie and Freddie with me, I'm the one running with the tail between my legs.

The next day Paula calls while I'm in the shower. I heard it while I was squeezing excess water out of my hair, but assuming it was Raj checking in or Mom calling for updates on Operation Get Rita Back Together With Milan, I let it ring.

I don't want to rehash what happened with him. I'm dreading Friday; waiting for him to show up and knowing in my heart that he won't.

After all, he didn't show up before.

After moisturizing and finger-combing the last tangles from my long hair, I dress in my oldest, softest black tee and oxblood hip-hugging shorts. As happy as my pups are to be home, I can't hide out here forever.

The sooner I finish up at Rosalie, the sooner I can never see Milan again.

Even if it means leaving a piece of my heart behind.

It's not what I want, but maybe it's what I need.

What's broken between us can't be fixed with a dab of glue or a clever bit of welding.

If only repairing broken hearts was that easy, Mom and Dad would be happy and in love.

Harrie butts his head against my just-lotioned calves. Despite the walk we took an hour ago, he still has energy to burn. Unlike me, who's ready to jump back into bed and pretend yesterday didn't happen.

I pick up my phone, surprised to see two new voicemails on the screen. Mom and Aji only call me on WhatsApp; Dad and I volley between iMessage and WhatsApp using emojis, gifs, and selfies with our food; Raj never leaves voicemails when she can just call me back incessantly until I answer. And no one else I know would call me when they could just DM.

Hey, it's Paula! chirps the voicemail. *How are you doing these days? You missed the neighborhood barbecue and my kids' lemonade stand! It was the cutest thing.* Her voice lowers to a hush, like she doesn't want anyone around her to hear. *Anyway, I saw you on a walk this morning and you looked a real mess, honey. Hope it's not that boyfriend of yours giving you heartache.*

She rambles on, spilling gossip that isn't that scintillating, about people whose faces I can't even recall, and it takes me a solid minute of half listening before I realize she's talking about a reality show she watches that for some reason she thinks I watch, too.

If I don't hear from you by this afternoon I'm going to swing by with some of that lemonade we didn't sell and a slice of my pine-apple upside-down cake to turn your frown upside down! She laughs at her own joke. *I saw some of your new posts on Instagram and I love the vibe, especially the painted table that looks like the Rosalie Island coastline? And I know we put a pin in your doing my home renovation, but if you're back home for good, I think maybe we should take a—*

The voicemail cuts off.

There's a long, pregnant pause before the automated voice begins: *Next message, received on—*

I end the call without thinking about it.

Something about what just happened is so familiar I could reach out and touch it.

My breath catches.

It's because of you, and I think maybe we should take a break—

Phone still clenched in my hand, I dash to the closet, throwing open both sides of the accordion doors. I don't find what I'm looking for at first. I tilt my upper body all the way in, rooting around the clothes still in shopping bags with receipts, ready to be returned if buyer's remorse or my credit card statement talk me out of keeping them.

I dig past the chest of dog toys, a box from Chewy, random old cables and empty iPhone boxes, the worn children's books I was too sentimental to give away, and a giant bag of cheap Amazon scrunchies.

Finally, my fingers close around the rough, all-weather fabric of a backpack I haven't used in years. *Success.* I pull it toward me. The keychains jangle, parting gifts from hostel friends who gave me a little piece of their home country.

In one of the inside pockets is my old iPhone 4s, the one I'd begged my parents for in high school. I'd taken it with me to Europe sophomore year of college, but had made the mistake of trying to pop it out of the case while on the plane to make sure I could do it. In the hustle of disembarking, I couldn't get the case back on in time.

Which meant that when I heard Milan's voicemail, the purple butterfly case had been stashed in my purse instead of protecting my phone. And when I'd dropped it in shock, the screen had shattered on impact. The long, jagged crack looks like a wicked grin.

It's because of you, and I think maybe we should take a break—

I'd assumed Milan's voicemail ended there.

But now I remember what he said yesterday: *I never broke up with you, Rita.*

It's a long shot. But maybe, just maybe, like Paula's voicemail had cut off, his had, too.

Maybe he had never broken up with me at all.

I think the five minutes it takes to charge the phone long enough to be able to check my voicemail are the longest five minutes of my life—until I'm on the phone with the customer service rep another fifteen to figure out why the mailbox is empty.

I'm transferred to someone else, a bored-sounding woman who couldn't care less that I'm trying to recover the proof to exonerate the man who broke my heart.

"You're trying to recover a voicemail from *how* long ago now?" Her tone is incredulous.

When I tell her, she whistles. I'm pretty sure that's not in her customer service handbook.

"If you haven't saved it somewhere, it's not on our server anymore," she says. "We purge old voicemails pretty frequently.

iPhones nowadays would be able to save voicemails indefinitely, but back then? Thinking you probably just had a month before it deleted."

My hope strangles in my throat, every last bit of anticipation ebbing away. So that's it? There's no way to get it back? To see if it came with a part two?

Try again, I want to insist. *Double-check with a supervisor.*

At my silence, the woman asks, more gently now, "Was it important?"

I don't want to think about how many other desperate strangers she's had to let down.

"Not anymore," I say, voice tight. "Thank you."

After hanging up, I'm strangely bereft without a wild goose to chase, so I decide to follow through on my plan to return to Rosalie Island with Harrie and Freddie. The boys would be content to stay, but suddenly my cozy little space seems squeezed and small, with an anticlimactic heaviness draping the air. I yearn for Bluebill Cottage with its high ceilings and rooms full of possibility, the way home settles in every nook and cranny.

I left the island only yesterday, but just like every time before it feels like I've left something important behind.

While my clothes spin in the dryer, the rest of the morning goes by in a flurry of cooking: crunchy Vietnamese-style chicken salad, lemony lentils with rainbow veggies, and heaping helpings of comforting spicy masala mac. The days of Milan coming over with lunch are, I'm afraid, in the past.

I lug my duffel and a cooler—heavy with portioned meals to last me through the final stint of home improvement—from my house to my car and then all the way to the New Bern ferry parking lot. That's when I realize that in my rush to get back, I got here too early. My head's fogged up with the past instead of the present.

With a short wait until the next ferry, I take the boys on a walk through New Bern. It turns out to be Harrie sniffing at every new flower growing through a crack in the sidewalk and making frequent stops to "talk" to the cats dozing in front windows. And somehow, without even realizing it, we wind up close to the historic district where my parents' fixer-upper used to be, a few streets away from the rows of Hatteras yachts near the ferry terminal.

How do I know? The fuchsia azalea shrubs shading windows and spilling through wrought-iron gates are the color of my very first lipstick from the Clinique counter. To Aji's consternation, I was drawn to the bright colors even then, eager to graduate from the tinted lip balms and Lip Smackers lip gloss that made it hard to kiss (not that I'd been kissed, but I trusted in Raj's pronouncement that gloss left a sticky mess everywhere, and as someone who had kissed a grand total of two boys and three girls, she should know).

Mom bought it for me, anyway. When she asked why I didn't choose the natural, soft pinks she'd selected, I told her it reminded me of the azaleas growing outside the windows of the New Bern house. We drove home the rest of the way in silence.

She forgot to take the turn to our favorite frozen yogurt place and when we got home, she disappeared into her bedroom with all her purchases instead of trying everything on for Dad like she usually did. That was when fourteen-year-old Rita realized that even though four years had passed since the house had been sold, Mom still carried something about it with her.

I never wore that fuchsia lipstick where Mom could see. And because she never saw me with it at home, Aji assumed she was right all along, that I was too young for lipstick. The truth was that I applied it before first period at school, craning over the sink in the girl's bathroom, and carefully wiped it off at the end of the day before Mom came to pick me up.

My heartbeat quickens. There's no logical reason I should have remembered how to get here, not when the last time I'd barely been tall enough to see over the window.

Nostalgia brings an image of the house to my mind.

I jangle the leash. "What do you think, boys?"

Harrie, always up for an adventure, wags his tail. Freddie raises one paw. *Okay.*

I walk along Middle Street in a daze, unable to shake how surreal it feels being back. Disloyal, too, maybe. Hand-in-the-Marie-biscuit-jar naughty, like I'm not supposed to be here.

The historic downtown is vibrant with upscale restaurants and teahouses, an art gallery selling local art only, florist and gift shops, cozy cafés oozing small-town charm, and, surprisingly, even an Indian takeout. The shade trees don't provide much protection and dappled sunlight warms my shoulders, but as we get closer to the first house that stole my heart, pink crepe myrtles canopy above us. They weren't this big when we left, nor did they droop low enough to touch.

My parents had been in a constant battle with the guidelines for the interior and exterior of the house, as per the National Register of Historic Places. With tempers flaring, they were constantly battling with each other, too. My mother, trying to keep her voice low so I wouldn't hear, gritting out that Dad should never have bought a fixer-upper that required so much research into what was appropriate for the historic district, and Dad, wounded, whisper-yelling back that he was doing this for her, for us, *didn't she see that*?

By some strange muscle memory, I see the house in my mind

before it even comes into view, shrouded behind mature flowering dogwoods and crepe myrtles. The gable-front Victorian is spiffier than I remember it. The white window trim of the high-peaked two-story and the front porch balustrade look recently refreshed, popping against the sky-blue of the painted clapboard.

Mom favored cream with lapis-blue shutters the same shade as the nearby Neuse and Trent rivers, but now that I'm here I can't remember in what state they actually sold the house. I don't remember much from the month Mom lived here by herself, either, and even less about how—why—she came back from this house that she and Dad never finished.

Whatever unhappiness lay within her, had she exorcised those demons? Had she exorcised her complicated feelings about Amar to let herself fall in love with Dad? My heart sinks. Or did she decide to come back only for me, using the month alone to brace herself for a lifetime living with a man she didn't love?

And Dad had taken her back. So had Aji.

And nobody ever spoke a word about it during or afterward. Even now, all these years later, it's like it never even happened at all.

Freddie rubs against my calves and Harrie whines, both of them picking up on my mood.

I stare long and hard at the fuchsia azaleas in front of the first-floor bedroom window that would have been mine. My heart twists. Someone else lives here now. The shrub has flowered even wider now, grown so much. Behind the Disney princess peel-off window stickers and the gauzy pink curtain comes a childish shout.

I snap out of my cotton-eared haze, blinking furiously.

Whatever Mom's reason for returning to us, she and Dad had found a way to grow their life together. After she came back, the two of them had gone away for a week, taking a couple's trip to

Niagara Falls that I'd later learn was their belated honeymoon. And though there had been several trips to Europe and Asia since then, the photo of them together on the *Maid of the Mist* is the only one Mom's ever used as her WhatsApp icon. And Aji, who gets pretty vocal whenever she isn't taken somewhere, for once didn't complain at all.

Somehow, my parents had fixed their relationship. And if they could do it, then maybe I could find a way to unpick the splinters of Milan from my heart, too. Maybe all those splinters put together could build a home.

"Bluebill," I say with a gasp. "Shit. We have to get back to the ferry."

Chapter 22

I get to Bluebill Cottage by a sheer stroke of luck. I'd raced to the ferry only to be told I'd just missed it since they'd just switched to their new end-of-August schedule, and there wouldn't be another one for three hours. Right as my eye began twitching at the thought of waiting around, I saw a family with children at the marina loading up their yacht, and asked to bum a ride with them on their day trip to Rosalie.

After I put the food away in the fridge, I'm surprised to find Milan's wallet and phone on the kitchen island. Why did he come back so soon? I strain to hear any sound of him, but the house is quiet. I didn't think anything could be worse than yet another house full of yelling, but the cold silence is definitely worse. Silence means not talking, not even caring to try, and we've already had six years of that.

If I could do our fight over, I would have called him back to yell at him some more. Let him yell at me. At least we'd be talking through our problems.

Through the glass-enclosed dining room I can see Milan on the back porch, unpacking an oversize picnic basket on the patio table. Harrie runs through the open door. Milan crouches down in surprise, ruffling his fur, then scans the area for me.

I follow Harrie out, amazed at the sheer quantity of food on the glass tabletop. It must have cost a small fortune. On a comically large charcuterie board, Milan's arranged different crackers, cubes and wedges of both hard and soft cheeses, and slivers of spicy cured salami and prosciutto. Little glass bowls hold rustic dijon mustard and deep colors of fruit preserves. I can smell tart cherry and make out smushed, jammy sweet apricots next to the baguette slices.

Before my eyes he brings out the sesame seed chikki that I love even more than the peanut brittle my mom makes at Christmas; sweet shankarpali, the deep-fried diamond-shaped sugar biscuits I used to eat by the fistful back in high school during an exam week; and spicy spirals of crispy bakarwadi stuffed with toasted coconut. All my favorite Indian snacks. There's enough food to throw a party for thirty, and he's still not done removing things from the basket.

I can only stare at him as he unloads a container of carrot sticks and plump red radishes, followed by a tub of perfectly round green grapes and small strawberries still on the vine. His lips are smudged berry pink as if he's already helped himself while waiting.

I look away from his lips when my stomach gives an unhelpful twist, focusing instead on his hands as he finesses the board arrangement, getting everything to fit.

A mistake. Who knew *knuckles* could be sexy?

His tentative smile turns into a nervous swallow when I meet his gaze. "Rita, I'm sorry. I was a dick about you having fun in Paris. Part of that is because you did it all without me, and I . . .

was a baby about that. So I thought, let me bring Paris to us. Oh, and the pretzels you like. Hearts, not sticks."

Hearts, not sticks.

"When did you get here?" I ask, smitten, as I slide into the chair he pulls out for me.

He did all this, not even sure whether I'd be here today.

Milan looks sheepish. "I wanted to surprise you. When I saw you coming up the drive I hustled out here to set everything up."

He proceeds to withdraw cornichons and garlic-stuffed olives, fig-and-olive crisps from Trader Joe's, salted almonds and crunchy wasabi peas, candied ginger, and red pepper hummus swirled with olive oil, then shuts the picnic basket.

"I know this isn't the real deal," he broaches again, "but I chose things I thought you'd like. A charcuterie board like you'd have had there."

"Just what the hell kind of budget do you think I had?" I help myself to a cracker, loading it up with hummus. "I was an only-slightly-better-off-than-broke college student who wrecked her souvenir budget because she had to buy a new phone the second she landed. I was mostly eating fresh bread, sidewalk Nutella crêpes, and farmer's market fruit. Nothing like this."

It's meant as a compliment, but his face falls. "So it's not the same?"

"No! That's not what I meant. This is lovely." I stare down at my lap, clearing my throat. "It wasn't, you know. As perfect as it might have looked. I mean, it was fun. But."

But it wasn't with you.

He sits, too. "Why did you need a new phone?" he asks, pulling some grapes off the stem. He offers me one, so polite. I take it, my fingers grazing his for a brief, electric second.

His hands tighten around the neck of a bottle of prosecco,

thumb stroking the narrowest part and coming away wet with condensation.

I pop the grape in my mouth, trying not to choke when I see Milan's eyes, dark and intense, watching me. Juice floods into my mouth.

He bites his lower lip as he drives in the corkscrew. "Are you enjoying it?" he asks, oblivious to the fact that I've turned into a live wire, and his thumb stroking is going straight between my legs.

Pop! The cork shoots out.

The grape skin sticks in my throat.

"So why did you need a new phone, anyway?" he asks. "You loved your iPhone like it was your baby."

Here's my opening. My chance to be that brave, fearless girl.

"Yeah, well, it was the same model as Serena van der Wood-sen's," I say, forcing a laugh. I want to ask him about the voice-mail, about that whole day, but I can't do it when he's looking at me with such undivided attention. "I even got her case to match," I rattle off.

Milan cracks a smile. "How could I forget *Gossip Girl* and all those dramas you'd get me to watch with you? *Friday Night Lights*, that one show you said was about basketball but it wasn't, and oh, that one about werewolves and vampires."

He's looking at me again, a question in his eyes. A simple question that I haven't answered yet.

"I dropped my phone," I answer. "The screen cracked. It was basically unusable. I had to buy one of those cheap ones with a European SIM at the airport."

Realization dawns on his face. "*That's* why you didn't return my calls. I tried reaching you a dozen times the first week, but it just kept ringing and ringing and ringing."

"To be fair," I say, drawing circles on the glass top, trying and failing to dodge his eyes, "even if I had gotten those calls, I probably wouldn't have answered."

"I *told* you I never broke up with you," he says in a rush, scowling.

"Your voice in my ear, telling me that it was all my fault . . . That was the first thing I heard when I got off the plane." I fidget with a piece of spicy salami, tearing it into shreds over a cracker. "The last thing I heard from you."

My breathing staggers. "That's why I dropped my phone. You broke my heart, and I had to gather the pieces back together and keep going, or fly home and explain things to my folks when I didn't even understand it myself."

The tortured expression on Milan's face almost undoes me, but I have to keep going. If I lose my nerve now, I'll never say it.

"So if it looked like I was having the time of my life without you, what you didn't see was that outside the frame, I was missing you in the pit of my stomach every time I had to do something alone, or with someone else, when all I wanted was to share that experience with you. A broken phone I could replace, but the rest . . ." I swallow. "Can I ask you something?"

He doesn't even have to think about it. "Anything."

"After the voicemail where you ended things, or, where I *thought* you ended things, what happened next? Did you— Did you get cut off? Did you call me back? Did you . . . regret it?"

He stares at me. The breeze picks up, ruffles his hair so it flops across his forehead à la sexy Hugh Grant. He drags his hand through it, pushing it back, but his hair has other ideas.

"I wasn't breaking up with you," he says finally. "I was trying to tell you I just needed a break that summer to get back on track academically, but I had maxed out the voicemail time limit. And by the time I realized it, I wanted to take back everything I said and apologize, but I didn't know what to say that would absolve all the other crap."

"*Was* it crap, though? You sounded pretty sure of yourself when you were blaming me."

His eyes flash, and I brace myself for him to launch a defense, but then he says, "I was twenty. I was a dumbass. Anything was easier than accepting responsibility for my own fuckups. I did leave another voicemail after that first one. I wish to god you'd heard it."

I wait for him to expand. After an agonizing lull, I ask, "That's it?"

He holds his hands out in front of me helplessly. "At best, all I have is justification, and that's not going to be helpful. I was wrong to blame you, Rita. I'm sorry."

There it is. I finally have my apology. But it doesn't make me feel any better.

"What did you say?" I ask. "In the second voicemail."

Milan's lips quirk into a sad sort of smile. "I don't remember. I wish I did. All I know is I'd calmed down by then and it hit me like a fucking truck that I'd been a jerk." He releases a bark of self-deprecating laughter. "The only part I remember is saying 'Please don't dump me, I know I'm a jerk.'"

Pressure builds behind my eyes. We each thought the other had dumped us.

He sighs with the weight of six years. "I should have pounded down your front door the second you came home. I should have rushed to the airport with flowers. There are a thousand chances I should have taken, and I still want to kick myself for letting all of them go without a fight. Letting *you* go without a—" He doesn't say it, but it lingers between us megaphone loud.

This was the truth I was so desperate to find earlier today. I feel pinched and small, flattened in a trash compactor.

"Six years lost," I say, stomach churning in an angry, sickening whorl. Is it grief? Is it anger? I can't tell. The two are joined too deeply now, too part of each other to separate and identify. "That voicemail . . . lost. Gone forever."

The ripped salami looks forlorn and unappetizing now, but I force it down, anyway.

"You asked me if I regretted it," states Milan. "Of course I did. How could I not? I regret it more than anything in the *world*."

But we'd both said nothing. We'd both done nothing.

The first real obstacle in our relationship and we'd folded like it wasn't worth a damn.

"The time we were apart is spent, but it's not gone," he says. "Tell me about your life. Catch me up to the day we met again at your parents' house. Give us that time back."

His last sentence engraves itself on my mind like the gel pen heart drawn on my Lisa Frank folder. Tracing the heart and the initials over and over, deeper and deeper until the baby-pink ink turned into an indent of magenta.

Give it back? This isn't a forgotten scrunchie that can be returned.

"I never thought of you as naive, Milan. It doesn't work like that."

He dips his head. "Tell me anyway. I want to know you."

I'm doubtful he wants to know about other boyfriends, the times something reminded me of him and I soaked a pillow with the tears, the sweet Chihuahua I almost adopted until I saw her collar said "Millie." I'd always thought if we'd had a daughter, we'd call her Millie. I'd even made us a *Sims* family in high school that I'd never told him about just in case he thought it was as weird as Raj did.

So I tell him some more about Europe, college, and starting Dharma Designs. Milan munches on almonds, asking questions at the right time, but my heart isn't in it anymore, walking him through memories with giant, gaping Milan-sized holes in them.

He's silent for a long moment, taking it all in, before he finally collects his thoughts enough to say: "There's one thing I don't understand. You helped me with *two* houses, all the while believing I'd treated you like crap." His eyebrows draw together. "The first house you were put on the spot, fine. But you could have said no to coming to Rosalie. In fact, you did, at first. What changed?"

I'd be lying if I said I hadn't posed the same question to myself a dozen times.

Each time came with a different answer, all true, but none quite the full story: I didn't want to see Neil while he was going on dates with MyShaadi girls, so Milan was any port in a storm; shitty service on Rosalie Island meant I could plausibly evade my mom's calls (and the demanded Milan play-by-play); I wanted a break from my life, taking a walk down memory lane before returning to the regularly scheduled programming.

"I did feel a little jerked around at first," I admit. "A marionette on a string. I don't blame my mom. She thought she was doing the right thing. A big part of me wanted to rebel against giving our moms what they wanted."

I crook my lips. "I don't want to be browbeaten or manipulated. I want to make my own choices, even if they aren't the right ones, because at least they're mine."

Milan nods and takes the carrot stick dunked in the hummus, forgetting that I was the one who'd put it there. "I had the same knee-jerk reaction. But I've spent too much time pissed at my parents. Our relationship finally feels good again. I couldn't be angry at my mom for this, too. Not when it's what I always—" He snaps the carrot stick in half, then looks down in surprise.

Worrying my lower lip, I say, "Speaking of choices, do you want to tell me why you failed your classes and lost your scholarship? In high school, you tied for valedictorian. You were the only kid who used study hall for studying and not sleeping. How do *you* of all people fail?"

It's been gnawing at me ever since I first heard his voicemail. It had never made sense that someone like Milan, so conscientious and thorough, would let his academics slide.

His jaw tightens and a wall goes up in his eyes.

It's clear I've hit a nerve, but what am I supposed to do? *Not* ask a question that's been plaguing me for six years?

"Milan," I say, vocal cords dry and tight and strangled. "I want to know about you, too."

He finishes chewing. "You don't want to know this version of me," he says. "Hell, there were times even *I* had trouble recognizing myself. I know you said you'd apply somewhere closer to UNC, but I was so damn proud of you for getting into such a prestigious program. It made no sense for you to give up your dream school just to stay local for me."

I start to protest but he shakes his head. "I had no idea what I wanted to study, so investment management seemed as good a career as any. And it's not even like I hated business classes, I just couldn't find a reason to get excited about much of anything without you here.

"We were used to texting over most of the summer when one or the other of us were in India visiting family, and I thought long distance would be just like that. But it wasn't. The first semester, I tried to be the one there for you. You were staying cooped up in your dorm room, convinced your roommate hated you, and you didn't want to sit by yourself in the dining hall. I was worried. So I'd message you during class instead of paying attention to the lecture, and assumed I could easily catch up on the material."

I jolted. I'd always assumed he was as lonely as I was, wanting to look busy on his phone so no else knew just how much.

"Eventually you made new friends, though," says Milan, "and . . . it sucked when you told me stories or talked about people I didn't know. I didn't want to get recaps for every story; I wanted to just *know* it, because I'd lived it with you.

"I could never bring myself to say goodbye in order to hit the books or go to class. I told myself I'd work into the night to get back on track, but with the time difference . . . you were three hours behind, and I hated not falling asleep together. So all those times we video chatted or watched movies together, you assumed I was done with my assignments, but the truth was I usually hadn't even started. And eventually I couldn't catch up anymore."

I've never felt smaller. Milan thought I'd see him in a different light when I knew the truth, but no, this speaks volumes about *me*.

In the beginning, aware of the time difference between California and North Carolina, I'd jokingly told him to go to bed, and he'd always waved me off by saying he didn't have an early morning class the next day. I'd just assumed it was fine, that he was managing his time well.

"So . . . um . . . now you know." He rubs at his nose, giving me a weak smile.

I can't return it. "I'm so sorry," I say.

His forehead scrunches into lines. "For what?"

I swallow. "I had no idea."

He shakes his head swiftly. "There's no reason you should

have. Like you said, I had good study habits in high school. You couldn't have known."

"But I took it for granted that you had a handle on everything. I feel so selfish now."

"You were eighteen," he corrects. "In a new, exciting place doing exactly what you wanted to be doing. It wasn't your job to look out for—"

"Of course it was, Milan! We were in a *relationship*." I shake my head.

"Rita, no. I was wrong to unload that voicemail when you had zero clue about what was going on. I could have told you at any time, but I didn't. The last six years are not on you."

But of course they are. How can they not be?

Maybe he sees some of the despair on my face, because he leans in, eyes softening. "I'm so sorry for that voicemail. And for not coming to see you when you came back home. And for freaking out on you yesterday. I was one hundred percent trying to pick a fight because it hurt too much to be that close to you and not tell you how I felt."

I understand. "But the longer we were here, the more you wanted to stay," I whisper.

His throat bobs as he jerks his head *Yes*.

"I want to show you something," I say, holding out my hand. "Come with me."

We go to the dining room so I can show him the trestle table. The wide legs are the perfect canvas for the beach panorama. Wild ponies trekking between sand dunes and tall, wispy beach grass painted in soft shades of brown. Bluebill Cottage overlooking the faded footprints that go from one side of the table to the other.

I hang back, let Milan follow the tracks around the corner.

His eyes widen when he sees the side view of the couple. They could be anybody; small and featureless, except for one thing.

The parakeet-green scrunchie worn in the girl's dark hair.

He crouches down, hands gripping the table edge.

"This is the scrunchie I returned to you at your house," he states.

"Yes."

He rises, meeting my eyes. "Is this what you've been working on?"

I nod. "There had to be some way to mark our time here. Leave a little piece of ourselves behind."

His lips crook into a crooked grin. "Like the forget-me-nots."

Back on the porch, Milan opens a second bottle of prosecco halfway through catching me up on everything else I've missed in his life. "I was irresponsible with my partial scholarship and their money, but I don't think I'll ever forgive my parents for stopping me going to the airport."

I sputter midway through sucking garlic out of the olive. *"What?"*

"It's why I left you that bizarro voicemail," he explains. "I procrastinated on signing up to retake some of my failed classes in summer because I didn't want to have to ask Dad for the money. So, some alarm bells went off when I asked them for a check to drop at the bursar's office the morning of the flight."

"Oh, Milan," I say with an exhale.

Desi parents do *not* react well to eleventh-hour surprises.

He gives me a rueful look as he taps his fingers silently against his glass, then refills it, as if he's building up to the rest of the story. "My dad asked what courses, and I told him, not thinking for a minute that he'd remember I'd already taken them."

I can see where this is going.

"But, of course, he recognized all the courses right away, and from there it all unraveled pretty quick." His breath comes out staggered, unsteady. "It was the worst fight we've ever had. I'm sure the neighbors thought someone was being murdered. Dad was shouting. Mom was screaming. I don't blame them. I deserved the fallout."

"Your voicemail was a mess," I murmur. "Stricken and panicked and so, so lost."

His lips part, incredulous. "You remember that?"

I remember every word, but maybe it's better to leave it in the past.

"Anyway," he says, rushed, like he's embarrassed, "I had to ask them for my passport a couple of hours later, and Mom hit the roof. She couldn't believe that I was still actually leaving, but I knew you were already in the air. I promised I'd buckle down after we got back home, but . . ."

"They weren't having it," I say.

Milan's forehead creases into a frown. "Mom flung the passport at my feet. Said if I walked out that door, I could forget about them paying for those summer classes, let alone any other semester."

My heart squeezes. So he stayed for money.

"No, that's not why I didn't meet you," he says, seeing the look on my face.

Most other Indian kids I know either got a full or partial scholarship, or a free ride on their parents' dime, with the implicit understanding that they would study what their parents wanted. It was hard to put your foot down when it meant turning your back on financial assistance you didn't have to pay back—at least not directly.

"I stormed off to my room pissed. At myself. At them. Even a little at you." He interlocks his fingers, clasps his hands as if in prayer. "The first thing on my mind was talking to you. Only I messed that up, too."

My heart twists. "I wish I'd known. That was *a lot* for you to handle on your own."

"There's nothing you could have done."

"Don't. Don't *do* that. I could have *been* there for you, damn it."

I don't want to center myself, but it tears at me that I didn't even have the chance to help him. In keeping his difficulties to himself, he robbed me—us—of the chance to make it through the dark clouds together. Stronger for it.

His laugh is bitter. "I went and spoke to my advisor right away, and while I didn't get my original scholarship back, he said a lot of scholarship money winds up just sitting there because people don't apply for the smaller ones."

I've heard that from Dad, too, ever since he started teaching.

"So that's what I did. I got a job as a department assistant and in the campus bookstore, working every hour I could get to pay my parents back for summer classes."

"They forced you to pay them back even after you canceled your trip?"

"Oh no, no," says Milan. "When I presented them with the check, they were mortified. The idea that I thought I had to pay them back for anything made them feel like bad parents. Dad refused to deposit it. But they were right—I wasted their money, and I know how hard they worked to save up for my education."

There's a sour film coating my tongue. He had to work so

hard to make up for how much I distracted him. I swallow past it. "It's commendable that you paid them back."

But his story's not done yet.

"The next semester," he says, "a real estate agent from High Castle came to talk in one of my elective classes, and they said their interns got paid twenty hours a week plus academic credit. Figured it didn't hurt to try?" A rueful smile takes over his face. "Josh Bell took one look at my GPA and almost showed me the door. Somehow I convinced him how badly I wanted it and he gave me a chance. Who would have thought that I'd be that *good* at it?"

For the first time, there's a note of pride in his voice. "I didn't accept another penny of my parents' money. Then Josh said if I passed the licensing exam, he'd hire me and pay me back the cost of the test. I loved the work, so . . . I had everything to gain."

Suddenly, his place on the High Castle Royalty wall makes sense.

"Wait, so is that how you got promoted to junior partner so fast?" I gape. "I *thought* it was weird, but you've been working there for years longer than I thought."

"I switched to the real estate concentration. I worked full time—more than full time, really—to put myself through school part time. I only graduated last year."

When I'm quiet a few beats too long, Milan gives me puppy-dog say-something-say-*anything* eyes.

He seems so nervous about what I'm going to make of all this, but how can I be anything other than awed? He's accomplished so much on his own to prove he wasn't a fuckup to his parents. He's done himself proud, and I don't know how to tell him that *I'm* proud of him, too.

I reach for his hand, settling my palm over his fingers and slotting my fingers in the valleys between his knuckles. He stills abruptly, breath caught on a gasp. His skin is warmer than mine, and even though there aren't any static shocks, my entire arm tingles. When I run my thumb over the inside of his wrist, *his* signature move, his upper body jolts, fingers flexing.

"Milan," I say, soft as down. "You're wrong. I want to know every version of you. The one who splurges on food because he knows I'll love it. The maddening man who will argue for the sake of arguing about two shades of blue tile that're almost exactly the same. The guy who uses even his failures to learn and succeed. We're both so much more than the sum of our parts."

Chapter 23

~~~~~~

I think this must be what closure feels like. The feeling follows me throughout the rest of the work week. I haven't been able to stop wondering what could have happened next if only he hadn't had to leave for a meeting so soon after our talk.

When I close my eyes and run the lightest of fingertips between my knuckles, my body comes to life the way it hasn't since—well, *since*. My cheeks flame. But all the same, it's no substitute for him.

To keep my hands busy, I get started stacking the shelves in the living room, intermittently texting Raj for details about her first date with Luke last night.

When I went back to the mainland for a tandoori dinner with my family for Aji's seventy-third birthday, Raj borrowed Harrie and Freddie ("But, Rita, think of the children! They need to socialize with their peers before they forget how!") to legitimize her presence at the dog park and stage a run-in.

It was utterly transparent, but from the goofy smile Luke wore when he saw her, apparently he was charmed by the subterfuge. Enough so that Raj asked if she could hold on to my doggos for longer ("Rita, you'll get so much more work done without them underfoot! *Pleeeeease*?").

I'm not sure what the past few days makes me and Milan. Friends? Or more than that?

Definitely more than friends. Raj sends. People who used to be as in love as you two were don't have a middle ground. You'll never be nothing to each other.

But that's what I'm afraid of. Now that he's back in my life, how can I say goodbye to him once this house is done if we've become "definitely more than friends" again? Bluebill gave us a shared space to orbit each other. Without it, what if we go back to the status quo?

That's why, trusting in fate to be on our side one more time, I logged in to MyShaadi last night to reset my old answers with true, honest ones. The kind I would fill out if I was really looking for the One. If Milan and I matched before with my bullshit answers, we *have* to now, too.

I chomp on my hearts-not-sticks pretzels while hoisting a stack of seven thin art books to a middle shelf of the bookcase. Their black and white spines compliment the monochrome world globe on the opposite end. I arrange more clusters of vertical books and separate them with an artsy bowl of pearlescent sea snail shells, framed around-the-world vintage postcards, and black horse head bookends. A spill of purple spiderwort trails down from the copper planter above.

When I'm done, I check my phone to find that Raj has sent me a picture of herself holding that horrific ceramic rooster to her face and feigning a horror movie scream while Freddie's buried his head behind the sofa cushions. And another of Raj and Luke out at dinner, sharing an appetizer plate of deep-fried ravioli.

A weird first-date present AND Italian food? I might be in love! reads her message.

Huh. Some guys bring flowers, some bring haunted roosters.

Smiling, I return to my shelves. A large purple geode goes on top of a leather-bound volume of poetry. They nestle between a Grecian bust pot with a thriving silvery green rex begonia and a framed floral needlepoint.

The rest of the books go up on the shelves in alternating horizontal and vertical stacks, leaving plenty of white space. I love to showcase books as art pieces, while using wire baskets to tuck away anything that doesn't quite fit my aesthetic. In my house in Goldsboro, it's usually the well-thumbed, dog-eared romance books featuring men with straining, sexy muscles, disheveled cravats, and just-ravished women in rumpled gowns that I don't want Aji to see. Not because she's a prude, but because she'll cheerfully make off with them in her purse.

The air shifts behind me. "These bookshelves are incredible."

My heart leapfrogs. "Hi, Milan." I hesitate, then say, "I really hoped you'd come today."

He's right about the shelves. Refinished to look brand-new, they seamlessly melt into the wall on either side of the blue-tiled living room fireplace. You can't even tell that these are the same junk bookcases Dad hauled from the curb.

The warmth of Milan's breath nips at my ear. "I remember when you painted them. They looked *nothing* like this before. So many clients, even the ones that don't even read a single book a year, want built-in bookshelves. It's a hot-ticket item."

His hand lands on my shoulder. Squeezes. "You added *a lot* of value to this house."

"I hope whoever moves in has the books to fill the space," I confess, not turning around. "Whenever I make something, I try to imagine the kind of person or family that's going to buy it. I imagined this shelf filled with yellowed, dog-eared paperbacks from a secondhand bookstore. Hardcovers that lost their dust jackets years ago, their corners worn smooth from rereading. Some picture frames up. Memories you'd want to see every day. Memories that take you back."

"This looks exactly like what you just described," says Milan, voice a low rumble. "Down to the well-loved books." A beat. "It's everything I'd want in my home."

He can't see me, so I don't need to bite back my smile, but I do it, anyway. "That's the perfect way to put it. Well loved. There's something about old things, right? Comforting favorites. A place in time you want to return to, revisit, like an old friend."

Like talking to him now, better than friends.

He touches my arm, warm fingertips on bare skin. I startle, whirling around.

He's standing close. Too close. I almost collide into him.

"Whoa," he says, hands coming up to steady my shoulders like I'm a spinning top. His warm thumbs slip into the sleeve of my black tee and he doesn't let me go.

Somehow, he seems more startled than I am.

My breath stalls in my throat when I see the look on his face. All masks dropped. Open, for-all-the-world-to-see yearning on his face. He lets me see it, doesn't throw the shutters up.

"That shirt's an old friend," he says, just the tiniest bit hoarse. He pinches the sleeve of my black tee between his thumb and forefinger. "You wear it a lot."

"I mean, I have a lot of black tees."

"Yeah, but you like this one the best," he states.

What a weird thing to say. I shoot him a confused *okaaaay* smile.

"You were wearing it the day we reunited, too," he says, an undefinable quality in his voice unlike anything I've heard before. "And about a dozen times since."

Curiosity leaps into my throat. If I asked, would he remember what I wore the first time he realized he was in love with me? The ditsy floral dress I wore when he gave me those forget-me-nots and teasingly made me promise not to forget him (as if I could even if I tried)?

His hands are still on my shoulders, and now I'm feeling dizzy for altogether another reason. His forehead is scrunched, intense, the way he looked when we were doing our homework together, only this time it's not a tough math problem he's trying to figure, it's me.

The warm pads of his thumbs inch further up my sleeves, gentle but a little rough, too, maybe from working on the house. My nipples stiffen against my bra and I instinctively strain forward, yearning to be crushed against the solid heat of his chest, but I draw back just in time.

"I remember what you were wearing the first time we reunited, too," I say instead, swallowing past the leapfrogs in my throat. "You looked like one of those hot, preppy guys in the American Eagle store windows. I was, like, he dresses like this on the daily just *because*?"

I think my comment flies over his head at first. No smart-alecky quip? No cocky comeback about the fact I called him hot and didn't try to backtrack?

Milan seems content to keep holding me, touching me. The friction of his thumbs skimming against my bare skin makes me jumpy and achy at the same time. These aren't his usual calming, trancelike circles. My cheeks burn. I want to know what this butterfly-light sensation would feel like in other places.

I'm pulsing for him. Though he's infinitely, teasingly tender,

I don't think he's aware of the arousal he's eliciting from me. That far-off look on his face, that restrained emotion in his eyes . . . These are new. If he picks up the tempo on his barely there caresses, I think I'd shatter right in his arms.

Belatedly, he laughs, but it's gravelly and strained. "I guess my color palette got more sophisticated since we dated. Figured out I liked colors other than gray and black."

I'd noticed. Has he cataloged the ways I'm different now, too?

I take his cue to pull out of the moment. I roll my shoulders away from him, and he lets me, but that contemplative expression doesn't leave his face once. A muscle in his jaw flickers when I rub my arms as if I'm warding off the cold, but in actuality, I'm trying to desensitize myself from the ghost of his touch.

"If only you'd realized that the million times I told you that when we were together," I say. "It would have made shopping for you so much easier."

"I mean, you could always buy me a present *now*," he drawls.

Back to banter and verbal sparring safe ground. Familiar, but possibly not any safer.

I roll my eyes. "Smooth. For what occasion?"

His smile is victorious. "Us, of course."

A giddy flutter of butterflies takes flight in my chest. Celebrate *us*? My startled laugh turns into a hacking cough. "What?"

He thumps my back. "For doing such a great job on this house."

It's an amazing job on this house, actually.

An hour later, right before we break for lunch, I've finished hanging a curtain of twinkly fairy lights against one of the glass panes in the dining room. It'll provide the perfect ambient lighting both inside and out. I switch them on before joining Milan at the old picnic table in the backyard.

We have some of the leftover charcuterie, mostly dried fruit, nuts, and cheese, to go with the simple tomato-basil soup and ham-and-cheese sourdough panini Milan made with some of my farmer's market produce.

He looks up from the screen of his Canon camera with a distracted smile as I drop into the seat next to him. My knee glances off his, but neither of us moves away.

"I was just about to call you to eat," he says. He notices the lights glittering in the window in front of him. "Wow. That's going to look terrific at night. Really romantic."

I reach for my sandwich. Some of the cheese has spilled out from the crust while frying, thin and crisp and deliciously golden. I snap it off and pop it into my mouth, where it crackles with the barest pressure. The cheese in the sandwich, however, is a different story, gooey with the nutty, buttery tang of swiss and the kick of pepperjack, multiplied with the crisp sharpness of dill pickles and dijon mustard.

Taste buds exploding, I close my eyes in satisfaction. Masala mac is without a doubt my number one go-to comfort food, but this piece of pure heaven is a close second.

"You're still a cheese fiend," Milan informs me, taking a sip from his Limca bottle.

I don't bat an eye. "Cheese is a very important food group."

His voice holds a smile. "I noticed you have a value-size bag of kid's string cheese in the fridge."

"Leave me and my cheese alone," I grumble good-naturedly.

He laughs, and oh my god, it warms me more than the oozing cheese. A reflexive, fizzy giggle rises in my throat. I shovel in a succession of quick bites until my cheeks bulge like a chipmunk's.

"Get anything good?" I ask around a mouthful, nodding to the camera he's holding.

He hums, angling the screen my way. "You tell me."

"You do realize an iPhone packs the same amount of power in a smaller package?"

One corner of his mouth crooks upward. "Who said I like small packages?"

I nudge his knee. "Quit being cute and show me."

It just slips out, but I'm big enough to admit that he's cute. He just *is*, no trying involved.

Milan's eyes flash like I've turned brown topaz in the palm of my hand to catch the light. He tries to hold back a laugh, but obligingly begins clicking through the pictures. He's done a great job with the composition and angles, showing the outside of the house to its best advantage.

He has the Before photos, too. Looking at the yellowing wall-paper and dull floors, the saltwater damage to the exterior paint-work, and the thick drapes smothered in so much dust Milan said he'd been on allergy medication for a week just reminds me how unloved Bluebill Cottage used to be.

Through spoonfuls of hearty, warming soup and bites of crusty panini, we discuss the listing, making sure to note every new update and improvement. We're listing it for so much more than he bought it for, so if we want any chance of recouping well over our costs, we have to show where the money went. Remodel-ing all the bathrooms and the kitchen, the professional cool blue exterior paint, the brand-new roof . . . It's unrecognizable from the Before pictures.

My heart wrings and my fingers tighten around the slim neck of the Thums Up glass bottle he handed me. Pictures mean we're one step closer to putting the house up for sale. One step closer to saying goodbye.

And maybe not just to the house.

"What do you think?" he asks eagerly. "I sent a few shots over to Josh because he was curious about the house that stole my heart, but— Oh, not that one." He hurriedly clicks through a handful of photos before I can see them.

"They're great. I . . . I really like them." I down the rest of my Indian cola drink.

The inevitability of our parting ways should have occurred to me when I was putting the final touches in the living room, arranging the bookshelves with objets d'art. We've ticked off just about everything on our to-do list. I don't even need to double-check on my phone's notes app, I just know.

I look to the sky, at the angry gray clouds rolling toward us, darker than they'd been on my way out here. Birds scatter above us, swooping over Bluebill Cottage as they head back toward the mainland. Fleeing like they sense a storm coming.

The first raindrop lands in Milan's scraped-clean bowl of soup. He hisses, reaching for the camera's lens cap. "Let's move this inside," he says.

We make it back with seconds to spare before the rain slakes down, hitting the windows hard enough for the house to tremble. As Milan secures the doors, I pile the last of our salvaged lunch on the kitchen counter, but my hand shakes at a sudden clap of thunder, sending the nuts rolling along the blue soapstone.

When our hands accidentally touch over the runaway almonds and he hooks his pinky around mine, it's hard to pretend it didn't happen.

"It's coming down hard," he says, pulling a bottle of bubbly from the fridge. "We can't get any work done, anyway, so might as well pop this open?"

I sink into the new emerald-green velvet settee that I'd covered with an old bedsheet for protection. "I— I thought you were saving that for our last day."

If we split it now, the sale of the house is all but inevitable. And while I always knew in my heart that this was going to happen, can't we put off the celebration until it actually sells?

"Let's seize the fucking diem," Milan declares, rifling through the drawers. "Where are the fresh kitchen towels?" he mutters under his breath.

I know where they are, but I don't tell him, hoping he won't find them.

No such luck. Older and wiser Milan doesn't give up that easy. "Success!" he crows.

Waiting for his return, I idly pick up Milan's camera. It's heavy in my palm, a satisfyingly solid weight. I can see why he prefers it. It hasn't turned off yet, so I go back to clicking through the images.

I click the wrong arrow button. There, between a picture of the freshened front porch and a coastal view of the house, is a picture of me.

My heart flies into my throat. I never posed for this.

And yet, you'd think I did. I'm working on the dining table, sanding it back, sweat glistening on my neck and damp baby hair slick on my forehead, but I'm smiling. Smiling big.

Not at Milan, and not even in the general direction of the camera, but I look happier than I've seen myself look, well, ever. And he caught it, immortalized the joy in that moment, with the most serendipitous of timing. As if he'd been watching me for a few minutes. Studying his subject. But he'd limited himself to just one photo. Why? Was that all he thought he could get away with before I noticed?

There's a muffled *pop!* and then a drawer in the kitchen

slides shut. I jump like I've been caught reading someone's diary. Quickly, I go back a few photos and set the camera on the end table without turning it off.

None the wiser, Milan joins me on the couch with a wide grin and two glasses of champagne. "To a job well done," he says, raising his glass to me.

I clink mine against his. "We're not finished yet."

"Spoilsport," he says, grinning against the rim of his glass.

When his mouth pulls away, there's a bead of champagne clinging to his lower lip that I absolutely don't notice, not at all.

"Hey, pass me the camera," he says suddenly. "I'll show you the rest."

"Oh, I— Okay."

With him on one end of the couch and me on the other, it's hard to view the small screen, so I scoot closer, only half listening as he enumerates the rest of the house specifications he's putting on the listing. I keep my eyes glued to the screen, nodding at the right intervals, waiting to see if he's sneaked in any more surreptitious photos of me.

He splits the rest of the bottle between us, giving me too much and leaving only half as much for himself. With a rueful, crooked grin, he shakes the bottle to get the last few drops out.

"Just take some of mine," I murmur, taking my eyes away from the screen.

My voice came out husky, inviting. The idea of his lips on my glass, maybe even overlapping where my mouth has been, is thrilling.

Milan stares at the glass I nudge toward him. His eyes are bright, maybe even feverish. "No, no, that's okay," he says, more to himself than to me, before he gulps down the remnants in his glass.

When his throat bobs with the swallow, my stomach up-downs, up-downs in a concurrent rise and fall. It's like being on a roller coaster on the way down.

"Um, should I put on the lights? It's gotten so dark outside." Milan switches on the table lamp closest to him, and then lunges forward to get the one behind me, but freezes when the side of his face brushes my cheek.

If I turn my cheek just a few degrees, we would meet. It takes every bit of self-control I have to stay still, waiting to see what he'll do.

"Uh, why don't you get that," he stammers, even though he's more than halfway there.

I sag with disappointment before forcing up a smile. "Yeah, no worries." My voice is twice the normal volume.

I twist around to turn on the lamp. By the time I face him again, he's pushed himself all the way back to his armrest, leaving the middle cushion in the no-man's-land between us.

The rain's coming down hard. The air electrified with the coming storm.

This wasn't on the weather radar.

"I swear it sounds like the roof is made of tin," he says, reading my mind.

I roll an almond between my thumb and forefinger. "It'll pass."

"I wouldn't mind if it didn't," he muses quietly. "If we could just stay like this." He darts a look up at me from under long, thick lashes.

He's been doing that ever since our foray to the farmer's market. Secret little stolen glances that I'm not meant to catch, but I do. Our eyes lock, and I'm the first to look away, embarrassed by the depth of the want in his eyes.

"Rita." There's a trace of panic in his voice. "Right now, us, here . . . It just makes me feel like this could be ours again. It's in our grasp."

When I don't answer right away, he jerks his head up. "Couldn't it be?"

It's what I've been asking myself since New Bern. A question that's burned my mind, hungering for an answer. I settle upon, "I wish it could be as easy as a yes or a no."

"Because you met someone on MyShaadi?"

I hesitate. "Not exactly. But there was someone I met on Tinder."

He sucks in a sharp breath. "Was it . . . serious?"

I have no clue how to answer this. What does *serious* even mean? Yes, I'd slept with Neil. He was my longest relationship since Milan. He'd wanted to marry me.

"Ish," I settle on.

We're sitting sideways now, our legs are tucked under us, knees close enough to bump if I move just a bit. His arm is stretched over the back of the couch, and every so often his fingers strum the air. As if he forgot himself for a moment, regressing to a time when he could reach out and tuck an errant strand behind my ear or massage the back of my neck.

To my disappointment, he catches himself every time, hand stilling as if he's struck the wrong chord and the discordant note is reverberating all around us.

"So then why are you looking on MyShaadi?" Milan asks. "Did you break up?"

He's doing his best to sound aloof, face a little closed off, but his eyes tell a completely different story.

So I tell him: about Amar, about Mom, about the chance meeting with Neil, about the Shaadi scam, and then, finally, about the breakup.

As I speak, he starts to play with my hair, idly, like he's not aware he's doing it. "What did you like about him?"

I tilt my head to lean against the couch. My hair, frizzy at the temples, wisps against his fingers. I feel a soft pull as his fingers instinctively curl. It takes every facial muscle I have not to grin like a clown at how incredible it feels.

"Do you really want to know?" At his nod, I say, "Neil seemed uncomplicated. No gross come-ons, no ego. And he was attractive. He made me laugh. Pretty basic reasons, I guess. Just a guy and a girl who met and talked and thought they'd maybe like to see each other again."

"So what changed?"

I roll my shoulders, getting more comfortable. "We wanted different things," I say. "He wanted a happily ever after and I wasn't looking that far ahead."

I tip my cheek into the path of his hand. I study him, his posture, the curve of his shoulders. In the soft, buttery lamplight, he's gilded in gold, light brown skin warm and honeyed.

"What about you?" I ask, stomach a writhing pit of snakes. "Have you dated much?"

Of course he has. Look at him.

"A few relationships," he acknowledges. "One that even lasted a year. Keiko was a little older than me, and had just got out of a nasty divorce. I found her a new place and we hit it off. But she wasn't looking for anything more than casual."

"Oh." A year is pretty serious. Longer than any of my boyfriends anyway. "Do you still love her?"

He shoots me a strange look. "I was never in love with her. Maybe I could have been, but I knew from the start she didn't want anything permanent. We're still friends. In the end, I think that's all she wanted, really."

Milan breaks into my thoughts when he asks, "Do you still love Neil?"

"I was never in love with him. I don't think he loved me, either. I think he saw it as the natural progression of our relationship. The obvious next step. And on some level, I knew it. I just ignored it, hoping he'd get the hint." I shake my head. "That was my biggest mistake."

"It can be hard when two people aren't at the same place at the same time," Milan offers. "Don't beat yourself up."

I know I will anyway, but I nod.

"Anyway, after Keiko, I joined MyShaadi," he says. "I used a junk email, you know, instead of my main one. The kind you sign up with for shit that you won't need more than once? I had some friends who'd met their then-girlfriends there and I figured, what the hell? But I wasn't looking to get married, and that's what most people on the site want."

"You weren't the only one who got suckered into giving it a chance. I did it purely for Aji, and got bombarded with matches I couldn't care twice about."

"Same," says Milan. "So I ditched the account without meeting anybody. That's why I was so shocked when you said you matched with me, because I thought there's no way they would be pimping me out after a year of inactivity. But then I remembered that after you told me you were on MyShaadi to meet 'reliable men,' I logged back in that same afternoon to see if by some chance we'd matched up, but we hadn't. It must have reactivated my status."

And he never got any of the email notifications that we matched multiple times because he used a junk email that he probably never checked.

"Do I know any of your exes?" I ask hesitantly.

Would we bump into them at Diwali parties, be forced to make small talk in line with them at the store? I want to cringe before I reality check myself. What am I *doing*? I'm already thinking in *we*, as if it's a given that Milan and I are a couple. Or that we will be, soon.

"No, you don't." He ignites my bones with the look he sends me now, all molten heat and shivery desire. Under the guise of stretching my back, I close the gap between us a little bit more.

Now two of his fingers graze my ear. Heat strobes over me when his pointer traces the edge without any urging. Soft and unhurried at first, then increasing the pace into an electric frenzy as the friction from the pad of his finger grows bold, traveling a featherlight caress to my lobe.

The unintended tickle wakes up my whole body, nipples peaking under my shirt. I lean into his touch, rewarded when his fingers slip into my hair, gripping hard. His wrist is nestled into the crook of my neck and shoulder, impossibly warm, exactly what I wanted, but now that I have it, I want more.

"Rita," he says in a rumble, maybe even a little exasperated. "What are you doing?"

"Something that is quite possibly a very bad idea," I whisper, inching closer and taking his hand with me.

"Definitely a bad idea," he agrees. His eyes draw me in like a tractor beam.

The thunder claps above us and we both startle, his fist grabbing hard enough to tug at my scalp. I gasp, arching my neck. It's a little rough, the way I like, and frenetic streaks of pleasure dart down my spine.

"Now," he whispers against my lips, throaty and sandpaper-delicious, "where were we?"

Milan's lips flutter over mine before touching down, moving slow and steady until my mouth opens to him. His hands run up my spine, soft fingertips dancing against the back of my neck as he pulls me closer, then closer still.

His hands settle on my waist, thumbs sliding up my heated skin. A soft mewl slips out of me when his warm tongue darts between my teeth. Our tongues meet, battle, then fall back. Tingles sweep over my jaw, electrifying and clustering in my ears until I'm cotton-eared and dizzy with want.

I bare my teeth and try not to cry in frustration. If I'm being honest, really honest, I'd love nothing more than to fuck him right here. But smarter, rational Rita is still in the driver's seat, and she talks me out of pushing him down and ripping off my shirt. Even if everything about being with Milan makes me feel as ravenous and giddy as I did as a teenager.

But there's still so much we haven't talked about, worked out.

I'm the first to break the kiss, gasping for breath. "We should . . . we should . . ." I can't seem to form the rest of the sentence.

"Keep kissing?" Milan suggests.

We should put up the new curtain rods and curtains.

God, I could just kick smarter, rational Rita's ass.

I could have spent the rest of the afternoon kissing him, but *nooooo*, I had to suggest getting back to work after we finished lunch. Now that I've kissed him again, I can't believe I ever stopped. My body is an ungrounded live wire, aching for Milan every time he looks my way, sending shooting stars down my limbs whenever he grazes my arm in passing.

When the last curtain goes up, Milan steps down from the stepladder with a regretful smile. "Rita, I hate to say it, but I have an open house tomorrow." He hesitates. "The rain's down to a drizzle. I could probably make the next ferry out. Plus . . . if I stay, I'm not sure we'd get anything else done. All I want is to—" He breaks off, turning away quick to walk to the door like he doesn't want to be talked out of it.

I don't want him to leave. I want the same thing he wants.

"Milan, I—"

He freezes, one shoe on his foot, the other hanging limp in his hand. "Yeah?"

"I don't know if the ferry will still be running."

It's not what I meant to say, and we both know it.

He hops into the other shoe. "Sure it will. It's not that bad out." He opens the door, letting in a gust of salt air. "See? No rain."

I peer out at the dark clouds gathering above. "I'm not so sure about that. Maybe you should stay—"

He grins at me over his shoulder, totally unfazed. "I'll text you when I reach mainland, okay? Lo— Later. See you later."

Chapter 24

The rain comes crashing down again ten minutes after Milan leaves. At first in dribs and drabs, light enough to be called a sprinkle, but then come the buckets. Sheets of rain hit Bluebill Cottage, mournful wind howling as the sky whorls a stormy black and gray.

I microwave a mug of tea for Milan, then hover at the window, mug clasped in my hands, and watch for his figure returning up the path.

By the time the herbal tea cools, Milan still isn't back, and he isn't answering his cell phone. Lightning breaks across the sky, splintering a dozen different directions. What if he's caught out in the storm and thinks he's better off continuing to town instead of turning back?

The next clap of thunder shakes the entire house. At this point, it's only a matter of time before the electricity goes out. Luckily Milan had already stocked plenty of flashlights, candles, and hurricane lamps just in case.

It's the *just in case* that's worrying me now. Planning for the eventuality of something bad happening.

Ugh. I should have insisted on calling ahead to make sure the ferry was still running before he left. There's no way they're making the trip in this weather.

I get through to Ken in the ferry office. "Hi, it's Rita. I'm out on Rosalie right now and I was wondering whether the ferries—"

He anticipates what I'm about to ask. "No. There's already more than a dozen dripping people taking shelter in here who didn't make it off the island in time. We're canceling service the rest of today."

"Um, would you happen to know if Milan made it to the office?"

Ken knows us. He's usually the one at the counter window when we buy tickets.

"Sorry, Milan's not here. Possible he ducked into a restaurant or something when it started to pour."

I thank him and hang up, trying not to panic. Yeah, that's gotta be it, he probably just found somewhere else to take cover. He's a grown man who can take care of himself and service on the island is spotty even on the best of days, but rationality is overridden by one thought and one thought only: Why isn't he calling me back?

I drink the tea just to have something to do, wash the cup, and then reuse the teabag. Forty seconds into microwaving my second cup, the electricity goes out.

I'm plunged into darkness, with my still-lit phone screen the only source of light.

BANG BANG BANG!

I jump. It's the first time since I've been on the island that I'm actually a little afraid to be all by myself, without even Harrie and Freddie here for comfort.

I peer through the peephole, heart going a hundred miles an hour. "Milan!" I exclaim, throwing open the door. "Oh my god, get in here."

He drips his way across the wood floor, muttering something about needing some more rugs in the entryway, which I ignore, working at the buttons on his shirt. He doesn't even make a wisecrack about me divesting him of clothing. He's shivering, arms wrapped tight around himself. He stays still and lets me peel his shirt from his arms.

"Wait here, I'm getting you a towel," I instruct.

When I return, I find that he's slung his shirt and shorts over his arm, but has stayed on his feet to keep from soaking the couch. His hair is plastered to his forehead in stringy wet-dog waves. While Milan towels himself off, I wring his clothes out over the sink and hang them to dry on the back of a chair I drag from the dining room. Jumping into action makes it easier not to think about the fact that he's two feet away, wearing nothing but boxers.

After he finishes the lukewarm mug of hot honey tea, he starts a fire in the grate and lights the hurricane lamps, casting the room in a soft, buttery glow.

"Oh, shoot, I should have gotten you a sheet," I say.

He gestures at himself. "No, I'm fine. See? I'm not cold anymore."

I run my eyes over him. He's finger-combed his hair to lie smooth, and except for the slight curl at the end, it does seem mostly dry. Likewise, his boxers have dried enough to tell they aren't black, as I first thought, but navy.

"Are you done eye-sexing me?"

My cheeks burn. I glare. "Stop trying to be cute."

His face is way too innocent for the way he purrs, "I don't have to try."

I get him a sheet, anyway, insisting he wrap it around himself if he doesn't want me to do it for him. He looks intrigued, but obliges, wearing it around his shoulders like a cape.

"Another second and I'd have run into the rain after you," I tell him, pulling a chair closer to the fire. The heat will hopefully take care of his clothes, but it'll take a few hours.

His eyes sparkle, or maybe it's just the flames dancing in his dark irises. "In that case, we'd both be sharing this. Darn. A missed opportunity."

"Ha-ha. If only the washer and dryer had been delivered on time, and the power didn't go out."

"What time do you think it is?" he asks, stifling a yawn.

"Dinnertime?" I check my phone. "Yup. It's almost seven."

What I really want on a cold, rainy night is hot soup and a crusty baguette, but we don't have either. So we scarf down some saltine crackers, apple slices, and manchego cheese, washing it down with the last bottle of lemon-lime Limca soda I'd stocked in the fridge, knowing how much he loved it.

Milan adds more logs to the fire. "I'm going to get some more. Want anything?"

"I'll just have some of whatever you're getting," I say, distracted by the sight of a red bubble on my email app. I tap it on reflex.

Sender: *MyShaadi.com*

Subject: *Rita, the only thing better than one match is two!* ❤ ❤

I don't even look at the preview, just open the email and follow the link to go to my account. My heart batters against my rib cage as I wait for the page to load.

I want it to be Milan. I want it to be him so bad.

By the time I remember the shitty reception here, Milan's returned to the couch with a tub of hummus and crackers. He gestures to the middle seat and makes as if to stretch his legs out. "Do you mind?"

I don't. "Go for it."

"Did you get service?" he asks while loading his cracker with hummus.

"N— Yes!" By some miracle, I have one bar. The shortest, tiniest bar, but it's *there*.

He looks amused. "I'm still out," he informs me.

The page still hasn't loaded.

Earlier today he wanted to know if I could see a second chance with him. But as the seconds tick by, I realize I don't need MyShaadi to tell me what I already feel.

It doesn't matter if an algorithm thinks we're a match. Even if we're one hundred percent perfect for each other. Many clever someones rigged dating science with data science to create MyShaadi, but the fact is Milan and I *aren't* perfectly matched.

That was always our mistake, thinking that we were.

We were together for six years and apart for six more.

If we're going to try again, to rebuild what was broken, we have to face that we weren't perfect then, and we aren't perfect now. It took us six years to talk to each other, to figure out what went wrong. To have a simple conversation.

"You're quiet," Milan comments. His foot nudges my knee.

I'm about to say *I'm thinking* when I realize I'm not thinking anymore.

"Is this what you hoped would happen from the moment we met at my parents'?" I ask.

Milan runs a hand over his face and into his hair as if he's suddenly shy. "I never stopped hoping. It just seemed like you had moved on. I mean, I used to look you up online. Eventually

I stopped because it didn't look like there was room for me anymore. But I should have fought for you, even fought *with* you. Should have talked to you, period."

"We're talking now." Tired of fighting the impulse, I reach out to cover his hand with my own. "I . . . I can't deny that I'm drawn to you. And this is the last thing I thought we'd be working on today. Us." I laugh under my breath.

"Oh, yeah?" His tone is deceptively light. "What did you think we'd be doing?"

I'm thinking of the work on the house still to be done. But his eyes are dark and smoldering, fixed on me. Without even being aware of it, he wets his lips.

He wants me. He's not exactly being subtle about it.

And that gives me a certain power.

I want to tell him—not that I love him, even though I think I maybe do—that high school sweethearts Rita and Milan are gone, we can't be them again, but that we can be who we are *now*. And maybe there *is* a second chance for older and wiser Rita and Milan.

Deliberately, letting him feel every inch of the innuendo, I say, "I guess I hadn't figured on us spending much time talking at all."

His eyes darken. After a long exhale, he says, "Right. Because we'd be hard at it."

My upper lip twitches halfway into a smile.

His eyes flare. "At work, I mean!"

Side-stitch laughter overwhelms me and I dissolve, clutching at my middle and hunching over. Without thinking about it, I nudge my toes against his ankle.

He yelps, but traps my foot under his hand. "How are your toes this cold in August?!"

I could pull back, but he makes no move to let me go.

There's nothing cute about my bare feet after weeks of hiding them in sturdy working boots and sneakers. There's one lone hair on my big toe, a little ashiness across the joints, and speckled remnants of old nail polish. My feet are nowhere near summer sexy, ready for sandal and flip-flop weather. But he doesn't seem to notice.

"It's just so easy to be with you. It's the ultimate illusion of no time having passed at all." He scrapes his front teeth over his bottom lip. "Don't you feel it, too?"

Of course I do. How could I not?

"Yes," I say quietly, even though what I mean is: I know there's no way we'll ever be able to afford to keep this house for us, but I'm still designing it like it is. I'm not nearly as fearless as you think I am, but you make me want to be brave and take a second chance on us.

"It's still coming down hard," he says finally, swiping his finger into the tub of hummus when he runs out of crackers. "Luckily there's enough food to see us through the weekend."

I eye his finger, which he's brought to his mouth. Right as he's about to stick it in, I say, "You didn't ask me if I wanted any."

He pauses. "Do you?"

"I want you."

"You should have told me before I finish— Wait, what did you say?"

I reach for his wrist, bringing myself closer. Keeping my eyes trained on his, I draw his finger into my mouth. His soft gasp as I scrape my teeth lightly over his slim digit is everything I remember it being.

That look of unguarded surprise he wears takes me back to the first time I went down on him and every time after, fingernails trailing over pale thighs, the tip of my warm tongue recreating the sensation. The way he didn't want to finish too fast and come in my mouth battling with the dazed look on his face, head thrown back and fists clutching in my hair, in his sheets, as he came undone.

"Rita," says Milan, voice impossibly strained. His eyes are dark and filled with want.

I swirl my tongue over the pad of his pointer finger, feeling his full-body shudder all the way in my mouth. My lips glide back and forth, taking him in all the way to the first knuckle.

"Rita," he says again, this time with more insistence.

I slip his finger free. "Do you want me to stop?"

The question in his eyes grows. "You want me for tonight or for forev—for longer than just tonight? Because I'm telling you right now, I don't want to be another Neil to you." Raggedly, "I want you. And, god, I can't believe I'm saying this, but not if sex is *all* that—"

I press my finger to his lips, cutting him off. "Sex isn't all I want."

"It's not?"

"No. I also wanted that hummus." I can't hold a straight face for more than a second.

"You also wanted—" He has to bite his lip to keep from laughing. "I am not laughing. This is me not finding that funny at all. You are terrible, Rita."

"Yes," I murmur, moving to straddle him. "I'm *sooooo* mean in my old age."

"Very mean," he agrees, sliding his hands up my shirt, around the curve of my breasts, and up my collarbone to finally settle around my neck. "It makes me almost not want to kiss you right now."

"Mmm, but that punishment doesn't fit the crime," I whisper. "You'll have to be a bit more creative."

His lips brush mine in a slow, lingering caress, but he denies me when I try to deepen the chaste touch. "I can be creative," he says in my ear, low enough for all the words to run together.

He trails his tongue down my earlobe to the shivery place where my pulse leaps to meet him. "I have protection," he says, nipping at my skin.

My neck arches, allowing him better access. "I'm on birth control," I say through a gasp, fisting his hair by the roots.

Milan breaks contact just long enough to grab a condom, returning to me with wild, flushed cheeks and a heady grin. He plants soft kisses along the column of my throat, working his way back to my jaw, and finally, *finally*, my lips.

When he pulls away for breath, he takes some of my lip balm with him, the gloss smudged across his swollen upper lip. I flash back to the fruity, sticky lip gloss I had to wipe off his chin when we were fifteen and hiding around hallway corners from teachers to kiss in peace.

He hisses when I adjust myself over him, pressing into his hardness. His fingers press against my hips, sliding under my black tee. "I've wanted to rip this off you the first time I saw you wearing it and every time since."

And then he does.

Chapter 25

I wake up on the floor rug with Milan's arm around me, tucked into the dip of my waist. My chin is warm from his chest as I wriggle off my stomach, yawning against him. The blanket slides down my back and I try not to yelp at the sudden cold. I have a vague memory of him pulling it off the settee in the night to cover us.

It's still dark outside, but with a silvery strip gleaming on the horizon, it must be early morning. I gingerly root around for one of our phones to check the time.

"What is it?" he mumbles, voice groggy and sleep heavy.

"I was trying not to wake you," I whisper back.

"Check between the cushions," he says with a yawn, not opening his eyes.

It's cute how sweetly boyish he looks, face slack and lips pouty. Hair tousled from my fingers. His chin is tucked into his chest and there are pillow marks on his cheek from the settee cushion he pulled off last night. I'm not ready to wake up, either, not if it means facing the day after what we did in the dark.

Everything could look different now.

But I don't feel any differently, my brain argues. If I had a chance to redo last night, I'd do everything the same.

Milan's arm tightens around me, nuzzling close. "I can hear you."

"I didn't say a word." I cast my eye around for my clothes and find my bra slung on the armrest behind his head and my black tee puddled on the floor along with my oxblood shorts.

I feel him smile into my hairline. "You think loud," he says.

I tilt my chin up, about to kiss him, when I remember the way Neil would freeze for a split second before returning it. "Sorry," I say swiftly. "Morning breath."

Milan's eyebrow quirks upward in a *Yeah, so?* expression. His eyes wear an expectant gleam, a what-are-you-waiting-for urgency, and I want to go for it, but something holds me back.

And then it's too late to recapture the moment.

"I need to pee. Have you"—I look around us—"seen my thong?" My nipples have pebbled hard enough to cut glass and shivery bumpies have prickled my breasts.

He shakes his head, lips downturned, so I pull my bra and shirt over my head and slip into my shorts.

I peck his cheek. "Back in a jiff."

He shoots me a slow, drowsy smile that morphs into a huge tonsil yawn.

When I get to the bathroom, I do more than that, brushing my teeth vigorously to get rid of the sour aftertaste. I rub my thumb to clean the bristles and make up my mind to offer my toothbrush and what's left of the squeezed-out toothpaste to Milan if he wants.

When I get back all the lights are on, flooding the downstairs with light.

"We got electricity back," says Milan, wearing only his boxers. "I started breakfast."

The cheap coffee machine is sputtering away on the counter next to the food we didn't stick back in the fridge, the microwave's clock has reset to zero, and my annoying seven a.m. alarm is going off with no sensitivity to the fact we only fell asleep a few hours ago.

"Ugh, would you turn that off?" I ask, massaging my temple.

"Yeah, no problem."

"Oh, and you can use my toothbrush if you want to, uh—" I use a finger to mime the back and forth motion.

My finger so close to my mouth brings back memories of last night for both of us, if his heated stare is any indication. Looking at him in the bright light of day is weirdly uncomfortable considering where his face was last night, but I can't look away. Heat suffuses my cheeks.

"It's okay. I finger brushed over the sink," he says, sounding hoarse.

While Milan starts cracking eggs, humming some catchy tune from the radio, I fold the sheet and start rearranging the settee cushions, mentally kicking myself for acting like an awkward first timer.

It's not like there weren't guys along the way, but my god, his moves last night were absolutely *nothing* like our first time. Where did he learn how to—

The memory of last night's double orgasm threatens to rock me again.

I want to know about the other women, but I also *don't* want to know.

The house is so goddamn cold. The fire went out sometime between sucking him off and his getting me off in *several* different ways, because with only one condom, we could just go the one round of missionary.

"See?" he had said, smug as a cat, head between my legs. "I can get creative."

A+++ for tremendous pluck and outside-the-box thinking in the face of adversity.

I try not to giggle; his boss truly has no idea what kind of asset he has in Milan Rao.

His shorts are still damp and his shirt is hopelessly wrinkled, and he's making scrambled eggs in the kitchen shirtless, with the same hands he did things with last night, and it's all so surreal that for a moment I can't breathe.

We said so much last night that I think we both feel inexplicably shy this morning. Milan plates up leftover cold salami and hot-from-the-pan scrambled eggs in silence, turning red when I mumble my thanks. His eggs are surprisingly soft and fluffy, unlike mine which end up either too wet or too dry.

"So," I say, breaking the silence as I spear some eggs on my fork.

He glances up.

I don't know where I'm going with this, so I let it stand at *So*.

He returns to eating, sneaking shy little peeks at me when he thinks I'm not looking. I guess I'm not the only one feeling a little out of sorts.

But then I catch him making a face at the coffee like it's rancid before swallowing.

"Did the creamer go bad?" I ask.

He struggles to clear his expression. "No, it's just . . . you bought the regular unflavored creamer."

"It's *hazelnut*." I take a tentative sip. "Milan, it's fine. You had me thinking it'd spoiled."

"You're still such a coffee purist," he says with a crooked smile. "Café Bustelo, cane sugar, and 'a creamer that won't compete with the flavor of the coffee.'"

That *does* sound like something I'd say.

He pushes the rest of the mug toward me. "I gotta admit, though, it's a relief that you're still exactly the same. Popsicle toes and too-strong coffee."

Something about the way he says "still exactly the same" gives me pause. Sure, there are parts of me that are still fifteen and sixteen and all the years leading up until now, but we have to be different, don't we, if we're going to make it work this time?

He thinks it's a good thing, a *comforting* thing that there are parts of each other that we still recognize. But we have to learn each other again. Map out more than just our bodies, but our hearts and minds, too.

I'm not sure he gets that.

I roll my eyes. "You can't even call it coffee with how much creamer *you* use. Do you have a new novelty flavor favorite?"

"Toasted marshmallow. No, wait. Cinnabon. Nah, it's gotta be peppermint."

I groan. "Milan."

We finish breakfast, half-heartedly arguing about the top ten list of flavors Milan has put *entirely* too much time into narrowing down. And since he cooked, I wash up.

My phone chimes while the water's still running. Figuring it's Raj updating me on last night, or this morning, depending on whether Luke's still there or not, I let it go.

"The sky's clear," says Milan, pushing aside the white linen living room curtains to peer outside. He had gotten dressed while I was at the sink. "I wish I had some fresh clothes."

I come up behind him to wrap my arms around his middle. "You know, you could just leave a spare outfit here."

He twists to look at me. "We're not going to be here much longer, Rita."

"No, there's still—" I falter, unable to think of more than a few things we have left to do.

He's right. Another few days and the house will be ready to list.

"Hey." He cups my face, his thumb tipping my chin up. "Don't be sad," he says softly.

I hug him to me a little tighter. "It's bittersweet, is all."

He inclines his head, agreeing. "Sure, but it doesn't mean the end of you and me. We made this house strong, set it up to last. Just like us."

How is he so confident? We weren't strong six years ago, the first time we were tested. Is it just faith that we'll make it another six years?

At least.

"Hey, got something kinda cool to show you." Milan pulls his phone from his back pocket. "I logged in to MyShaadi last night."

"Oh?" I already suspect what he's going to show me.

The screen faces me. I'm his newest match, my name and photo at the very top.

I'm in a knee-length pink chiffon dress with a nipped waist, caught in motion looking over my shoulder, hair styled piece-y and askew, blurred rows of vineyards behind me.

It's an old photo, but a favorite, and one of the few where I'm wearing a dress, looking like an Anthropologie girl.

"Is this from the trip to your roommate's family's vineyard in the Bay Area you took sophomore year?" he asks softly.

I nod against his back before remembering he can't see me. "Yeah. It was a good trip."

"We'll have to plan something of our own pretty soon," he says, giving me a quick glance to gauge my reaction.

"Yeah. I'd love that."

The smile splits across his face. "Great." His thumb hovers over the accept button. "Wanna make it official?"

Without waiting for an answer, he pushes the button. Fireworks explode around my picture, something I've never seen before, and linger around the frame.

I blink. "Is that what happens when you accept somebody? It's so . . . cheesy."

"I don't know, it's kind of sweet, isn't it?" Milan shrugs. "Celebrating that you could have found the One." He twists around to face me, arms enveloping me into his warmth. "You've always been that person for me, Rita. I didn't need MyShaadi to tell me that."

I feel like we're on the precipice of something big, and rise on my tiptoes to brush my nose against his. "Good."

I ghost my lips over his, a featherlight barely-there caress, but the moment shatters at a loud, familiar WhatsApp beep from one of our phones.

"It's not me," he whispers against my mouth.

"I should check who it is."

He groans, tightening his arms around me. "No, don't. I promise you it won't be as important as this."

I laugh at the abject disappointment on his face. "I'll be *right* back."

But when I open the app, all color drains from my face. I think I'm forming words, but what comes out is a series of unintelligible mouse squeaks.

Milan surges forward. "Rita? What is—"

I show him the message from my dad, too shaken to even make a smart-ass quip about how my dad signs all his messages -*Dad* as if he wasn't a saved contact.

> Hi, chinu-minu, Mom wanted it to be a surprise (shhhhh) but
> we just stepped off the ferry. Getting a taxi with the Raos
> to visit the house we keep hearing about. Hope the warning
> helps. -Dad

"*Hurry up!*" I hiss, sweeping the curtain aside. "The taxi's here already."

I tamp down the terror when not just Mom and Dad pile out, but a grumpy-faced Aji, too. Milan's parents get out from the other side, and both men start to argue about who's going to pay the driver. That'll buy us a minute or two, at most, before they climb up to the house.

Milan's thrown all the cushions off the couch. "Rita, I still haven't found your underwear."

My hair starts to sweat at the thought of one of our dads finding the wisp of red lace. Or worse . . . Aji. She'd probably pick it up and ask what it was.

Would anyone believe me if I said I'd been folding laundry and lost it? Somehow?

"Oh my god, this is how we die," I moan.

Thanks to Dad's message, we had some time to frantically clean up, but we're cutting it close.

"Listen," says Milan, "in no way am I saying one of our parents finding your panty is an ideal situation—"

"Ha! You think?" I scoff.

"But what's the big deal if they know we're back together?"

I let the curtain drop. We've been dancing around it, but it's the first time it's been crystallized.

Back together.

My brow furrows. Is that what we are?

"We already know our parents want it to happen," he says, getting up. As he rearranges the cushion seats, he flashes me a grin and dangles the condom wrapper between two fingers. "Success!" he crows, carrying it to the trash. "Hey, maybe we could even fill out one of those MyShaadi testimonials, huh?"

It's a joke—I think—but the warning bells go off, panic sprinting in my chest as Neil's voice echoes *It's in the goddamn name.* Just because Milan and I reconnected yesterday doesn't mean we're anywhere close to having a shaadi of our own. Why would he even *go* there?

I can't *not* say something.

Slowly, I say, "Milan, those testimonials are for couples who have decided to get married. Shaadi success stories. Not dating stories."

"Yeah, yeah, I know," he says, fluffing a throw pillow before setting it back on the couch at an angle. "But our parents stopping by the morning after we work everything out? That's pretty coincidental." His grin turns teasing. "One might even throw the word *fate* around."

"Oh, might one?"

He hears the caustic bite to my words and peeps at me from under lowered eyelashes.

Tempering my voice, I say, "We talked, sure, but I wouldn't say we worked absolutely everything out. 'One' might even say we didn't work anything out."

"But we slept together."

"Milan." I give him a look. "Sometimes sex can just be sex."

"Not to me," he says. "And you said you wanted more than just sex." He goes still all of a sudden. "No, wait," he says haltingly. "You made a joke. You didn't actually say you wanted to get back together. You knew what I was asking, but you sidestepped it."

"I wasn't sidestepping anything," I tell him. "Last night was step one. But you're racing to step, oh, I don't know, five?"

Confusion clouds his eyes. "I thought we were on the same page," he says carefully, like the wrong words might spook me.

"I do want another chance with you, Milan," I say. "But we need to talk about our past. I don't want to pretend that the last six years apart didn't happen."

"Why not? I don't want to waste another second. You're the same girl I loved then and the same woman I love now. You're the one I want to spend the rest of my life with, Rita."

I love him for his conviction. But Rita-from-then and Rita-right-now are two separate people, and he doesn't see it that way. Or maybe he just doesn't want to acknowledge it.

"I don't want to jump into anything," I say. "I want to keep this for ourselves right now. Can you imagine how insufferable our moms will be once they find out that they pulled this off?"

Tension snaps into his shoulders. His jaw takes on a mulish set. "So you can pull the Shaadi scam to trick your mom, but our moms joining forces to set us up, to get us in the same room again, *that's* a step too far?"

I didn't tell him about Neil and MyShaadi so he could use it against me. I flatten my lips into a thin line. "That's not even close to the same thing. What *I* did was a defense tactic. Our moms' play was totally on the offensive."

"But it worked out," he argues.

"Worked out? We only talked, *for real* talked, yesterday. It hasn't even been a full day yet. We haven't even given this a chance to see where it goes."

"'Where it goes'?" he repeats.

He says that like it was already a foregone conclusion.

Didn't he hear anything I told him about Neil? Didn't he *listen* when I said I wasn't looking to be rushed into marriage?

There's a loud one-two, one-two thump at the front door. We're out of time.

"Just tell me this," he says as I move to open the door. "Do you even love me?"

Another knock. Women's voices blur together. I can hear my mom ask whether she should call me, make sure I'm even here. In a moment, my phone will ring.

Milan's waiting for my answer.

"Yes," I say. My heart plummets into my stomach.

Joy blooms over his face. He doesn't see the *but* coming.

I wish I didn't have to say it like this. I wish my next words won't rob that walking-on-the-moon elation that crinkles his eyes, curls his lips.

"But it's like my furniture, Milan," I say in a rush. "You can't just take something broken and magically decide to fix it. You have to sit with it, figure out if it's even doable. Some jobs need glue, some might need a stronger fix. Some things are too broken to be fixed at all, but you *can*—"

When my WhatsApp ringtone goes off, he cuts in. "Got it. We're the broken furniture. You think at the slightest provocation, the slightest weight, we're going to collapse." His mouth twists. "Like a badly assembled flat-pack dining table."

My heart crumples like an unwanted love letter. "No, that's not what I was saying at *all*."

Just as I'm about to explain where I was going, what he didn't let me finish, he beelines to join me at the front door with an arm outstretched, about to let our families in. His hand glances mine, a surreal echo of meeting at High Castle when he tried to open the door I was perfectly capable of getting for myself. This time, though, he doesn't prolong the moment, the shared limbo of not breathing for a second because we're standing so close.

He shatters it like a toppling pane of glass and doesn't bother to pick up the pieces.

"Hey, Mom," he says, throwing open the door. "What a surprise!"

Chapter 26

~~~~~

Once everyone's in the living room, our parents exchange curious glances with each other—and at us.

"Since we caught the first ferry of the day, and we didn't see *you* on it, Milan, you must have spent the night," says Aji, with her usual penchant for saying what everybody is thinking.

Milan's dad visibly shrinks from secondhand embarrassment, but his mom perks her head toward us like she wants all the juicy details.

Dad coughs and gives a little shake of his head.

Aji, unperturbed, fixes Milan with a shark-eyed I've-got-your-number-buddy look.

Our families have spent a lot of time together since high school, but this is definitely the most awkward scene I've ever witnessed.

"Well, with the storm, ferries probably weren't running last night, right?" Mom asks, breaking the silence.

"Yup," I say, latching on quick. "He got drenched trying to make the last one, and had to turn back."

Everyone looks at the wrinkles in Milan's shirts as if they're noticing them for the first time. His mother makes a dismayed sound and tries to smooth his collar, but it's hopeless.

While they're distracted, I cast a quick glance over the living room floor for my underwear. Try to peek in the crevice between the couch cushion and the armrest. How can a wisp of red fabric be so difficult to find?

Mr. Rao is taking in the room decor with undisguised interest. When he catches my eye, he gives me a broad, encouraging smile. What he makes of my squirrelly eye contact, heaven alone knows.

I swallow. On the other hand, thank god my red thong *is* hard to spot.

Then his eye travels to the fireplace surround, the beautiful blue tiles, the vintage poker stand, the ship in a bottle perched on the mantel . . .

Red thong wadded up in the corner of the rug where no one thought to look.

Please let no one see it.

Slowly, I start edging toward it, hoping I can swipe it before anyone's the wiser.

Unfortunately, this is the exact moment that the conversation dwindles and everyone turns to look expectantly at me.

Dad looks toward the fireplace with a trace of desperation. "I'm glad you stripped first."

I freeze in horror. I was wrong. *This* is the most awkward conversation I've had to date.

I follow Dad's gaze to the two old bookshelves he had found discarded on the sidewalk.

Oh thank god. He's talking about the finish.

Aji gets a Harrie-like gleam in her eyes. "Rita, chunnu, is that—"

"I was folding laundry last night," I blurt out at the same exact moment Milan says, boisterously loud, "So that's where my dust rag went!"

"Arey deva," whispers Mrs. Rao.

Mr. Rao proudly claps his son on the back. "We taught him well."

"Because I taught *you* well," says his wife.

To the rest of us, Mr. Rao adds, "Since childhood, he's seen me doing little jobs around the house. In my mother's house, I was a prince, but when I got married . . ." He grins.

"Yes, I can see *exactly* where he's been applying himself," says Aji.

"Okay, then!" says Milan, slapping his thighs. "Time for a tour?"

I don't know how we get through the next half hour of giving our families the full tour of Bluebill Cottage. Milan takes them from room to room, back in real estate agent mode, giving me another glimpse of the man he became when I wasn't looking. He's generous with praise, making sure to give me credit for every idea and addition I brought to the house, and is patient with our parents' questions.

Mr. Rao avoids eye contact, focusing on a spot somewhere beyond my right ear when he directs anything to me, and Mrs. Rao keeps glancing between me and Milan with a feverish anticipation, trying to spy any affectionate gestures or touches that will give us away.

Little do they know we're currently in a cold war (and trying so hard not to look like it that we've gotten marionette smiles on our faces and wooden stiffness in our shoulders).

His parents don't know a whole lot about woodworking or

restoration, so they're content to listen and nod, wandering the rooms with naked interest. Dad, not Milan's biggest fan after our breakup, quizzes him about things he doesn't have the faintest idea about, and Aji demands chai, which I don't have, but I grab on to it as an escape hatch.

"I don't have any loose tea. Herbal okay?" I ask when Mom returns to the kitchen where I'm laying out snacks left over from Milan's charcuterie board. We've gotten ridiculous mileage out of his extravagance.

She eyes the peppermint packet I tear into and pulls her mouth to one side in doubt.

Oh well. That's what the old bat is getting.

"What do you think of the place?" I ask, sticking my only mug in the microwave.

"It's the kind of house I could imagine you living very comfortably in."

"Yeah, that's what I was going for. A house anybody would be thrilled to call home."

"Not just anybody." She slants me a sharp look. "It has you written all over it."

"Oh. Huh. Cheese?" I hold out a cube of mango-habanero cheddar.

She shakes her head. "Barely any glasses, but three different kinds of crackers and cheese," she says mildly.

"I wasn't expecting company," I say, a little embarrassed that all we have to offer tap water in are two regular water glasses, two wine goblets, and a mug that up until a half hour ago was filled with coffee.

And then I'm annoyed with myself, because these aren't my in-laws and I'm not their hostess, but I'm stressing like I am, especially with my parents added to the mix. Who even shows up uninvited anymore?

But it's not them I'm mad at so much as Milan. Who had an opportunity to talk through our issues, but chose to run from them. I grit my teeth together to keep my lips from trembling.

I will not cry. I will *not* cry.

"Honey, it's fine." Mom's eyes soften. "We didn't come here to be waited on."

"Why *did* you come?" I hear how waspish it sounds, but it's too late. "Sorry. I'm just a little cranky this morning."

She lays her hand on top of mine. "Don't be so suspicious. You weren't answering your phone last night so Dad and I decided we'd come out here to see how you were doing. That storm got a little scary, and when we couldn't get through to you—" She swallows. "Well. I worry."

I pull her into a one-armed hug. She sinks into my side like she was waiting for it, but it's more for me than for her. I take in the fresh, bright scent of orange-blossom shower gel and the smoky sweetness of sandalwood incense and for one outrageous second, I feel like I could tell her anything right now, even the history with Neil.

"Something is different between the two of you," she states.

Panic flares down my neck that she knows, that there's some weird post-sex glow that people can see sticking on my skin. Raj has a good instinct for it, but Mom? Can't be.

Mom's face settles into sympathy. "You've had a fight."

"I—yeah."

She clucks her tongue. "You've been working too hard."

I make a noncommittal sound, plucking the mug out of the microwave when it beeps.

"No, it's true," says Mom. "When two passionate people work closely together—"

"This sounds creepily like the 'when a man and a woman really love each other' talk—which was totally heteronormative, by the way—you gave me when I got my first period."

She pulls her gray wool cardigan around her and straightens to her full height. "Rita."

"Mom. I don't want to talk about this. Okay?" I plead.

She doesn't relent. "Let's go outside for a minute." There's a steel in her voice that isn't often there, and so, after a moment of hesitation, I follow her to the porch.

We sit on one of the benches, which was once broken and unloved, that I refinished with a deep walnut stain and plenty of Danish oil to bring back its shine. The seating cushions are too new and plump to be comfortable, but Mom doesn't say a word.

In fact, she's quiet for so long that I wonder if she forgot why she called me out here at all. She stares at the water, at the dreary gray sky, a tenseness to her mouth like she's weighing what she's about to say. Then she expels a breath so long and so heavy that I can't help but wonder what demons have been exorcized with it.

"Sometimes people, even when they're suited for each other, even when they love each other, scrape against each other in small spaces. Friction. Especially when—"

I lean toward her. "Yes?"

"—you live in the same place as you work. The way the two of you were just now in front of everyone . . . I recognized myself in you," Mom says, sighing as though the admission costs her. "I knew at once we'd interrupted something. And no, not what Aji none too subtly hinted at. We'd walked into a moment that wasn't over. From the way you two were so rigid, after all these weeks of working together, I knew, I just *knew*, that something had just happened before we arrived. That you two were waiting for us to leave to continue the argument." She peers at me, worried. "Am I right?"

I jerk my head up down, up down.

Her eyes sadden. "When Milan's mom and I got talking at the temple's Holi festival last year—all about you kids and what you were up to these days—we didn't set out to set you up together. We only became close again recently, and we thought we were doing the right thing by not involving you kids in our friendship. But then, when we chatted again at the potluck and she said Milan had a problem-house, well, it seemed like the perfect solution to give you both a second chance. Things were so awkward between our families those first few years when you broke up. His parents always acted so, now that I think about it, guilty."

I know why. The failed grades that led to the voicemail that led to us breaking up. I can imagine how they blamed themselves—how *Milan* must have blamed them.

Mom purses her lips. "You were both so adamant about not talking to each other . . . But then when neither of you seemed to find anybody to get serious with, we thought, why not help you two along, if it meant you'd be with the one you love?" She clasps my hands between hers. "Did we do wrong?"

I stare at our joined hands. "No, you didn't do wrong. I fought against it for so long, but I . . . I'm glad he's in my life again. I just wish it was because *he* set all of this in motion."

"What I never understood is," says Mom, "if the breakup was mutual, why you didn't stay friends afterward."

I think about all the things we don't understand about each other. The secrets we've kept.

Maybe it's time to share one of my own.

"I told you and Dad that the breakup was both of our decision because I didn't want to tell you what really happened. He dumped me." When fire sparks in her eyes, I add hastily, "At least, that's what I thought at the time. It turned out to be both our faults for assuming the worst of the other. He thought I dumped him; I thought he ended things with me."

Mom still looks fiery. "What do you mean? When did this happ—*right before your trip?*"

"Don't get mad at him. Some of it was my fault, too."

The set of her mouth tells me she disagrees. "How did both of you *think* you'd been dumped and not talk it out further?" Her laugh is mirthless as she says, "Rita, my love, when you've been dumped, trust me, you'll know it."

Somehow the subject has become more sore for her than it is for me.

If I didn't know she was thinking about Amar right now, I'd snark back *Yeah? You and Dad were such great role models about talking out problems, I guess? That's why you moved out for a month? Why we never talk about the fact you lived in the New Bern house without us, like you were trying it on for size, leaving us forever? Talk it out like that, Mom?*

But this is another thing my mom and I never discuss. The past is whisked out only when it suits her. It hurts her enough; it's not for me to use it against her.

"Your aji will be wanting her tea," Mom says abruptly, standing up and taking the mug out of my hands. She gives my shoulder a squeeze, and I *get* it; I get that she's trying to give me all the strength and love that she can't put into words without feeling too much.

I give her enough time to go back upstairs, readying myself to go back "on," too.

Tap, tap tinkles out behind me.

Oh no. My insides writhe like a pit of snakes.

The tapping becomes more insistent.

I turn, coming face-to-face with Aji on the other side of the window.

She crooks her finger. *Come here.*

Stomach sinking, I go back inside. Aji's sitting in the plaid cream-and-green armchair to the right of the fireplace, feet propped up on a woven belt footstool.

Her wrinkled hands are empty. No mug.

"Esha didn't see me sitting here," she says, answering my unspoken question. She points to the armchair opposite, a denim-blue fabric patterned with white, bell-shaped snowdrops. "She went upstairs looking for me."

I cross my arms and raise an eyebrow. "You could have told her you were right here."

A pained expression flashes across her face. "Your mother," she says, "would not have liked me to overhear any of that."

I should let it go, but I'm still in a fight-y mood. "You could have left the room."

Aji doesn't even dignify that with a response, just gestures at me to sit again. "I am going to tell you," she says when I do, "something that should have been obvious. I don't like people who treat the women in our family badly."

She gives me a pointed look. "Your Milan should have fought for you. Amar should have fought for your mother. And both of *you* should have fought for the men you loved. Do you know how much your father fought me and your aba to marry Esha?"

Out of all the family stories I've heard, this one is new. "What do you mean?"

"I mean," says Aji. "I told your father not to pursue a girl so freshly heartbroken."

I startle. The idea that my grandmother opposed Mom feels like a betrayal.

"I told him he would never be first in her heart," she continues. "That her parents were pressuring her to marry so the family wouldn't look bad, so her younger sisters could marry instead of waiting for the eldest to have her shaadi first."

"And Dad didn't listen?"

She smiles. "Would you be here if he had?"

I duck my head and blush. "Right. But he . . . he knew about Amar and stood up to you two, anyway? He didn't care that he was a rebound?"

"Your aba and I were arranged. We thought we knew what was best. But *your* father, your stubborn, stubborn father," she says, shaking her head, "he insisted on Esha and no one else. He spent years convincing her of his love. Brick by brick you can build a house. I saw that when he called me here to help with you when they were going through"—she darts me a look as if to gauge what I know—"some troubles."

"When Mom left," I say flatly.

Aji shakes her head, impatient. "Yes, she left, but she also came back. I told your father to offer her a divorce if that's what she wanted. Esha refused. She said she had what she wanted."

"And time alone made her realize she loved him after all? That's why she came back?"

My throat tightens, grows scratchy as a sweater. I'm eager for the answer I want.

If Mom loves Dad, it means she didn't come back just because of me.

It means I wasn't the reason she felt forced into staying.

Aji studies me for a long moment. "Your mother loves the life they've built together. Ruthvik standing by her side and giving her strength when she needed it, and loving her enough to give her solitude. Of raising a strong, beautiful daughter."

I frown, trying to keep the wobble from my voice. "But that's not what I asked."

"Is that not love also?" asks Aji, voice level.

Her comment makes me feel childish. Like I'm missing an important point that's glaringly obvious to everyone else.

"But what *happened*? She must have said something when she came back. You would have asked. You wouldn't have just accepted it. It was a *month*."

Her face takes on a mulish, cranky set. I can tell I've annoyed her. "You're asking the wrong person," she says. "But if you ask me, you shouldn't be asking at all. A child doesn't need to know everything."

That's bullshit.

Maybe she reads it on my face, because she sighs and stands up, looking older and more weary than I've ever seen her. "I'm thirsty," she announces. "Get your mother, Rita. I'll take that horrible tea you made me now."

"*Well, that wasn't* as bad as I thought it would be," I say, forcing a heartiness to my voice the moment we wave our parents off. With the sun out it's a balmy seventy-seven degrees, but there's a coolness to the air that has nothing to do with the weather.

"Yeah," says Milan, lips pursed and rounded, as if he's about to say something, but doesn't.

The pressure builds to fill his silence. "I'm sorry about before," I stumble out.

He's starting to tidy away the kitchen, taking the used glasses to the sink and sweeping crumbs into his palm. "What do you mean?" He isn't looking at me when he starts the tap.

"It wasn't fair to expect us to finish a conversation when our parents were right outside," I say. I wish he would stop rinsing and just *look* at me. "It's just that you seemed to take what I said in a totally different way than I intended, and I—"

I get my wish. He twists around, expression eerily detached. "I don't think I did, Rita," he says, voice calm. He sets everything upside down in the draining rack and rubs his hands dry on his pants. "I think I heard you loud and clear. Despite the fact that I've known and loved you for most of my teen years and all of my adulthood, you still think—somehow—that we're 'jumping into things,'" he says, with air quotes.

"Milan, when we're together, you know how easy it is to slip back into old habits," I plead. "And I love that. I love that so much about you, that you're my best friend who I can just fit back into, no matter what. But that's also what scares me."

Hurt flashes in his eyes. "I scare you?"

"Yes. Because I'm scared we'll fall into *all* our old habits. The ones where you don't tell me what you need from me and pretend you're fine when you're not. Where I don't even *know* to ask how you are because you don't let me see you faltering." My voice cracks. "Because you think you need to be strong for me instead of letting me save you sometimes, too."

"You *have* saved me. You saved me with the house I couldn't sell and you saved me again with this place."

"Anyone with a bit of knowledge could have done what I did," I fire back.

With a disbelieving scoff, he spreads his arms. "How can you say that? You are in *every* room in this whole damn place. I've walked into rooms you've left and followed the scent of the perfume in your wake like some kind of hound."

"But you have to face it," I say. "*You* didn't reach out to me. Our mothers came up with a way to get us in the same room again—not you. If they hadn't set us up, who knows how many years would have passed before we saw each other again? Another six?"

His stance changes, becomes defensive. With his arms crossed and jaw set, I can tell he's a second away from butting in with a "Well, actually," so I race ahead, nearly spitting the words.

"Milan, you can't take credit for me being back in your life. I'm here in your house right now not because you wanted me, needed me, couldn't live without me, but because your mother opened the door and my mother pushed me through."

The silence screams loud.

"I want to be with you," I say. "But I'm not ready to jump into a commitment without getting to know you again. We can't keep playing house and pretending that this is how our life would have played out if we'd never broken up. You're ready to let our parents know about us, but what if we break up again?"

"We won't," he says fast, like he was coiled for an opening. "I swear we won't. I get what you're saying. I hear you. But we can't be so afraid of the past that we rule out having a future together. Throwing away a second chance for love because you think we haven't been punished enough is—"

"That's *not* it."

"Yes, it is," he says, louder. "Because you're not scared to be with me because you think we're doomed to make the same mistakes again. You're scared because you've spent the last six years blaming me. But the truth is that you're equally as guilty of letting the time pass by, Rita."

"What?" I stare at him.

"Six years," he says, enunciating each word an unholy amount. His heated gaze lasers into me. "Six years that you could have come to me. Yes, I was wrong in assuming the worst and letting you go without a fight, but you make it sound like it was only on me. It wasn't. I was here all those six years, Rita. It's not like you came running, either. You're being unfair."

"Oh my god, that's exactly what I'm trying to say! Neither of us took the first step."

His laugh is humorless, so sure he's right.

I try not to scream, but it still comes out jagged and sharp. "How is it unfair to want to see where things go before we tell our folks? We fit as a holiday couple, maybe, seeing each other on weekends. But day in and day out? We haven't had that in more than six years and, honestly, part of me thinks that, at this rate, we won't even last six months."

It's the wrong thing to say, even if it felt right flying out of me.

Stunned hurt splashes over his face. "Right," he says, hoarse. And no, it's *not* right, *none* of this is right, but the breath is sucked out of me. When I say nothing, he says, in a voice devoid of any emotion, "This is it, then."

No, we're not done here. We have to work this through. We have to be better than before.

But by the time I pry my lips apart, he says, "Let's just get back to the work at hand. We're pretty much done here. We can just . . ." He swallows. "Go back to our lives."

Our lives without each other. Again.

"If we rally, we can finish the last touch-ups and catch the ferry home," he says.

Home. In a way that Bluebill Cottage can never, will never, be.

A hot tangle tightens in my throat, drops into my stomach. And then keeps going, plummeting like the Twilight Zone Tower of Terror ride at Disney World, until I can't feel my body anymore.

This house, filled with all my beautiful finds and memories of Milan in every room, turns into a mausoleum the second his eyes flick away from me. His back muscles ripple as he wipes down the counter, putting way more shoulder into it than he needs.

We haul the last new mattress upstairs, rip it out of its plastic, and lift it onto the bed without saying a word. He disappears as soon as the job is done, taking with him the old mattress I slept on, leaving me to straighten crisp white sheets snug over the mattress corners and to lay one of the quilts I bought at Luke's antique mall at the foot of the bed.

When I see him next, he stinks of bathroom cleaner and hands me my packed toiletry bag. The toothbrush I'd offered him this morning—oh god, was it only this morning that things looked so full of promise?—is nestled inside, taunting me.

By some unspoken agreement, neither of us wants to spend another night on Rosalie Island. I pack up everything I brought with me, folding up my used sheets and wrapping them around my crockery for safety, setting each item into my weekender duffel.

We walk to the ferry, still not speaking. My feet drag, the finite clicking of the lock as Milan closed up the house playing in my head over and over again.

His profile is devastatingly handsome, but whenever I look at him, he's not looking at me. So when tears prick at my eyes, I let them fall. Tears will dry. They always do.

"Guess you found him," Ken in the ferry's ticket office says with a cheerful smile when he sees us walk up.

"Yes," I say, swallowing past a lump in my throat that's about six years and a few odd months' old. "I did."

Tickets in hand, we wait with the other day-trippers and tourists.

Yes, I found Milan.

But then I lost him again.

Chapter 27

The next three mornings I wake with the rush of the sea in my ears and the kiss of the salt in the air. But I'm not on Rosalie anymore. I'm back in my own house that smells like the reheated idli sambar and spicy chicken Alfredo Mom brings over, and overpriced scented candles that are a pale imitation of being by the coast.

The fourth day I shake myself out of my funk long enough to return Paula Dooley's voicemail. Miffed at being ignored, she plays hard to get until I get sick of phone tag and go over there myself with a plate of warmed-in-the-oven store-bought cookies we'll both pretend I made from scratch.

We sit next to the window at her kitchen table with her fancy Keurig coffee and the raucous shouts of her children coming from the backyard. She glances outside, frowns, then taps the glass sharply to catch the attention of whoever is misbehaving.

"I was going to be mad at you for another day or two at least, but you caught me on my cheat day and I haven't had sugar all week," Paula explains as she sinks her teeth into a cookie. "So are you home now? For good?"

It's so weird to think of this as home. I mean, it is, but it isn't. For two short months, it felt like Bluebill Cottage was my would-be home. But now it's just a dream I wake up from, drifting away before I can cling it tight.

"Yeah, I finished my other project," I say, tasting sawdust. "It's finished. All of it."

She nods and blows on her coffee. "What happened to Scrunchie Hunk?"

"The job's done. The house is already listed."

She gives me an arch, amused smirk. "I meant what's going on between you two?"

When I busy myself with a long gulp of Seattle's Best Toasted Hazelnut that's too scalding hot to swallow, she adds, "Things seemed pretty intense, from what I remember."

"Let's just say I've learned my lesson about mixing business and pleasure."

Paula rolls her eyes as she swishes her cup. "Rita, business should always be a pleasure. We wouldn't be small business owners if we didn't believe that in our hearts. We'd be back at our soul-sucking multinational marketing jobs."

I cough on a sip. "You used to work at a—"

"In another life, when climbing the corporate ladder was all I aspired to," she says, waving a hand. "I had a ten-year plan and everything. God, I wasted so much of my thirties. But after I met Rick and had kids, we decided he made enough money for me to pursue my dream of being a YouTuber. It took a few years but now I have my own skincare line that's going to pay for my kids' college."

It's hard not to gape at her. "You were—in your thirties—"

She looks like she had her kids when she was eight. A tiny bit scandalized, I lower my voice. "Paula, how old *are* you?"

Her lips twitch. With an arch tone in her voice, she quips, "A lady never tells. Still on the fence about my moisturizer and serums?" Without missing a beat, she adds, "So I guess you'll be looking for something new to start working on." She eyes me over the rim of her cup.

She's being more subtle than usual.

"Yes," I say. "So I thought, if you're still interested—"

"When can you start?"

So much for subtlety.

But it's so familiar and so Paula that, on impulse, I reach out to touch her hand.

"I can start right now," I tell her. "I mean, if I'm going to buy your whole line of products, I'm going to need some money coming in."

She gives me her sunniest smile. "Good, because I know just what I want." She pats both palms against the kitchen table. "I want that mural-style table you made for the beach house you put on your Instagram Stories. The Before and After was just phenomenal. I mean, how did you even come up with that? All those little details . . ."

I shift in my seat. She's still talking, waxing poetic about how much she loves the trestle table, but all I can think of is that I'm leaving it behind. A piece of me. I'm leaving memories behind, moments that are precious and meaningful to no one but me and Milan.

Before being reunited with him, it was like pulling teeth to sell special pieces. In the midst of falling back in love with him, in the cocoon of that new-crush feeling, I forgot myself. Allowed myself to think that Bluebill could be mine. Ours. The place where we'd raise our children with his get-out-of-jail-free tongue and honey eyes and endearing dimpled chin.

And for the most part, I'm okay with letting go of almost everything in that house.

But not him.

And not that table.

After leaving Paula's I get started organizing my Pinterest boards, putting together the country-chic kitchen she has in mind and creating a checklist of places where I plan to source everything from. Interior decorating comes easy the third time around.

No taped-together sheets of computer paper this time. I set out to impress with a trifold project board, layered with Polaroids of furniture and art from Lucky Dog Luke's and other nearby antique and flea markets, wallpaper samples, fabric swatches, and 3D room renders made in SketchUp, a recent gift from Mom. Well, I call it a gift. *An investment in your future* is the way she put it. *Dad and I have faith in you.*

Enough to let me take a whack at your *house?* I'd teased.

Her face blanched at the idea of me ripping apart her recently renovated French country–style house, replacing the soft whites, muted mauves, and cool grays with my own bold taste. *Y-yes* she'd managed to get out, uncertain if I was kidding but trying so hard to show her support.

Maybe we won't ever be as in sync as Raj and Una, and maybe a day won't ever come that Neil will be an anecdote that brought us closer together, but even if we aren't there yet, we're getting *somewhere*. And that's the important thing, trying.

On day five, Mom stops by with Dad, Aji, and all the fixings for vegetarian tacos in tow. It's a squeeze in my tiny house with four humans and two dogs underfoot, but the hubbub is a welcome respite from the zombie-like monotony of the last few days.

Aji casts a critical eye over my somewhat untidy housekeeping but doesn't say a word—Mom must have coached her on the way over.

While Harrie lolls on the living room rug begging for scratches and cuddles from Dad, the three generations of Chitniss women sit around my kitchen table with steaming, fragrant chai ("Made the *right* way," Aji couldn't resist pointing out) in my prettiest mugs. My latest Etsy purchase: Tuscan-yellow glazed ceramic with a honeycomb texture and a bee perched on the handle. And unless I line up some more projects and sell more of the furniture I already have, probably my *last* purchase for the foreseeable future.

Then we get to work: Mom mixes the taco seasoning and garam masala to marinate her homemade paneer cubes before stir-frying; Aji steals my apron to chop onion and roasted green and red bell peppers; I start the sauce, blending a huge cilantro bunch, a whole bulb of garlic, jalapeño and serrano peppers, lime juice, a hearty dollop of mayo, and cotija cheese.

Over the final whir of the blender, I call out "Who's ready for aji verde?"

My grandmother scowls.

Dad catches my eye and winks.

The green Peruvian sauce, aji verde, is our favorite for paneer tacos: bright, tangy, and pungent. We explained the name—and the fact it's correctly pronounced *ah-hee*—to Aji several times, but she constantly forgets and thinks we're making fun of her somehow.

It's turned into a running gag for me and Dad, but this time, Mom lightly scolds, "Not funny, you two."

No one's more surprised than Aji, who turns away to wipe her eyes with my pug-patterned apron when Mom's not looking. "You put in too many spicy chili peppers, Rita," she complains in a crotchety voice that's at odds with the smile not quite hidden behind the fabric.

I sling my arm around her shoulder and kiss her cheek. She makes a sound at the unfamiliar gesture, then relaxes. "I love you all," I say to the whole room.

"We love you, too," says Dad. He gets up, brushing dog hair off his jeans, and heads over to join Mom at the stove, where she's charring corn tortillas on the burner. Harrie whines and follows, acting like he's starved for attention when we literally *just* met Luke and his pups at the dog park this morning. Freddie's content to stay in his bed with his favorite plushy and watch us.

"Need any help, Esha?"

She's got it, but she smiles and nods, handing him the tongs.

They stand next to each other, just like that, Mom passing him a tortilla from the packet while he turns it side to side over the burner. Two people doing the job of one. Mom puts her right arm around his waist, tips of her fingers tucked into his front pocket.

It's a quiet gesture, so soft and so intimate that it could easily have gone unnoticed.

See? say Aji's lofted eyebrows and pointed stare. *Is this not love also?*

"Ruthvik, why don't you take the boys for a walk?" Mom suggests as we finish the washing up. Aji's already left to gossip with Mrs. Jarvis about gardening and grandchildren, and Dad looks like he's ready for a nap, so I can only assume she wants to talk to me alone.

I help her out. "Harrie could definitely burn off some of that endless energy."

"Taking over my mother's agenda of making me and Freddie get some exercise, huh?" Dad rises from the couch and holds his hand out for the leashes I give him. "But Freddie's got to carry his own weight. I'm getting too old and decrepit to lift him," he jokes.

"Nonsense, you're in your prime," Mom says crisply, turning off the tap and drying her hands. "And take your phone with you to count your steps."

When he leaves, Mom fixes me with the kind of stare that only a parent can. "Now, am I *finally* going to get a real answer out of you as to what happened with Milan?"

I give her the same answer I gave Paula: It's over.

"Now that," says Mom, "I don't believe for a minute. You both still love each other."

There's a sizzle of resentment under my skin. She's never talked with me candidly about Amar, woman to woman, not even last week when she came to Bluebill, but she expects me to bare my heart just because I'm her daughter? Doesn't it go both ways?

"Mom, it's my life."

"And you're my daughter," she counters. "You're *my* life."

"Why does my second chance matter to you so much?"

She blinks at the edge in my voice. "What do you mean?" she asks carefully.

"Is it because you still wish you had a second chance with Amar?"

Her lips part. I've shocked her, I can tell. It's the first time I've used his name in front of her. The second time I've said it out loud *ever*. Since I was a teen, I've always sensed that this one word would shell-shock a room more than an f-bomb.

Finally, Mom swallows. "Sweetheart, no, is that what you think?" Her eyes grow glassy. "Oh, baby, yes, I champion you and Milan. But not because I want a second chance."

"Then why—"

"Because I had my second chance already with your dad. Amar might have been my first love, but your dad is my last."

For the first time, the silence between us doesn't have a single ghost.

"Rita," says Mom, opening her arms. It's only then that I realize I'm crying.

On day six, after finalizing the plans for Paula's remodel and working my way through the last complimentary deluxe skincare samples she sent me home with, I make up my mind.

I'm going to engage my best friend in crime.

"Rita, would you please hurry up? Please don't tell me you're chickening out when we're already *here."* Raj shivers in her striped sweater minidress and black-cat tights when the Rosalie Island wind picks up. "It doesn't look like any of the lights are on inside. It's a quick in and out, you said. You still want to get your table back, right?"

It's the first week of September and the listing has been live for a while, so if I'm really doing this, I need to do it now. I swallow hard.

I still have the key, so sneaking back inside Bluebill Cottage isn't technically a break-in. Although it certainly seemed like a much better idea *before* we were standing outside of it. I'd expected to feel a sense of rightness once we were finally here, but the second mini rental van I notice parked in the driveway is all kinds of wrong.

The house was *just* listed. How could he have sold it already? Even worse, without even *telling* me?

"Oh my god, it's cold out here," Raj whines, stamping her feet. "Can you have your quarter-life crisis *after* we get inside?"

Leave it to her to make me face my demons head-on. Grimly, I set my shoulders.

We've already spent a ridiculous amount of time pro-and-conning this: last night during Girl's Night (a misnomer, really, what with Harrie and Freddie cuddled up with us through tipsy-on-tequila-and-making-fun-of-hot-rom-com-leads-for-not-realizing-what-they-had-when-they-had-it and then despondent-on-tequila-and-wishing-the-rom-com-leads-would-just-kiss-already); the whole drive and ferry ride over to Rosalie Island; the last ten minutes in my moving van; plus, the last five minutes we've been hovering on the porch.

In any case, I trusted Raj to keep track of the pros and cons on her notes app, and her typing devolved from full, coherent sentences to drunken keyboard smashing. Since multiple variations of "jahsdfhjan" doesn't count as a con, the pros have it.

Time to steal my table back.

The second I take the plunge and turn the key in the lock, everything comes rushing back.

Along with every reason this is a bad idea.

But Raj pushes in before I can chicken out, making a big show of rubbing her arms and chattering her teeth. "Finally. I thought we were going to leave without the criminal activity you promised me and I was *not* looking forward to that."

I hide my wince. I regret enticing her with crime so, so much. "It's not criminal," I protest. "It's . . . liberating the dining table that Milan only paid cost of materials for, so as long as I replace it with the identical table from Second Chance Shores tomorrow when the store opens, all I'm really taking back is my labor. Plus, I have"—I dangle the key between us—"this. So it's not a break in."

"In other words, we're here to be gay and do crimes," says Raj. "I wish I'd worn more black. We're like the younger, sexier cast of *Ocean's 8*." She pauses. "Wait, no, I take it back. No one is sexier than Cate Blanchett."

I groan because I'm definitely an Anne Hathaway girl, but we can argue about who does slick heists better when we *aren't* currently trespassing. Regardless of my justifications, I really don't want to get caught out here by Milan or anyone else.

"Come on, let's grab my table," I say.

I'd called earlier today to ask the store owner to reserve the matching table for Bluebill Cottage and that I'd pay cash—the *last* of my cash, thoroughly blowing this month's budget—when I picked it up tonight on the way to the house. But just like the changing of the ferry times, the store had also reduced their open hours for the low season.

The owner had forgotten to mention that, but because she had customers waiting in line, she also forgot her usual nosing around in what I and "my handsome young man" were up to these days in "our" new house. She's seen us together so many times and seems to ship us, so telling her there is no Rita-and-Milan anymore is a conversation I don't want to have.

But if my plan works . . . we won't be apart for long. Hopefully, anyway. Fingers crossed.

Raj is right, though. There's not a single sign of anyone living in the house. That moving truck outside could be here for any number of reasons. It doesn't *have* to mean someone bought Bluebill.

So the plan is still the same. Spend the night here and say my last goodbye, swap the tables tomorrow when the store opens, and then mosey back to Goldsboro with the only souvenir of the last two months on Rosalie Island that would, with any luck, get Milan to chase after me.

I'm not letting him go without a fight. I'm making the first move, showing him I won't pretend the last three months never happened. I won't make the mistake of waiting, waiting, waiting like he accused me of doing.

But if he wants me, he has to prove it, too.

While I stand in the living room, taking it all in for the last time—the blue fireplace tiles we'd argued about, the couch where we'd kissed (and more), the bookshelves where we'd had an *almost*—Raj pipes, "Gotta pee!" and jets.

And by that, I mean she goes upstairs to pee even though there's a downstairs bathroom *right there*, probably as a ruse to test out each bed like she's looking for a pea. She rejoins me at least ten minutes and five Milan memories later, as though she'd been right behind me all along.

Honestly, she could have just *said* she wanted to snoop.

"Did you know," she says conversationally, flinging herself onto the couch, "that when it comes to toilet paper, Milan is an under?"

"What? I put them over so you could see the pretty pattern." When he cleaned the bathroom he must have put it the way he wanted it. Typical. "Did you fix it?"

She makes a rude snorting noise. "Of course. Who do you take me for?"

Thank god for Raj. I take back every mean thought I had about her tipsy-typing skills.

Without skipping a beat she hauls a bag of Little Shop donuts from her vegan-leather purse. "Dinner first? I need sustenance before I do any manual labor." She holds out a chocolate icing donut with a gummy worm on it to entice me. "You know, I could have cashed in a girlfriend favor for this and asked Luke to come over and help us."

At least one of us is getting somewhere with a significant other.

I gesture for her to move her legs so I can sit. I pluck off the gummy worm to eat first. "So we're officially at the calling-each-other-for-big-favors phase of the relationship?"

She gets a glint in her eye. "Let's just say he owes me."

"Ew, Rajvee!" I mimic in an Alexis Rose voice that sends her into peals of giggles.

"It's not a sexy thing!" she insists. "He crowned that awful rooster on our mantelpiece and Mom adored it. It's an official part of the family. I tried to move it somewhere less conspicuous and Mom moved it back, but not before I freaked out that it was some kind of haunted doll I couldn't get rid of like in that *Goosebumps* movie we watched at my house when we were kids? Luke even threatened to 'find' its matching mate for her."

"Must be serious if there are threats involved," I tease.

Raj cheerfully takes a big chomp of her donut and throws her legs over my lap to stretch out. "I was kidding. I wouldn't make him come all the way over here just to help steal."

"We aren't—"

"Oh, sorry. *Liberating*," Raj says with an exaggerated drawl.

The second we finish eating, I get her off the couch. "So you grab the far end and we'll get her out of here," I say as we enter the dining room. "Milan and I did it with no problem."

It's hard saying his name, but it's nothing compared to the shock waves that hit me when we reach the dining room.

"Oh, fuck," whispers Raj.

I move too quickly on jellied legs, almost weaving. The table, or what remains of it, is bare. Back to its natural wood. No hint of the mural I'd painted. Not a fleck of blue water or a strip of sand. I run my hands over the smooth, almost soft, legs, disbelieving.

I taught him too well.

"I don't understand," I say, staring at the table like I'm deciphering a clue.

I can feel my heartbeat in my ears. My head pounds.

He sanded it down.

He *SANDED* it down.

He sanded it *DOWN*.

What happens next is a blur. Raj's arms are around my shoulders, pulling me up. She's trying to get me to walk, to leave the room. She's repeating my name, insistently at first, then crooning. Somehow she coaxes me back to the living room. Sits me down on the couch.

"That rat bastard!" seethes Raj.

I don't want to be here. Not on the couch, not in this room.

Not in this house.

I *ache* to demolish every single memory associated with this place that healed my heart before it broke it again.

If only I could take a sledgehammer to the day I showed him how to use the sander.

I *wish* I'd taken Paula up on the offer she made at the beginning of summer so Rosalie Island and Milan never happened at all.

I *need* to get out of here.

Chapter 28

~~~~~~~

There's no way to access the back porch without passing through the dining room first. I realize my mistake when I see the erased table, but I don't falter. I stride past it, finally able to breathe when I push the glass door open and take in my first gulp of cool, salt-filled air.

God, I was such a fool. I'd been looking for signs in all the wrong places, when the universe had already given me the biggest one of them all.

Broken things can't be fixed.

"I'm going for a walk," I say over my shoulder to Raj, who's followed me. *"Alone."* The word punctuates the fog in my mind. "By myself," I amend. Same meaning, but it makes me want to claw my heart out of my chest a little less.

I thought nothing would be worse than losing the opportunity to know Milan again. But no, *this* is worse. Because this makes it so everything new and tender between us this summer never happened at all. And now it won't ever happen again.

I wait for the coil of anxiety and upset deep in my belly to loosen, dissipate. Surely now that my head's made peace with saying farewell to even the tiniest wisp of a happy ending for us, my heart and the rest of me will fall in line?

But if anything, the coil squeezes even tighter.

My feet slip in and out of the sand as I walk. Frustrated, I hop along on one foot, ripping off my shoes without breaking stride. This side of Rosalie Island is ablaze with poppy-red color and marigold-bright rays. I almost make it to the nearest neighbor's house before the urge to vomit passes and the horizon starts to swallow the sun along with my last shred of hope.

God, I'm a *literal* walking-into-the-sunset cliché.

I whip around. It's time to go ho—go back and face things.

The plan to take my table back failed. No romantic candlelight dinners and playing footsie under the table. No dimpled children eating waffles and Milan's perfect scrambled eggs. No birthday cakes and Christmas roasts. No families squeezed around my table, bickering over the crackling and the last dinner roll. No Milan. No life together. Everything I dreamed . . . gone.

I'd believed in him—in *us*, in what we shared. So much that I hadn't let myself doubt for a moment that he would come chasing after me. That he wanted everything I wanted. It feels unreal how wrong I was. How disconnected my dream was from our reality.

Maybe I should have trusted in historical precedents instead of fresh starts.

I pad through the sand, heart sinking faster than the sun at my back. A hermit crab races to keep up with me, then scuttles across my path to join a second, smaller crab waiting near the water. My eyes sting, then blur, as I watch them together. It's hard to believe that this is the same beach Milan and I jogged on with the pups not so long ago.

"Rita?"

I stop short. Milan's walking up the beach, holding his flip-flops in his hands.

Face full of confusion and no trace of guilt, he asks, "What are you doing here?"

He's asking me that? He has the gall to ask me that?

"You sanded my table," I say, voice quivering. "You could have given it back to me or you could have— Anything but that. How *could* you? You had to get rid of everything that reminded you of us?"

He stops in his tracks, mouth falling open. "What are you talking about?"

"The trestle table in the dining room. The one I painted. For weeks."

"It's still here."

"No," I say vehemently. "It's not."

"Rita," he says, voice rough with frustration, "I promise you that it is."

"'Promise'? Ha!"

His jaw clenches. "Why do you think I'm here? With a moving van? Do you really think I would let you—or your table—go?"

I stare at him.

He sighs. "Your table's out front. Do you want proof?"

I give him a jerky nod.

This time we don't go through the house, but around it, navigating through the tall beach grass. My van is in full view. There's no way Milan can miss it, but with single-minded determination, he goes right to his own to unlatch the roll-up door at the back and shines his phone's flashlight inside.

I can't hold back my gasp.

The mural table *is* inside. My gaze zeroes in on the couple walking together in the sand the way we'd just done and on the green scrunchie in her hair.

The knot in my heart unravels, and hidden in its center is a terrifyingly small bud of hope.

But it's growing larger by the second.

"Believe me, now?" His voice holds a trace of annoyance. "Why are you here with your own van?"

Before I can answer him, apologizing for my rant, Raj shouts from inside the house, "If you're here to steal anything, you should know I called the police!"

"What the fuck?" Milan takes off for the front door, me on his heels.

He uses his key to get in, to his credit not blinking at Raj wielding a fireplace poker and a cranky expression. He sucks in his cheeks and looks from her to me before asking, "Does someone want to tell me what the two of you are doing here?"

"What are *you* doing here?" Raj counters.

He plays the trump card. Folding his arms across his chest, he says, "It's my house."

I swallow. Right. It's his house. He has every right to be here, unlike us.

Raj lets the poker clatter back into the stand and huffs back to her seat.

He's still waiting for an answer. I cast around for something that would explain why I, my best friend, and a *second* moving van are in front of his house.

"I, ah, forgot something here," I say finally.

He half smiles, then remembers to steel his face again. "Another scrunchie?"

"Uh, not exactly."

Milan lifts a brow. "Is it bigger than a bread box?"

He's teasing me. I gnaw my lower lip, replying in kind. "Considerably."

"Fine! You don't have to interrogate us!" Raj bursts out. "We came for the table and that's it. Rita was even planning on a replacement we were going to swap out for it, and maybe it's wrong, maybe the word 'stealing' was thrown around, but this is important to her, okay?"

Wow. Miss Cat Burglar didn't even hold up to three questions without folding like *that*.

I pass a hand over my eyes. "You are the worst criminal ever."

"At least now I know why you're here," says Milan.

Anxiously, I ask, "You didn't really call the police, did you, Raj?"

The blush rises on her cheeks. "No. It seemed like the smart thing to say to scare off an intruder."

The tension in the room evaporates.

"Well, then," says Raj. "I'm gonna give you two some space. And fair warning, I'm not coming out until someone gives me the all clear."

Well, that's one way to avoid awkwardness.

And oh god, awkward it is. Now that the fright and anger has faded, I'm left with the awful memory of the way we ended and that stony ferry ride home when we'd locked Bluebill Cottage up for the last time. And now, arguing again only thirty seconds after laying eyes on each other. It's embarrassing. We should be better than this.

"I'm sorry. I didn't exactly break in. I still had my key. Which, um, I should probably give back to you." I pull it from my pocket, the metal warm to the touch, and hold it out.

I'm sure I don't imagine that moment of hesitation before he takes it.

It's a small key. It would be so easy for our fingers to brush, but he seems as tentative with his acceptance as I do in my offering.

"Thanks." His Adam's apple bobs. "So, were you seriously going to steal our table?"

My mind latches on to the *our* and brings it close. "*Steal* is a strong word."

His mouth crooks. "Liberate, then?"

"It doesn't mean anything to anyone but us," I say. "Or, well, I guess just me. I'm the only one who'd want it."

"You're not the only one."

I wring my hands. "Oh, did you— I mean, is there an offer? Someone who saw the pictures and wants— I know the whole point of bringing me in to flip this house was to sell it furnished, but—"

"Rita," he says gently, ceasing the flow of my babble. "I meant me. *I* want the table."

"So *you* came here to steal it?"

His cheeks flare with color. "I know what you put into it. I didn't want someone else to have it. I was planning on smuggling your table out, replacing it with its twin we saw at the store, and retaking the dining room picture for the website."

"You got a little streak of deviousness in your old age," I say to lighten the mood, but all it does is reignite our banter, which last time led to . . .

We both find ourselves looking at the couch and then at each other.

"I was planning on giving it to you," says Milan.

"But we had a fight," I say. "You said we were done. Time to go back to our lives."

"It was in the heat of the moment," he says, hanging his head for a moment. Then he shoots back up and I'm taken aback by the fierceness in his eyes. "I was a jackass, Rita. I almost walked away from you again— No, I *did* walk away. I was hurt that you weren't ready to be out in the open with me, outside of the fairy tale of this house. And instead of examining why you were hurt, and the role I played in it, I did the same exact thing you were afraid of."

"You did," I say quietly.

"But, Rita, try to see it from my point of view. You didn't want to tell your folks about Neil. And I get why. But you wanted to keep me on the DL, too. It felt like a pattern. Worse, like a punishment. And I know that isn't how you intended it, but if our breakup has taught us anything, it's the thin line between intent and effect."

"You always call me on my shit," I tell him. "All of it. And it is *infuriating*. Especially when you're right. I tried to break that pattern by coming here."

"By turning to a life of crime?"

"By giving you a reason to come after me." I grab Raj's phone from where she left it on the coffee table, bypass the security code, and open the notes app. I turn the phone to face him. "The first pro on my list."

I love him. I could learn to live without him again, but I really don't want to.

He reads the list silently, ignoring the other random strings of letters.

"I waited for you a long time, Milan. I don't intend to make the same mistake again. You're right. I could have come to you any time over the last six years and I didn't." I give him a tiny smile. "We knocked down those six years apart into just six days, for what it's worth."

A slow, unsure smile spreads over his face. "And we're both here. Does that mean . . . No, *you* tell me what it means."

"It means I want to be with you. I want everything you want, everything I've ever wanted, ever since I was fifteen years old." I press my hand to my chest. "I want my heart to always beat like *this*. For you."

He closes the distance between us in two long strides. His arms are around me in an instant, crushing me to his chest. "I wish—" He breaks off, a frustrated crease appearing in his forehead. "I wish we could live here. Start fresh. But I can't afford to, not after all the money invested in flipping it."

I've had a lot of time to think about this. What comes next.

"What if we leased it?" I find myself asking. "If we're both doing okay for money right now, then maybe we could find someone willing to rent, and maybe we could put our money toward paying down the mortgage and, one day . . ."

"One day live here ourselves," he breathes.

I nod, a rigid, jerky thing. I don't even dare to hope.

"I'd have to take a look at the numbers. See what we could rent it out for. Maybe downsize my apartment, find someplace cheaper. Figure out how long we'd have to wait until—" He stops again. But I can still sense he's crunching numbers in his head, trying to work out whether the impossible could actually be within our reach. "This is what you want, Rita? Is that what would make you happy?"

"You make me happy," I say. "And I love this house. But I love you so much more. And I'm willing to fight and make up with you every day to prove that, if I have to."

His arms tighten around me. Our foreheads rest against each other, noses bumping. "Tell me more about the making-up part. Does it go like this?"

He kisses the question off my lips with a sweet, searing intensity that I feel all the way down to the tips of my toes and a hundred other places, too. The kiss deepens as our tongues touch, and his abdomen tenses against my stomach when I breathe his name into his mouth.

"Rita," he rasps in return, devouring me in another kiss, digging his fingers into my hair. I gasp, pressing myself against the solid feel of him, feeling the hard heat of his torso and the bump of his nose as he makes his way along the shell of my ear and down my neck. Everywhere his lips linger alights with fireworks, setting me up to soar, knowing he'll catch me if I fall.

The kiss goes on for what feels like minutes, and maybe it does, because the next thing I hear is Raj shouting, "I hope the silence means you're kissing each other!"

"It does!" he calls back.

I stifle my laughter. "You can come out now, by the way."

In a strangled voice, Milan calls, "Please don't!" Then, to me, in a voice that promises another six years and another and another, "I think we still have some making up to do."

I hum under my breath. "Six years' worth, if we're keeping track. And I want it with interest."

He looks somber for a moment before nodding as if he's come to a decision. "Gone but not forgotten." His expression turns impish on a dime. "Kind of like that shirt of mine you're wearing. I always wondered where it went."

"Yours?" My mouth drops. "Uh, you are very much mistaken there, buddy."

He runs his warm hands up my arms, then folds back the left sleeve. "Look familiar?"

I glance down, breath stolen by the sight of a small embroidered black heart. It's almost invisible against the black fabric, scarcely bigger than a thumbnail, and pressed almost flat.

I remember stitching this. Back in the days he only wore gray and black, when he was so difficult to shop for, I'd made this birthday gift a little bit more special by giving him my heart on his sleeve. When I look back at his face, Milan knows I remember.

"Wait, how did you even know the heart was—*oh*. That day in front of the bookshelves."

The memories whoosh back like a plug's been unstoppered. That pensive, preoccupied look on his face that I couldn't place. The way he'd seemed to be putting something together while I trembled on the precipice of coming apart under the roughened pads of his thumbs.

I take in a long, controlled inhale, then let it out, heart expanding about a dozen sizes. All these years, all these long six years, I'd been reaching for him and I never even knew it.

He grins. "Don't worry. I don't want it back. Looks cuter on you, anyway."

"Good, because you're not getting it." My eye catches on movement through the glass-enclosed dining room. "Milan, I think I see a pony out there."

"From here?" He taps his foot against the living room floorboards.

I'm already moving for the porch. "I swear I saw something."

But when we get there, the beach is empty. I scan up and down the coastline, but whatever was there is gone now. Only our footprints remain.

Milan waits a respectful .02 seconds before saying, "I bet it was a *real* cute dog."

I elbow him good-naturedly, trying not to laugh. "Shut it, you. Let me have this."

He can't stop smiling. "Your imaginary wild pony?"

"Are you going to tell this story to *everyone* we meet?"

He wraps his arms around me, bringing me flush against him for a soft, unhurried toe-curling kiss. His hands are clasped at the small of my back, thumb working erotic little circles on my tailbone. "Oh, only for the rest of our lives."

I tilt my head back to look into his eyes. The teasing smile is gone, replaced by a solemnity he doesn't often wear. "You and your cheeky declarations," I whisper, flattening my palm against his cheek, savoring the hint of stubble. "Maybe it wasn't a Banker. Can't have everything, I guess."

The smile in his eyes spreads, breaking over his entire face. "Yes," he says, sliding an arm around my waist and bringing me close for another toe-curling kiss. "I'm making you a promise, Rita. We *can* have everything. Our new beginning. Everything your table and the house represents, not just now, but in the future. And I'm going to prove that to you."

"Our table," I say, giving him a peck on the lips. "Our house." I repeat the kiss.

"Ours," he agrees.

"And we'll prove it to each other," I say, and then reach up on my tiptoes to kiss him.

Three Years Later

MyShaadi Success Story Testimonial

Rita & Milan!

It's so weird to be writing this. Three years ago we would never have thought we'd be here today, announcing our engagement on MyShaadi! It's funny, you know, because we were pretty torn on whether we wanted to fill out this testimonial. See, unlike most people who find love here, we had met and fallen in love many years earlier, so our situation was . . . well, pretty unconventional!

It was a huge surprise to both of us to find ourselves matched by MyShaadi. Ironically, this was a double whammy because our mothers had already conspired to get us in the same room together to see what should have been obvious: We were still very much in love with each other.

It took us a long time to rediscover each other as the new people we'd grown into and there were some growing pains along the way, but once we decided to get engaged we both thought it made sense to bring our MyShaadi journey full circle.

P.S. We are super stoked to share that while we are still working in realty and interior design, we will also be starring in our new

HGTV show, *Make Yourselves at Home*, this spring! Join us as we move into the homes of in-over-their-heads homeowners who don't know the first thing about renovation or luxe-for-less DIY, and turn their "oh hell no" into "welcome home"!

~~~

Rita and Milan are planning a June wedding at their beautiful property, Bluebill Cottage, on Rosalie Island.

Acknowledgments

By the time this book releases, (I'm sure) you'll all be sick and tired of hearing its droll origin story, so I'll leave it at this: *The Shaadi Set-Up* is the book I've always wanted to read about the Indian-American diaspora experience, but since it didn't exist, I knew I had to write it.

In the past, I've struggled to relate to South Asian characters and narratives that I'm told are supposed to share my experiences, instead yearning for more stories where a Desi character gets to just *be*, where their ethnicity isn't the most interesting thing about them and they aren't culturally torn in two. Where they are *of* their heritage and traditions, but it is not wholly *theirs*. Where being *enough* isn't even a thought that crosses their mind because they are everything they are meant to be and everything they strive for is within reach.

So the first thank-you is for you: anyone who sees a part of themselves—maybe, like me, for the first time—in the characters who inhabit the world of *The Shaadi Set-Up*.

It is still surreal and mind-boggling that I somehow managed to sell and write (in that order!) this book during a global pandemic, after a confluence of incredibly serendipitous events during the most unimaginable circumstances. The heart of this book has always been a love letter to the places we call home and the people we find our way back to, and it felt especially affirming to draft this book during a time when so many of us were looking for comfort and connection. Writing is solitary at the best of times, but publishing is very much not, so it's hard to write a book about love and friendship and family without thinking about all the people who made it possible in the first place:

Thank you to my extraordinary agent, Jessica Watterson, for all-caps BELIEVING in this book from the start and finding it the perfect home. I count myself lucky to have your unwavering guidance, enthusiasm, and fierce heart. Thanks also goes to Andrea Cavallaro and the rest of Sandra Dijkstra Literary Agency for their knowledge and savvy.

Thank you to the entire team at G. P. Putnam's Sons, starting with my editor Gabriella Mongelli, who is so tremendously wonderful to work with and without whose support this book wouldn't be what it is today. Our shared love of HGTV (thank you *Island Life* and *Flea Market Flip* for being such an inspiration!) made this book extra fun to work on!

Margo Lipschultz, while we didn't get to work on this book together, your first enthusiastic *Yes!* meant the world. I will always be thankful.

My gratitude also goes to the publicity team, including Sydney Cohen and Kristen Bianco; to the marketing team, including Nishtha Patel; to copyeditor Lara M. Robbins; to production editor Joel Breuklander; to the art director and jacket designer, Vi-An Nguyen; and to the publisher, Sally Kim. To anyone who helped bring this book to life, I appreciate you.

Big thanks to Alex Cabal, who illustrated such a gorgeous cover and perfectly captured the impish and dead chuffed expressions (respectively) on Harrie and Freddie's faces. AND THE KEY CHAIN. Still swooning.

I'm immensely grateful to Rachel Lynn Solomon, Sarah Hogle, Farah Heron, Elizabeth Everett, and everyone else who gave their time so generously. Thank you for gracing me with your words.

Nicole Aronis and Kate Holliday, thank you for reading the very first draft!

Thank you to my parents, both of whom were the first in their families to marry for love, and who have never made me question that love as Rita does her parents'. Thank you again to my mom, first and best beta reader. Thank you to Granny, who is just as charming and wily as Rita's aji, and is in no small part her inspiration.

Thank you to my grandfather, who didn't get to see me publish my first book, but who truly lived the most storied life of anyone I know: he taught on a naval ship; he was an inventor and entrepreneur; he was an engineer on the Canadian Pacific Railway; he traveled the world with the eyes and spirit of his favorite author, Louis L'Amour; and he even met Queen Elizabeth. At my birth, he gave me my first-ever book, and continued to make sure I was well stocked with plenty of Enid Blyton. But his ultimate gift was in passing down his love of stories to my mom, who passed it down to me, which is undoubtedly why I'm an author today.

Thank you to the booksellers, librarians, and bloggers who have championed this book—I appreciate your hard work and passion so much. Thank you to my friends in the Romancing the 20s group chat and all the '21/'22 authors with whom I've found so much support and solidarity. LlamaSquad, meeting all of you gave me a community I can't imagine myself without. You all remind me every day that it really does take a village. I'm blessed to count you as mine.

Thank you to absolutely none of my exes. I don't want a second-chance romance with any of you! ☺

My final thanks is for you, my readers. Thank you for buying, borrowing, tweeting, hyping, and supporting me on this journey, but most of all, thank you for the privilege of letting my words make you feel things. Thank you for this most incandescent and ordinary of magics.

Photo of the author © Lillie Vale

Lillie Vale is the author of the young adult novel *Small Town Hearts*. She writes about secrets and yearning, complicated and ambitious girls who know what they want, the places we call home and people we find our way back to, and the magic we make. Born in Mumbai, she grew up in Mississippi, Texas, and North Dakota, and now resides in an Indiana college town. *The Shaadi Set-Up* is her debut novel for adults.

~~~~~~

CONNECT ONLINE

lillielabyrinth.com

 @LillieLabyrinth

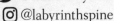 @labyrinthspine